PENGUIN BOOKS
PRINCE OF AYODHYA

Ashok K. Banker is a well-known Indian writer. For the past few years he has been working full-time to realize his childhood dream of retelling the great tales of the Vedic Age. He plans to follow the Ramayana with imaginative retellings of the tales of Krishna, Ganesha, and the world's longest epic, the Mahabharata.

Ashok is married with two children, and lives in Mumbai.

BY ASHOK K. BANKER

Prince of Ayodhya
Siege of Mithila
Demons of Chitrakut

Prince of Ayodhya

Book One of the Ramayana

ASHOK K. BANKER

PENGUIN BOOKS

PENGUIN BOOKS
Published by the Penguin Group
Penguin Books India Pvt Ltd, 11 Community Centre, Panchsheel Park, New Delhi 110 017, India
Penguin Group (USA) Inc., 375 Hudson Street, New York, New York 10014, USA
Penguin Group (Canada), 90 Eglinton Avenue East, Suite 700, Toronto, Ontario, M4P 2Y3, Canada (a division of Pearson Penguin Canada Inc.)
Penguin Books Ltd, 80 Strand, London WC2R 0RL, England
Penguin, Ireland, 25 St Stephen's Green, Dublin 2, Ireland (a division of Penguin Books Ltd)
Penguin Group (Australia), 250 Camberwell Road, Camberwell, Victoria 3124, Australia (a division of Pearson Australia Group Pty Ltd)
Penguin Group (NZ), cnr Airborne and Rosedale Roads, Albany, Auckland 1310, New Zealand (a division of Pearson New Zealand Ltd)
Penguin Group (South Africa) (Pty) Ltd, 24 Sturdee Avenue, Rosebank, Johannesburg 2196, South Africa

Penguin Books Ltd, Registered Offices: 80 Strand, London WC2R 0RL, England

First published in India by Penguin Books India 2005

Copyright © Ashok K. Banker 2005

Printed at Baba Barkhanath Printers, New Delhi

Ganesa, lead well this army of words

For Biki and Bithika Banker,
The Gemini twins.
One saved my life,
The other gave me
Two new ones

For Ayush Yoda Banker,
Friend, son, Jedi Master.
When you were born,
I was born again.

For Yashka Banker,
Devi, daughter, princess.
You made me believe in luck again,
And, more important, in love.

ACKNOWLEDGEMENTS

The author thanks

Ravi Singh, and everyone else at Penguin India, for building the bridge across the ocean that brought Rama back home.

R. Sriram, and the wonderful staff at Crossword Bookstores.

Hemu Ramaiah and her terrific staff at Landmark, Chennai.

Pallavi Joshi, Anuradha Anand, and Lushin Dubey.

All those readers and reviewers who came out in such numbers to make this one of the most popular as well as bestselling series of books in the country in such a short time. You understood that it's not about 'hindutva' and the religion of politics, but about 'Inditva', Indian pride, and a story too great to be either saffronized or sanitized.

The vanar sena, led by my dearest friend Sanjeev Shankar, and the fantastic fans of epicindia.com, who overwhelm me daily with encouragement, praise and valuable insights.

And again and always, my wife Bithika, my son Ayush, my daughter Yashka. Love you all.

AUTHOR'S NOTE

Adi-kavya: The first retelling

Some three thousand years ago, a sage named Valmiki
lived in a remote forest ashram, practising austerities
with his disciples. One day, the wandering sage Narada
visited the ashram and was asked by Valmiki if he knew
of a perfect man. Narada said, indeed, he did know of
such a person, and then told Valmiki and his disciples a
story of an ideal man.

Some days later, Valmiki happened to witness a hunter
killing a kraunchya bird. The crane's partner was left
desolate, and cried inconsolably. Valmiki was
overwhelmed by anger at the hunter's action, and sorrow
at the bird's loss. He felt driven to do something rash,
but controlled himself with difficulty.

After his anger and sorrow subsided, he questioned
his outburst. After so many years of practising meditation
and austerities, he had still not been able to master his
own emotions. Was it even possible to do so? Could any
person truly become a master of his passions? For a
while he despaired, but then he recalled the story Narada
had told him. He thought about the implications of the
story, about the choices made by the protagonist and
how he had indeed shown great mastery of his own

xi

thoughts, words, deeds and feelings. Valmiki felt inspired by the recollection and filled with a calm serenity such as he had never felt before.

As he recollected the tale of that perfect man of whom Narada had spoken, he found himself reciting it in a particular cadence and rhythm. He realised that this rhythm or metre corresponded to the warbling cries of the kraunchya bird, as if in tribute to the loss that had inspired his recollection. At once, he resolved to compose his own version of the story, using the new form of metre, that others might hear it and be as inspired as he was.

But Narada's story was only a bare narration of the events, a mere plot outline as we would call it today. In order to make the story attractive and memorable to ordinary listeners, Valmiki would have to add and embellish considerably, filling in details and inventing incidents from his own imagination. He would have to dramatise the whole story in order to bring out the powerful dilemmas faced by the protagonist.

But what right did he have to do so? After all, this was not his story. It was a tale told to him. A tale of a real man and real events. How could he make up his own version of the story?

At this point, Valmiki was visited by Lord Brahma himself. The Creator told him to set his worries aside and to begin composing the work he had in mind. Here is how Valmiki quoted Brahma's exhortation to him, in an introductory passage not unlike this one that you are reading right now:

> Recite the tale of Rama . . . as you heard it told by Narada. Recite the deeds of Rama that are already known as well as those that are not, his adventures . . . his battles . . . the acts of Sita,

known and unknown. Whatever you do not know will become known to you. Never will your words be inappropriate. Tell Rama's story . . . that it may prevail on earth for as long as the mountains and the rivers exist.

Valmiki needed no further urging. He began composing his poem. He titled it Rama-yana, meaning, literally, The Movements (or Travels) of Rama.

Foretelling the future

The first thing Valmiki realised on completing his composition was that it was incomplete. What good was a story without anyone to tell it to? In the tradition of his age, a bard would normally recite his compositions himself, perhaps earning some favour or payment in coin or kind, more often rewarded only with the appreciation of his listeners. But Valmiki knew that while the form of the story was his creation, the story itself belonged to all his countrymen. He recalled Brahma's exhortation that Rama's story must prevail on earth for as long as the mountains and the rivers exist.

So he taught it to his disciples, among whose number were two young boys whose mother had sought sanctuary with him years ago. Those two boys, Luv and Kusa, then travelled from place to place, reciting the Ramayana as composed by their guru. In time, fate brought them before the very Rama described in the poem. Rama knew at once that the poem referred to him and understood that these boys could be none other than his sons by the banished Sita. Called upon by the curious king, Valmiki himself then appeared before Rama and entreated him to accept Sita back.

Later, Rama asked Valmiki to compose an additional part to the poem, so that he himself, Rama Chandra, might know what would happen to him *in future*.

Valmiki obeyed this extraordinary command, and this supplementary section became the Uttara Kaand of his poem.

Valmiki's Sanskrit rendition of the tale was a brilliant work by any standards, ancient or modern. Its charm, beauty and originality can never be matched. It is a true masterpiece of Indian literature, the 'adi-kavya' which stands as the fountainhead of our great cultural record. Even today, thousands of years after its composition, it remains unsurpassed.

And yet, when we narrate the story of the Ramayana today, it is not Valmiki's Sanskrit shlokas that we recite. Few of us today have even read Valmiki's immortal composition in its original. Most have not even read an abridgement. Indeed, an unabridged Ramayana itself, reproducing Valmiki's verse without alteration or revisions, is almost impossible to find. Even the most learned of scholars, steeped in a lifetime of study of ancient Sanskrit literature, maintain that the versions of Valmiki's poem that exist today have been revised and added to by later hands. Some believe that the first and seventh kaands, as well as a number of passages within the other kaands, were all inserted by later writers who preferred to remain anonymous.

Perhaps the earliest retelling of Valmiki's poem is to be found in the pages of that vast ocean of stories we call the Mahabharata. When Krishna Dwaipayana-Vyasa, more popularly known today as Ved Vyasa, composed his equally legendary epic, he retold the story of the Ramayana in one passage. His retelling differs in small but significant ways.

Sometime later, the burgeoning Buddhist literature, usually composed in the Pali dialect, also included stories from the Ramayana, recast in a somewhat different light. Indeed, Buddhist literature redefined the term dharma itself, restating it as dhamma and changing the definition of this and several other core concepts.

In the 11th century a Tamil poet named Kamban undertook his own retelling of the Ramayana legend. Starting out with what seems to have been an attempt to translate Valmiki's Ramayana, Kamban nevertheless deviated dramatically from his source material. In the Kamba Ramayana entire episodes are deleted, new ones appear, people and places are renamed or changed altogether, and even the order of some major events is revised. Most of all, Kamban's Ramayana relocates the entire story in a milieu that is recognisably 11th century Tamil Nadu in its geography, history, clothes, customs, etc, rather than the north Indian milieu of Valmiki's Sanskrit original. It is essentially a whole new Ramayana, retold in a far more passionate, rich and colourful idiom.

A few centuries later, Sant Tulsidas undertook his interpretation of the epic. Tulsidas went so far as to title his work Ramcharitramanas, rather than calling it the Ramayana. By doing so, he signalled that he was not undertaking a faithful translation, but a wholly new variation of his own creation. The differences are substantial.

In art, sculpture, musical renditions, even in dance, mime and street theatrical performances, the story of Valmiki's great poem has been retold over and over, in countless different variations, some with minor alterations, others with major deviations. The tradition of retellings continues even in modern times, through television serials, films, puppet theatre, children's versions, cartoons, poetry, pop music and, of course, in the tradition of Ramlila enactments across the country every year.

Yet how many of these are faithful to Valmiki? How many, if any at all, actually refer to the original Sanskrit text, or even attempt to seek out that text?

Should they even do so?

So many Ramayanas

Does a grandmother consult Valmiki's Ramayana before she retells the tale to her grandchildren at night? When she imitates a rakshasa's roar or Ravana's laugh, or Sita's tears, or Rama's stoic manner, whom does she base her performance on? When an actor portrays Rama in a television serial, or a Ramlila performer enacts a scene, or a sculptor chisels a likeness, a painter a sketch, whom do they all refer to? There were no illustrations in Valmiki's Ramayana. No existing portraits of Rama survive from that age, no recordings of his voice or video records of his deeds.

Indeed, many of the episodes or 'moments' we believe are from Valmiki's Ramayana are not even present in the original Sanskrit work. They are the result of later retellers, often derived from their own imagination. One instance is the 'seema rekha' believed to have been drawn by Lakshman before leaving Sita in the hut. No mention of this incident exists in the Valmiki Ramayana. Then there is the constant process of revision that has altered even those scenes that remain constant through various retellings.

For example, take the scene where Sita entreats Rama to allow her to accompany him into exile. In Valmiki's Ramayana, when Rama tells Sita he has to go into exile, and she asks him to allow her to go with him, he refuses outright. At first, Sita pleads with him and cries earnest tears, but when Rama remains adamant, she grows angry and rebukes him in shockingly harsh terms. She refers to him as a 'woman disguised as a man', says that 'the world is wrong when they say that there is no one greater than Rama', calls him 'depressed and frightened', 'an actor playing a role', and other choice epithets. It is one of the longer scenes in Valmiki's Ramayana, almost equalling in length the entire narration of Rama's early childhood years!

Tamil poet Kamban retells this incident in his more compressed, volatile, rich style, reducing Sita's objections to a couple of brief rebukes: 'Could it be that the real reason [for Rama not taking her into exile] is that with me left behind, you'll be free to enjoy yourself in the forest?'

By the time we reach Sant Tulsidas's recension, Sita's rebukes are reduced to a few tearful admonitions and appeals.

Were these changes the result of the change in the socially accepted standards of behaviour between men and women in our country? Quite possibly. Tulsidas's Ramcharitramanas depicts a world quite different from that which Valmiki or even Kamban depict. In fact, each of these three versions differs so drastically in terms of the language used, the clothes worn, the various social and cultural references, that they seem almost independent of one another.

Perhaps the most popularly known version in more recent times is a simplified English translation of a series of Tamil retellings of selected episodes of the Kamban version, serialized in a children's magazine about fifty years ago. This version by C. Rajagopalachari, aka Rajaji, was my favourite version as a child too. It was only much later that I found, through my own extensive research that my beloved Rajaji version left out whole chunks of the original story and simplified other parts considerably. Still later, I was sorely disappointed by yet another version by an otherwise great writer, R. K. Narayan. In his severely abridged retelling, the story is dealt with in a manner so rushed and abbreviated, it is reduced to a moral fable rather than the rich, powerful, mythic epic that Valmiki created.

English scholar William S. Buck's 19th century version, dubiously regarded as a classic by English scholars, read like it might have been composed under the influence of certain intoxicants: In one significant departure from Indian versions, Guha, the tribal chief of the Nisada fisherfolk, without discernible reason, spews a diatribe against brahmins, and ends by kicking a statue of Lord Shiva. To add further confusion, in the illustration accompanying this chapter, Guha is shown kicking what appears to be a statue of Buddha!

If you travel outside India, farther east, you will find more versions of the Ramayana that are so far removed from Valmiki, that some are barely recognizable as the same story. In one recent study of these various versions of the epic across the different cultures of Asia, an aging Muslim woman in Indonesia is surprised to learn from the author that we have our own Ramayana in India also! The kings of Thailand are always named Rama along with other dynastic titles, and consider themselves to be direct descendants of Rama Chandra. The largest Rama temple, an inspiring ruin even today, is situated not in India, or even in Nepal, the only nation that takes Hinduism as its official religion, but in Cambodia. It is called Angkor Vat.

In fact, it is now possible to say that there are as many Ramayanas as there are people who know the tale, or claim to know it. And no two versions are exactly alike.

My Ramayana: A personal odyssey

And yet, would we rather have this democratic mélange of versions and variations, or would we rather have a half-remembered, extinct, tale recollected only dimly, like a mostly forgotten myth that we can recall only fragments of?

Valmiki's 'original' Ramayana was written in Sanskrit, the language of his time and in an idiom that was highly modern for its age. In fact, it was so avant garde in its style—the kraunchya-inspired shloka metre—that it was considered 'adi' or the first of its kind. Today, almost none of us can understand or read it in its original form.

Kamban's overblown rhetoric and colourful descriptions, while magnificently inspired and appropriate for its age, is equally anachronistic in today's times.

Tulsidas's interpretation, while rightfully regarded as a sacred text, can seem somewhat heavy handed in its depiction of man-woman relationships. It is more of a religious tribute to Lord Rama's divinity than a realistic retelling of the story itself.

In Ved Vyasa's version, the devices of ill-intentioned Manthara, misguided Kaikeyi and reprehensible Ravana are not the ultimate cause of Rama's misfortunes. In fact, it is not due to the asuras either. It is Brahma himself, using the mortal avatar of Vishnu to cleanse the world of evil, as perpetuated by Ravana and his asuras, in order to maintain the eternal balance of good and evil.

My reasons for attempting this retelling were simple and intensely personal. As a child of an intensely unhappy broken marriage, a violently bitter failure of parents of two different cultures (Anglo-Indian Christian and

Gujarati Hindu) to accept their differences and find common ground, I turned to literature for solace. My first readings were, by accident, in the realm of mythology. So inspired was I by the simple power and heroic victories of those ancient ur-tales, I decided to become a writer and tell stories of my own that would be as great, as inspiring to others. To attempt, if possible, to bridge cultures, and knit together disparate lives by showing the common struggle and strife and, ultimately, triumph of all human souls.

I was barely a boy then. Thirty-odd years of living and battling life later, albeit not as colourful as Valmiki's thieving and dacoit years, I was moved by a powerful inexplicable urge to read the Ramayana once more. Every version I read seemed to lack something, that vital something that I can only describe as the 'connection' to the work. In a troubled phase, battling with moral conundrums of my own, I set to writing my own version of the events. My mind exploded with images, scenes, entire conversations between characters. I saw, I heard, I felt...I wrote. Was I exhorted by Brahma himself? I had no reader in mind, except myself—and everyone. I changed as a person over the course of that writing. I found peace, or a kind of peace. I saw how people could devote their lives to worshipping Rama, or Krishna, or Devi for that matter, my own special 'Maa'. But I also felt that this story was beyond religion, beyond nationality, beyond race, colour, or creed.

Undertaking to retell a story as great and as precious as our classic adi-kavya is not an enterprise lightly attempted. The first thing I did was study every available edition of previous retellings to know what had been done before, the differences between various retellings, and attempt to understand why. I also spoke extensively to people known and unknown about their knowledge of the poem, in an attempt to trace how millennia of verbal retellings have altered the perception of the tale. One of the most striking things was that most people had never actually read the 'original' Valmiki Ramayana. Indeed, most people considered Ramcharitramanas by Tulsidas to be 'the Ramayana', and assumed it was an accurate reprisal of the Sanskrit work. Nothing could be farther from the truth.

For instance, Valmiki's Ramayana depicts Dasaratha as having three hundred and fifty concubines in addition to his three titled wives. In keeping with the kingly practises of that age, the aging raja's predilection for the fairer sex is depicted honestly and without any sense of misogyny. Valmiki neither comments on nor criticises Dasaratha's fondness for fleshly pleasures, he simply states it. When Rama takes leave of his father before going into exile, he does so in the palace of concubines, and all of them weep as copiously for the exiled son of their master. When Valmiki describes women, he does so by enumerating the virtues of each part of their anatomy. There is no sense of embarrassment or male chauvinism evident here: he is simply extolling the beauty of the women characters, just as he does for the male characters like Rama and Hanuman and, yes, even Ravana. Even in Kamban's version, the woman are depicted in such ripe, full-blown language, that a modern reader like myself blushes in embarrassment. Yet the writer exhibits no awkwardness or prurience in these passages—he is simply describing them as he perceived them in the garb and fashion of his time.

By the time we reach Tulsidas and later versions, Rama is no less than a god in human avatar. And in keeping with this fore-knowledge, all related characters are depicted accordingly. So Dasaratha's fleshly indulgences take a backseat, the women are portrayed fully clad and demure in appearance, and their beauty is ethereal rather than earthly.

How was I to approach my retelling? On one hand, the Ramayana was now regarded not as a Sanskrit epic of real events that occurred in ancient India, but as a moral fable of the actions of a human avatar of Vishnu. On the other hand, I felt the need to bring to life the ancient world of epic India in all its glory and magnificence, to explore the human drama as well as the divinity that drove it, to show the nuances of word and action and choice rather than a black-and-white depiction of good versus evil. More importantly, what could I offer that was fresh and new, yet faithful to the spirit of the original story? How could I ensure that all events and characters were depicted respectfully yet realistically?

There was little point in simply repeating any version that had gone before—those already existed, and those who desired to read the Ramayana in any one of its various forms could simply pick up one of those previous versions.

But what had never been done before was a complete, or 'sampoorn', Ramayana, incorporating the various, often contradictory aspects of the various Indian retellers (I wasn't interested in foreign perspectives, frankly), while attempting to put us into the minds and hearts of the various characters. To go beyond a simple plot reprise and bring the whole story, the whole world of ancient India, alive. To do what every verbal reteller attempts, or any classical dancer does: Make the story live again.

In order to do this, I chose a modern idiom. I simply used the way I speak, an amalgam of English-Hindi-Urdu-Sanskrit, and various other terms from Indian languages. I deliberately used anachronisms like the term 'abs' or 'morph' because these were how I referred to those events. I based every section, every scene, every character's dialogues and actions on the previous Ramayanas, be it Valmiki, Kamban, Tulsidas, or Vyasa, and even the various puranas. Everything you read here is based on actual research, or my interpretation of some detail noted in a previous work. The presentation, of course, is wholly original and my own.

Take the example of the scene of Sita entreating Rama to let her accompany him into exile. In my retelling, I sought to explore the relationship between Rama and Sita at a level that is beyond the physical or social plane. I believed that their's was a love that was eternally destined, and that their bond surpassed all human ties. At one level, yes, I believed that they were Vishnu and Lakshmi. Yet, in the avatars they were currently in, they were Rama and Sita, two young people caught up in a time of great turmoil and strife, subjected to hard, difficult choices. Whatever their divine backgrounds and karma, here and now, they had to play out their parts one moment at a time, as real, flesh-and-blood people.

I adopted an approach that was realistic, putting myself (and thereby the reader) into the feelings and thoughts of both Rama and Sita at that moment of choice. I felt the intensity of their pain, the great sorrow and confusion, the frustration at events beyond their control, and also their ultimate acceptance of what was right, what must be done, of dharma. In my version, they argue as young couples will at such a time, they express their anger and mixed emotions, but in the end, it is not only through duty and dharma that she appeals to him. In the end, she appeals to him as a wife who is secure in the knowledge that her husband loves her sincerely, and that the bond that ties them is not merely one of duty or a formal social knot of matrimony, but of true love. After the tears, after all other avenues have been mutually discussed and discarded, she simply says his name and appeals to him, as a wife, a lover, and as his dearest friend.

'Rama,' she said. She raised her arms to him, asking, not pleading. 'Then let me go with you.'

And he agrees. Not as a god, an avatar, or even a prince. But as a man who loves her and respects her. And needs her.

In the footsteps of giants

Let me be clear.

This is not Valmiki's story. Nor Kamban's. Nor Tulsidas's. Nor Vyasa's. Nor R.K. Narayan's. Nor Rajaji's charming, abridged children's version.

It is Rama's story. And Rama's story belongs to every one of us. Black, brown, white, or albino. Old or young. Male or female. Hindu, Christian, Muslim, or whatever faith you espouse. I was asked at a press conference to comment on the Babri Masjid demolition and its relation to my Ramayana. My answer was that the Ramayana had stood for three thousand years, and would stand for all infinity. Ayodhya, in my opinion, is not just a place in north-central Uttar Pradesh. It is a place in our hearts. And in that most sacred of places, it will live forever, burnished and beautiful as no temple of consecrated bricks can ever be.

When Rama himself heard Luv and Kusa recite Valmiki's Ramayana for the first time, even he, the protagonist of the story, was flabbergasted by the sage's version of the events—after all, even he had not known what happened to Sita after her exile, nor the childhood of Luv and Kusa, nor had he heard their mother's version of events narrated so eloquently until then. And in commanding Valmiki to compose the section about future events, Rama himself added his seal of authority to Valmiki, adding weight to Brahma's exhortation to recite the deeds of Rama that were already known *as well as those that are not*.

And so the tradition of telling and retelling the Ramayana began. It is that tradition that Kamban, Tulsidas, Vyasa, and so many others were following. It is through the works of these bards through the ages that this great tale continues to exist among us. If it changes shape and structure, form and even content, it is because that is the nature of the story itself: It inspires the teller to bring fresh insights to each new version, bringing us ever closer to understanding Rama himself.

This is why it must be told, and retold, an infinite number of times. By me. By you. By grandmothers to their grandchildren. By people everywhere, regardless of their identity. The first time I was told the Ramayana, it was on my grandfather's knee. He was excessively fond of chewing tambaku paan and his breath was redolent of its aroma. Because I loved lions, he infused any number of lions in his Ramayana retellings—Rama fought lions, Sita fought them, I think even Manthara was cowed down by one at one point! My grandfather's name, incidentally, was Ramchandra Banker. He died of throat cancer caused by his tobacco-chewing habit. But before his throat ceased working, he had passed on the tale to me.

And now, I pass it on to you. If you desire, and only if, then read this book. I believe if you are ready to read it, the tale will call out to you, as it did to me. If that happens, you are in for a great treat. Know that the version of the Ramayana retold within these pages is a living, breathing, new-born avatar of the tale itself. Told by a living author in a living idiom. It is my humble attempt to do for this great story what writers down the ages have done with it in their times.

If anything in the following pages pleases you, thank those great forebears in whose giant footsteps I placed my own small feet. If any parts displease you, then please blame them on my inadequate talents, not on the tale itself. Several previous infelicities and minor errors have all been meticulously corrected by my excellent editors and myself. We trust that this, the first Indian edition, will stand as the definitive edition of my Ramayana series.

Mumbai   ASHOK K. BANKER
January 2005

Om Bhur Bhuvah Sivah:
Tat Savitur Varenyam
Bhargo Devasya Dhimahi
Dhiyo yo nah prachodayat

Maha-mantra Gayatri
(whispered into the ears
of newborn infants at
their naming ceremony)

The Moon is
a Harsh Mistress

ONE

Rama.

The blow-heat of rancid breath against his face, guttural whisper in his ear. He snapped awake. Sweat-drenched, fever-hot, bone-chilled, springing from his satin bed, barefoot on the cool redstone floor. Sword, *now*. A yard and a half of gleaming Kosala steel, never out of reach, a bolt of lightning in his fist. Soft rustle of the silken gold-embroidered loin-cloth around his tight abs. Naked feline grace. Taut young muscles, supple limbs, senses instantly attuned to the slightest hint of threat.

He scanned the moonlit expanse of his bedchamber with the sharpness of a panther with the scent of stag in its nostrils. Barely three seconds after rising from deep, dreamless sleep, he was ready to take on a dozen armed men. Or worse.

But the bedchamber was empty. The moon was full tonight and the room was caught in a silvery net, more than sufficient for his trained eyes to scan the princely apartment. Jewelled ornaments and regal furnishings gleamed richly in the silvered dimness. The far wall, some twenty yards from where he stood, showed him a pale imitation of his own reflection in an oval mirror framed in solid gold. He had heard enough descriptions of his appearance in kavyas composed by the royal bards to know what the mirror would have shown had the light been sufficient. A distinct dynastic resemblance, unmistakably related to one of those towering portraits of his illustrious ancestors adorning the walls of Suryavansha Hall. Classically handsome (the bards would sing), a fitting heir to the dynasty of the Sun. The reality was harder, leaner and more austere. His piercing brown eyes, as sharp and all-seeing as a kite-hawk's thousand-yard gaze, scoured every square inch as he traversed the apartment with quick military precision, his movements graceful and flowing. Bedchamber, clear. Gymnasium, clear. Bathing chambers, clear. Enemy not sighted, repeat, not sighted.

Circuit complete. Return to bedchamber.

Breathing in the pranayam style, he executed a martial asana that was part attack and part spiritual discipline. In three breathtakingly graceful leaps, it took him to the veranda that ringed one side of the circular chamber. Sword slashing through the gossamer folds of the translucent drapes that could conceal an assassin. Turn, turn, breathe, slice, follow-through, recover, resume stance. Guru Vashishta had trained him superbly. A quad of assassins striking with two weapons apiece would have been hard-pressed to put a scratch on his lithe body.

The veranda was empty.

He checked his perimeter in a sweeping three-hundred-and-sixty-degree arc that put him back precisely in his original position, and scanned over the ornately carved redwood balustrade, first checking topside then below. Above, the complex vaulting architecture of the mahal rose up in an ingeniously layered design that allowed efficient guard-watches without the royal residents ever seeing their vigilant protectors, out of their line of sight. But he had to be sure; the sense of mortal dread was too real, too powerful. He vaulted out on to the lip of the ledge that encircled the veranda, flicked the sword from

4

one hand to the other, gripped the sculpted corner of the balustrade, then leaned out over a twenty-yard fall into darkness. In the bright wash of the purnima moon, he could see the helmeted heads and spear tips of the night-watch patrolling the south grounds, moving in perfect unison in the regular rhythmic four-count pattern of a normal chowkidari sweep. Ground level, clear. Topside, clear, all the way to the roof. Silvery gleam of the tip of a lance held in defensive position: roof watch on guard and alert.

Leap down to the veranda. Turn, arc sword in a sweeping action that clears the first circle of personal safety. Circle clear.

Hold stance. Sword blade flat on right shoulder. Cold steel on sleep-warm skin. Breathe. Exhale. Scan down. Move to the far end of the long veranda, twenty yards running the length of the princely chambers, covering the distance in a cheetah-swift instant. From here, he could see down to the western grounds, the distant front gates of the palace and the darkened length of Raghuvamsha Avenue beyond. Again, deserted, except for the night-watch, patrolling alertly even at this silent hour. Armour and sandalled feet clinking and tramping in precisely coordinated rhythms. Quads of four armed and armoured royal guards scouring every square yard in an endlessly overlapping pattern. Squares interwoven with squares interwoven with more squares, in a grid extending outwards in every direction. The grid extending to the seventh wall, the outermost defence of the greatest fortress city ever built by the Arya nations. Ayodhya the Unconquerable.

From the south, a gentle wind, carrying the scent of battle elephants, horses, camels, buffaloes, boar, deer, cow, fowl, a thick murky soup of animal odours. Source: the royal stables and stockyards behind the palace.

Somewhere in the still, silent night, a domesticated wolfhound baying uneasily, as if feeling the same sense of not-quite-rightness that stirred Rama's hackles. An elephant trumpeting sleepily in response. A rooster clearing its throat, croaking once irritably, then lapsing into silence, stealing a last few moments of sleep before the imminent dawn.

He forced himself to stand down from the martial asana of full alertness, changing the pattern of his pranayam breathing, dialling down his biorhythm using yoga techniques. From battle readiness to mere watchfulness. There was no danger anywhere to be seen.

The night breeze was cool on his sweat-limned body, the air damp with the sweet mist of the river, barely thirty yards from where he stood. As eldest prince—by mere weeks, but eldest all the same—he had the corner suite in the maharaja's palace, giving him a view of his beloved Sarayu. Even though coyly concealed by his father's palace, he could smell her. That invigorating mineral tang of glacial flow, a smell that brought back memories of a childhood spent on its banks. The gentle murmur of the river helped him calm himself. His body released its tension in carefully graded stages. Warming down. Sweat cooling on his heated skin. Odour of the royal stables fading away as the wind changed, coming now from the north, carrying the frosty bite of the distant snow-capped peaks of the Himalayas and the delicate fragrance of nightqueen blossom, raat ki rani, from the palace gardens.

Your women ravished, your children enslaved, your city sacked and razed to ashes.

His eyes widened. Full alert instantly. Turn, turn, slash, clear first circle, second, third, turn, turn, slice, jab, breathe, always breathe. In moments, he had covered the seven circles of personal safety. If this had been a battlefield, a dozen men would lie dead or dying around him. Nothing could survive the seven-circle asana. Nothing human at least.

But still, there was nobody there. Neither man, beast, or Asura. What was going on here?

Then he felt it.

A foul presence, like the nostril-clogging stink of wild Southwoods boar five days rotted and worm-infested. Maggots seeping out of blood-encrusted orifices. Mulch and mildew. The raw, fetid stench of deep jungle.

He felt the heat of a living breath on his face, heard the rasping gravel of a voice in his ear. A voice like rock scraping across glass. It isn't my imagination. Someone— something—is here with me. Invisible, unseen, venomous as a stepped-on cobra.

You will watch your birth-mother savaged beyond recognition, your clan-mothers and sisters impregnated by my rakshasas, your father and brothers eaten while still alive, your race massacred, your proud cities pillaged and razed—

'Who's there? Show yourself, you coward! Face me and fight!'

—and when you think you can endure no more, when the horror is over and every living mortal is enslaved or converted to my cause, when you have suffered as much torture as any of your kind can endure and still live, then I shall snuff you out and start all over again. The samay chakra, your sacred wheel of time, will repeat the cycle of birth and suffering infinitely. You will wish you were in hell then, for even the underworld of Narak will seem a blessed escape from the living nightmare of mortal existence.

'Damn you! Show your face!'

Boy. You still do not understand. See for yourself then. See the future and tremble.

And in a flash of blinding light, Rama was transported.

7

TWO

He stood in the Seers' Tower, the highest point in Ayodhya.
The stone tower rose like a sword in the sky, an awe-inspiring achievement of Arya architecture as well as a
perfect lookout post. Such a tower existed in every Arya
city from Gandahar to Ayodhya, to alert the citizens to
an approaching enemy host. But it had been more than
two decades since the Arya nations had tasted the bitter
salt of war. And Ayodhya itself had not once in its proud
history been under siege. Hence its title, Ayodhya,
literally, the Unconquerable. Even the seven legendary
seer-mages who had raised the tower with the mystical
power of brahman had not found reason to assemble
within its impregnable walls for hundreds of years.

This circular chamber of the tower's topmost level,
nicknamed the Seers' Eye, was damp and musty with
disuse, the grey flagstone floor frosted over by night
dew beneath Rama's bare feet. He turned and turned
again, sword proscribing the arc of the first circle. The
elements were wilder here in this edifice of sorcerous
architecture, carrying a sense of ancient times when war
was a way of life and places like this were all that kept
the Arya nations a sword-length ahead of their mortal
enemies. He listened carefully, but at first all he heard
was the whistling breath of Vayu, the wind god, blowing

through the windowless openings and the distant growling of Indra, the god of lightning and thunder, threatening to unleash a storm even though the monsoon season was months away.

Then he heard it.

There. Below the howling of the wind and the distant growling of thunder. A sound like nothing he had heard before in his fifteen years of mortal life. Yet he knew at once what the sound meant.

War.

It was the sound of war.

Within Ayodhya.

For the first time since coming awake, he felt a needle of fear pierce his heart. He started to freeze, muscles locking reflexively; then, with an effort of will, he forced himself to maintain his breathing pattern. He moved forward, towards the dark maw of the windowless aperture, and faced the most shocking sight of his life.

Ayodhya was being raped.

A great war raged in its streets. A huge army of Asuras had breached the seven gates and invaded the city. The three defensive moats were choked to overflowing with the corpses of the inhuman races of the Asura army as well as the bodies of the city's mortal defenders. The rich crimson of human blood mingled with the multi-hued life-fluids of the alien invaders, lying splattered in swathes everywhere he looked, flowing into and polluting the sacred life-giving Sarayu herself. The river was dark and heavy with the offal of death, her pristine purity turned into a corpse-gutter.

Asuras of all sizes and shapes butchered Ayodhyans. Rama had heard countless tales of Asura atrocities before, nightmare tales from the Last Asura War that he knew still haunted his father on moonless awamas nights such

9

as this one—for awamas was the night when evil flourished—but never had he heard of or envisioned such atrocities taking place within the walls of his home city, mighty Ayodhya herself. In a single glimpse, his entire world tilted and went out of balance. A thousand impossible sights filled his vision, threatening to drive him insane.

Rakshasas twice as tall as men, roaring with exultation as they impaled human soldiers on their enormous antlered horns, then using their curved yellow talons to tear open their bellies and suck the steaming entrails into their hungry mouths.

A quad of palace guards encircling a rakshasi, her sagging breasts suckling two hairy infants that clung with tenacious stubbornness to her waist. The guards jabbed the rakshasi with their longspears, trying to contain her and shepherd her away from the palace gates. He guessed that they were squeamish about killing a female, a mother at that. Their moral strength was their downfall. The rakshasi grasped their spears and twisted them around the necks of the soldiers as easily as winding wool. She grabbed a soldier in each hand and held them high in the air. Her infants screamed with delight and tore the guards open, one feeding greedily on dripping intestines, the other sucking the spray of blood jetting from an unfortunate soldier's throat with relish, as if it were mother's milk.

Everywhere Rama looked, rakshasas were killing and devouring Ayodhyans with terrifying ease. For every rakshas that fell or was wounded, a hundred of Rama's fellow countrymen died horrible deaths. Most of those eaten weren't even killed off properly; he could see hundreds lying with their bellies torn open, crying for merciful death. Rakshasas strode over them, trampling their wounds underfoot as they sought new victims on whom to inflict their terrible butchery. They were the forerunners of the Asura army, heading the invasion and leading the rest of the inhumans into the city.

Pisacas followed in their wake, clicking their insectile mandibles as they swarmed noisily through the streets, seeking out and destroying their prey. They inflicted a double violation upon their victims: first tearing open their soft flesh with their razor-sharp claws, then squatting above the agonised Ayodhyans to deposit their loads of greenish-black crystalline eggs. Then they exuded a viscous fluid that instantly sealed the gaping wounds. Only then did they move on to other victims—a single Pisaca impregnating dozens of humans in this manner. Their victims would survive the few hours it took for the eggs within their ruined bellies to hatch and the tiny swarms of crab-like infants to feed on their warm-blooded hosts, eating their way out of their bodies. Most Asuras combined warfare with the eating of enemies. Only the Pisacas used their enemy to breed as well.

Nagas, giant cobra-like beings with a human head and torso but with yard-long forked tongues and serpentine lower bodies and long tails. They slithered through the alleyways and up walls, finding the strays and those who tried to flee the more organised invaders. Rama saw a group of Nagas converge hissing on an unarmed brahmin mother and her two shaven-headed sons. The raised hoods mercifully hid what happened next. When the hoods parted, the three brahmins lay prone on the street, their skin turning blue from several twin-puckered bites.

Uragas, enormous reptilian brethren of the Nagas, flowed slimily among their cousin species, their enormous python bodies swollen with telltale lumps—the Ayodhyans they'd swallowed alive. Their deceptively human faces were cast in the appearance of beautiful girl-children, a detail that only added to the horror of their violations.

11

Yaksas, the Elfish races. Even though Rama had grown up with tales of their magical antics, he had never heard of Yaksas being openly malevolent. They were generally benign, lovable but mischievous pranksters who used their morphing abilities to tease and entertain, not to kill and maim. Here, their mischief was vicious, their antics deadly. He saw a group of Yaksas morph into a herd of horses as they turned a corner and came face to face with a troop of citizens armed with an assortment of farming implements and kitchen weapons. The Ayodhyans paused to let the horses ride past, realising their mistake only when the Yaksas tore into them like predators rather than the gentle herbivores they were masquerading as. Hooves flailed, smashing skulls like ripe pumpkins. Powerful equestrian teeth ripped necks and bit off limbs. Half-ton heavy battle-horse bodies trampled screaming humans underfoot, shattering bones and smashing organs. Elsewhere, other Yaksas were using their morphing abilities to disguise themselves as elephants, camels, deer, dogs, swine, even an unlikely band of murderous buffalo, loping along with horns dripping blood and gore.

There were other Asura races too, committing other unspeakable acts of violence and desecration. Defiling holy icons, demolishing temples, and slaughtering, always slaughtering.

A rumbling sound forced Rama to raise his gaze to the extremities of the city, where he saw the king's highway boiling with more intruders. The Asura forces covered the road all the way to the edge of the Southwoods, a distance of a full yojana. They flowed from the high rises of the Southwoods down to the city like a boiling black river of pestilence. Even at a glance, it was clear that the invaders vastly outnumbered the defenders. And yet, more kept coming in a constant seething flow. There seemed to be no end to their unholy numbers.

A screeching cry startled him from his horrified reverie. He looked up to see the early dawn sky darkening. Great hulking shadows coalesced into the winged shapes of flying bird-beasts, humanoid creatures out of myth and fable. He stared in disbelief at what seemed to be Garudas and Jatayus, named after the gigantic mythic man-eagle and enormous fabled man-vulture of ancient folklore. Their slender, lightly feathered bodies were strikingly humanoid, except for the bird-like eyes and beaks, and the incredible muscular wings growing from their backs. Some had a wingspan as much as ten yards or more. They swooped down to the streets below, down to the killing floor of the slaughterhouse that Ayodhya had become. Rama scanned the sky and saw hundreds, perhaps thousands of the flying creatures, flocking to the carnage, calling to each other exultantly in their proto-human speech. As they reached street level and a new wave of horror began, he shut his eyes and staggered back, away from the aperture, unable to absorb any more.

Now do you see the futility of resisting me and my forces? Would you like to see your kith and kin ravished and slaughtered like your countrymen below? Your brothers, perhaps? Or your birth-mother? Or—

Rama lashed out. This time he struck without discipline or stance. Pure rage fuelled his actions. The sword slashed through empty air. He came to his senses a moment later, at the far end of the tower chamber, sword vibrating in his double-handed grip. He had traced an interweaving mandala pattern that covered every square yard of the chamber. There was no living being here. His eyes misted with impotent rage.

'Who are you? Why do you show me these monstrous visions? Reveal yourself, damn you!'

Boy. You still haven't seen the real horrors. The best part comes later, when the survivors are taken back to Lanka as my slaves and whores. Shall I show you that now?

'What do you want from me, demon?'

The cry was torn from his throat by an emotion more powerful than simple rage. It was an attempt to understand, to make sense of the evil that confronted him.

Now, you begin to learn. Yes, I do want something from you. A vow of allegiance. Bend your knee to me now, this instant, and swear fealty to me. Do this now, and perhaps I shall see fit to spare Ayodhya when my armies lay waste the nations of Arya. Kneel, boy, and live.

He forced his breathing to stay measured, his voice as steady as he could keep it. It took more strength than wielding the sword.

'The only time I would bend my knee before you is when I kneel to aim an arrow at your cursed brain. Show yourself and face me like the man you claim you are, coward!'

Lightning shattered the sky above the Seer's Tower. Lightning out of a pitch-black sky. Thunder boomed and echoed an instant later. When the voice resumed, it sounded like giant teeth gnashing in frustration.

Boy. Still just a boy. But you will learn. I will teach you the song of pain and terror. And you will bend your knee then. You will beg and cry for the honour of kneeling to me. Until then, sleep your childish sleep, boy. And remember this well: Ayodhya will fall.

Another blinding flash of white light.

He woke in his bed, chest heaving, sweat-drenched, fever-hot, bone-chilled. He sprang to his feet, stood naked on the cool redstone floor—he had tossed off his loin-cloth as the night grew warmer. Even as he reached for

14

his sword, he knew that it was still there on the bed where it had lain all night, untouched.

Just another bad dream, he thought, willing himself to calm down. He remembered the perfection of his movements and asanas in the dream, and also how futile all his training had proved. Who was this faceless beast that tortured him this way? This was the third time this week alone that the monster had appeared and shown him similarly horrible dream-visions. Too horrible to discuss with anyone else. He hadn't even told Lakshman, and he always told Lakshman everything. Just another nightmare. As real and terrifying as all nightmares usually were.

But this time, it felt like something more.

It felt like a prophecy.

15

THREE

The traveller reached the top of the rise and paused.

Ayodhya.

He was clad in the simple garb of an ascetic. The coarse white dhoti girding his loins, wooden toe-grip slippers on his feet, matted unkempt hair swirling around his craggy face, the long straggly white beard, the red-beaded rudraksh mala around his neck, all marked him for a hermit returning from a long, hard tapasya. His gaunt face and deep-set eyes completed the portrait of a forest penitent, a tapasvi sadhu.

Yet there was something about him that set him apart from any ordinary sadhu or hermit. An indefinable quality that belied the obvious first impression. An alertness in his intense predatory eyes, a sense of banked power in his fluid movements, a hint of hidden strength, and most of all, an unmistakable regal air.

He had been a warrior once. A king even. Lord of an ancient and illustrious northern Arya clan, master of a great throne and monarch of a rich dynasty. He had given it all up millennia earlier to pursue a life of total dedication to the pursuit of brahman, the life-force that knit the universe. Now, he wielded this wooden staff instead of a sword, voiced mantras instead of royal edicts. His kingdom was the realm of atman and brahman, spirit and power. His name had passed beyond history, across the boundaries of legend, into the misty realms of myth. A guru among gurus, a seer that other seers looked up to reverentially. A Brahmarishi. Yet the regal bearing and manner had not left him entirely. And at this fateful moment, this cusp of history, as he stood sketched against the sky on that high peak, gazing down at the lush, epic beauty of the Sarayu valley, he looked every inch the king he once was.

Leaning lightly on the head-tall wildwood staff, his large frame silhouetted against the dusky purple of the pre-dawn sky, he resembled nothing so much as a warrior king surveying his battlements. He would have looked at home on a royal chariot, gripping the carved bonewood of a longbow, polished armour gleaming in the cold sunlight, contemplating the battlefield's lie.

Even the gentle northern wind that rustled the vast rolling banks of kusa grass below seemed to pause briefly, awaiting his command. The waters of the Sarayu, ice-pure and crystal-clear, stilled their gurgling momentarily. The world grew silent, marking the moment, as he spoke aloud a sacred mantra. Not just a mantra, a maha-mantra. The sacred and omnipotent Gayatri.

As he spoke, the lines of destiny swirled around him. The faint blue hue of brahman, the raw energy of spiritual enlightenment, caressed his form, an invisible cloak of power. From here on, every step he took closer to Ayodhya would bring about change, historic change. For on this cool, crisp morning, the last night of winter, the first day of spring, he was about to make a king. Perhaps the greatest king of them all. What he wrought today in that city by the river would reverberate down the corridors of human history.

Gripping the hefty staff more firmly, the seer-mage Vishwamitra stepped back on the well-worn cart track of the king's highway and began the long downward trek to the first wall. The city itself was still a whole yojana distant and he wished to be there before daybreak. But first he had to alter his appearance. It would not do to appear as himself. The unannounced appearance of a seer-mage of his legendary status would become the talk of the city, bringing brahmins by the hundreds out of doors to pay their respects, which would only delay his urgent mission.

Without slowing his pace he spoke the mantra of transformation. The glow of brahman grew brighter around him as nature itself responded to the sacred incantation. Countless tiny motes of bluish light began to swirl around him, blurring his form. A large boulder lay off to one side of the road and he stepped off the path and into the knee-deep kusa grass, droplets of dew clinging to his dhoti like beads of quicksilver. As he strode around the rock and passed out of sight, his body shimmered as if seen through a curtain of smoke.

When he emerged scant seconds later on the far side of the boulder, it was no longer as the great seer-mage Vishwamitra. The man who stepped back on to the cartwheel-ridged mud road was a muscular, dark-skinned young man with the traditional animal-skin loincloth, bone necklace and body-pierce adornments of a sudra hunter. A bulging game bag was slung over one shoulder, a gleaming sickle-spear clutched in the other hand. A few scattered motes of blue light trailed behind him, winking out slowly like fireflies extinguished by rain.

The hunter strode towards Ayodhya.

FOUR

High on the hill, a dark shadow detached itself from a small grove of eucalyptus trees. It hopped forward cautiously, reached a mossy ledge overhanging the path below and peered over the rim. Its keen eyes easily picked out the figure of the sudra hunter far below, striding north at a determined pace.

The disguise did not deceive it. It was familiar with creatures that changed their bhes-bhav at will. Even at this distance, the seer-mage's aura was as keenly visible to its preternatural senses as a halo around a blue-skinned deva. Its bright golden eyes followed the hunter's striding form until he disappeared over a rise a mile distant. Then it chittered and scratched repeatedly at the mossy ledge underfoot. Its yard-long talons drew deep grooves, sending the thick damp moss flying in shredded strips, exposing the rock. The tips of its claws drew sparks from the rock as it raised its head and issued a blood-curdling scream. The cry was almost human and the traveller on the path below heard it and recognised its source, but strode on without slowing. An ordinary sudra hunter would have been terrified out of his wits; the great seer-mage Vishwamitra barely gave the cry a second's attention.

The creature chittered again, frustrated. It now wished it had attacked the traveller while he was still in the dense jungles of Bhayanak-van, the darkwoods. The seer-mage had been aware of its presence from the very outset, it knew, so it had made no attempt to conceal itself. But rather than glance up fearfully at the gigantic shadow lurking overhead as most ordinary mortals would have done, the sage had simply strode on relentlessly, as if it had been a mere raven or crow flying overhead, not the legendary Jatayu itself, first of its name, a name that struck terror into the hearts of mortals across the Arya nations. Furious at being ignored, weary of circling endlessly to compensate for the far slower pace of the earth-bound mortal, Jatayu had longed to plunge down, down, strike at the dhoti-clad human and rip him to shreds.

But its orders had been clear: *follow and observe.* Nothing more, nothing less. The Dark Lord of Lanka had been explicit in his instructions.

It scratched the ledge one last time, hard enough to draw a cracking noise like a dry twig being split. Its great talons had caused a fissure in the rock. Turning its enormous bald head skywards, it considered its next move. It had a long way to travel, in the shortest time possible. Lanka was a whole sub-continent away and the news it carried was important. The Lord of the Asuras would not be pleased to learn the seer-mage Vishwamitra's destination, but he would certainly be pleased at his spy's diligence.

It spread its wings; first the left one, then the right, unfolding them slowly, painfully, sighing as it did so. They were weary from the long journey. What was more, its belly rumbled with hunger. It had been able to snatch a few small prey on the wing, a pair of parrots, a duck that had strayed from its fellows, even a juicy pregnant bat. But they were barely snacks for its enormous appetite.

If it could just stay awhile, forage around until it found the burning ghats where it knew these Ayodhyans must cremate their dead, it would have food aplenty. After all, if it was part-human, it was also part-vulture. And the vulture part craved human flesh.

But Lanka was thrice as far as the distance it had flown already. Even with brief rests, the journey would consume precious time. Hopefully, the seer-mage would stay in the city that long. These holy men usually took their time when they made their rare forays back into civilisation. And this particular one had broken his retreat after a considerable time, even by Jatayu's count. Over two hundred mortal years, it reckoned. Which meant there had to be a very good reason for Vishwamitra's visit to Ayodhya. Which meant in turn that the Lord of Lanka would not appreciate the news being delivered late.

Sighing in frustration, Jatayu began the arduous task of flapping its mighty wings, trying to work up enough wind to elevate itself off the ground until it found an air current. For yards around, the grass was flattened by the tremendous force of its flapping. A family of hares creeping from their hole were pressed to the ground, their long ears laid flat on the earth to either side of their heads. With a final ear-splitting screech of effort, Jatayu launched itself off the ledge, plummeting downwards like a boulder for several heart-stopping seconds before it found a small wind-wave and clung to it fiercely. The wave strengthened and it straightened out scant yards above the trail the sage had taken. With one more massive effort, it rode the wave out into the Sarayu valley.

Airborne at last, it drifted for several minutes, climbing steadily higher to find a current flowing in the direction it wished to go. It saw the seven gates of Ayodhya far below, ringing the mortal city like a set of concentric necklaces around a queen's throat. The river Sarayu undulated like a silver cord through the lush valley. The magnificent palaces and mahals at the centre of the city straddled the roaring river with a variety of vaulting arches and inbuilt bridges in a large complex system of architecture. It was an amazing sight and Jatayu accepted grudgingly that it had never seen a mortal city as intricately designed as this one. So this was the great Ayodhya the Unconquerable. As it drifted on a strong up-current that flowed parallel to the river, the sickly-sweet odour of mortal flesh came clearly to its hunger-heightened senses. All the beauty and splendour of the magnificent Arya architecture was forgotten as its appetite was provoked again. To Jatayu, that was what this great city was ultimately: a giant feeding trough. Soon, it knew, its lord and master would beat down the proud walls of this so-called unconquerable city, and Jatayu and its kind would feast to their heart's content.

The giant man-vulture issued an ululating cry, mocking the city and its inhabitants and their puerile quest for immortality before riding the air current southwards to its distant destination.

The sound that issued was a single word, split into three extended syllables by the bird-beast's cry:

'Ra-van-a!'

The guards on watch at the city walls below heard the cry of the bird-beast and started involuntarily.

A grizzled veteran at the seventh gate glanced up and glimpsed the shockingly large silhouette that was sketched briefly against the deep-blue pre-dawn sky.

'What in Shiva's name was that?' asked his companion, a much younger man, barely old enough to sport a beard. 'Did you see the size of that thing? It must have a wing-span of at least twenty yards!'

The veteran shrugged. 'Trick of the light. Like I told you before, this is the time of day you see the strangest things.'

The young guard stared at his companion. 'But you must have seen it. It was right above us. It looked like a giant vulture. That round head, long hooked beak, that hunched back. But there was something odd about the body. It was broader than a bird, differently shaped, almost like a—'

'A man? A giant man-vulture, is that what it looked like, young novice?' the older man responded sharply.

'Exactly!' The young soldier looked eagerly at his senior. 'Then you saw it too?'

The old man hawked and spat over the rim of the stone wall. The gob of phlegm glistened in the light of the gate-lamps. He watched it splash into the still waters of the moat far below before he answered in a disinterested tone.

'There are no giant man-vultures, boy. Not any more. A trick of the light is all we saw. One sees strange things on purnima. The full moon dazzles the senses. Now, get your thoughts back on your work. It's almost time to open the gates.'

Still the young guard pressed on.

'But Somasra, you saw it too! It was a Garuda. Just like the ones in the frescoes at the War Museum. From the Asura Wars.'

The veteran snorted derisively, choosing not to reply. It was a silent message to the young novice to let the matter drop. First of all, the veteran thought to himself, if that thing they had glimpsed had indeed been a man-vulture, it would have been called a Jatayu. A Garuda was a man-eagle, the great flying mount of the devas and a holy icon. A Jatayu, on the other hand, was not man's friend. But one of the failings of youth was that it tended to be slow to heed warnings, or heeded them too late.

The novice spoke impetuously, ignoring the silent message. 'You were there, Somasra. You fought in the Last War with my father. You've seen creatures like that before, haven't you? How can you say they don't exist?'

That was more than the veteran could take. He turned on his companion sharply. 'Because they don't, is why! You talk about the Last War? What do you know of it? You were not even a seed in your father's gonads when the Last Asura War ended. That was twenty-two years ago this past Shravan. Who are you to speak of such things?'

The young soldier's face turned sullen. He knew how sensitive the old veterans were about talking lightly of the old days and old ways. His father had thrashed him once for simply repeating a play-yard rhyme about rakshasas; he had been only seven at the time. He never made fun

24

of Asuras or the Asura War ever again. Still, he knew what he had seen just now. And it was no ordinary bird.

It was the old guard who spoke again, gruffly, after several minutes of tense silence. 'What do you greenhorns know of Asuras and suchlike? Giant man-vultures? Jatayus? Jatayus, not Garudas, mind you!' He laughed bitterly. 'Aye, I fought with your father, shoulder to shoulder. If not for him, I would not be standing here manning this wall today. Your father was a good man, Vishnu take his atma. He and I saw enough beasts out of hell to last a hundred lifetimes. That's why Maharaja Dasaratha formed the PFs, to give us veterans a regiment of our own. He almost disbanded the entire army, that's how much he wanted to put the war behind him. We all did. Because some things are best forgotten.' He stared into the distance, as if seeing straight into the past. He shuddered once, shook his head, and spat again into the moat.

The young soldier spoke cautiously. 'I didn't mean to be disrespectful, Somasra. It's thanks to you all that we live in times of peace today. I know that. Every Arya in the seven nations knows it.'

The veteran nodded once, acknowledging the apology. 'You're lucky, is what you are, to be born in the first time of peace since the rise of the Arya nations. But don't just thank us PFs. Thank the good Maharaja Dasaratha. He was always at the forefront of the Arya armies, fighting right beside us, and it's thanks to him and Maharaja Janak and the other clan-chiefs that we were able to rid the land of the last Asuras. Why, Dasaratha was away fighting so long, he was in his fortieth year by the time the wars ended, and he hadn't even begun a family yet! Imagine that if you will! Most of us are grandparents by that age, and his queen, bless her atma, had not produced a single heir till then. Even after his return, it took another ten years and two more queens to give him his heirs.

Truly, he gave his best years and best men to the cause. He planted the banyan tree of peace and prosperity beneath which we all shelter today.'

The young soldier nodded, abashed. 'I must have seen a vulture, that's all, and my imagination ran away with me. I've been listening to too many stories in the Veterans' Inn, I guess.'

Somasra laughed, clapping the young man on the back almost hard enough to knock the novice off the wall and into the moat. 'Stories are necessary, young 'un. Even the seers teach us that katha, the art of story, is the food and drink of an intelligent mind. But that's all the tales of the Asura War are now. Stories. And may they always stay just that, Vishnu be praised.'

He looked up abruptly, squinting at the eastern sky. 'Past gate-opening time. Move to it, greenhorn. Time enough for stories and wine when the shift's ended.' He winked, his grizzled features a grey shadow in the dusky dimness. 'You want Jatayus? I'll tell you a story about Jatayus that'll turn your blood to icemelt, over a matka of the maharaja's bhaang at the Holi feast today. Now get back to work.'

The gates opened a few minutes later and the two mismatched guards had no time to discuss mythical giant vultures again. They were busy working the heavy winch-wheel that lowered the enormous wooden gate. The gate also served as a bridge across the moat outside; when lowered fully, it spanned the fifteen-yard gap. The sound of it settling in its iron cradle was like a giant thumping his fist. Then they worked the levers that drained and refilled the moat with fresh water directly from the river. This was done weekly to avoid diseases breeding in the water.

A small crowd was waiting outside the gate when it came down. The brief chatter between the two guards had delayed gate-opening by a few minutes. The other six gates had already opened and allowed in the travellers eager to enter Ayodhya.

It was a motley bunch. Mostly bullock-carts carrying entire families from the outlying northern farms, children squealing excitedly at the thought of spending a feast day in the great city. A few kshatriyas, professional armsmen, also arriving for the festival or simply passing through. A courier from Mithila, Ayodhya's sister city in the eastern region of Kosala, with Maharaja Janak's royal seal on his leather bag. A few brahmins on foot or riding mules and asses, their enormous bellies murmuring at the promise of the feast ahead. A vendor leading three camels laden with bagfuls of rang, the brightly coloured powders used during the Holi festival. An assortment of street entertainers—a snake charmer, a family of acrobats carrying their paraphernalia, a rope climber, two jadugars, a flautist, a Shaivite self-flagellator wielding a five-yard-long set of metal-tipped whips, a bear-and-monkey show-man. They were just the early birds. By sunrise, there would be an incessant flow of traffic into Ayodhya. In recent years, it seemed as if every citizen in the kingdom of Kosala wanted to come to their capital city to avail themselves of the king's open-house policy of free food and drink to all for the day. Holi was the biggest festival day of the Arya year apart from Deepavali. And while Deepavali provided one last opportunity to celebrate and feast before the onset of winter, Holi marked the celebration of the first day of spring. A new beginning to a new harvest year.

The two seventh-gate guards watched the ragged caravan of travellers trundle excitedly through the open gates. It was Somasra's ageing but still sharp eyes that saw the figure in the thick of the crowd, a tall white-bearded man clad in the red-ochre robes of a seer, carrying a wildwood staff. Somasra peered at the seer and blinked, startled.

27

The crowd cleared, turning right and left as their business took them, and for a moment the seer was clearly visible, illuminated in the flickering torchlight from the mashaals bordering the gate. He strode purposefully into the city, heading up Harishchandra Avenue. Somasra rubbed his eyes, unable to believe he was seeing right.

If his eyesight hadn't failed him at last, then that old seer over there, now already several dozen yards down the main street of Ayodhya, was none other than the legendary seer-mage Brahmarishi Vishwamitra himself. The famous likeness was unmistakable, a mirror image of the huge portrait in the Seers' Gallery. But how could it possibly be Vishwamitra? The great seer hadn't been seen by human eyes in over . . . how many years was it? Two hundred? Two hundred and fifty?

Several minutes later, while Somasra was still trying to decide whether he had seen correctly, the real Vishwamitra, still disguised as a sudra hunter, strode through the gate, following the same route as the impostor who had assumed his form. This time, even Somasra's alert vision failed to recognise the visitor.

SIX

Manthara hated her own shadow. It was one thing to be a hunchback and quite another to see the deformed evidence of her own misshapen form projected ten times lifesize on to a wall. But the serving girl holding the mashaal had been slow in getting out of the carriage after her, and was following Manthara when she should have been ahead of her. The flickering flames of the backlight sent Manthara's shadow fleeing ahead of her, dancing across the cobbled street then up the wall that marked the end of the blind alley. At this dark hour, after yet another sleepless night in a succession of sleepless nights spent in anxious anticipation, the sight was more than Manthara could bear. She turned abruptly to face the startled serving girl and laid her hand across the wretch's face. The girl cried out, whimpering, but kept her hold on the mashaal. Even in the flickering glow, the marks of Manthara's long bony fingers stood out as clearly as lashes on the girl's pale young cheeks. She stared wide-eyed, not knowing what her error had been, and Manthara didn't bother to inform her. She had already turned back and was shuffling the last yards to the door at the end of the alley.

Manthara paused for a moment to listen for the sounds of the night patrol. But her sharp ears heard nothing except

29

the faint sound of the seventh gate being lowered with a booming like distant thunder. It was getting dangerously late. She must return to the palace before the change of guards which took place at dawn.

She raised her hand to knock on the door but it opened even before her knuckles fell on the battered and scarred wood. A short dark figure clad in a flowing black chaddar gestured her in impatiently. She entered a small room dimly lit by a foul-smelling pair of candles and sparsely furnished. The serving girl followed her, extinguishing the mashaal as usual. The walls of the windowless room were painted black and appeared bare of any decoration, but Manthara knew from past experience that when illuminated by a violet light, phosphorescent writing would be revealed, covering virtually every square inch of those apparently blank surfaces. Forbidden tantric symbols in a tribal dialect long since forgotten by most Aryas, pagan markings from a primitive age when the thousands of deities in the Vedic pantheon were regarded not as manifestations of the One True God but as individual gods in their own right, a polytheistic outlook that was considered blasphemy in these civilised times. Even worse, these wall markings professed allegiance to the darkest and most forbidden of those ancient deities. Not the benign and just devas that civilised Aryas worshipped, but the primordial spirit-lords that the Asura races bowed to—and a few discontented Aryas like Manthara herself. Manthara herself was shrewd enough to keep her worship of Asura gods a secret; there were no blasphemous symbols painted on her walls, in phosphorescent paint or otherwise. Even her yagna chamber was secret, unknown to even her mistress and ward, Second Queen Kaikeyi. By painting his walls with such symbols, this tawdry tantric was inviting trouble. The kind of trouble that came dressed

30

in the purple and black uniform of the Purana Wafadars whose job it was, among other things, to seek out and arrest such demon-worshippers.

She turned to the man. 'Do you have what I need?'

He didn't reply. He rarely talked, this one. Most tantrics affected that posture in the belief that it gave them an aura of great wisdom. Manthara didn't care. She didn't have much to say to him anyway, and there was nothing he could say that she would want to hear.

He went over to the far end of the room, bent down and picked up a gunnysack filled with something heavy. Dragging it across the room, he dumped it at her feet. A subdued moan issued from the coarse jute sack and faint movements caused it to billow outward. The tantric frowned, looked around, picked up a short wedge of wood, bent down and clubbed a rounded bulge that was distending the mouth end of the sack. At the unmistakable sound of wood striking bone, the moaning and agitated movements subsided. Satisfied, the tantric dropped the makeshift club and stood, dusting his hands.

Behind Manthara, the serving girl gasped out a brief prayer for forgiveness to the Mother Deity Sri. She was forever offering prayers to the Devi, despite Manthara's specific orders forbidding her. She would have to be reminded later. Manthara unknotted the calf's-leather purse that she wore at her waist and fished out the coins she owed the tantric.

He reached out silently for the rupees but she held them clutched in her fist a moment longer. His eyes registered the delay and rose slowly to meet her own. She realised at once that the man was under the influence of some drug. Ganja, most likely. Tantrics always seemed to favour ganja for some reason. She wrinkled her face with distaste. She disapproved of drugs and intoxicants; they made one careless, and when employed in such undertakings, a careless man was a dead man. She held the money back, bitterly aware of how easily this wretched fool could ruin everything.

She questioned him sharply.

'Were you seen or heard?'

He stared dully at her, his black pupils dilated far more than warranted by the dim light. She waited.

He shook his head at last.

She gestured at the gunnysack.

'He will not be missed?'

She waited another eternity for another dumb shake of his head.

'He was an orphan like the others? Taken from an anarth-ashram like the five before him? No parents or known relatives?'

Another shake of the head.

'And yet you made sure he was a born brahmin, with his naming ceremony and thread ceremony performed correctly, as well as his coming-of-age ceremony performed in the past week, just like the other boys before him?'

A longer pause this time, followed by an up-down affirmative nod.

'And nobody has questioned you about any of the earlier disappearances? You haven't talked to anyone about any of these kidnappings, or about your dealings with me at all? No PFs sniffing around asking funny questions?'

He seemed unsure whether that required a shake or a nod. He settled for moving his head diagonally. His eyes had drifted down to her fist, still clenched tightly around the six silver coins, one for each year of the boy's age.

She wasn't satisfied. Far from it. But if he had been stupid or overtly careless, she wouldn't be standing here bantering right now; PFs would be breaking down the door and hauling them all away to the maharaja's dungeons. And he had delivered a half-dozen brahmin boys to her thus far. It wasn't easy to find someone to kidnap a fresh six-year-old boy every month in a city as priggishly self-righteous as Ayodhya. Even the outlaws and waylayers she had interviewed over the years balked once they learned what was to become of the boys, spitting viciously at her feet. She didn't understand how murderers and thieves could claim to be so righteous, but that was Arya morality for you.

She had found this tantric after great effort and risk. But now, she realised, she had dealt with him once too often. He knew too much of her affairs. With the great day so close at hand, that much knowledge could be dangerous to her. Yes, she decided, she would have to make sure he didn't have an opportunity to share his knowledge with anyone else. She had come much too far to be thwarted now by a pathetic bhaang-addled tantric who thought that a few painted symbols were sufficient to show his devotion to the Dark Lord.

The sound of him clearing his throat distracted her from her thoughts. She realised she was still holding the money and her work here was finished. *Move, Manthara. It will be daybreak soon. There's much to be accomplished today, and it can't be done standing around in this stupid man's shack.*

'Here,' she said disdainfully, holding out the money. To her surprise, he didn't take it.

Instead, he raised his eyes to look at her. Insolently. 'You promised,' he said. His voice was hoarse and cracked. It told her that he took his ganja through a hookah rather than through a chillum.

She frowned. 'Yes, I promised six silvers. Here they are. Take them quickly. I am in a hurry.'

33

He shook his head, straining to express himself better. Speaking in a dialect of commonspeak so chopped and garbled as to be almost incomprehensible. No wonder he didn't talk much. 'Promised, I join you. This yagna. Dark Lord, welcome, into Ayodhya.'

She stared at him. Had she promised this lout that she would let him aid her in performing her yagna? How did she know that this was the crucial rite, the penultimate sacrifice with which she would welcome her lord on the eve of His entry into Ayodhya? Why in the three worlds would she have revealed this much to a ganja-addicted tantric? Then she remembered. It had been his insistence, not her revelation. He had guessed without being told. Had put two and two together over the months—it wasn't hard, given the task she had hired him to do—and had added rumour, dark gossip, and word brought by tantrics from the Southwoods of strange developments afoot. He had come up with this smart but wholly logical conclusion: that she was a worshipper of the Dark Lord of Lanka, who demanded the sacrifice of a threaded brahmin boy at every interface, and who was prophesied to rise from his ignominious failure in the Last Asura War and launch a great new campaign of conquest.

Starting with the invasion of Ayodhya.

Yes, she recalled how eagerly, excitedly, nervously this fool had blurted out his findings and eventual conclusion at their last exchange, and how impatiently she had waved him away, hardly caring whether he thought she was agreeing to his requests or simply dismissing him. She hadn't expected the wretch to have the gumption to actually follow up that ill-voiced demand.

And yet here he was, voicing it again, mumbling on in his fractured ganja-scattered syntax about how his talents and hers would make a perfect union of yoni and lingam shakti, the meshing of female and male energies that resulted in the perfect circle of tantric power. How they would form a new order together, the Order of Lanka, and after the Dark Lord's arrival, they would preside as the high priest and priestess of their new religion.

She resisted the urge to laugh aloud at his impudence. High priest and priestess indeed! This fool would drop dead with terror if the Dark Lord appeared before him even for an instant. And did he really think that by helping feed her sacrificial fire with a few young brahmin boys—for which he had been well paid—he had earned the right to make these ludicrous demands? Really, the human capacity for arrogance was only exceeded by its capacity for ignorance. *Arrogant, ignorant gaddha*!

Sensing that he wasn't getting through to her quite as effectively as he desired, the tantric stopped his rambling and looked at her dully. He was waiting for her response.

She surprised him by smiling warmly. Or as warmly as her wizened, paralysis-stricken right side allowed.

'Of course,' she said, 'you have great vidya, great kala. This knowledge and art would be an immense aid to me in my rituals. The Dark Lord desires acolytes such as yourself to join His cause. We are islanded here in the midst of these deva-worshipping hordes, tiny isolated islets in an ocean of wretched brahman. We must join together and ensure our lord's victory.'

She paused, opening her purse and reaching into it once more. 'As recognition of our new alliance, I offer you in our lord's name this special dispensation. Use it as you see fit to recruit new acolytes to His cause. There is much, much more where this came from. The Dark Lord knows how easily these mortals are seduced by the lure of gold. Keep as much as you think fit as your own reward. You have served Him well and He is greatly pleased.'

She held out a handful of gold and silver rupees that would be enough to purchase a comfortable house in the upper avenues of Ayodhya. His pupils dilated even more as he stared roundly at the small fortune in her fist. His throat jumped as he swallowed, and he nodded dumbly, acquiescing. He held out his hands, cupped together, to receive the lavish payment, probably more money than he had ever seen in all his wretched life.

She turned her hand to drop the coins into his open palms, then pretended to lurch sideways, spilling the money across the floor. It jangled and clanked and rolled in several directions at once. He stared dully at the coins for a moment, then dropped hard to his knees and began scrambling around frantically.

Manthara watched him for a moment, then she parted the folds of her thick robe and pulled out the long curved dagger she had sheathed in a specially made leather-lined pocket. She had poured several drops of a potion of her own making into the sheath before sliding the dagger in before she left the palace a half-hour ago, a precaution she took whenever she went on one of these illicit nocturnal forays. As she exposed the dagger to the smoky candlelight, the tip of the wavy blade gleamed yellowish-green with the lethal poison. She gripped the dagger's hilt tightly in both hands, the double-grip ensuring a steadier stance with her deformity.

Then she bent and struck the tantric on the back of his neck with the dagger. Just a prick, barely enough to break the skin. He seemed not to feel it at first, still pawing the floor in search of his lost reward. Then, after a moment, he stopped, grew still, and slowly reached up to touch the back of his neck. The tiniest spot of blood came away on a fingertip. He stared at it for an instant, then put the fingertip in his mouth, sucking. Slow recognition dawned on his scrawny features. He started to raise his eyes, seeking out Manthara. Before he could find her, the poison—admitted through his blood as well as through his mouth by now—took effect. His nerves spasmed and he fell face-down on the floor, the coins he had managed to gather falling again noisily.

Manthara watched his death throes for a moment, then turned to the serving girl. Her face had turned as white as a brahmin's dhoti. She was pressed back against the door, as if trying to melt into the wood and disappear.

'Take the bag to the carriage,' Manthara said harshly. 'Make sure the footmen don't know what it contains. Place it in the usual khazana box inside. Carefully. You bruised the last one.'

The serving girl looked as if she would bolt. Her hand crept down to the door latch. But at the last moment, her eyes returned to the spasming, choking tantric on the ground and she remembered the fate that befell those who crossed Manthara. She darted forward, picked up the gunnysack, threw it over her shoulder like a bag of potatoes, and preceded Manthara out of the door.

Manthara stayed a moment, surveying the foul-smelling candle-lit room. There was something here that could be used to her advantage. There was always something. She pulled a scarf from within the folds of her robe, an anonymous silk garment used by the titled and untitled queens alike in the maharaja's palace—but only by them. With a smile as sly as a mongoose toying with a cobra, she reached down and placed it in the dead tantric's fist, as if he had snatched at his assailant in his last moment. There. That would fox his fellow tantrics, give them something to get worked up about. Anger could be useful.

Leaving the shack, she was caught unawares by the brightness. She raised her deformed right hand, snarling.

The wretched purnima moon. Full and bloated as a pregnant witch, it glared down at her, omniscient and grim as a judge. In her clan, Chandramukhi, the moon deity, had been a revered and feared totem. All clan panchayat judgements had been passed on purnima nights like this one. Even though her loyalties had changed long since, it was difficult to shrug off the instinctive fear drummed in by those youthful rituals. She drew the cowl of the robe over her head and walked as quickly as her hunchbacked gait would permit.

Her moon-cast shadow danced before her all the way down the alley, mocking her silently. She spat on it before climbing into the carriage and kept the drapes drawn tight all the way back to the maharaja's palace.

KAAND I

Childhood's End

ONE

'Kausalya!'

The winding corridors of the First Queen's Palace reverberated with the booming voice. The female guards at the entrance goggled at the large barrel-chested man striding towards them, then hurriedly lowered their spears and bowed to their king. Men were forbidden in the First Queen's Palace, with only one exception. Maharaja Dasaratha, ruler of the kingdom of Kosala, was that solitary exception, yet it had been so long since he had last entered these chambers that some of the female attendants stirring sleepily or peeping through silk curtains and ornately filigreed panels took several startled moments to identify the loud-voiced visitor. Some scrambled to cover their modesty with whatever was at hand—satin cushions, a billowing drape, a silver flower vase—while others deliberately flaunted their nudity, seeking to attract the eyes of the maharaja by posturing coyly in doorways and on luxurious shaasan. They knew that apart from the three queens in their individual palaces, there were three hundred and fifty more wives in the king's palace. Yet it never hurt to try.

But the maharaja's eyes did not stray to those distracting feminine bodies or those alluring almond-shaped eyes. He strode through the First Queen's Palace with an energetic gait that belied his considerable bulk and age.

'Kausalya,' he called again. The calling was more by way of giving her advance warning of his approach. It had been a long time since he had come to these chambers and he covered up his anxiety and nervousness with bluster and authority. It was an effective disguise; to the startled serving girls, it seemed the most natural thing in the world to see the maharaja striding through the palace, calling his maharani.

He passed through the last of the forerooms and emerged into a small chaukat, a square without a roof. Glancing up at the sky as he stepped around the delicate sculptures and the marble fountain in the centre of the chaukat, he saw that dawn was just breaking, turning the sky several shades of purple. A soft dewy precipitation made the air cool and fragrant here, carrying the aroma of the first queen's famous gulmohur gardens. He glanced nostalgically at the statue of Kama that towered above the fountain and the lotus pool, smiling wistfully at the sugarcane bow and flower-arrow held daintily in the marble god's chubby hands. He remembered when Kausalya had first installed this fountain, showing it off with great pride—she had personally conceived the whole arrangement, as she had the interiors of most of her palace. He had watched wonder-struck, holding her in his arms at the base of this very fountain, beneath the midnight-blue sky of a Varsha night, as a gentle drizzle fell on them. Seventeen long years separated that day from this one. And yet, the sight of the fountain brought back the memory as clearly as if it had been just days ago.

'Kausalya,' he called again, gently this time, as he passed into the inner chambers. A young serving girl, lying virtually naked on a shaasan despite this being the end of winter, squealed and sprang to her feet, then froze, wide-eyed as a doe before a chariot, transfixed by the sight of her king bearing down on her. Dasaratha noted her large breasts and spare bony ribs tapering down to a waist slender enough for his hands to go around. He put a hand out, gripping the girl gently by the shoulder—and moved her aside gently. His elbow brushed her breasts as he passed her, and he heard her emit a tiny gasp. He walked on without a backward glance.

He noted the distinct change in decor as he entered his queen's private chambers. A muted, almost sombre effect achieved through sober colours and exquisitely chosen furnishings and artefacts displayed at perfect aesthetic intervals. Even the mashaal stands and candelabra were arranged artistically, their fluted vents designed to conceal their true purpose, which was simply to provide an upward exit for the smoke and heat of the flames. He shook his head wryly as he trod carelessly over intricately embroidered eastern carpets without even noticing their unusual weaves and patterns. It was like stepping through a doorway between ages, back into the past.

He paused, struck by the sensations coursing through his body. Once he had spent almost every single waking hour in these chambers, and all his sleeping ones. It was startling to see how little it had changed.

The chamber was empty. He was about to turn away, about to look elsewhere for Kausalya, when something caught his eye. The flash of a familiar face at the far end of the room. There, by the window, in an alcove where the flickering light of the mashaal barely reached. It drew him like an apsara drawing a traveller to her enticing embrace.

It was a portrait of Kausalya and himself. From back then. He winced at the difference between himself then and now, the slender, tautly muscled limbs that had thickened and softened, the torso that had seemed sculpted

43

and so sharply masculine then and was now filled out and almost rounded, the face that was so clear and bright with ambition then, now turned dark and fleshy, the hair . . . Enough, enough. Bad enough that his physicians berated him constantly for his excess weight and lack of exercise; he didn't need a picture from the past to rub salt into the wounds. At sixty-three years of age, physical appearance was the least of his concerns.

But he could stand to look at Kausalya a moment longer. Or an eternity. Her beauty still took his breath away. He reached out, compelled to touch that soft face, that smooth cheek unlined by years of care, childbearing and motherhood. She was a picture of Arya perfection: doe-eyed, raven-haired, wheat-complexioned, delicately featured, small-limbed, large-breasted . . . In her carefree smile, he could see himself, young, strong, unaffected by these mystery ailments and unaccountable fainting spells.

The sound of bells brought him out of his reverie. He turned with a rustling of his silk dhoti to see Kausalya, a pooja thali in her hands, standing in the doorway of her bedchamber. Unlike his own weary, illness-plagued body, Kausalya's beauty had matured like a ripening mango, swelling just enough to enhance her femininity. And her eyes, those deep dark eyes he had once swore he could see his soul mirrored in, those eyes were still the same. Still smouldering. Except that right now, at the sight of him standing uninvited in her private bedchamber, they were closer to blazing.

'Ayodhya-naresh,' she said, using his formal title. 'What brings you to this forlorn part of the city?'

He grimaced as the barb struck home. The First Queen's Palace was right beside his own, linked by a common corridor, no more than a few hundred yards away.

'It's good to see you haven't lost your wit, Kausalya,' he said, walking towards her. 'Nor your sense of dharma.' The second comment was directed at the pooja thali in her hands.

She raised her eyebrows, feigning surprise. 'Dharma, my lord? A big word to use for a small act of daily habit. Surely all your queens begin their day by offering a few basic prayers to the ancestors, the gods, and to their lord and master? No decent married woman in Kosala would do any less.'

He shifted his gaze, pretending to examine the view through a latticed window. The dawn was just breaking and he could glimpse the neatly arrayed rows of flowers and smell the strong, arousing odour of jasmine, always her favourite. He knew her comment was directed at the fact that his second queen, Kaikeyi, was more likely to be sleeping at this hour than performing the ritual dawn prayer. He resisted the provocation in the comment with a small effort. It had been a long time since anyone had dared to rebuke or taunt him.

'Kausalya,' he tried again, 'how have you been, my queen? I trust all is well with you? You do not want for anything?' He tried to put as much sincerity as possible into his voice, to sound suitably regal and king-like to deflect any further arrows of sarcasm.

But she was not done yet. Barely begun. Her still lovely face twisted slightly in a small moue of mock surprise. 'Me, great naresh?' she said, using the Sanskrit word for lord this time—anything but his first name, he noted. 'What is there about me that could possibly interest you any longer?'

He smiled with an effort. 'Come, come now. You know that you are my first queen, my first bride.' He gestured at the large empty bed that dominated the chamber. 'We have shared so many happy nights here on this playground of pleasure.'

'And we do so no more.' The rebuke was as sharp and brief as a whip-crack.

His smile faded. 'Let me come to the point. I came here this morning because—'

She shook her head. 'Not yet, my king. Not all your wives may be as diligent in their duties, but I was brought up better than that. There are traditions to be followed.'

Before he could protest, she clapped her hands. A serving girl, perhaps the same one he had passed in the hallway outside, appeared instantly, bowing low enough to almost strike her forehead on the floor. She had clothes on now, but he didn't notice.

'Arghya,' Kausalya said, and the girl scuttled away, returning at once with a large metal bowl and jug of water.

He sighed as he took the seat Kausalya indicated. 'My queen, this is ridiculous. Arghya is done to greet a guest honouring your house with a rare visit. Not your own husband!'

She looked up from her crouched posture as she washed his feet. 'I could name guests who have visited our house more often, raje.'

That one cut deep. He reached down and grasped her arms, stopping her in the act of wiping his feet dry with the end of her own sari pallo. 'I have to speak to you on a matter of great importance. Dispense with these foolish games.'

She looked down at her hands. At his large hairy fists gripping her wrists, pressing her gold bracelets into her slender forearms. 'You are truly a great king, Ayodhya-naresh. You visit your first wife's chambers after such a long absence, and this is how you show your affection towards her.'

46

He released her wrists at once, stung with shame. Even if she had goaded him, it was his own guilt that had provoked his temper. He turned away, unable to look her in the eyes for a moment. He had been away from her for too long; had forgotten that she was not Kaikeyi. And now, in re-entering her little circle of power, he had granted her the opportunity to taunt him, rebuke him, make him feel as guilty as a young bridegroom stealing a kiss from his sister-in-law. He willed himself to stay calm. After all, he had been prepared for this when he made the decision to visit her this morning. Whatever the provocation now, he would stay within the bounds of chivalry.

But her next words were completely unexpected, as was her tone. Her voice was gentle and soft and sincere. And it came from right beside him. Her hand touched his bare arm and the very touch brought sense-memories flooding back.

'Raje,' she said, again using the affectionate 'e' suffix instead of the more formal 'maharaja'. 'I apologise if I spoke harshly. It has been a long time since you graced me with your presence. I have been so long in my own company, I seem to have forgotten how to behave in the presence of my king.'

He was startled to find his eyes turning moist. The nape of his neck creeping with shame.

She went on. 'Please, do me the honour of sitting with me in my akasa-chamber. Together we shall watch the new day dawn and you may speak your mind freely. I shall not forget the rules of royal hospitality again.'

He turned and gripped her shoulders so unexpectedly, so strongly, she gasped at first. Then she saw the look in his eyes. Not anger. Far from it.

'Please,' he said, making no attempt to sound regal any longer, 'say no more. Not another word. I am ashamed enough as it is.'

Her eyes widened. 'Raje?'

'Please. Believe me. I have never stopped loving you. Not a day, not an hour, not a moment has passed when I did not think of you.'

She stared. For once, Kausalya the silver-tongued was at a loss for words.

'I know,' he went on, 'that I acted foolishly, even cruelly. I neglected you without cause or reason, explanation or excuse. It is shameful in a kshatriya, unforgivable in a king. But even after I realised it, I did not know how to express my regret to you. How to make amends. Even the gurus are not so wise in matters of men and women, Kausalya.'

She shook her head slowly. 'I had no idea.'

He hung his head. 'You do not know how many times I desired to come to you, to beseech you to forgive me. To let me start afresh.'

She looked at him as if seeing him now for the first time since he had entered her chambers. 'You should have come. I would have forgiven you in a trice. If only you had come.'

'Yes,' he said hoarsely. 'I should have come. But I had not the heart. You know, you alone know, how much I fear rejection. I hesitate to venture where I might not find certain victory. For grieving as I was—yes, that is the word, grieving for our lost love—I could not bear the thought of you turning me away, pushing me out. Then I should have been lost utterly.'

'How could I?' she cried. 'Turn you away? Push you out? You fool? You royal fool! I would have taken you in with open arms. I could never turn you away.'

He stared at her. 'Is it true then? Would you have forgiven me so easily?'

She looked down for a moment. There was a ragged edge to her voice when she spoke again. 'Perhaps forgiveness would have taken a while. I am no devi, just a woman. A woman still trying to be a queen. But I would have let you stay. Of that much you can be certain.'

They were both silent for several moments. Thinking of the nights they had lain awake in their respective beds, so near to one another, yet so emotionally distant. Longing, wanting, fearing.

'I *am* a fool,' he admitted. 'An old fool now.'

She looked up anxiously. The deterioration in his health had been no secret around the palace. 'Have you had more attacks? The royal vaids—'

He snorted. 'The royal vaids find my ailment fascinating to study, and impossible to cure!' He shook his head. 'I am being uncharitable. They do their best, it is true. Yet even the great medical science of Ayurveda doesn't have all the answers.' He shrugged aside the topic brusquely. 'We will speak of that later, I promise. But right now, I am better than I have been in years.' He gestured wistfully at the portrait of his younger self. 'Not what I was once. Never again that strength, that burning ambition, that war-lust, that—' He coughed once. 'But I feel good. Better than I have felt in a long time. Perhaps that is why I was able to find the strength to come to you at last.'

He looked at her, a gentleness in his moist eyes that was more than mere politeness.

'And I thank the ancestors that I did.'

She felt his gaze move down her face, to her breasts, her still slender waist, her flaring hips, her navel . . . He saw her fair almond-white complexion turn scarlet, the flush spreading from her cheeks to her throat . . . He moved closer.

'Kausalya,' he whispered in her ear.

Her knees buckled and gave way. She slipped down, her sari rustling, bangles clinking against each other.

49

She crumpled in a heap at his feet, boneless, breathless. He sighed and bent with an effort. He caught her hands and pulled her to her feet. She came easily, not resisting, and he caught a whiff of jasmine and was instantly flooded with memories. Of their first years together, their first nights, when there had been only she and he, no second or third queens, no three hundred and fifty other wives, just a young prince and his princess, lying on a flower-bedecked bed in the open chaukat beneath the stars. The jasmine brought that back with a suddenness that was all the more shocking because he had blocked out the memories for so long.

She looked up at him with eyes that were as wide, as beautiful—no, far more beautiful—as the ones in the portrait. No amount of artistry could capture the way the light caught her eyes, this glowing inner flame that made her seem both angel and conquering warrior princess. It was as if the years had never passed, as if she had never borne a son, as if he had never lost interest in her and grown distant, as if . . .

He shook his head and released her, stepping back. His bare feet trod on the edge of the arghya bowl and tipped it over, spilling water and making a clattering sound that echoed hollowly in the large chamber. Neither noticed or cared.

He drew her to the bed. As he did, he saw her reach out and yank on a slender tasselled cord tied to a post of the bed. A shower of cool, delicately scented rose petals coated the bed and their bodies. He was amazed. How many years had she waited, night after night, replenishing that cache of petals daily, for just this one moment when he would come to her again? He could not conceive of such infinite patience. He was astonished to find himself weeping with pleasure and pain both at once, the pleasure of her clasp and the pain of their long separation.

He remembered then that he had not yet spoken to her of the real reason for his coming to visit her. Afterwards. He would tell her immediately afterwards.

TWO

Second Queen Kaikeyi was being murdered by a rakshas.
The horned demon was sitting astride her chest, crushing
her lungs with his bear-like bulk, hammering away at
her head with his pounding paws, as rhythmically as a
dhol-player at a Holi celebration. Bam-bam-bam-bam,
pause, bam-bam-bam-bam, pause.

He would have continued until her skull cracked open
to spill out her brains but her thought of Holi seemed to
interrupt his rhythm. He growled angrily and squeezed
his thighs, making her ribs ache unspeakably.

She struggled to open her eyes. Holi. What was it about
the festival of Holi that had angered the rakshas? It was
sometime soon, wasn't it? She knew it was, because just
the other day Manthara had told her that this was Bharat's
first Holi at home since the age of seven. Kaikeyi had been
startled to hear this. She knew Bharat and his brothers
had spent several years at Guru Vashishta's gurukul, being
schooled in God knows what. But they had been home
for three seasons now, and it seemed like he had always
been here with her. Had he really been away for eight
years? Manthara couldn't be mistaken, she was never
mistaken. That was why Kaikeyi trusted her to decide
everything for her.

Where was Manthara now anyway? Why wasn't she doing something about this damn rakshas sitting on her chest? And this head. Blessed Earth-Mother Sri. She wished the rakshas would just tear off her head and be done with it. Decapitation would be a blessed relief after this pounding. Then she might dare to open her eyes and resume her life once more. Of course it might be awkward to pursue a normal life without a head. Although of course the great god Ganesha had managed fine with a baby elephant's head.

Perhaps she could have a doe's head attached, or better still, a stag, one of those giant Nilgiri stags, ten feet high at the shoulder, antlers bristling menacingly. She could picture herself, standing naked, her neckline ragged and blood-smeared, with the head of a Nilgiri stag, proud and black-eyed, antlers rising like a bizarre crown. Interesting. In a strange gods-and-monsters kind of way. Like a mythic victim of a terrible curse. Arousing, like those strange paintings of twisted creatures she had once seen at a foreign merchant's stall on the road to Janakpuri.

'Kaikeyi!'

Or like those tribals she had watched performing that dance inspired by the forbidden shakti-pooja ritual. The dance had been so shockingly coarse, she had wondered what it would have been like to witness the ritual itself. Or even—bite your tongue—participate in it. The tribals had worn animal pelts, complete with heads and glassily staring eyes. That was how she would look if she had the head of a Nilgiri stag and the body of a woman, a perfect body like she used to have, before marriage, before motherhood, before living well and eating even better took their toll. What a formidable, terrifying, awe-inspiring thing she would be.

'Kaikeyi, if you don't wake up this instant, I will pour this ice-cold water on your head.'

And if she danced for Dasaratha then, really danced, not the cautious, precisely choreographed natya performances designed for royal viewing but the wild abandoned frenzy of the Gandaharis or Kazakhs or Krygziks, then even his long ailing would not be able to suppress the urges he would feel. Yes, she would have that power over him once again. That sense of complete and utter control.

'Kaikeyi, this is your last warning, girl. Next comes the water. Brace yourself.'

Why did the stupid hag always call her 'girl'? Just because she had tended her since childhood. It was ludicrous to call her that at this age. She was a mother. A queen no less. And yet Manthara still treated her like she was nothing more than a snivelling, spoilt little—

'Aaaah!'

She sat up in bed, opening her eyes to a watery hell. No, not hell, for hell would be hot and blazing. This was cold, ice cold, and the stupid hag had splashed it across her face and her chest—she still had the jug in her hand, as she stood there, grinning her crooked-toothed grin—like she was washing down a horse or, or, or . . .

'Manthara,' Kaikeyi spluttered, wiping water from her eyes. 'You witch!'

Manthara's grin widened. 'Yes, me witch.' She dropped the arghya jug with a clatter and shuffled forward, reached out with one wizened, claw-like hand. Slapping Kaikeyi once across each cheek, hard enough to sting. 'And you hussy. Now wake up, and see where your master has gone while you slept the dawn away.'

Kaikeyi blinked rapidly, the slaps completing the wake-up process the water had started. Manthara's use of foul language told her at once that something was seriously wrong; the hunchback wasn't above using bad language to express herself at times, but when she addressed Kaikeyi in such terms, it always meant that Kaikeyi had made a serious mistake, one that had repercussions on her, Manthara's, own life and fortunes. And while Manthara could overlook a mistake that affected Kaikeyi alone, she would never, ever forgive a mistake that affected herself. That was a lesson Kaikeyi had learned a very long time ago, as a girl barely tall enough to reach Manthara's knee, staring up with large infant eyes at the hulking hunchbacked woman who had absolute power over her life and needs, or so it had seemed then.

Kaikeyi scooted to the far side of the bed, her miserable headache suddenly forgotten. Suddenly she was that little girl again, clinging fearfully to Manthara's sari, completely at the mercy of her daiimaa. It had been years since Manthara had thrashed her physically but Kaikeyi suspected she intended to make up for lost time. She had that familiar diamond-bright gleam in her eyes and the part of her lower lip where her overhanging upper teeth rested was shiny with spittle.

Kaikeyi drew her knees up to her chest, crouching at the far edge of the large luxurious bed, watching Manthara with feral darting eyes. She didn't know what she might have done to enrage her surrogate mother-cum-nanny but she didn't intend to sit still and accept whatever new brutality Manthara was planning to dish out.

To her surprise, Manthara's next words were a question, not the string of four-letter words she'd expected.

'How long is it since he came to you?'

Kaikeyi rose to her knees and stared suspiciously at Manthara, wiping away the water seeping from her drenched tresses into her eyes. 'Who?'

The hunchback snorted. 'Who? Foolish woman, your husband. The King of Kosala, master of Ayodhya, Maharaja

55

Dasaratha, who else? How many other men do you share your bed with?'

Kaikeyi wasn't sure if that was meant to be a real question or a rhetorical one. She had never been good with subtlety and the pounding in her skull had only become worse. Oh, what cheap brew had that lout at the inn poured into her cup last night? She held her head in her hands and struggled to frame a good answer instead. What was the question again? Ah yes, how long had it been since Dasaratha had visited her bed? Good question. How long *had* it been?

'I don't know,' she replied at last, truthfully for once. 'A long time. Maybe a year, maybe longer.'

Manthara nodded thoughtfully, setting the jug down on a chaupat table—Kaikeyi never actually played the game, but Dasaratha sometimes did. Several pieces— an elephant, a rook, and a few foot-soldiers—tumbled off the squarish board and clattered on the floor. 'That was what I thought. Naturally, I assumed it was because of his health. An ailing septuagenarian does not desire physical intimacy as frequently as a robust young man.'

Manthara wagged a finger. 'But you can never tell with men. They often feign weakness only to conserve their lustful energies for other, newer conquests.' Her face twisted in a snarl. 'I was fooled just as you were, believing his health kept him from your bed. Now, I see, he's had his own agenda, the shrewd bastard.'

Kaikeyi's eyes widened. Manthara's abusive outbursts had never included the maharaja before. She shuddered. Whatever this was about, it was something she didn't want to deal with right now. Not with a splitting headache.

The old hunchback went on sharply, 'What are you gaping at, girl? Standing around here won't do us any good. We have to find out what the old man is up to,

56

and quickly. Get dressed, Kaikeyi.' She gestured at the suit of clothes she had placed on a couch. 'Go on then. Jaldi! There's work to be done.'

Kaikeyi did as she was told without argument. She had endured a lifetime of such bossing about, being told what to wear, what to say, how to say it, what to do and when and to whom. It was almost a relief to fall into this easy obedience. As she wiped the water from her face—this was to be the extent of her morning ablutions today, it seemed—she glanced repeatedly at Manthara, trying to read the daiimaa's mood more clearly.

Manthara stared at a diya beside the bed, her eyes fixed directly on the flickering flame.

'What happened?' Kaikeyi asked as she stripped off the loincloth in which she had slept and put on a fresh one. 'Why are you asking about Dasaratha? What did he do?'

Manthara's attention remained on the lamp, her small glassy pupils transformed into tiny pinpoints of yellow fire by the twin reflections of the diya's flame.

Kaikeyi wrapped the sari around her waist with quick, practised efficiency. 'Manthara,' she said, starting to feel really scared now, 'what's wrong? Talk to me, won't you?'

Manthara looked up at last. The reflected diya flame in her eyes seemed red now, deep fiery ochre, the colour of blood, if blood could flow upwards like a flame.

'The maharaja is in the first queen's bedroom,' she said.

Kaikeyi paused in mid-fold, one hand at her hip, the other holding the bunched material at waist-height. She stared at Manthara, trying to absorb the implications of her words. It must be a joke. Dasaratha hadn't entered Kausalya's chambers in years! Except . . . except . . . Manthara never joked.

'Doing what?' Her voice screeched on the second word.

Manthara's face twisted in another grimace of disgust. 'Doing what men do to women.'

Kaikeyi started. Whatever she had been expecting or fearing, this was not it. 'But . . .' she began, confused and bewildered. She looked around, found the silver lota of water kept on her bedside table, picked it up and downed it in one long swallow. Her tongue worked again, although her throat still felt desert dry. 'But why? Why her? I mean . . . I thought . . . You said he was too ill to . . .' The implication struck her like a sledgehammer. A surge of anger rose like bile in her throat. 'Why *her*, Manthara? Dammit! Why *her*?'

Manthara looked at her grimly. With the flames dancing in her eyes, she eerily resembled the rakshas in Kaikeyi's dream. 'That's what we have to find out, you stupid woman.'

THREE

Pradhan-Mantri Sumantra saw Guru Vashishta levitating a moment before he entered the yoga chamber.

He glimpsed the guru's white-clad long-bearded form between the closely bunched stone pillars that ringed the central chaukat. And for one startled moment, he could have sworn the guru was levitating. Not very high, perhaps just a foot or so—but rising steadily, definitely rising—above the ground. Sumantra's view was blocked for an instant, just a fraction of a second as he rounded the last pillar, but when he reached the chaukat, the guru was firmly seated on the ground, eyes half-shut in the classic yoga-nidra asana of deep transcendental meditation. If it had been anyone else, Sumantra would have thought he'd imagined it and put it out of his mind at once. He was a scientific man, the most pragmatic prime minister the kingdom had ever had. Not given to tales of the Seven Seers and their fantastic mastery of brahman sorcery. But he had never known quite what to make of Guru Vashishta. After all, the brahmarishi was a legend among legends. It was said he had been ordained by the Creator, mighty Brahma himself. Even Sumantra's pragmatic outlook faltered momentarily before such a reputation.

'Namaskar, gurudev.' His message delivered, the prime

minister carefully kept his gaze directed at the guru's feet, waiting silently for the sage's response.

Vashishta remained in the lotus posture for a few moments longer, his eyes shut, breathing slowed to the point of stasis. Out of the corner of his eye, Sumantra imagined he could glimpse a faint bluish tint to the sage's white dhoti. Even the guru's toenails seemed to glow briefly with the electric-blue tint.

Sumantra blinked.

The blue tint was gone. The dhoti's edge was pristine, white as a sesa rabbit and spotless. He swallowed and resisted the urge to rub his eyes. Perhaps he needed to have the royal vaids check his vision once more.

He heard the the sage's breathing gradually assume a more normal rhythm. He sensed rather than saw the sage's eyes opening.

'Kaho, Sumantra.'

The prime minister glanced up, startled. The guru's voice had seemed to come from within his brain itself, rather than from his lips. There was a faint hint of a twinkle in the brahmarishi's eyes as he gazed serenely at Sumantra. And for an instant, Sumantra thought he glimpsed a faint sizzle of electric blue, like two very tiny bolts of blue lightning, within the orb of the seer's pupils. Sumantra blinked twice and they were gone.

'Kaho, Pradhan-Mantri. Kya samasya hain?' *Speak, Prime Minister. What seems to be the problem?*

Sumantra bowed his head, admonishing himself for giving in to his imagination once again. This always seemed to happen when he met Vashishta alone: it was as if the seer-mage was secretly toying with him, testing the limits of his scientific rationality.

'Shama, mahadev. Forgive me for interrupting your sacred meditation. There is a visitor who wishes to have your audience at once. Normally, I would have told any visitor to come back at a more suitable time, but this is no ordinary lord or lady seeking your ashirwaad.'

'Who is it then? Speak, noble Sumantra.'

Sumantra could contain his excitement no longer. 'Mahadev, it is none other than the great sage Vishwamitra himself! The famed seer-mage in person! He is standing at the gate of the royal palace, refusing to take a step inside. He says he cannot enter until invited by the lord of the abode. I pray I did nothing to offend him. I rushed directly here to inform you.'

'You did the right thing as always, Sumantra.' Guru Vashishta was as calm as Sumantra was excited. 'Now you must go and inform the maharaja. Protocol demands that he and I must both go to the gate and welcome this illustrious visitor with all due formality. You understand what an honour this is. Vishwamitra has been in the deep forest, meditating for a great length of time. If he has interrupted his meditation, there must be a very good reason. It is imperative that all the necessary traditions and rituals be followed to the last detail. Go quickly and fetch Maharaja Dasaratha. I will make the other arrangements and meet you both in the foyer in a few minutes.'

Sumantra was not a nervous man and matters of protocol were his daily bread and butter, but he had never been confronted with the dilemma he was in right now.

'Mahadev, the maharaja . . .' He paused, considering how to phrase the rest of the sentence.

Vashishta saw the expression on his face.

'Sumantra? Aakhir samasya kya hai?' he said with no trace of impatience. *What exactly is the problem*?

'Guruji, the maharaja is not in his chambers.'

'So? You must know where he is then. You always know, Sumantra. You are the eyes, ears and conscience of the throne.'

Sumantra nodded. 'Yes, I have an idea where he might be.'

When the mantri did not go on, Vashishta asked with infinite patience: 'Sumantra, where is the king?'

Sumantra raised his eyes reluctantly.

'Guruji, the maharaja is with First Queen Kausalya in her private sleeping chambers.' The slight emphasis he placed on the word *with* left no doubt as to his meaning. 'For the first time in fifteen years.'

There was silence for a minute.

Then, slowly, like the first flush of dawn creeping across the benighted sky, a smile appeared on the face of the mahaguru.

FOUR

Dasaratha and Kausalya reclined on comfortable cushioned floor-mats in the first queen's beautifully designed akasa-chamber. The room was perfectly circular, with an enormous domed roof that filled his entire field of vision when he lay back and looked up. The dome was made of the finest, most translucent glass in the kingdom, so flawless he could see the first flush of dawn spread across the eastern sky as clearly as if he had been lying on a grass mound out of doors. In fact, he mused, when he was young, akasa-chambers were not furnished. Their floors were carpeted daily with freshly scythed kusa grass, soft and dew-dampened, still smelling of earth.

'Raje.'

Kausalya's gentle voice roused him from his daydream. Dasaratha raised himself on his elbow and looked at his queen. She looked contented and sleepy-eyed after their time together. Kausalya was a traditional Arya woman, brought up never to reveal her desires, yet not constrained from enjoying them when a legitimate opportunity presented itself. She was pleased by their joining, he saw, and her pleasure gave him pleasure. With Kaikeyi, his second queen, it was always a challenge. To see who could outdo whom, in what exotic manner. Almost a

63

circus. And with Sumitra, his docile youngest wife, the third queen, it was like lying with a naïve gandharva, a forest nymph, so innocent and guileless was she, almost to the point of being unexciting. And with his other wives, it was only the sport of Kama.

But this . . . what he felt now, lying in this state of bliss in the akasa-chamber, staring up at the new day washing the sky clean and preparing to paint a gorgeous sunrise, the first spring sunrise of the year, he felt . . . at home. It had been a long time since he had felt this good.

'Much as I would love you to come to me every day like this,' she said softly in his ear, 'you did mention something you wished to discuss with me. What was it?'

He smiled up at her.

'Yes, my rani. I do indeed have something of great importance to tell you. But any discussion about it will have to wait for later. Already I have spent almost an hour in your beguiling embrace. Much as I hate to leave your company, our good Sumantra and mahaguru Vashishta will already be seeking me out. And in another hour or two, the festival celebrations will begin in earnest and then the usual endless queue of court nobility and well-wishers will start arriving with their rang thalis.'

What he said was true. It was customary to visit a colleague or superior's house on Holi and apply a little rang on their face; in Dasaratha's case, all of Ayodhya looked upon it as a golden opportunity to share a rare moment of friendly intimacy with their king. Kausalya smiled at the mention of the rang thalis. She remembered nights spent massaging him with warm, gently scented coconut oil to cleanse the rang stains and soothe his tired nerves. Behind the public pomp and ceremony of the maharaja's throne, there were a million such private inconveniences.

She touched his arm affectionately, stroking the curling silver growth that sprouted thickly along the back of his hand. 'Dasa, just tell me what's on your mind.'

He took his first queen's hand in his own and looked into her eyes. He wanted to see her initial, most natural reaction. He was not a great patron of the performing arts—to him hunting wild boar was a sport, not dancing with silver bells attached to one's feet—but he was a great observer of human behaviour, a necessary skill for anyone dealing with the machinations and politics of high office, and he had considerable ability in reading human faces and reactions, particularly at unguarded moments. He spoke in an almost flat tone, denuding his voice of all stresses or emotions. He could have been asking her to bring him a paan, specifying what supari he wanted in it and whether he wished the betelnut flaked, cut or sweetened.

'Today, after the Holi parade, I will announce the coronation of my successor. I will name our son Rama crown prince of Ayodhya.'

Of all the possible responses Dasaratha had expected, the expression on Kausalya's face and the words from her lips were the last ones imaginable. In fact, they weren't even in the range of responses he was expecting.

Her face drained of all colour, turning her already pale complexion into an almost albino whiteness—she had always had a tendency to iron-lack in the blood, he recalled. His first thought was that she was fainting with shock. But then her hand, the one that had been caressing him so gently an instant ago, tightened on his forearm in a grip stronger than he had felt in years. Leaning forward, she looked at him with tears misting in her eyes and said in a voice choked with sudden shock:

'But you're still young, Dasa. You still have many years of life and vigour in you. Your father Aja, his father

Raghu, your ancestors, almost all the Suryavansha kings, reigned well into their grey years. Why, Raghu was almost thirty years older than you when he crowned Aja prince of Ayodhya. It's too soon to step down from the throne. It's much too soon, Dasa.'

Dasaratha found himself filled with an emotion so powerful, he was unable to find his voice for a moment. When he could speak again, the tremor in his voice betrayed his inner feelings.

'My queen, what breed of woman are you? I tell you I am going to crown your birth-son Rama prince of Ayodhya and you try to dissuade me! Is this the way a mother speaks?'

'No,' Kausalya replied. 'This is the way a queen speaks, out of love and concern for her husband and king.'

Dasaratha was silent. Suddenly the smells and sights of the akasa-chamber seemed unbearable. Was it possible for any woman to love her husband this much? To be more concerned about her liege's health than about her son's inheritance?

Dasaratha was no philosopher or sage, but he knew that what he had just witnessed, was still witnessing, was a hallmark in his long illustrious life. Kausalya had passed his test and proved herself a perfect wife.

His eyes brimmed with an emotion that was simultaneously sorrowful and joyous. 'You are like no other woman I have ever known, Kausalya.' He didn't need to add the obvious corollary: and like no other wife.

Kausalya ignored the compliment, eyes still shining with anxious concern. 'Raje, I beg of you, reconsider your decision.'

Dasaratha shook his head. 'It is already marked on the royal calendar, my queen. Guru Vashishta has even picked an auspicious date for the coronation. The tenth day of the first half of the month of Chaitra.'

Kausalya sat up. 'On Rama's sixteenth birthday?'

'Not just his birthday; it's the most auspicious day of the year apart from the usual feast days.' He appealed to her maternal side. 'Almost as auspicious as the day he was born to you, my queen. That night was truly a great tryst of the stars and planets. It was as if the devas themselves graced his birth with good omens.'

Her eyes softened. 'It was a miraculous moment.'

'Miracle is the right word. He came to us when we had lost all hope of progeny. After all the yagnas and pooja rituals had failed to produce results. All of Kosala celebrated for a week.'

He saw her yield and pressed home his advantage. 'What better muhurat to announce Rama's coronation than the sixteenth anniversary of that miraculous day?'

She hesitated, torn now between her spousal concern and maternal pride. 'But that's this month. Less than half a moon from today! Dasa, all I'm asking is why so soon? It's barely been a year since he's been home from the gurukul. Give him a little time to grow, to learn. To marry even. Once the cares and weight of statehood fall upon his shoulders, he will no longer be a boy. Give him a little more time, Dasa.'

Dasaratha did something unexpected. He bent forward and kissed Kausalya's maang, the tip of the centre parting of her hairline where a husband customarily anointed his wife with blood-red sindhoor powder, symbolic of the blood oath of marriage. He kissed her there, at that symbolic spot, with tenderness. When he drew back, he saw the surprise and pleasure in her eyes. And she saw the tears in his own.

'There is no more time, Kausalya. I am dying. The vaids and Guru Vashishta agree that my remission is a temporary reprieve before the end. The illness that plagues me has run its course, as I have run mine. Before I die, I will see Rama crowned prince, if it's the last thing I do.'

FIVE

Before Kausalya could respond to Dasaratha's shocking revelation, the drapes at the entrance to the akasa-chamber stirred and a small female voice spoke deferentially. Kausalya replied at once, her wits always about her. Dasaratha made out a half-familiar phrase in the queen's native eastern dialect, Banglar, then the girl left them.

Kausalya turned to him. 'You are needed. Guru Vashishta has sent for you urgently. He waits in your palace.'

Dasaratha frowned. Guru Vashishta would never disturb him in his queen's private chambers unless it was a matter of great urgency. He hoped it wasn't another territorial dispute over river waters and dams; he didn't think he could stand another raging debate in a multitude of local dialects. He tried to conceal his weariness with jocularity. 'Something to do with the coronation announcement this morning, no doubt. Probably he wishes to add yet another ceremony to the list. You know how brahmins love ceremonies, my queen. They won't let anything be done without elaborate never-ending rituals with lots of chanting, agar-incense and bells! Why are they always so fond of bells? I can barely pray with those bells clanging in my ears!'

He rose with an effort, impatiently waving away Kausalya when she attempted to aid him. He was more tired than he realised, but he would have died rather than admit it to her. Still, it had been worth it. He looked at Kausalya's face, still faintly flushed, crow-black tresses loosened and falling about her shoulders, and felt a twinge of desire despite his condition.

She smiled, as if sensing his thoughts. 'It would not do to keep Guruji waiting.'

He was tempted to reply with a suggestive retort but said instead, 'Do me the honour of accompanying me in the official ceremonies.' Adding with a boyish grin, 'It will make the bells more bearable.'

Kausalya kissed him on the cheek. He was touched to see tears brimming in her eyes. 'Do you even have to ask? I will be at your side every minute if you but permit me. And if the devas permit, I would go with you to Lord Yama's domain as well.'

He looked at her wordlessly. Her comment needed no explanation: only the dead travelled to the underworld domain of Yama, Lord of Death.

Kausalya touched his arm gently, urging him to move.

'Go with grace, Dasaratha.'

He turned to leave, afraid to attempt any response. Even regal restraint had its limitations when it came to emotional borders.

'Dasa?'

Her voice was small, the voice of a tremulous young bride rather than a queen of the mightiest Arya nation. He stopped at the doorway of the chamber.

'Yes, my love?'

'As always, I respect and shall uphold your decision. Yet do not fault me if I continue to hope that you will yet rule another forty sun-years.'

He replied without turning his head. If he looked at her face now, he would be lost, he knew. His voice was

70

as tender as that of a young groom greeting his new bride for the first time in their marital bed, soothing her inevitable fear of the unknown male whose bed and life she was sworn to share until death undid their holy knot.

'My beloved, there is nothing more anyone can do. The vaids and the seers have done all that is humanly possible. The matter is beyond the abilities of all vedic science and Arya knowledge.'

There was a brief pause as if she might have shaken her head slowly or gestured.

'Then let us appeal to those whose abilities are more than human.'

She stepped up beside him, hands folded in a namaskaram, and bowed to a point directly above his head.

He raised his eyes and saw a portrait of the sacred trimurti—Brahma, Vishnu and Shiva—looking down at him, their open palms extended in blessing.

The image stayed with him as he hurried through the connecting corridor, the torches flickering in an unexpectedly cool draught of wind. His shadow fled before him, then ran behind each time he passed a torch, playing tricks with his mind. He thought about the events of this morning and wondered if he had been wise to go to Kausalya as he had.

In his heart, he had no doubt at all, only a warm glow. Making love to her again had been like nothing else he had ever experienced. And that look in her eyes when he had told her of his decision to step down? Would he see that expression in Second Queen Kaikeyi's eyes when he told her the same news? He didn't think so. And that last gesture, her determination to pray to the gods despite the final analysis of the physicians, that had caused his throat to choke with emotion. How could he have frittered away so many years in the arms of Kaikeyi and not come to Kausalya even once? All those times they had stood, sat or walked side by side at official functions and ceremonies and he had felt a kinship with her that he didn't feel with any other woman; that feeling had been so right, and he had been so wrong to ignore it. But he had his reasons for that long absence and his only prayer now was that Kausalya would not press him to reveal those reasons. It was that he had dreaded most of all these many years: her questioning. He was grateful to have accomplished this much without being subjected to it. Yet he was filled with conflicting emotions, his guilt over the long absence vying with the lush sensual fulfilment he felt at being rejoined with his first true love.

The mixture of regret and joy was still visible on his face as he emerged from the connecting corridor and came face to face with Guru Vashishta.

'Gurudev, pranaam,' he said, joining his hands respectfully before the seer.

'Pranaam, raje,' the guru replied. 'I see that you have been binding old wounds and weaving fresh bonds this morning. It is a good beginning to an auspicious day.'

Dasaratha bowed his head silently, not sure what to say to that observation and knowing from long experience that it was best to say nothing rather than blurt out a foolish remark. The kshatriya code demanded that even the proudest and fiercest warrior caste must bow before the spiritual superiority of a brahmin. Yet Dasaratha bowed his head not simply to uphold the code but out of simple respect. Guru Vashishta had mentored fifty kings of the Suryavansha dynasty before Dasaratha, every single one of his ancestors dating back to clan-founder Ikshvaku and even beyond to Manu Lawmaker, the first Arya. For one thousand years, the greatest Suryavansha kshatriyas had bowed before Vashishta. It was a formidable heritage.

The sage turned and began to walk, inviting Dasaratha to accompany him. Dasaratha found he had to strive to keep pace with the agile and slender guru who walked as decisively as he spoke. One thousand years older than me and I'm the one who walks like an ailing old man, he thought ruefully. Yet there was a time, not ten years ago, when he could at least keep up with the seer. For the tenth time that day, he cursed the nameless canker that had brought him to this decrepit state.

If the guru noticed his struggle to keep pace, he gave no sign of it. His manner was as businesslike as always when discussing formal matters with the maharaja.

'Ayodhya-naresh, I am pleased to inform you that an even more auspicious event has occurred this fine first day of spring. A very great and divine personage has chosen to grace us with his presence. I do not yet know what his arrival here means, but certainly it is an auspicious and momentous visitation. Maharaja Dasaratha, count yourself among the few fortunate kings of Ayodhya. For you have none other than the renowned seer-mage Vishwamitra standing at your gates. Come with me, and let us receive him with all ceremony.'

It took every ounce of Dasaratha's will not to stop dead in his tracks.

SIX

Lakshman and Shatrugan woke at the exact same instant. They finished their ablutions quickly, dressed and came out of their bedchambers at the same time. Falling into step beside his younger brother—by twenty minutes—Shatrugan slapped him on the back affectionately.

'No sword today, Luck?'

Lakshman gestured at Shatrugan's hip. 'You neither, Shot. Because it's forbidden by maharaja's law to carry arms on a feast day. Or did you forget that during your long, rigorous training in the forest at Guru Vashishta's gurukul?'

Shatrugan mirrored Lakshman's toothy grin. 'I don't know about rigorous, but it surely was long. I was beginning to think we would spend the best years of our lives in that hermitage in the middle of nowhere.'

'Well, now you're back in the lap of luxury.' Lakshman gestured at the opulence of their surroundings, the princely annexe, a section of the king's palace. 'You must feel like you died and went to swarga-loka.' He corrected himself: 'Or came back to swarga-loka.'

Shatrugan shrugged. 'Yes, it is heavenly, isn't it? But somehow, brother, it doesn't seem real any more. I mean, I remember it from when we were little. Then it was all we knew, our entire cosmos. But after eight years in the forest, living off the land, sleeping on clay floors, dirt under our fingernails all the time, straw in our hair, all this feels . . . you know . . .'

'Maya. An illusion? Like it could vanish at any time?' Lakshman snapped his fingers, the sound echoing in the silent corridors they were walking through. Except for the occasional curtsying serving girl or maid, the vast halls were empty. Each prince had a suite of seven chambers to himself, with several more additional ones. 'Yes, brother,' he agreed as they passed the library and then the akhada, where they worked out together with their brothers every morning. 'That's the whole point of those eight years of training. To make us realise the illusive seductiveness of luxury and wealth.'

Shatrugan nodded without slowing. 'That's one way of putting it. Although I thought we also learned the vedic sciences and humanities. Everything from vedic mathematics, physics, geography, ayurveda and the study of human physiognomy, cosmology, astronomy and astrology, military strategy, self-defence and hand-to-hand combat, mastery of weapons, engineering and architecture—'

Lakshman clapped his brother on his muscled shoulder. 'Enough already! I was there too, you know, right beside you, learning all that you learned.'

'I was just trying to point out that after all those years of study and training, it seems so strange to be here again.' Shatrugan stopped suddenly, turning to Lakshman, a strange expression darkening his features. 'Do you ever wonder what it would be like to be a free-archer?'

Lakshman almost choked on his surprised laughter. 'What? You mean a mercenary? Like a wandering bow-for-hire?'

'Or a sword-for-hire,' Shatrugan mused thoughtfully. He looked up at the ornately carved ceiling painted with a fresco depicting the deva of storms, Indra. 'Sometimes I feel like maybe I was born in the wrong age. Like if I was born a thousand years earlier, I would have been out there battling Asuras, slaying rakshasas by the hundreds.' He looked down at his empty hands, turning them over. They were veined and taut from daily weight and weapons training. Nobody, perhaps not even Rama, trained and exercised as hard as Shatrugan did. It was starting to show. 'I feel as if I was made for something more than just governing a kingdom and touching silken robes.'

Lakshman stared at him. He wasn't sure what to make of this extraordinary admission. At a loss for words, he turned the revelation into a joke. 'What did you eat for dinner last night, brother? Because I fear you've been stricken with food poisoning!'

Shatrugan's hand flashed out faster than Lakshman could dodge, grabbing his younger twin's shoulder in an iron-vice grip. The strange expression was still on his angular features. Despite their identical appearance, there was a sense of hardness about Shatrugan that was curiously absent in Lakshman. It was as if an artist had drawn them each in turn, aiming for identical similarity, but had been in a different mood each time. The same features that came across as hard and grim in Shatrugan appeared gentle and light-hearted in Lakshman. It was a subtle contrast visible only to those who looked closely enough, yet once you were keen enough to see it, it was unmistakable. Only when they smiled did the differences vanish.

They smiled now, at the exact same instant. And became two perfect profiles of the same face.

'Speaking of dinner, brother,' Shatrugan said in a deceptively casual tone, 'are you planning to gorge yourself full to bursting on Susama-daiimaa's sumptuous morning naashta savouries, or did you have other more pressing plans?'

Lakshman shrugged, the weight of Shatrugan's hand still on his left shoulder. 'Actually, I thought I'd skip naashta and make for the mango groves. Rama and I fixed up to meet there at sunrise and it's almost time.'

Shatrugan's smile deepened. 'All right then,' he said slowly, building up momentum with his deliberate pauses, playing a game they had played every day since they had first learned to walk and talk—the very same moment, it had been, in fact. He yelled suddenly, as Lakshman had known he would: 'Last one to the stables is a camel's rear end!'

Even before he finished, he let go of Lakshman and ran down the corridor, not towards the bhojanshalya where they had been heading, but towards the rear stairway which led to the stables and eastern gates. His ploy to surprise and delay his brother was no more successful than usual: Lakshman's lighter, less thickly muscled form gave him the edge, carrying him easily ahead of the bulkier akhada-built physique of his brother. Even before they reached the head of the stairwell, the outcome of the race was a foregone conclusion.

The eastern sky was suffused with luminous soft light, turning the enormous white-marble fountain in the centre of the circular driveway into quietly gleaming bronze. The first strands of light of the rising sun—barely peeking its head over the crags of the distant Gharwal Hills—caught the polished edges of the effigy of Surya, sun god and the progenitor of the eponymous Suryavansha dynasty, standing at his chariot, one hand gripping the twin reins of his magnificent Kambhoja stallions, the other holding his Suryachakra, the magical golden disc.

The twins slowed to a walk, Lakshman two whole lengths ahead, laughing and slapping one another on the back as they circled the courtyard and rounded the enormous lotus pool containing the fountain. The sculpture itself rose a good seventy feet in the air, towering above the entire courtyard and driveway, casting a shadow that seemed to point proudly at the palace. The brothers turned right towards the chariot-stables where their grooms were waiting, ready and alert. The princes were all early risers and their charioteers knew well enough to keep their raths ready and waiting. The raths, elegantly designed two-horse Arya chariots built for speed and manoeuvrability, gleamed in the early-morning sunshine, their gold-plated iron armour polished to a mirrored sheen.

Shatrugan dismissed his driver with a curt gesture, leaped up on to the platform of his rath, and was off instantly. He called out to Lakshman as he manoeuvred the rath smartly in a ninety-degree turn.

'See you at the games, brother. When I win the shield in the archery contest!'

'You mean when Rama wins the shield!' Lakshman shouted back.

Shatrugan waved as he rode off, his rath taking the curve of the fountain easily. Lakshman watched him pass through the rear gates and turn right on to Aja Marg, heading for the royal games field. Their older brother Bharat—older by two weeks—would be there already, waiting for him. Twins they might be, but from infancy, Shatrugan had veered towards Bharat's company, and Lakshman had sought out Rama's companionship. The bonds of these pairings had only been strengthened during their eight years away from home.

Lakshman turned back to the stables.

He spent a moment speaking affectionately to his horses. He loved animals and they seemed to know this at once. It was one of the many qualities he shared with his elder brother Rama—elder by four weeks, and eldest of all four of them. Shatrugan, on the other hand, neither liked nor disliked animals.

Lakshman returned the respectful namaskar of his charioteer. 'Ayushmaanbhav, Samar. How long ago did Rama leave?'

The charioteer grinned. 'Long life to you as well, my prince. Rajkumar Rama left very early, just before dawn. We were only just starting to groom the horses. I knew you would ask after him, so I spoke to his charioteer and Samin says he rode out in the direction of the river.'

Lakshman frowned. If Rama's charioteer was still here, then that meant . . . 'He rode his rath himself then?'

'Nay, Rajkumar Lakshman, he declined to take his rath.'

'Horseback then?'

'Yes, my prince. He said that the rath horses should be fresh and rested before the Holi parade, so he took an old battlehorse from the king's stables.'

'That must be Airavata,' Lakshman said at once.

His driver grinned again. In the dim early light his teeth flashed brilliantly white against his dark face. 'Right as ever, my rajkumar. You and Rajkumar Shatrugan are womb-brothers, yet your kinship with Rajkumar Rama is no less a bond. You are twins in all but appearance.'

Lakshman smiled back. 'So I have been told.' He thanked his charioteer for the information. Samar and Samin, like the charioteers of Bharat and Shatrugan's raths, were not just excellent rath-drivers and warriors, they were also fellow-shishyas from Guru Vashishta's gurukul. In the reign of Dasaratha, it was mandatory for all kshatriyas to acquire the gifts of Saraswati, devi of knowledge. Samar was as much a peer and a friend as he was Lakshman's rath-driver.

Lakshman took Marut, another old battlehorse that had seen better days and greater challenges. Sometimes while astride the ancient destrier he felt as if he was riding back through time itself, into the ancient days Shatrugan had spoken of, a time when war was a simple fact of daily existence and a kshatriya was a warrior not just by birth and name, but in his daily actions. To defend the Arya nations and die defending them, that was all a kshatriya was expected to do. It was his dharma, just as the brahmins or priest-class must maintain the sanctity of Arya dharmic rituals and traditions, the vaisyas maintain the trade and commerce that were essential for Arya economy, and the sudras perform the less desirable yet necessary duties of cleaning, foraging, hunting, and otherwise ensuring the health and maintenance of the community. In those days, caste divisions had been a vital part of survival. Today, even a sudra could rise to kshatriya status through diligent effort and application. In the age of Dasaratha, being a kshatriya was no less honourable, yet it was much less exciting than the days that Shatrugan found so attractive.

But Lakshman wasn't Shatrugan. He didn't fear war, yet he didn't desire it either. He could do without battling Asuras and slaughtering rakshasas, all his life if need be. To do one's duty as a kshatriya was inevitable and desirable, yes, but this was fine too, to live in a time of peace and calm.

'We're bred for war, you and I, old kshatriya,' he said, leaning to nuzzle and pat Marut's neck as he rode down the empty marg. 'But what else do we fight wars for, if not to win peace? Let's hope we get to enjoy this well-deserved peace for another thousand years, right, brave one?'

The battlehorse flicked his head and whinnied, his powerful strides belying his age as he found his wind.

80

As he turned his head briefly, Lakshman caught a glimpse of Marut's forehead, still marked with the grisly scar of an axe-wound that would have felled lesser horses. He understood the gesture: even the old battlehorse would take peace over war any day.

SEVEN

Sumantra had arranged the arghya items Guru Vashishta had ordered and was waiting at the palace steps. The sky had turned crimson and saffron in the east and the deep midnight blue Dasaratha had seen from the akasa-chamber had turned to a lighter blue, the exact shade of the white-and-blue china vase he had been gifted by the Greek envoy just last week. It was an auspicious blue, the blue of brahman, and Dasaratha felt a stirring in his heart as he walked with his mahaguru and pradhan-mantri towards the gates of his palace.

Vashishta continued speaking softly as they walked, his voice audible only to Dasaratha's ears. They often adopted this method to get Dasaratha through the rigorous rituals of official ceremonies. Dasaratha had long since accepted the impossibility of remembering every minute detail of the intricate chain of actions and words that were strictly required by vedic tradition. Yet he wondered how Vashishta could recall these hundreds of thousands of details with such flawless ease. This was only one of the many reasons that kshatriyas gratefully and gladly accepted the spiritual guidance of the brahmins. This way a kshatriya was free to concentrate on his real duties rather than clutter his precious time and mind space with countless details. Yet sometimes even Dasaratha wondered if that wasn't precisely the reason why brahmins made these rituals so intricate and complex!

Still, after a lifetime of listening unobtrusively, he was comfortable with receiving the guru's constant flow of instructions and advice. It was not a matter of who was in command, as some foolish clan-chieftains made it out to be, but simply who possessed the best knowledge on a specific matter. Besides, even the palace guards saluting them as they walked in the pleasant dawn breeze were not aware of the guru speaking in Dasaratha's ear. It was as if, Dasaratha often mused, the guru could telepathically transmit his words directly into Dasaratha's brain.

'And lastly, even by error, do not mention my old association with him, back when he was a king, before he became a spiritual man. Since his reformation and his subsequent elevation to brahmarishi stature, Vishwamitra does not like to be reminded of his former life.'

Dasaratha jotted a mental note to look up Vishwamitra's 'former life' in the royal library later. All he knew of the legendary seer-mage was that he had been ordained some fourteen hundred years ago by the great god Shiva himself. Before that, he had been a king, Dasaratha knew. Not a maharaja of united clans but a maharaja of some princely clan housed far to the north-west. Guru Vashishta's cryptic reference—'his reformation'—suggested he had led an interesting life back then. Certainly more interesting than spending two hundred and forty-two years meditating in the deep forest.

The gates of the palace were wide open as always. These were peaceful times and Ayodhya took pride in the fact that its houses were never barred or locked, not even the king's palace. In his entire reign, Dasaratha had never needed to lock them against anything or anybody. Even the palace guard, highly trained and alert though they were, were completely decorative. They were compelled

83

to hold weekly athletic games to keep in shape and had developed a complicated choreographed ritual for the change of watch that had become a tourist attraction. The quad of four guards at the guardhouse by the gates had been joined by an entire platoon as was customary when the king emerged from the palace. Moving in perfect unison now, they performed an impressive variation of the changing-of-guards ritual, flipping their short spears and passing them from one hand to the other before setting them back on to their shoulders and saluting their king smartly as he approached.

Dasaratha saluted back as best as he could manage, his chest and shoulder muscles protesting. He was the commander of all armed forces after all, the supreme senapati. He felt painfully ashamed of his overweight, decrepit body. Once, he would have been able to take on four armed kshatriyas bare-handed, disarming them all in a matter of minutes. Now, he could only recall those martial asanas with deep regret and thank the devas he could still walk about and stand erect.

'Focus, Dasaratha,' Guru Vashishta's sub-audible voice said in his ear.

Again that sense that the guru's instructions were within his head rather than in his ear. The calm, iron-steady voice forced the maharaja to shed all his needless emotions and thoughts and concentrate solely on the task at hand. It was harder than it used to be.

'Focus.'

The guru's voice was firmer this time, a coiled reprimand. Unknown to Dasaratha, who regarded tales of the legendary brahman power of seers with healthy scientific scepticism, the guru possessed not just telepathy but complete mental control. He had 'heard' the maharaja's distracted thoughts about his decaying physique. Just as he could now 'hear' Dasaratha's thoughts straying back to the morning's dalliance

84

with his first queen . . . It would not do to have the maharaja's distraction lead to an error in protocol or a misspoken word. This was no ordinary visitor they were receiving. Vashishta put the weight of his considerable personality into one final command.

'*Focus.*'

Dasaratha focused. Forcing his mind to clear itself and direct its attention outwards.

The figure standing just outside the palace gates was like a painting come alive. The striking twice-as-large-as-life-sized one hanging in the palace foyer, perhaps. That work of art had been painted over four centuries earlier by a king of the Suryavansha dynasty, Dasaratha's illustrious ancestor Dilipa. The official chronicles of the Suryavansha clan, to which historical record Dasaratha himself had contributed from time to time, noted in its entry that the noble Dilipa had painted this portrait entirely from memory. Dilipa had returned from a chance visit to the ashram of the great sage Vishwamitra, greatly impressed by the sage's insightful advice. That encounter had changed his life and fortunes, and the future of the Suryavansha dynasty itself, and as a tribute Dilipa had poured every gram of his considerable artistic talent into rendering the magnificent portrait. Since the great sage Vishwamitra had never actually set foot in the city of Ayodhya, that painting had stood as his representative likeness for these past four hundred years, becoming the basis for several lesser imitations, and even a statue in Seers' Square. But today, at long last, Dilipa's descendant Maharaja Dasaratha could vouch with pride and a strange swelling emotion that the painting's accuracy was amazing. Perfect, down to the last detail, Great Dilipa. Absolutely perfect.

The figure before him looked as if he had just this minute stepped out of that enormous canvas.

He was clad in the simple garb of an ascetic: a coarse red-ochre dhoti hand-woven from beaten jute, battered wooden toe-grip slippers, matted unkempt hair swirling around his craggy face, a long straggly white beard, red-beaded rudraksh mala around his neck. At a glance he could have passed for any of the dozens of tapasvi sadhus that emerged from the Southwoods each spring, gaunt and wasted from their rigorous abstinence and penance. Yet he possessed that same striking air of great inner strength and power that Dilipa had captured in that historic portrait. The appearance of a seer-mage who had once been a great kshatriya and maharaja. The unmistakable arrogance and dignity of Arya royalty.

He was facing away from them when Dasaratha, Vashishta and Sumantra approached. Staring out at the high slopes of the northern hills, the sloping ridges that eventually rose to become the foothills of the Himalayas. His long beard and weathered garments flapped in the wind. The attendant following on Sumantra's heels gasped and muttered an exclamation of disbelief in Awadhi commonspeak. The startled servant, obviously shocked at the sight of a legend from history books come alive, clattered the arghya bowl and basin together and the sound rang out on the still clear air. There was no traffic on the vast expanse of Raghuvamsha Avenue this early on a feast day and the sound was as grating as a cartwheel cracking.

It attracted the attention of the visitor.

He turned, holding his hefty staff easily in one powerfully muscled hand. Dasaratha felt a tremor of anticipation. A sense of history in the making. He would be the first king of Ayodhya to be graced with the visit of this legendary seer-mage. And on a most auspicious day. Despite his resolve to keep his thoughts clear, it occurred to him suddenly that if he could convince the great sage to stay until the coronation, a fortnight from today, it would lay the ultimate seal of approval on his last act as king. His first-born, Rama, would go down in Arya history as the first prince of Ayodhya to be blessed at his coronation by not one but two of the greatest seer-mages and brahmarishis ever, Vashishta and Vishwamitra. Now that would be an epoch-making coronation!

He opened his parched lips to speak the appropriate greeting, lowering himself to his knees to prostrate himself before the great brahmin. But before he could say a single word, the living legend spoke first, breaking protocol and surprising Dasaratha.

'Maharaja Dasaratha, in keeping with the ancient tradition of guru-dakshina between kshatriya and brahmin, I have come to ask a boon of you. As is the custom, I exhort you to agree without hesitation or pause to grant me my heart's desire, regardless of what I ask for. Honour your caste, your clan and yourself, and agree without delay. I, Vishwamitra, sage of sages, command it.'

EIGHT

The doe leaped out of Rama's arms. He had enfolded her in a gentle embrace, careful not to grip her too hard, and when he sensed her muscles tensing for the leap, he made no attempt to stop her. She jumped upwards and away, bounding across the grassy knoll in the direction of the river. Reaching the rim of the knoll, she paused and turned her head. Her ears flicked as she looked back with wide alarmed eyes. He smiled and rose to his feet, speaking softly, his voice barely audible below the sound of the river.

'Did I scare you? That was not my intention, little beauty. I was only eager to be your friend. Will you not come back and speak to me again?'

The doe watched him from the edge of the precipice, her body still turned towards the path that led down to the river, only her head twisted back towards him. She made no move to return, yet she did not flee immediately.

Rama took a step towards her, then another. She did not run. He took several steps more, but when he was within twenty paces or so, her flank rippled and her ears flickered at a faster rate. So he stopped again. He called to her. She stayed where she was, watching him. For a long moment, they stayed that way, the boy and the doe, watching each other, the river rushing along, the sun breasting the top of the northern hills to shine down in its full glory. In the distance, the city caught the light of the new day and sent back a thousand glittering reflections. Towers and spires, windows and arches, domes and columns, glass and brass, silver and gold, copper and bronze, crystal and shell, bead and stone, all were illuminated at once, and Ayodhya blazed like a beacon of gold fire, filling the valley with a luminous glow. In the light of this glorious new day, it was easy to dismiss the nightmare as just that, a bad dream. And yet . . . he could still hear the screams, see the awful wounds, the gaping—

Stop!

He straightened and stared at the city, the deer forgotten, the mango he had been about to pick before he saw the doe abandoned. It took a moment of steady pranayam breathing to restore him to the sense of calm he had experienced when stalking and catching the deer.

He focused on the sight before him. His beloved Ayodhya resplendent in the sunlight of a new day, a new season, a new harvest year. He walked forward, eyes fixed on the blazing city. Before they had grown old enough to be sent to gurukul, he and his brothers had spent any number of days here in the shade of this mango grove. Playing, fighting, racing, all the things that young boys and young princes alike were wont to do. He had come here today hoping these nostalgically familiar environs would cleanse his mind of the nightmare that had broken his sleep. So far he hadn't been entirely successful.

His feet found the edge of the knoll and he stopped, poised ten yards or more above the raging river. It was the point where the Sarayu roared around a bend in the valley, tumbling over rocks and boulders with the haste and energy of a river still in the first stage of its lengthy course. The sound was thunder sustained. He spread his arms, raised his face to the warm golden sunlight, and laughed. Droplets of spray drifted up slowly, catching his hair and simple white dhoti, like diamonds glittering in the sunlight.

When he returned to the grove, the ache at the back of his neck was lessened considerably. He thought he could manage some naashta now. Not the lavish buffet that Susama-daiimaa laid out each morning, enough to feed an army garrison, but just a fruit. His eyes sought out the large green kairee he had been about to pluck off a low-hanging branch when he had spied the deer. Found it, plucked it and smiled as a few loosened leaves fluttered down around his head like a bridegroom's welcome. Ah, now there was a question that could easily be answered. How did a raw green mango taste on the first day of spring? A question worthy of one of his Uncle Maharaja Janak's famous philosophical councils at Mithila court. He would solve the mystery in a moment.

He nursed the kairee in his palm. It was heavy, firm, filled with the thick juice of the king of fruits. But this was not truly a king yet. Not even a crown prince. Simply a prince in waiting. And yet, a kairee was more than a mango. For you had not truly lived until you had tasted the unspeakably teeth-keening sourness of a kairee, bitten into the mustard-yellow flesh, green skin and all, tearing bits with the edges of your teeth, teasing the fruit, sucking on the succulent sourness within. He patted his waist, checking that the small packet of salt was still there. He drew it out and opened it carefully, seating himself cross-legged on the dry grassy earth. Kairee and salt. He was ready to discover heaven on earth once more.

He licked the kairee's tip, wetting the skin. Then dipped it into the salt. Grains of brownish-white namak stuck to the parrot-green fruit. The tart aroma of the kairee mingled with the earthy smell of the rock salt now. He raised it to his mouth, shutting his eyes in anticipation of the sourness that would explode on his palate in a moment.

The small downy hairs on the backs of his arms—he had his mother's smooth near-hairlessness rather than his father's hirsuteness—prickled in anticipation.

The fruit was almost at his mouth when he heard the high, keening cry. Followed by laughter and hoarse yells. And, even above the roar of the river and the cacophony of birds singing in the thickly growing trees of the mango grove, the unmistakable sound of a bow-string twanging.

He frowned and listened. The hand holding the kairee froze. The other hand, poised above the salt, ready to dip the kairee the moment his teeth had broken the skin, scooping up more salt to cut the sourness, hovered.

A moment later, he heard it again, the distinct quaver of a tautly strung bow speaking to the wind. And this time there was an answering voice, as familiar as the first: a dull thwacking sound. A metal-headed wooden arrow striking flesh. And the squeal of a beast in pain.

Rama shot to his feet with a swiftness that the doe would have envied. The unbitten kairee was tossed aside, the salt packet overturned. An instant later, he was speeding up the knoll. He stopped at the rise, leaning out with the easy confidence of a fifteen-year-old in perfect command of his bodily reflexes.

The scene below couldn't have been clearer had a gypsy nautanki troupe been performing it with puppets for toddlers.

The doe lay by the edge of the river, within reach of the grass. In a few seconds it would have been in the grass and virtually invisible. The arrow had struck it high on the foreleg, stunning it. There was a lot of blood but Rama thought the wound wasn't fatal. Most deer died of shock at the moment of impact, slow blood loss or infected wounds. His fists clenched as he saw the doe struggle to rise again, bleating with pain then flopping back on the glistening stones of the river bank.

The perpetrators of the crime—he thought of it as nothing less—were a group of at least a dozen burly, fair-skinned northerners. They were clad in the wolf-pelts and bear-pelts of the Garhwal tribes, a loosely related clan of mountain people who lived on the lower slopes of the Garhwal Himalayas, some yojanas north and west of Ayodhya, outside Kosala borders. They came a few times a year to trade at the melas. They were probably here for the Holi celebration; Ayodhya's Holi feast was renowned throughout the Arya nations, and the city had always maintained an open-house policy during festivals and melas. But that didn't include hunting within sight of the city. From the wineskins they all carried—and kept swigging from—Rama knew they were drunk and seeking good sport. One of them, a young loutish oaf who could barely hold his bow straight, was trying to finish off the doe. The others were egging him on with yells and sadistic suggestions, speaking the crude pahadi dialect of the mountain tribes.

Rama sprinted along the knoll, running down to a point where the overhang doubled back upon itself. He leaped down to the lower path, deftly dodged a cobra sunning itself on a rock—the snake hissed in warning but made no move to attack him—and bounded down the last two yards, landing in the thick, bouncy kusalavya grass. In a moment, he was at the bank of the river. He ran without care for arrows and reached the wounded doe. He knelt by its side, examining it. Above the roar of the river, almost deafening now that he was down here, he heard the surprised shouts of the Garhwalis.

The doe turned her head to stare up at him. His heart broke when he saw the fear and confusion in those large terrified eyes. Her lips parted as if she wanted to speak, to explain her plight, but only a sharp mewling sound emerged. He tore a strip from his kurta, glad he had

92

worn it in expectation of a nippy wind. Wrapping the cloth around her injured leg, he tied it tightly enough to staunch the bleeding until the arrow could be removed. The doe kept turning her head, her teeth baring as she reflexively tried to reach and remove the thing embedded in her flesh. Rama touched the top of her downy head, and whispered softly: 'I will be back to help you.'

Then he stood and turned to face the men.

NINE

Dasaratha looked up at the tall, imposing figure that stood before him at the front gates of his palace. He knew he couldn't delay his response by even an instant.

'Mahadev,' he began, using the universal term of respect that elevated the honoured visitor to the level of a great god. 'My adherence to tradition is as sincere as any of my illustrious ancestors. You have my unhesitant and joyful agreement to fulfil any desire you name. As is the custom, whatever you wish to ask of me, I shall give it without question, be it my proudest possession.'

The seer's craggy face, brighter now in the growing daylight, smiled at the king's words. He brought his heavy staff down hard on the packed earth of the avenue, punctuating his first words with a solid thud.

'Ayodhya-naresh, hum prasan huye. You have pleased me greatly with your reply, lord of Ayodhya. Now, I exhort you to remember this promise you have made me in the sacred presence of your own mahaguru and marg-darshak Vashishta himself, as well as these other associates.'

Vishwamitra gestured at Sumantra and his attendants, who had been so terrified when the seer began to speak that they had dropped flat on their faces in the dust of the avenue, where they still lay, too scared to even look up at the fabled brahmin.

'They shall be my witnesses,' Vishwamitra added, and struck the ground once more with his staff, underlining the pact with the gesture.

Dasaratha wanted desperately to steal a glance at Guru Vashishta, who hadn't uttered a word since they had emerged from the gates. But he guessed correctly that this was one situation where his protocol was clear and unambiguous.

'Mahadev,' he said, bowing once again with his hands folded. 'I beg of you, give me the honour of performing the customary arghya and welcoming you into my humble abode.'

The brahmarishi looked up at the palace, towering above all other structures on the vast avenue. 'Of course,' he said thoughtfully. 'Of course. But do you not wish to know what boon I am about to ask of you?'

Dasaratha kept his hands joined and his eyes directed downwards at the seer-mage's dusty bare feet. 'Mahadev, I have already sworn to give you whatever your heart desires. It would honour me greatly if you would utter your sacred request within the walls of my abode. It is not seeming of me to keep you, a great and esteemed guest, standing on this public causeway. Please, do me the honour.'

And without further ado, he gestured to the attendants, who were still frozen. After a sharply whispered order from Sumantra, they scurried forward with the arghya bowl and items, almost falling over their own feet in fear. They were so nervous that the attendant holding the heavy jug filled with Ganga-jal, the sacred water of the Ganges, almost spilled it on the maharaja himself. In silent exasperation, Sumantra took the jug from the attendant and bent down himself, indicating to Dasaratha that he was ready to pour.

But before Dasaratha's fingers could make contact with the visitor's dust-caked feet, an oddly familiar voice rang out across the silent avenue.

'Stop, Ayodhya-naresh! Do not debase yourself by touching the feet of this vile creature. Rise to your feet at once!'

Kausalya was in her pooja room when Kaikeyi burst in. She was absorbed in praying to the Mother Goddess Sri in her avatar as Devi the Provider, patron deity of married women and mothers. The room was dense with the fragrant smoke of agarbattis. The thick agarsticks were delicately scented with jasmine, musk, pinewood, ashwood and lotus, and they mingled to form a heady cocktail of aromas that helped Kausalya empty her mind of everything except the countenance of the devi.

The room was silent except for the occasional ringing of the bell placed before her on the wooden altar. As she reached the end of a cycle of mantras, she picked up the bell and shook it rhythmically, filling the chamber with its sweet pealing.

She was ringing it when the door—shut but not bolted; there had never been any need to bolt the door—was struck a blow by a hand heavy with bangles. She knew this without turning around. The exact instant that she finished ringing the bell, the intruder entered. Kausalya heard the harsh clattering of heavy gold bangles and knew at once that a woman had entered, and the woman could only be Second Queen Kaikeyi. The bangles were solid gold and Third Queen Sumitra always favoured silver. In any case, Kausalya couldn't imagine timid Sumitra entering her chambers without announcing herself well in advance, let alone barging in like a roughneck at a cheap tavern. There was no doubt in her mind that this rude invader was Kaikeyi, even before the intruder spoke loudly and harshly.

'You hussy! I know what you're up to. You won't succeed.'

Kausalya put the bell down carefully and bent forward to touch her forehead to the feet of the statue of the devi. She smelled the familiar reassuring aroma of the red clay used to mould the effigy and the scent of the vegetable pigments with which She had been painted in the traditional bright parrot green, peacock blue, red ochre, yellow ochre, seed saffron and lavender. She sent up a silent prayer to the devi, asking for succour and calm.

It occurred to her at that instant that she was in the perfect posture for a decapitation. But she wasn't afraid. Kaikeyi's tongue was sharper than her dagger. Kausalya joined her hands together one final time as she rose to her feet, then turned to face her rude intruder.

Kaikeyi was a portrait of feminine rage that would have inspired any Kali worshipper. Except that Kali was never this self-indulgent or luxuriously bedecked.

The second queen was overdressed as usual, burdened by heavy gold ornaments and ritual symbols of her regal position as well as her marital status. The large red bindi on her forehead blazed angrily against her flushed pale skin, like the third eye of Shiva rather than a symbol of bridehood. Kausalya almost expected her to have four arms and a divine weapon poised to strike in each hand.

Instead Kaikeyi struck with her tongue.

'You temptress. Seductress. Like a cheap devdasi you lured my husband away from my chamber and into your clutches. Did you think I wouldn't know, witch? Did you think I'd give him up without a fight?'

Kausalya stared coldly at her husband's second wife. She walked towards Kaikeyi, the gold pooja thali in her hands. Kaikeyi started, as if fearing that Kausalya was about to attack her with the thali, and raised a hand protectively. Her heavy gold bangles jangled. Kausalya marvelled that the woman was able to lift her hand at all with that weight. Where did she think she was going decked up like that? To her own marriage?

Kausalya walked past Kaikeyi and emerged from the pooja room. She set the thali down on the raised wooden lectern, gently extinguishing the diyas. A coiled satin rope hung by her bedside. She tugged at it thrice in quick succession. Bells rang out faintly somewhere in the bowels of the palace. Then she stood with her back to the doorway from which she had just emerged and waited for the other woman to follow her out. When she heard the jangling of the jewellery, she turned with the speed and intensity of a fevered nagin, a queen cobra, striking without giving Kaikeyi the chance to speak first.

'How dare you violate the sanctity of my prayer room? You have no right to even step into my chambers uninvited. And as for calling me those names, well, you probably picked them up from palace gossip over the years, all addressed to your own slinky back. They fit you quite well. You're the one who tempted my husband from my bed fifteen years ago, binding him with a warrior's obligation to repay a life-debt. You used your seductive wiles as boldly as any woman from the back streets, luring him to your arms. As if that wasn't enough, you decided you couldn't share his affections. You plotted and conspired against me and poor Sumitra, poisoning Dasa's ears with God alone knows what rot, until he began spending his time only with you. How dare you come in here and accuse me of your own sins? May the devas strike you down as you stand! Now get out of my chambers before I have the guards pick you up and throw you out bodily!'

Kaikeyi stood astonished and speechless, stunned by this unexpected outburst. Even before Kausalya's words had ended, the clattering of wooden sandals echoed down the corridor leading to the first queen's bedchamber.

An instant later the drapes parted and an entire platoon of female guards, part of the special division of the palace guard that was assigned to the three titled queens and the three hundred and fifty untitled wives of Dasaratha, filed in quickly, taking in the situation at a glance and bearing down on Kaikeyi. At a flick of Kausalya's finger they surrounded Kaikeyi, their short spears held at a diagonal upward angle, not lowered to attack but in a warning posture. They were Kausalya's personal guard, hand-picked from her own clan back east to ensure unquestioning loyalty. Every one of them was an Amazon among women, tall and muscular as any Arya man, and as capable of holding her own in battle, sport or mortal combat as any male warrior.

Kausalya watched grimly as Kaikeyi looked around with startled eyes at her unexpected response and weighed her next move. She guessed that never before in her pampered life as a crown princess of Kaikeya and then a queen of Kosala had Kaikeyi ever been faced with a hostile guard under her own roof.

Except that it wasn't her roof. These were Kausalya's private chambers. And Kaikeyi had violated her title, her dignity and her religious feelings with her abusive intrusion.

'Take her away,' Kausalya ordered sharply. 'If she resists, drag her by the hair, and throw her out into the courtyard.'

As Kaikeyi blanched and swallowed silently, still debating her next course of action, Kausalya smiled grimly and asked: 'Well, Kaikeyi? Are there any other names you'd like to call me? I'm sure my personal guards and kinswomen would love to hear you abuse me in their presence.'

Kaikeyi shot a look of pure hatred at Kausalya. Her red-rimmed eyes blazed in her feverish face.

Kausalya checked the temptation to rub the insult in with salt: *That's enough. You've already hurt her enough to make her a blood-enemy. End this now.* Aloud she said to her guards: 'The second queen wishes to leave now. Escort her to her own palace.'

As the Amazonian guards reached for Kaikeyi's arms, she came alive once more, slapping their wrists furiously, punishing them for her humiliation.

'Don't touch me!' Her voice rode up an octave, shrill and on the verge of hysteria. 'The first one to lay a finger on me will be executed within the hour!'

She turned to look at Kausalya. Her eyes flashed like twin flames in her fleshy face, her chin quivering with rage.

'This isn't over yet, you snake mother. I'll not give up my husband without a fight. Before nightfall, he'll be back with me and you'll be just another unnumbered concubine in the palace of untitled wives!'

And with that threat still echoing off the walls, Kaikeyi turned and walked out of the chamber. The guards followed close behind, but Kausalya knew they were redundant now. The second queen wouldn't be back. She had achieved what she had come for, to threaten and intimidate Kausalya. The sequel to this scene would be played out in circumstances of Kaikeyi's choosing, and Kausalya had a feeling she would be the one facing sharpened steel at that encounter.

TEN

Kausalya sank to the bed, releasing an involuntary sigh. She was a strong woman and in her youth she had been trained in warfare and the use of arms, just as Kaikeyi had. But Kaikeyi was a born warrior, a female kshatriya who had ridden at the head of her father's army at the age of fourteen and had conquered barbarian hordes. She was already a feared and formidable warrior queen when Dasaratha's path and hers had crossed those many years ago. It had never been a secret that her very ferocity and kshatriya prowess had been the source of her attractiveness to Dasaratha's roving eye. And even now, fifteen years later, it was that same ruthless ability to take life and to slaughter without hesitation that gave her the edge over Kausalya.

Despite her own kshatriya origins, Kausalya's inclination had always turned more towards artistic pursuits. Whatever her strengths, the willingness to kill to achieve her goals was not one of them. It made the brief, potent encounter with Kaikeyi that much more exhausting.

She fought the temptation to lie back on the bed and rest for a while. So much had happened already, but the day itself had barely begun. There was much to be done yet. The Holi parade. The coronation announcement.

101

And that visitor that had compelled Guru Vashishta to send for the maharaja so urgently—surely it must be an important personage for Guruji to have Dasa interrupted during a private audience with his queen. And then there was Rama. She needed to see Rama before the parade.

When she heard the tinkling of delicate silver payals, she smiled. She could identify the approaching visitor by that dainty sound as surely as she had recognised Kaikeyi by the harsh jangling of her heavy gold bracelets.

The drapes at the doorway parted for the third time that morning and Sumitra's small doe-shaped face looked into the chamber cautiously. She saw Kausalya alone and looked relieved.

'Come in, my sister,' Kausalya called softly. 'Don't be afraid, the myini's gone.' She smiled self-consciously at her use of the word for 'witch'. Speaking roughly didn't come naturally to Kausalya, even when provoked.

Sumitra emitted a small gasp as she scuttled in, her diaphanous choli rustling musically as she sat on the bed beside Kausalya. She was so light, the bed hardly shifted.

'I heard the commotion and the shouting. My guards told me Kaikeyi was attacking you in your chambers! I came at once. Is it over? Are you hurt? What did she want, the hussy?'

Kausalya smiled. Even after fifteen years of marriage and two grown sons, Sumitra had hardly changed. She was still just an older version of the breathless, girlish young woman who had come nervously to ask Kausalya's permission to marry her husband and become her sister in bridehood. Kausalya had felt a maternal protectiveness for the young girl that had never completely faded: could this waif be the answer to Dasa's prayers for an heir? Kausalya had accepted the ancient Arya custom permitting a reigning monarch to take more than one wife into his home in order to ensure progeny. Accepting Sumitra as her husband's new wife had been like welcoming a sister home, not a rival. How different it had been when Dasaratha announced that same day that he had brought another bride home as well, and how differently had Kaikeyi glared at her as she descended from her wheel-house and strode arrogantly up the steps of the palace on that fateful day, seventeen long years ago. Had Kausalya known then that Kaikeyi's shadow that morning would cast the next decade and a half into virtual darkness, she might have asserted her spousal right under Arya law to disallow her husband's choice and compel Dasaratha to send Kaikeyi back to her father's house. But seeing the gentle, childlike Sumitra had disarmed her and she had failed to realise the threat that Kaikeyi posed until it was far too late for lawful redress.

She brought her attention back to Sumitra's question. 'She's upset because Dasa came to me this morning. She thinks I manipulated him somehow to do so.'

Sumitra's large eyes, as dominant in her face as the eyes of a rabbit, widened even more than usual. They seemed to take up half her little heart-shaped face. 'And did you do that? Manipulate him, I mean?' She realised what she had said and coloured instantly. 'I mean, of course you wouldn't do such a thing! But I mean, did he really? Come to you this morning?'

Kausalya took Sumitra's hand in her own. Her hand was a half-size larger than Sumitra's little mitt. How on earth had this waif given birth to two strong and muscular saplings like Shatrugan and Lakshman?

'Yes,' she admitted.

Sumitra stared at her uncomprehending for an instant, and then her little mouth opened wide. 'No! You're pulling my leg!'

'If I was, then you would be flat on your back, my little sister!' Kausalya laughed, starting to relax after the unexpected anxiety and emotional upheaval of Dasaratha's visit and the sudden shock of Kaikeyi's verbal attack. 'It's true, my sister. You can see for yourself.' She gestured at the crumpled bedsheets and mashed petals.

Sumitra picked up a handful of petals and stared at them. 'By the Goddess alive!' She bounced up and down on the soft downy bed, absorbing the news like the overgrown child she still was. 'In the name of blessed Lakshmi, wife of divine Vishnu!'

She laughed and hugged Kausalya. To her surprise, Kausalya found herself responding easily, laughing and hugging Sumitra back. How different we three are, she thought. One wants Dasa all to herself, the second is willing to share him with whomever he pleases to be with, and I . . . what do I really want after all?

Suddenly, Sumitra detached herself from Kausalya and knelt down by the bedside. Before Kausalya knew what she was doing, she had bent and touched Kausalya's feet, then touched the tips of her fingers to her own forehead.

'Bhagyavan Kausalya,' she said earnestly. *Blessed of the devas, Kausalya.*

'Sumitra,' Kausalya started to protest. Then stopped. She felt a lump in her throat as she embraced her friend— *yes, my dearest friend*—affectionately, feeling her emotional warmth, as heartfelt and benevolent as Kaikeyi's attitude had been malevolent. Sumitra was right. On this auspicious feast day of Holi, Kausalya *was* bhagyavan, blessed by the devas. Through some inexplicable turn of the wheel of samay, her husband had returned to her after a long and bitter estrangement and her son was about to be crowned prince-heir. Nothing could darken such a day.

Let Kaikeyi do her worst now, she resolved fiercely. This time, she'll have to kill me to get him back.

There were eleven of them, Rama saw, not quite a dozen. A tall, massively muscled man with a face disfigured by hideous scars appeared to be the leader. They were all looking to him, then back at Rama and the doe, shouting in their pahadi language. The young man they had been egging on still had an arrow in his bow, trained directly at Rama now, and he was grinning as if this was all a big adventure. Three others also had their bows in hand, two of them with arrows ready to be strung.

'Ayodhya ke aas-paas shikhar karna mana hain,' Rama said in high Sanskrit first, then repeated the same message twice more, in commonspeak as well as in the pahadi dialect. 'Hunting is forbidden within sight of Ayodhya city.'

The men looked at each other for one startled moment, then burst out laughing. Only the leader stared impassively, his milky-grey eyes meeting Rama's across the twenty or more yards that separated them.

Rama pointed at the doe. 'You men have committed a crime under Kosala law. You must surrender yourselves to the city magistrates. If you are unaware of the laws of our state, some leniency might be shown. But you must put away your weapons at once and hand them over to the guards at the first gate. No weapons are permitted beyond that point.'

Another wave of laughter rose from the group. The youngster with the arrow aimed at Rama laughed too, evidently imitating his older companions rather than because he found Rama's words funny. His hands were unsteady on the bow, and he almost released the arrow without realising it.

Rama called to him.

'You, young one. Put down that bow and arrow. Right now. All of you do the same with your weapons at once. If you do not obey, this will go badly for you.'

The youngster looked uncertain. The hand holding the fletch of the arrow quivered, then eased. The bow dipped, pointing at the river. He looked around to see the response of his older companions.

They looked unimpressed by Rama's warning. A pair standing off to one side spoke to each other and spat together into the river. They drew knives, large curved hunting knives that had been sharpened so often their blades were honed to fine needle points at the tips. They held the knives in the pahadi fashion, blade under the fist, pointed sideways.

A fat man with a head full of blond hair and a beard to match strung an arrow into his bow. 'Methinks this will go badly for *you*, boy! You're holding up our sport, you are!'

'Yes,' shouted another man, brandishing a khukhri that gleamed dangerously in the bright sunlight. 'You move out of the way and let us have our sport with the deer. Unless you want to join in its fate, in which case we'd be happy to oblige you!'

The others all shouted similar challenges and comments, some adding abuse and insults against Ayodhyans and their city. Three more men drew bows and strung them with drunken arrogance. Rama counted seven arrows in all now pointed at him. He looked at the leader and addressed him directly.

'Do you speak for these men?'

One of the men called out: 'We're free men, we speak for ourselves.' But they all glanced up to see their leader's response.

He stared at Rama for a moment, his eyes flicking up and down, taking in every detail. The sun caught his

106

eyes and turned them into two pinpoints of white light, like reflections off quartz stones. He hawked and spat out a lump of phlegm streaked with blood. It travelled a good five yards to the river, and fell in, carried away by the swirling waters. Somehow, that offended Rama far more than the spoken insults and abuses. It was one thing to wash or bathe in the Sarayu, but by spitting in it the pahadi leader was mocking the entire Ikshvaku clan that had originally settled this valley and cared so well for its ecology these past two thousand years. Rama noticed the peculiar slash-shaped scars on the man's face, the lines of shiny scar tissue and gouges where the flesh had been damaged too deeply to repair itself, and recognised them as the marks of the great Himalayan brown bear, a giant of a beast that spared nothing and nobody in its path. It was commonly known as rksaa. Looking at the man's hideous scars, Rama wondered how anyone could have suffered such a mauling and survived. The military training ingrained in his mind concluded that a man who had faced a rksaa and lived to tell the tale would most likely make a dangerous adversary. The other men clearly looked to him as a leader, and addressed him as Bearface.

'You go find your mother and bring her to us, boy,' Bearface said in a hoarse rasping voice that meshed with the river's grinding roar. 'We'll find something to keep her busy.' His eyes flicked to Rama's lower body. 'And you as well, pretty one.'

The burst of laughter that greeted this comment was the loudest yet.

Rama's voice was clear and unflecked with emotion, carrying across the laughter and the roar of the river.

'For hunting the deer and refusing to put down your arms, you will be arrested and tried under Ayodhya law.

107

The most severe punishment applicable will be meted out to each and every one of you.' He paused and pointed at the one they called Bearface. 'But for that last comment, pahadi, you are answerable to me.'

The fat blond man yelled exuberantly: 'You hear that, Bearface? You're answerable to him now!'

The leader grinned, revealing slits in the scars down his face where the skin and flesh had been torn through completely, exposing parts of his cartilage and jawbone. 'I like that. Answerable, hey? Come closer, boy, I've got the answer you're looking for right here in the crotch of my langot.' He clutched his loin-cloth with a gesture that left no room for doubt.

Rama picked up a stone and hefted it in his hand. It felt just about right. At the movement, the seven men with bows grew alert in a drunken, amused way. Several of them had relaxed enough to begin drinking again from their wineskins, slopping wine down the front of their chests. Rama shook his head regretfully. He had been taught never to fight with men under the influence of liquor; but he wasn't being given a choice. Still, he tried once more to appeal to their better sense.

'I ask you one last time,' he said, his voice as calm and steady as the hand holding the rock. 'Throw down your weapons and surrender to me and I will not pursue this further.'

This time, the laughter was ragged. The pahadis were tired of talk. One of them loosed an arrow carelessly. It shot a whole yard over Rama's head, burying itself with a soft sigh in the grassy side of the knoll behind him. Rama ignored it.

'Pursue that, if you can,' the man yelled, and reached back to pull another arrow from his quiver.

Rama decided that the time for talk was past.

ELEVEN

Dasaratha raised his head to stare at the person who had so rudely interrupted him.

A man dressed in animal furs was striding up Raghu-vamsha Avenue towards the palace gates, a hunting spear clutched threateningly in his hand. His dark skin and body piercings identified him unmistakably as a common hunter, a sudra no less.

Dasaratha blinked repeatedly, unable to believe that this low-caste would have the gumption to shout orders at him, maharaja of Kosala. He almost turned to look around, in case he had misheard the stranger's impudent command. There was no need to: the broad avenue was deserted at this early hour on a feast day, except for the street sentries standing guard at intervals of thirty yards all the way down the long causeway. Raghuvamsha Avenue led nowhere except to the palaces and treasury houses. Even the tradesmen and staff used the rear entrances.

In case he had any doubt, the man spoke again, even louder and more forceful in his exhortation this time.

'Dasaratha! Rise to your feet at once! Do not debase yourself by bowing before this vile filth. Rise, I command you!'

Dasaratha stared at the man in stunned silence for a moment. His upper lip trembled with sudden anger. He rose to his feet, joining his hands together before the seer-mage who still stood awaiting his arghya.

'Shama, mahadev. Forgive me for pausing in my hospitable duties. But I must deal with this insolent intruder who so rudely interrupts our ritual.'

Vishwamitra nodded, his eyes seeming to stare distantly at some point above the maharaja's head. Dasaratha was relieved that the seer hadn't taken offence at the interruption—not yet. Dasaratha took three steps sideways, to face the rude stranger directly, and pointed at the hunter who was approaching at a steady pace. He was still a good twenty yards away when Dasaratha summoned up his most imperial voice to issue a command.

'Guards! Stop this man and put him on the ground on his belly. He has interrupted the sacred arghya reception of our noble visitor. By committing this violation of our ancient ritual, he has forfeited his rights as a citizen. Arrest this man at once!'

Even as the words left his lips, the alert palace guards ran forward in perfect unison. In scant seconds, they had fanned out into three main formations: four quads of four men each encircled their king, walling him inside four concentric squares, a formidable defensive wall that would have to be hacked down a man at a time before they would allow any harm to come to their maharaja.

A second unit spread across the avenue in a V formation designed to catch the hunter at its lowermost point, wrapping themselves around him in seconds, closing the gap behind him until he was enveloped by hard flesh and sharpened steel. And a third unit, made up of two additional platoons which had been brought up the minute Dasaratha stepped out of the palace gates, blocked the way to the palace, shutting the gates with quick military efficiency to prevent any risk of intrusion.

The trumpeting of elephants and rumbling of chariot wheels grew audible and Dasaratha knew without looking that reinforcements had already been summoned. In moments, a force capable of resisting a small army would take up defensive positions all around the palace, in the event, however unlikely, that this commoner's challenge might herald a larger threat. For all its open spaces and free access, Ayodhya was nevertheless a formidable fortress designed to withstand any violent assault, large or small.

A conch shell sounded behind the barred palace gates, and Dasaratha knew that it was heralding the first alarm. Three miles away, beyond the great games field, the army cantonment would be put on first alert. Ayodhya city itself maintained a standing army of four akshohini. If a second conch sounded, all four divisions would mobilise within the hour: close to half a million foot soldiers, a quarter of a million armoured cavalry, a hundred thousand archers on chariots, and over eighty thousand war elephants. And if Ayodhya were under invasion, the rest of the army would arrive within days, summoned from garrisons at various strategic points across the kingdom.

But this was no invasion. There would be no need for a second alarm. Even the first was only sounded as a matter of routine. All because of a lone sudra hunter! Some insolent fool who had drunk too much bhaang too early on a feast day and had some petty grouse against his king. Dasaratha would sort this fellow out in a moment, punish him for his impudence—after he made sure the man didn't have any companions as unpatriotic as himself following close behind—and resume the arghya he had been about to perform.

Dasaratha looked at the chief of the quadrant immediately surrounding him. The captain standing before him was a pleasant-faced young fellow whose face suggested he was related to an old and illustrious senapati who had led part of Dasaratha's army in several campaigns.

'Drishti Kumar—it is Drishti Kumar, isn't it? —I wish to speak with him for a moment. Please make way.'

The man saluted. If he was pleased at being recognised and acknowledged by his king, he did not waste time showing it now. 'Maharaj, may I advise that you and your esteemed guest retire to the safety of the royal palace. We shall interrogate the low-caste commoner and bring you full details within minutes.'

Dasaratha shook his head impatiently. 'Thank you for your concern, captain. But this is just some bhaang-drunk citizen with a grouse. I can deal with him myself. Move aside.'

Reluctantly, the captain issued a secret signal and a corridor appeared before Dasaratha. He walked down the gauntlet of gleaming spears until he found himself within sight of the sudra. The hunter was still encircled by soldiers, but Dasaratha could see him well enough.

'Citizen, who are you and why do you dare to address your king so insolently?'

The sudra hunter took a step forward, unmindful of the spears fencing him in. He spoke in a voice that was strangely familiar. Completely unlike the western plains accent that Dasaratha would have expected, based on his appearance and caste marks.

'Dasaratha, listen very carefully. That man standing over there is an impostor. I am the real Vishwamitra.'

Dasaratha resisted the impulse to laugh aloud in disbelief. Was the man completely insane? He clearly needed some straightening out and quickly. Keenly aware that he was being watched by over a hundred of his personal palace guard, Dasaratha replied in his most formidable baritone.

'Insolent man! Do you wish to be put to death right here on the street?'

'Dasaratha, look at me closely. I changed my bhesbhav to enter the city without attracting the attention of your enemies. I did not know that this foul demon had already preceded me here by scant moments. If I had not come in time, you would be lying dead right there before your own gates. Even now, I urge you, step away from him!'

At the mention of harm coming to the king, the soldiers guarding the sudra moved forward. Their training demanded they deal with the stranger as a hostile traitor now, and they quickly disarmed him and twisted his arms behind his back. He made no move to resist, as if he had been expecting this action.

'Maharaj,' said the captain's voice from behind Dasaratha. 'This man is ranting. Let us take him to the dungeons where he will be suitably *interrogated*. He may be part of a conspiracy.'

Dasaratha nodded sadly. He felt pity for the man now, not anger. He turned his back on the citizen.

'Take him away.'

The sudra shouted fiercely, the veins on his neck and upper shoulders standing out with his intensity. 'You must believe me. That man is an impostor! He is an assassin from Lanka sent to kill you before you have a chance to announce the coronation of your son Rama. Tell your soldiers to unhand me or I will have no choice but to use my powers against them.'

Dasaratha stopped still. For a moment, it seemed as if time itself stopped with him.

He had recognised the hunter's voice the moment he turned his back. It was the voice of Vishwamitra, identical in every respect. It had taken him a moment to place it, having just heard the sage himself speak for the first time a few seconds before this insolent madman had begun yelling. But once he realised the similarity, there was no doubt at all. The hunter spoke in precisely the same cultured and modulated tones as the great seer-mage himself, a former kshatriya warrior king of a great dynasty, not like a low-caste killer of four-footed animals. What strange magic was abroad here? Dasaratha resisted the urge to turn back and reassess the sudra. He kept walking away.

'Dasaratha!' the sudra called out again, his anger clearly audible now. 'Do not force me to destroy your soldiers. I have sworn a sacred vow not to take a life until my tapasya is complete. Order them to move away and let me deal with the impostor. Look. Even now, he pretends to be me, the foolish creature, but his disguise is merely excellent, not perfect. Ask Guru Vashishta if you do not believe me. Vashishta! Speak and save lives!'

Dasaratha continued walking back down the corridor of guards. Ahead, he could see the trio of men still arranged in the same tableau. Guru Vashishta standing still as a statue, arms crossed in front of him. The sage Vishwamitra, proud profile limned against the growing light of the rising sun. And off to one side, eyes goggling at this incredible turn of events, Pradhan-Mantri Sumantra.

'Ayodhya-naresh.'

The seer-mage barely turned his head to look at Dasaratha as he approached. But the tone of hurt pride was unmistakable.

'Is this how you greet a visiting seer? With insults and abuse from a common citizen? I would turn my powers on the insolent wretch and reduce him to ashes in an instant.'

And then, with a calm that was almost preternatural, Guru Vashishta spoke his first words since emerging from the palace gates.

'An excellent idea, Vishwamitra. Why don't you do just that? Use your power of atma-brahman and punish that wretched mortal over there for insulting you. The code of the seers demands it, as you well know.'

In the sudden deathly silence that followed these words, Dasaratha heard a peculiar sound from behind. A sound like men grunting and choking.

He spun around and saw an amazing sight.

The sudra hunter had somehow managed to throw off the two men holding his arms, and they lay on their backs on the street, clutching their throats, gasping for breath. The rest of the guards surrounding the hunter raised their spears and drove them forward without hesitation. Dasaratha saw the foot-long tapered steel blades of the spears strike the sudra's body—and break off!

The snapping spears made a loud and shocking sound. The baffled soldiers, not quite comprehending what had happened, stared down at their broken weapons, then at the sudra. Not a scratch marred his bare upper body. As their unit leader shouted an order in commonspeak, the guards dropped their broken spears and reached over their shoulders for their back-sheathed swords.

The sudra raised his palms and pushed outwards, like a man shoving at the walls of a narrow corridor. With a burst of blue light, the ring of soldiers surrounding him exploded into the air, rising up and back and falling several yards away in a stunned heap. Their armour clattered noisily on the street, leaving a clear circle around the sudra.

He lowered his hands and strode towards the seer standing before the gates.

'Come on then, impostor. Vashishta speaks wisely. Destroy me. Or be destroyed yourself. But know this first: you face none other than Brahmarishi Vishwamitra.'

And before Dasaratha's astonished eyes, the sudra hunter cried out a Sanskrit mantra as fiercely as a general

calling out a battle cry, and in a burst of blinding blue
light morphed into the spitting image of the seer-mage
Vishwamitra.

TWELVE

Several things happened simultaneously. Rama pulled back his hand and threw the stone. It flew directly at its destination—the leader—and before Bearface could blink, it struck him squarely in the centre of his forehead with a sound like an axe striking a teak tree. Bearface grunted, his eyes rolled up in his head and he fell bonelessly to the ground.

At the same time, two of the other men loosed arrows directly at Rama, these ones aimed to hit, not miss. Rama's hand was still at the end of its throw when the arrows left their bows. Moving with the pull of the throw, he turned his body sharply to the right, presenting his slender silhouette rather than his broad front. Both arrows whizzed past him, the rusty iron head of the second one nicking and shredding the seam of his kurta, and buried themselves in the side of the knoll. He had judged their trajectories correctly: both were too high to harm the deer lying helpless behind him on the ground.

Even before the two arrows had struck the knoll, three more were loosed. At the same time, the men not firing realised their leader had been downed and paused, surprised and confused. A few of them could not understand how Bearface had fallen at all; they were too drunk to connect the rock thrown by Rama with the man's fall.

117

Rama was still poised sideways, presenting his silhouette to the pahadis, when the three arrows left their strings. He had been looking back to see where the first arrows landed, and there was not enough time to turn and judge the trajectories of the new ones. So he did it by the sound of their loosing and the hiss of their metal heads as they flew through the air, barely audible above the roar of the Sarayu. At the same time, he completed the half-turn he had begun, now presenting his back to the men, while bending over backwards, his hands shooting up towards the sky as he did so.

He clenched his fists as if grabbing mosquitoes, then straightened up slowly, still with his back to the men.

Two arrows were clutched in his right fist, one in his left.

The pahadis blinked, astonished.

'By the shakti of Kali,' one of them said.

Another man dropped his wineskin. Blood-red wine splashed from the open mouth, staining the damp ground of the riverbank.

The youngster, his bow still unfired, hiccuped loudly and lost his grip on his arrow. It shot upwards into the air, arced gracefully, and fell into the river.

The other men all looked at their fallen leader, then at Rama. He turned to face them, the arrows still clutched in his fists. He tossed the single one in the air, spinning it around and catching it by the tail. He judged its heft and balance. It was a well-made shortbow arrow, about half a yard long and reasonably well balanced. He tossed it again and caught it by the head this time, raising his arm to aim it at one of the men who had shot at him.

The man fumbled at his back, his hand seeking his quiver. His eyes were still wide with shock, his drink-addled brain unable to comprehend what he had just seen. Working by instinct, he found an arrow and pulled it from the quiver. Before the pahadi's arrow could even reach the string of his bow, Rama tossed his first arrow back at him. Thrown like a dart knife with just the right force and the perfect angle to bring it around the force of the wind blowing downriver, it struck the man in the shoulder. His bow and arrow fell from his hands and he fell with them, clutching at his shoulder, his face contorting in a silent scream.

In quick succession, Rama tossed the other two arrows, taking care to aim only at those who had loosed missiles at him, avoiding the ones with blades who had simply swaggered and threatened. Both arrows found their marks—one hitting its target in the ample flesh of his side, away from any internal organs, the other striking a man in his upper thigh. He was standing on a rock a yard high, which accounted for the difference.

One foolish Garhwali pahadi, still not comprehending what they were up against, spat a curse and loosed a fresh arrow, aiming directly at Rama's throat this time. Rama snatched the arrow from the air in a gesture like yanking off a neck-chain, and tossed it back at its owner in one single fluid motion. The arrow took the man in the throat. He sank to his knees, a gurgling liquid noise bubbling from his gashed windpipe, blood pouring down the front of his chest to merge with the winestains on his wolf-pelt. He fell forward on his face and lay still.

The nine men still alive and conscious stared at Rama silently. For several moments, none of them spoke. The youngster who had shot the arrow upwards was breathing heavily, as if he had run a yojana non-stop. His panting was punctuated by hiccups at irregular intervals, large lurching hiccups that made his entire body shake. Finally, he fell to his knees and lost the contents of his stomach.

The sound of the river grew very loud.

Rama spoke to the pahadis, looking them in the eyes one by one.

'Cast down your weapons and there will be no more bloodshed.'

The clattering of wooden bows and metal blades on the rocky riverbank made an almost musical counterpoint to the river's sound.

Lakshman was less than a hundred yards from the grove when he saw the ragged group coming towards him on foot. They looked like pahadis from their pelts but he had never seen pahadis behave in that fashion. The men were walking in a straight line and displayed none of the boisterousness of mountain folk. One of them was supporting a companion who seemed to be ill. Another pair were carrying a makeshift sling between them, in which a man with an obvious arrow wound lay—even from here, Lakshman could see the shaft sticking out. At the end of the line, another pair were carrying what appeared to be a dead companion wrapped in furs. And finally, bringing up the rear was a slender young form in white, walking behind the ragged line like a govinda shepherding his bleating flock home. Except that this particular flock was unusually silent.

Lakshman whispered to his horse, Marut, who immediately responded, slowing to a light canter. They reached the peculiar procession in moments. The pahadis stared sullenly up at Lakshman but offered no greeting or comment. Now he knew something was off here. Pahadis were notorious for their loquaciousness. Even their funeral processions were accompanied by incessant chanting and singing. Only one particularly large pahadi, the one being supported by his companion, glared hotly at Lakshman through a terribly scarred face. Bear slashes, Lakshman thought. During the years in Guru Vashishta's gurukul, he had seen several examples of the work of the great Himalayan rksaa before, but they had all been the mauled corpses of waylaid pilgrims that he and his fellow shishyas had found on the slopes of the lower Himalayas. This pahadi had the worst scarring he had seen on a man still living.

Lakshman reached the end of the line and halted Marut.

'Well,' he said to Rama. 'Looks like you've been busy this morning.'

Rama was holding a kairee in his hand, sucking on it with an excruciating expression on his face. He nodded at Lakshman. 'Pass me some salt.'

Lakshman pulled out the small packet of salt that every kshatriya carried to fend off dehydration as a matter of habit. He tossed it to Rama, who caught it and opened it one-handed, and then dipped the kairee into it. He sucked on the salt-encrusted fruit again, and this time he shook his head with delight. 'Sundar. Ati sundar.' *Beautiful. Truly beautiful.*

Lakshman smiled as he turned his horse around. Rama's fondness for sour kairee was so legendary it had made him the butt of many jokes in the past. Lakshman leaped off Marut, leading the horse by the reins as he walked by his brother. 'So what did these scoundrels do to deserve their wounds?'

Rama shrugged, still intent on his kairee. 'They were hunting a deer by the riverbank. I told them to stop. They didn't listen.'

Lakshman glanced over the sullen group trudging silently towards the first wall-gate. 'Three wounded, no, four. And one dead. And that young badmash there looks like he's been throwing up more wine than he's been drinking. And they all look like the nasty kind, the kind

121

who poach on the king's lands and don't hesitate to murder wardens over a rabbit snack.'

Rama nodded, eyes shut as he relished his kairee. 'Good thinking. Have some of the wardens take a look at them. They might find some familiar faces. Repeat offenders. Sumantra did say something about poachers on the king's lands this past winter.'

'So how did you do it?'

Rama grinned up at him, displaying lips and teeth yellowed by the sour fruit.

Lakshman sighed and nodded. 'Ask a stupid question . . .'

Rama pointed down the long raj-marg. The king's highway wound through the groves and sloping valley road of the north bank of the Sarayu for another full yojana before reaching the city gates. 'Why don't you ride to the first gate and have them send an escort for these wretches? Then maybe we can get to the practice session we'd planned. I bet you Bharat and Shatrugan are hard at it already. They're determined to top us in archery as well as the chariot race.'

Lakshman snorted. 'They can dream.' He took up the slack in Marut's reins gently. 'Why don't you give your flock a rest for a few moments? I'll be back before you can finish that kairee.'

Rama grinned and patted a bulge in the pocket of his kurta. 'That's okay,' he said. 'I have more.'

THIRTEEN

Dasaratha was seeing the impossible. Two Vishwamitras? One claiming the other was an impostor, an assassin? What was going on? And if the sudra hunter was just an Asura in disguise, how did he have the use of brahman? Dasaratha had seen the sacred force used enough times in his lifetime to recognise that bluish light.

The man who said he was the real Vishwamitra stopped a few yards from the first Vishwamitra, the man whose feet Dasaratha had been about to wash with holy Ganges water a few minutes ago. He raised his hand and Dasaratha heard a whooping sound, the sound of heavy wildwood whipping through the air. He turned to see the sudra hunter's spear, which had been lying on the street beside the stunned guard who had confiscated it, flying through the air towards its owner. As it flew, making that whooping sound, it transformed into a hefty wildwood staff, identical to the one in the hand of the first Vishwamitra. The staff reached its destination and the man who claimed to be the real Vishwamitra raised it in a threatening stance at the amazed soldiers blocking his path.

'Move aside, Ayodhyans. I have no wish to harm you. My business is with that impostor over there. He is the intruder and a threat to your king and city, not I.'

The soldiers looked at their captain uneasily. Dasaratha knew that scenarios such as this were not part of their training. He himself had never seen anything like it before. To his credit, Captain Drishti Kumar, swallowing his obvious puzzlement, shouted to the men defending the maharaja and the gates to hold their positions. Then he barked an order to the rest of the platoon to attack the stranger without hesitation or mercy. Dasaratha nodded approvingly. This was the result of *his* training, *his* army.

A moment later, he lost all faith in his own experience.

The challenger, seeing that his warning hadn't been heeded, calmly sketched two half-circles in the air with his staff.

An explosion of blue light filled the avenue, visible for a mile in every direction.

The entire contingent of soldiers blocking his path, some forty-odd hefty armed men, were thrown up into the air like a child's rag dolls. They flew to either side like sods in a field riven by a plough, and fell in a crumpled heap of tangled spears, armour and bruised limbs. Even in this moment of crisis, Dasaratha's battle-hardened eyes noted that none of them were actually harmed by the sorcerous bolts. *But if he could do that to them, he could easily have killed them too.* He recalled what the sudra hunter had said about not wanting to break his tapasya by taking a life, and the first seed of real doubt began to sprout.

Now, nothing stood between the challenger and the first Vishwamitra. The man whom the sudra hunter had accused of being an impostor had turned to face his accuser. Dasaratha saw that the moment his back was turned, a quartet of soldiers rushed up and escorted Pradhan-Mantri Sumantra aside, out of harm's way. The prime minister was trembling like a leaf. Dasaratha had seen Sumantra fight like a veteran in the heat of battle, but sorcery of this magnitude was any kshatriya's nightmare come true. Flesh and metal were poor armour against seers' sorcery.

The soldiers did not attempt to lead Guru Vashishta aside. If there was anyone here who could deal with the situation, it was he, Dasaratha knew. Why had he not acted yet? It was this rather than anything else that made Dasaratha himself hold his tongue and wait before giving another order. He needed to hear the guru speak again.

Preternaturally sensitive to the maharaja's mind as always, Guru Vashishta spoke again into the thick silence that followed. He addressed his words to the man who stood before him, the first Vishwamitra. His tone was calm, almost casual, as if he was discussing the weather and harvest with his seer colleague.

'There seems to be a question of identity, my esteemed friend. This man has challenged your authenticity. Aren't you going to respond in some way?'

The man whose feet Dasaratha had almost washed with his own hands looked at the guru silently. Then, with a perceptible reluctance, he turned and faced his challenger.

'I am Vishwamitra. You are the impostor.'

The challenger smiled grimly at those words. 'You will have to do more than claim now, assassin. Prove it!'

The seer-mage looked at him intently. 'My word is my proof. Now be gone or be ruined.'

If he was acting, Dasaratha thought, it was one hell of a performance.

But then the other Vishwamitra spoke.

'I cannot perform an aggressive act, impostor. It will negate my entire penance. I have not endured two hundred and forty years of tapasya in the fetid swamps of the Bhayanak-van just to be tricked by a shape-shifting Asura

125

such as yourself. As I did with the soldiers, I will only defend myself. Unleash your black sorcery. Do your worst.'

Guru Vashishta nodded and looked pleased, speaking again.

'Well said, old friend,' he said approvingly. The guru's voice turned harsh as he turned back to the first Vishwamitra standing barely a yard before him. 'It is time to show your true self now, impostor.' And with a penetrating, bone-chilling cry, he uttered a mantra: 'Reveal yourself, rakshas!'

With a shock, Dasaratha realised the guru was siding with the second Vishwamitra! Vashishta believed that the insolent sudra hunter was the real seer-mage! Which meant *the other man was the impostor*. Dasaratha watched, transfixed, as the drama at the gates took its unexpected new turn.

Just at that moment, reinforcements arrived. Out of the corner of his eye, Dasaratha could glimpse a senapati shouting orders to a quartet of elephant-mounted spearmen, while several chariot-borne archers blocked every ingress and exit. A second squadron of his personal guard began to ring Dasaratha, eager to spirit him away from this incomprehensible but obvious threat. It took two successive orders from the maharaja, spoken quietly but firmly, before they reluctantly settled for a defensive position around him. Dasaratha twisted and turned to get a better view. The sound of armour rattling and feet running echoed from all around. Whatever the impostor's goal may have been, he would not get into the royal palace now. Not without killing several thousand of the finest warriors in the Arya nations. Behind the palace gates, Dasaratha saw a crowd of servants and staff being kept back at a safe distance by guards, while at the far end of Raghuvamsha Avenue a growing crowd of citizens had begun to gather and were similarly being kept behind a line of spearmen. Word spread fast in Ayodhya, especially when the army alert was sounded. By now, the entire city would know that a crisis had arisen at the palace gates—a crisis involving their king himself.

The man who was the centre of all this attention, the first Vishwamitra, slowly raised his staff. For a moment Dasaratha thought he was about to sketch a mantra in the air, blasting the other Vishwamitra to ashes, proving his own authenticity.

But with a tired sigh, the man simply threw the staff lightly up into the air and caught it. It was the gesture of a court juggler and it had the same effect. For an instant, every pair of eyes followed the rise and fall of the staff, shifting away from its owner.

In that instant he changed back to his true form.

FOURTEEN

A medley of gasps and exclamations rose from the massed soldiers surrounding the avenue. Dasaratha heard his own voice uttering a hasty invocation to Lord Indra, patron deity of warriors, general of the army of the gods.

The thing standing before Guru Vashishta was no longer a man, let alone a legendary seer-mage.

It was a rakshas. A demon from the netherworld, the third and lowest plane of existence, of which Lanka was the capital city and gateway. Its blackish-red skin, garments made of human skin, necklace of human infant skulls, wild snake-mouthed hair and blood-red eyes left no doubt at all. No seer would assume this form, even in jest. This was a born rakshas, and from the size of its horns, two-yard-long antlers formidable enough to match the headgear of a Himalayan black stag, he could see that it was a very aged and powerful rakshas. It towered at least thrice as high as Guru Vashishta, and the guru himself was over six feet tall.

The rakshas laughed, revealing a mouthful of splintered black fangs. The sound it emitted was nothing like human laughter. Dasaratha's hair curled and his teeth keened at the sound. Somewhere beside him, a soldier moaned and uttered a brief prayer. Dasaratha added his own, but silently.

Guru Vashishta was the only person on the avenue who seemed unperturbed by the apparition that had appeared before him. The fact that the creature was barely a hand's reach away didn't seem to bother him in the least.

He spoke, cutting sharply through the demon's laughter. 'Kala-Nemi, it's been a while since we last met.'

The rakshas turned to look at Vashishta. His antlered head was too heavy even for his bulky muscular body, and the action was slow and deliberate. Dasaratha realised with a surge of disgust that the rakshas's skin was *alive*, a crawling carpet of living tissue that bulged and boiled and seethed like the surface of a volcanic mass rather than an epidermal covering. And there were *things* living inside the beast's body, he saw, their blind white worm-like forms snaking into and out of his flesh, his form undulating as they writhed.

'*Vashisht. Still alive, old fool?*'

The rakshas's voice was like the sound of gravel grinding with glass. It hurt the ears physically.

Vishwamitra addressed Vashishta.

'You know this beast, old friend?'

Vashishta replied without taking his eyes off the rakshas, who kept turning his antlered head slowly to look at each of the seers as they spoke.

'He and I have had . . . encounters over the millennia. He comes from a very illustrious line of Asuras. I'm sure you know him by his family name at least. Pulastya.'

Vishwamitra snorted.

'You must be joking. This stinking foulness is descended from the sage Pulastya?'

'Yes. Through his son, Visravas. This handsome fellow is Visravas's brother, in fact.'

'How interesting. So that would make him . . . uncle of Ravana, the self-proclaimed king of the rakshas clans?'

129

At the mention of Ravana, the rakshas raised his antlered head and opened his mouth wide. A slimy, maggot-infested serpent with snapping jaws emerged a foot out of his open mouth and emitted a high-pitched scream that jarred Dasaratha's ears. The serpent retreated as quickly as it had come, dropping one wriggling greenish-white maggot on to the dust of the avenue. Dasaratha saw the ground boil with a frenzy like soup bubbling, and the maggot dissolved into a tiny puddle of steaming fluid, unable to survive outside the fetid environment of its natural habitat.

'I am Kala-Nemi, king of rakshasas. Ravana is merely my nephew. I roamed the three worlds long before he was even a mote in my sister's eye.'

An elephant reared in fright, startled by the unnatural sound of the rakshas's voice. An old veteran, Dasaratha thought, just like me, hearing and seeing things it has tried desperately to forget for many years.

Suddenly, he wanted a sword in his hand. The sight of the rakshas sickened him to the belly. He had almost washed this thing's feet! Bent his head before its vile presence like a goat bowing before a butcher. Close enough to be struck down with one treacherous blow. At the gates of his own palace, in the heart of the most impregnable Arya city ever built. Unbelievable. He turned to Drishti Kumar and asked him for a sword. The captain responded without a word, eyes fixed on the tableau unfolding before the palace gates.

Dasaratha clutched the sword in his fist, and strode forward, trailing his squadron of guards. He wanted to confront this stranger who had dared to humiliate him on his own turf. But as he moved forward, Vishwamitra and Vashishta exchanged a glance, and Vishwamitra gestured in the maharaja's direction. To his chagrin,

130

Dasaratha found himself locked into a bubble of immobility, unable to speak or move.

The guru inclined his head marginally in the maharaja's direction, his tone apologetic. 'This matter cannot be settled with swords, Dasaratha. Allow us to deal with this intruder in the manner that best befits his race.' He gestured at the rest of the army contingent gathered all around them. 'I have done the same to all your brave soldiers as well, with your royal permission.'

For a moment, Dasaratha felt an irrational surge of anger at the guru. But he realised at once that Vashishta was right. He had fought enough rakshasas to know that to bring down one such beast could cost a dozen or more kshatriya lives. And he had never faced a rakshasa as formidable as this Kala-Nemi before. As his anger subsided, he felt a brief pulse of gratitude to the guru for yet again helping him save face, and saving his life as well.

It is my dharma, my king, came the unspoken reply in Dasaratha's brain, reminding him for the umpteenth time that if Vashishta's actions and words sometimes seemed curt and brusque, it was because the sage bore the weight of great responsibility. The responsibility of being the world's oldest living seer, one of only three of the original seven seers who had been present at the dawn of civilisation, and by extension, the oldest living repository of the unwritten vedas, the cumulative knowledge of the Arya peoples since the beginning of their race.

Aloud, Vashishta continued calmly, as if he was accustomed to having conversations with rakshasas at the palace gates, surrounded by Ayodhya's army and the watching populace. 'So, Kala-Nemi. You believe yourself to be the true leader of the rakshas clans, do you? And yet, I would wager my seven thousand years of knowledge that it was on your nephew Ravana's orders that you came here on this foolish mission.'

131

'*It was my idea. I go where I please, do as I please. If I choose to let Ravana sit on the throne of Lanka, it is because I prefer to roam free and ravage the cities of you mortals. He likes to enjoy the company of his stolen queens and toys. It pleases me to leave him to manage my kingdom while I strike terror and cause ruin among your kind.*'

Vishwamitra commented scornfully, 'Is that what you intended to do here? You don't seem to have been very successful.'

'*If your canny colleague had not exposed me when he did, I would have been within the walls of your palace wreaking havoc even at this moment. You were fortunate to have been spared my wrath this time.*'

Both sages laughed together.

'Foolish creature,' Vashista went on. 'Did you really believe you had fooled me? I saw through your disguise the moment I laid eyes on you. Just as a true sage, seer or seer-mage has an aura of brahman around his form, you Asuras have a stench of evil around you. I smelt it a mile away.'

The rakshas roared again in frustration, spitting maggots into the air. '*You lie! If you saw through my disguise you would never have let me come so close to Maharaja Dasaratha!*' He extended a large clawed hand and made a slashing motion barely inches from Vashishta's face. '*I could have slit his throat just by flexing my arm!*'

The guru looked unperturbed by the threatening gesture. 'But then you would never have come close to your real target. And your mission would have been a failure.'

Kala-Nemi grunted. Dasaratha thought he heard disgust in that alien sound. Although it might have been just an acid belch.

'If you know who I intended to kill, then know this also, old seer. I will accomplish my mission, sooner or later. And a day will come not far from now when this gaudy eyesore of a city will lie in smouldering ruins. Even as we speak, the greatest army of Asuras ever assembled is preparing to march north. Ayodhya will fall. And after it, all of the proud Arya nations. We masters of the netherworld will possess the world of Middle-Earth that you call Prithvi. We will crush you like the pathetic bags of meat-and-water you are, mortals! And when we have rid all Prithvi of every last one of your kind, we shall rise to overpower the plane of swarga-lok as well, land of the devas. No power in the three worlds of hell, earth and heaven can stop us!'

Vashishta glanced at his fellow seer-mage grimly.

'I think we have bantered enough with this pretty boy, Vishwamitra. Time to show him how we *mortals* deal with skulking assassins and rude rakshasas who threaten us with genocide.'

Vishwamitra nodded, and both seer-mages raised their arms high, chanting a mantra that even Dasaratha had never heard before. Blue streaks of light shot from the tips of their fingers, coiling together to form a thick rope of brahman. They lowered their hands, and the rakshas was entwined in the rope of mystic energy. He screamed with rage, twisting in the grip of their power.

'Do your worst, fools. I will be back. And you will learn as countless mortals before you have learned the painful way, that it's not for nothing He is named Ravan-a. He Who Makes The Universe Scream!'

'But for now,' Vishwamitra said softly, 'you are the one who will scream.'

Together both mages raised their hands. Lifting the rakshas on the thick, coiling beam of blue light, they elevated him a dozen yards above the avenue. Dasaratha heard gasps of wonder from the crowd assembled at the far end of the avenue as well as muttered exclamations and invocations from the soldiers.

'In the name of Brahma, Vishnu and Shiva,' cried the mages together in a single voice that seemed to boom like thunder from the clear skies, 'consign this demon to the lowest level of the netherworld, to everlasting agony!'

One last mantra. And with an explosion like a volcano erupting, the blue beam shot the rakshas downwards into the ground. He struck it like an arrow piercing water, and a hole appeared. Dasaratha felt a sucking force drawing himself and everything around him, the very air itself, into the hole. Darkness swirled like a vortex into infinity. The blue light blazed blinding bright, forcing everyone to cover their eyes; a deafening thunderclap sounded, and suddenly the rakshas was gone, the hole had disappeared, and the world was normal once more.

A giant roar of applause and cheers exploded from the watching hordes, soldiers and citizens alike. Elephants trumpeted, echoing their mahouts' joy. Guards clattered their swords against their shields.

Dasaratha found he too was free to move once again. The spell binding them all had been released the instant the rakshas was dispatched. He pushed his way past the soldiers encircling him and ran to the seers. They stood together speaking softly, their faces looking more lined and anxious than when they had been fighting the rakshas.

'Mahadev,' Dasaratha blurted, bending to touch the tips of his fingers to Vishwamitra's dusty feet. 'Forgive me for not recognising you at first, and for treating you so rudely. You have saved my life and done all of Kosala a great, great service. My debt to you can never be repaid. But if there is any way I can show my gratitude, then you have but to ask.'

Vishwamitra touched Dasaratha's forehead, blessing him, then raised him to his feet gently.

'That natural error is not even worth mentioning, Ayodhya-naresh. As for being in my debt, don't be too quick to offer me gratitude. I am about to ask you to give me your most precious possession.'

Dasaratha smiled, joining his hands in pranaam.

'Great One, whatever you ask for, it is yours. I swear this in the presence of my mahaguru Vashishta, by the honour of the Arya nations, the Suryavansha dynasty and Ikshvaku clan, the kingdom of Kosala and its capital city of Ayodhya. Today, you have ensured the survival of all these great lineages. Name your dakshina and I shall grant it without hesitation.'

Vishwamitra glanced at Guru Vashishta. The older seer looked troubled but did not speak. Vishwamitra looked at Dasaratha again.

'Raje, I come to ask for the life of your oldest and most beloved son, Rama. I need him to accompany me on a mission of the greatest danger and importance. A mission that could save Ayodhya itself. Surrender his life to me and you shall be forever blessed for your sacrifice.'

Lakshman brought Marut to a halt. Rama, riding double-saddle behind his brother, dismounted and ran to the tree where he had tethered Airavata.

'I couldn't herd the whole bunch of pahadis up through the grove to get him,' he explained to Lakshman. 'It was simpler to walk them straight to the first gate. If I hadn't met you on the way, I would have just left them with the gate-watch, turned around and come back for him.'

Lakshman nodded, peering over the rise at the river-bank below. 'Where did you say you left the deer anyway? I don't see her down there.'

Rama joined him, scanning the rocky bank. 'Right there. Look. You can see the blood-stains from her wound. She must have been well enough to return to the forest after all.'

'Good for her. Now we can go back to the city and play Holi!'

Rama frowned. 'What about practice?'

Lakshman sighed. 'What about it? You're already the best in your class, Rama. Besides, in case you've forgotten, today's a feast day! Everybody's looking forward to a day of celebration, masthi, bhaang and roast meat! And it's Holi! Our first Holi in Ayodhya in eight years!'

Rama grinned, wiping a last stain of kairee ras from his chin. 'It is, isn't it?' He paused. 'Luck, do you think we're too old to play Holi?'

Lakshman chuckled. 'Too old? Don't you remember all the stories Father told us about playing Holi with our mothers and all his other wives as well, all three hundred and fifty of them? Or how the entire cabinet of ministers got drunk on bhaang and danced the bhangra with each other—and these are statesman who are at each other's throats at every cabinet meeting! You're never too old to play Holi, Rama! Holi was created for even the old to act young, just for a day at least.'

'That's good,' Rama mused. 'So if we act like little brats today, nobody would mind, right?'

Lakshman grinned. 'What did you have in mind?'

Rama shrugged. 'Oh, nothing much. Just thought we might find Bharat and Shatrugan and turn their faces as purple as monkeys!'

Lakshman clapped his hands. 'Now you're talking like a true Arya! Let's do it!'

'Okay!' Rama yelled, rising to a half-crouch. 'Come on, kachua. Race you back to the horses!'

Lakshman laughed and raced his brother. As they leaped on their horses, startling the old stalwarts with their suddenness, they sang out together in perfect harmony:

'Holi hai, Holi hai! Rang-birangi Holi hai!'

They had just reached the point where the raj-marg undulated from its curving path and ran straight as an arrow the last half-yojana to the first gate when they saw the dust-cloud approaching.

'That's Bharat and Shatrugan,' Rama said.

In a moment, the dust-cloud cleared to reveal two gleaming gold-plated raths, each drawn by two fine Kambhoja stallions. As the chariots neared and slowed,

Bharat's muscular bulk and Shatrugan's only slightly less developed physique became clearly visible.

Bharat's voice rang out across the dusty highway. 'Where in the three worlds have you been?'

Rama grinned as his brothers halted their chariots smartly, barely a yard before Airavata and Marut's noses. The old battlehorses stood their ground calmly. Rama replied, 'What's the matter, bhai? Impatient to get your face coloured?'

Bharat grinned back at him. 'We'll see who gets his face coloured first. But first we're needed back in the palace. Father's orders.'

Rama and Lakshman exchanged glances. 'Probably heard about your little escapade with the pahadis,' Lakshman commented under his breath.

'What pahadis?' Shatrugan asked as he started to turn his chariot around, clucking encouragingly to his horses. 'Are the pahadis invading us too?'

'Invading? Who said anything about invading?' Rama asked, his voice suddenly sharp. Lakshman glanced at him, surprised.

This time, Bharat and Shatrugan exchanged glances.

'Don't you know anything?' Bharat replied, turning his chariot as well. 'The city is on full alert. The army was called out.'

Rama's expression darkened abruptly. Lakshman saw him and thought of a barkha cloud passing across the sun. 'Tell me what happened.'

Shatrugan chuckled. 'It was almost funny at first. There were two Vishwamitras, but one was a sudra hunter. It was only when he started throwing whole quads of soldiers around that Father realised he wasn't a sudra hunter. And then—'

'Be quiet, Shot.' Bharat's voice was quiet but firm. He had seen the expression on Rama's face. 'It's all under

138

control now, bhai. The seer-mage Vishwamitra arrived to visit Father on an urgent mission. Only a rakshas arrived at the same time, disguising himself as Vishwamitra. There was a lot of confusion. But the real Vishwamitra and Guru Vashishta exposed the rakshas and dispatched him using brahman sorcery. Father's called us all back to the palace just in case there are more intruders around. We should go.'

They were all silent, watching Rama closely. Lakshman had never seen his brother grow so serious so suddenly. Rama had nodded distractedly during Bharat's explanation. It was as if Rama had expected to hear something along those lines.

'What is it, bhai?' Lakshman asked gently.

Rama glanced at him. He seemed to realise that they were all staring at him and that he might not be behaving quite as might be expected. 'Nothing. It's nothing. I just . . . Bharat's right. We should return to the palace as soon as possible. We should be within the seventh wall at a time like this.'

Lakshman saw Shatrugan frown and look at Bharat questioningly. Bharat shook his head, silencing Shatrugan again. Shatrugan shrugged.

They began trotting their horses down the raj-marg. After a moment of tense silence, Rama seemed to shrug off his sudden cloak of tension with a visible effort. He glanced around at his brothers, giving them a smile. Lakshman felt relieved. He had been worried there for a moment. The news from the city was shocking enough, but Rama's reaction had been even more alarming. It was good to see Rama looking like his brother again.

'Hey,' Rama called out in a more cheerful tone. 'What say we race back to the first gate? Order of arrival decides who gets to colour the others' faces first, agreed?'

'Agreed!' cried the three of them in happy unison, ululating and crying encouragement to their horses as they began raising a dust-cloud that filled the breadth of the raj-marg.

The four brothers shot forward like a single arrow from the same bow, heading home to Ayodhya.

On the uppermost rise of the mango grove, high above the raj-marg, the doe lowered her head and watched the four mortal boys ride away. The head of the arrow still stuck out from her leg, but the wound had stopped bleeding; Rama's hurried tourniquet had been rough but effective.

Still reluctant to endure the pain of changing that might well open the wound once more, the doe licked around the edges of her injury, trying to come to terms with what had happened today. She had been sent here to Ayodhya on a mission. That mission itself was simple enough: to accompany her uncle Kala-Nemi on the long journey north, aid him in infiltrating the great mortal city of Ayodhya, and wait until he accomplished his own assignment, which was to assassinate a certain mortal named Rama Chandra, first-born son of Maharaja Dasaratha. So when Kala-Nemi had assumed the bhes-bhav of the seer-mage Vishwamitra, a brilliant idea suggested by her cousin Lord Ravana during their briefing, she had taken the form of a deer, a favourite disguise that had fooled humans many times before, and waited in the woods outside the city. In the event that Kala-Nemi failed—unlikely but certainly possible, given the presence of that ancient enemy of the Asuras, Guru Vashishta—she would take up and execute the same assignment.

But something very peculiar had happened as she waited for her uncle's return. That strange mortal boy had found her unexpectedly. Taken her by surprise. Even her heightened rakshas senses had not warned her of his

140

presence until he had her in his grasp. That itself was so unusual as to be a first in her lifetime. She was young by rakshas standards—barely five hundred years old to her cousin Ravana's five thousand years—but like all rakshasas, she was preternaturally tuned to any risk or threat. Yet she had sensed nothing, just the pleasant northern wind, the spray from the river, the scents of flowers and unripened mangoes—and the next instant, the mortal boy had her in his arms, enfolding her like a lover in his warm embrace. It had taken her breath away, shocking her speechless and immobile for several vital seconds. She, Supanakha, who was called the river-tongued by her fellow rakshasas back in Lanka!

The only explanation she could conceive of now, coming to terms with that bizarre capture, was that he had posed her no threat or risk, and hence his body odour and aura had been so benign that her finely attuned senses had included him as part of the environment itself. It defied everything she had learned and experienced about mortals, but there it was, the only logical answer. And when he had touched her, had there actually been affection in that embrace? Could a mortal, those brutal, rapacious two-legged beasts, actually feel affection for a four-legged mute animal?

But there was more confusion, and other questions too. When those vile intoxicated men—behaving more like normal mortals in her experience—had attacked her without provocation, once again the boy had behaved uncharacteristically. He had saved her life. And dressed her wound. And risked his own life and limb to stop her attackers. Altogether, it was too much for one morning.

Now, she licked one last time at her healing gash and prepared herself for the change. Painful as it might be, she must return to her true form. She needed hands rather than hoofs to remove the arrow before it festered.

She focused on the change, using the emotions swirling within her to try and distract her mind from the inevitable pain. Even so, when it came, it was tortuous. The arrowhead, deeply embedded in her doe form, remained where it was as her living flesh and tissue morphed and transformed around it, cutting and tearing her changing flesh and tissue, causing greater internal bleeding and damage than the original flesh wound.

Finally, she could take no more. She screamed. A scream neither wholly deer-like nor Yaksa-like. Simply the scream of a living being in terrible agony. *Damn you, damn you mortals all to hell!*

The change complete, she stood naked at the edge of the forest, tears rolling down her furry anthropomorphic face. Her large curved ears twitched several times as she reached gingerly for the arrow. Her clawed fingers probed cautiously at the edge of the torn skin. The good news was that the arrow hadn't gone into bone yet, just flesh. If she could just pull it out, the wound would heal naturally. That was one of the benefits of being a Yaksa: she would heal the wound in a day or two and in a week the scar would be barely visible. But right now, that didn't console her much.

She screamed again when the arrowhead tore its way out of her arm. This time, it was less the bleat of a wounded doe and more the shriek of an outraged rakshasi. The birds and creatures of the riverbank sensed the difference and grew silent and still.

The cry echoed in the sunlit valley, rippling down to the river and the raj-marg that ran alongside it. By the time it reached Rama, a good chariot-length ahead of his brothers, it had almost faded to nothingness. Still, he raised his head a fraction, his grin of triumphant concentration fading as he sensed the suffering of another living creature.

A moment later, the faint echo was driven out of his mind as he saw what lay ahead, and he held up his hand, calling a halt to the impromptu race.

SIXTEEN

Maharaja Dasaratha paused at the entrance of the sabha hall. He had expected the news of the morning's events to spread like wildfire through the city; already, the captain of the guards had brought word that a substantial crowd was amassing outside the palace gates. But it had barely been half an hour since he and Guru Vashishta had escorted Vishwamitra to the reception hall of the palace. How on earth had all these people collected here so soon? The sabha hall was designed to accommodate two hundred seated official court delegates and a thousand observers. As far as he could tell at a glance, it was filled well over capacity in both respects. The sheer press of the crowd forced him to pause at the entrance to take in this unexpected scenario.

The crowded hall buzzed with the chatter of a hundred excited conversations. Dasaratha caught the words 'rakshas' and 'Vishwamitra' spoken by several different voices with varying degrees of awe and amazement. What was that old Arya saying? 'Yesterday's rumour, today's legend?' Never truer.

Even the court crier, a young stripling with a high-pitched falsetto voice that grated on Dasaratha's nerves, was distracted enough not to have noticed his maharaja's arrival; leaning on the court standard, he was whispering energetically to a particularly attractive serving girl bearing a water jug. The crier seemed more interested in looking down the girl's blouse than in keeping the Suryavansha emblem aloft. In ages past, that lapse alone would have cost the youth his life. But Dasaratha settled for clearing his throat gruffly. The serving girl gasped at the sight of the king and instantly melted away into the crowd. The crier leaped to attention, blushing bright crimson, as he struck the standard thrice on the wooden floor and sang out the traditional entree.

'Kosala-narad Ayodhya-naresh Suryavansha Raghu-vansha Aja-putra Shrimati Maharaj Dasaratha rajya sabha mein padhaar rahein hain.'

King of Kosala, lord of Ayodhya, heir of House Suryavansha and House Raghuvansha, Son-of-Aja, The Honourable Emperor Dasaratha now graces the royal assembly with his esteemed presence.

By the time the litany of ancestral lineage and royal titles had ended, the chatter had died away to a whisper which also subsided as Dasaratha strode the forty-yard length of the ceremonial red carpet to the royal podium. As he climbed the seven silver-plated rose-petal-bedecked steps to his raj-gaddhi, he was rewarded by a dignified silence: his presence still commanded enough respect to ensure that nobody chattered once he entered a room. His right knee wobbled slightly as he reached the top and he resisted the urge to grip the ornately carved arm of his throne for support. For the first time in his long reign, the enormous gold-filigreed bulk of the Suryavansha throne seemed much too large for his frail and weary body. As he reached the seat of Kosala unaided, he sent up a silent prayer to his ancestors, asking for strength to endure the rest of this startling and difficult day. He turned around to face his court.

145

Sumantra had done the impossible as usual, assembling all the important officers of the court within the short time it had taken Dasaratha and Guru Vashishta to complete the welcoming formalities to honour their great visitor. Every single one of Ayodhya's eight cabinet ministers was present in the front row—Drishti, Jayanta, Manthrapala, Vijaya, Siddhartha, Jabali, Arthasadhaka, Ashoka—and Sumantra made nine. It was odd to see them dressed today in uncharacteristically commonplace homewear—spotless white cotton dhotis and kurtas—until he reminded himself that it was Holi and an official holiday. Obviously, they had been preparing to begin the Holi celebrations when summoned to court. No doubt, if Sumantra's hard-riding chariots had arrived a few moments later, the eight chosen representatives of Ayodhya's eight major constituencies would have been washed in rainbow hues, faces and clothes stained with the coloured rang powders and tinted waters symbolising the arrival of spring. As it was, they all looked unusually fresh and alive today, clearly infected by the same excitement that was sweeping the entire congregation. Only Jabali, the stern Grekos-influenced rationalist, looked sour-faced. But then Jabali always looked sour-faced.

Guru Vashishta and Brahmarishi Vishwamitra had followed Dasaratha on to the podium. As the seer-mages turned to face the sabha together, a collective murmur rose from the sizeable contingent of brahmins that made up more than half the mass of the crowd. They were witnessing a sight that their forefathers would have given a right arm to view. Dasaratha's eyes flicked across what seemed to be every last one of the city's prominent brahmins and purohits, all clad only in the traditional white dhoti with the black thread marking their caste criss-crossing their bare chests and bellies. And quite considerable bellies they were, Dasaratha noted wryly. From the expressions of devotional ecstasy on their well-fed faces, he could see that they were struggling to keep from prostrating themselves and kissing the sacred feet of the divinely ordained Vishwamitra.

Out of the corner of his eye, Dasaratha caught Pradhan-Mantri Sumantra stealing a sideways glance. The court recorders sitting off to one side, their quills poised over their parchment scrolls, were watching him intently, waiting for his first words. The ministers were waiting, their attendants and secretaries were waiting, the brahmins were waiting, the courtiers were waiting . . . even the royal guards, present in five times their usual strength, were clearly stiff-necked with anticipation even though their discipline compelled them to stare directly ahead.

Dasaratha drew himself up as straight and tall as he could manage. He had rigorously followed every formality of protocol so far, prolonging the inevitable as long as possible. Now, he could dally no longer. It was time.

'Ayodhya ke vasiyon, sada khush raho,' he said, uttering the customary prayer for an auspicious beginning to the sabha. *Ye all who dwell in Ayodhya, may you live happily here for ever.*

Sumantra responded with the customary 'Maharaj ki jai hon!'

'Long live the king!' echoed the assembly lustily.

The court crier then introduced their visitor, adding an extra flourish to his litany: 'Brahmarishi mahadev saprem swami tapasvi mahantya Vishwamitra atithi satkar ka swagat hai.' *Brahma-anointed great master, supreme lord of penance and wisdom, our honoured guest the sage Vishwamitra now graces us with his esteemed presence.*

Guru Vashishta now made a formal introduction of their great guest, presenting him to the sabha at large

147

and to the king in particular. Dasaratha knew that this was all for the benefit of the assembled observers and court recorders, but he had never been so glad of the time-taxing formalities of royal protocol. Vishwamitra turned and offered a namaskara to each minister and pundit in turn as Guru Vashishta called out their names. Even Jabali managed to reduce the sourness on his horsey face to about a third of its usual grimacing disapproval as he was presented to the seer-mage.

Dasaratha used the time to try to think through all the various options available to him. But the introductions went surprisingly quickly and before he could even concentrate properly, Sumantra was at his side again, whispering to him to commence with the formal agenda of the sabha.

With an invocation to his guest to be seated, Dasaratha enthroned himself, resisting the urge to sigh as the massive gold-plated sunwood throne took the oppressive weight of age and indulgence off his weary feet.

'Khamosh! Sabha jaari hain!' the crier sang out. *Silence, court is in session.*

With an uncharacteristic absence of sound—no lavish silks to rustle noisily or elaborate court jewellery to tinkle and clatter today—the occupants of the sabha hall bowed to the maharaja and seated themselves. A fifth of them took the gaddhis provided, the rest simply sitting cross-legged on the ground in traditional Arya style.

Mahaguru Vashishta spoke in formal Sanskrit high-speech. 'We are greatly honoured to have with us here such an illustrious and legendary guest. On behalf of this sabha and every citizen of Kosala, I offer Brahmarishi Vishwamitra every courtesy and respect—sampurn atithi satkar—that Ayodhya has to offer. We are your humble servants, mahadev. Please, grace us with your wisdom and tell us how we may serve you.'

Vishwamitra rose, took a small step forward and addressed Dasaratha directly.

'The blessings of Brahma, Vishnu and Shiva be upon you and your lineage, Ayodhya-naresh Dasaratha. I am pleased to be here in the nation of the Suryavanshas. Sadly, my business here is not pleasure, but necessity. As time is of the essence, I will come straight to the point. It is my unfortunate task to inform you all that the greatest crisis in the history of the Arya nations is upon us.'

SEVENTEEN

The princes had begun to slow the instant Rama's hand went up. Bharat's chariot, barely behind Rama's lead, came up beside Airavata and Bharat began protesting about Rama unfairly calling a halt. He broke off as he saw what lay ahead of them. All four princes brought their horses and chariots to a halt.

'The first gate is shut,' Lakshman said incredulously. 'That hasn't happened on a feast day since . . . well, since the Last Asura War.'

The gate was indeed shut. Or raised, to be more accurate. The enormous drawbridge of the first gate had been hauled up to wall the only gap in the fifty-yard-high stone abutment that was the city's first line of defence. The raising of the bridge exposed the twenty-yard-wide moat which teemed with magarmach and gharial and deva knew what other water-dwelling predators. The moat walls were ten yards straight down, making it impossible for the deadly beasts to climb out—they had little islands in the moat on which to rest and breed and fight amongst themselves. Lakshman had always wondered what would happen if the moat was neglected during one of those pounding seven-day monsoon downpours and allowed to overflow its banks. But it had never happened in Ayodhya's history. Ayodhyans took great pride in maintaining their city.

Had the moat creatures been able to crawl ashore right now, they would have found considerable prey to feed on. A large crowd of travellers was gathered on the raj-marg, milling about restlessly, chattering to one another. They had quietened and turned at the sound of the approaching horses and chariots, but none of them seemed fearful. *These are people grown in a time of peace*, Lakshman thought. *They've forgotten the horrors of war already, barely twenty-two years after the last invasion. Or perhaps they just want to forget.*

As the dust cleared, the travellers recognised the crown heirs of Kosala and several of them started forward, calling out anxiously in commonspeak.

'Rajkumaron! Aap hi kuch kijiye, na. Hummey andar jaane nahi de rahey hain.' *Princes, do something. They're refusing us entry into the city.*

The brothers exchanged glances.

'I guess we should talk to the gate-watch,' Bharat said, preparing to get off his chariot.

Rama stopped him. 'You and Shot wait here. Lakshman and I will go and talk to them.'

'Whatever you say, bhade bhaiya,' Shatrugan said, but grinned to show he didn't mind. The reference to 'big brother' was a long-standing joke on the few weeks' age difference between Rama and his siblings. They all accepted his evident maturity as far more important than those crucial weeks, but even had they not been so convivial, Arya law left no room for doubt. First-born was first-born. And first-born always led. Bharat, the second-oldest by two weeks, had long ago got over any childish sibling envy at this fact and come to accept Rama's seniority.

151

Rama and Lakshman dismounted and tossed their reins to their brothers, who caught them deftly and tied them loosely to their chariots. Then they turned to make their way through the crowd, a task not as easy as it seemed. Besides the desperate pleas of the commoners to grant them access into the city, they were hampered by the surprising amount of luggage and cartage that blocked the raj-marg.

'Looks like these Holi revellers came to spend more than just a feast-day in our fine city,' Lakshman said as they manoeuvred through the carts, buggies and mounts—and the foot-travellers sitting cross-legged on the road.

'The Holi celebrations last seven days. It takes most people twice that long to recover from all that carousing and feasting.' Rama's voice sounded distant and distracted.

Lakshman shot him a glance, waving away a Tamil who was trying to show him his pedlar's licence. The man was dressed in a lungi and had a coconut-cutter's scythe tucked into his waistband. Lakshman wondered how the flimsy waist-cloth managed to stay up and hold the weight of the knife.

'Are you all right, bhai?' Lakshman asked quietly. 'You looked like you'd seen a rakshas yourself when Bharat and Shatrugan told us about the happenings in the city.'

Rama glanced at Lakshman. His eyes contained a faraway, lost expression, not their usual alert sharpness. 'I had a dream something like this would happen.' He seemed about to say more but was silent.

'Something like this? You mean a rakshas invading Ayodhya? That's quite a coincidence, isn't it? When did you dream this dream? Maybe if you tell Guruji, he can interpret it properly. After all, seers can see visions of things to come. Maybe your dream was a prophecy.'

'I'm no seer.' Rama's voice was cold. 'It was just a stupid dream. I don't want to talk about it.'

Lakshman was surprised. 'Why are you so touchy about it? I was only suggesting— In the name of Shiva!'

Lakshman was face to face with the rear end of a mithun, a buffalo-bison crossbreed from the north-eastern hills. The mithun was all of seven feet tall, even at the flank, and as Lakshman stared at the unexpected apparition that had seemed to appear in his path out of thin air, the mithun's shaggy tail rose suddenly. Rama laughed as his brother side-stepped quickly to avoid whatever might follow that ominous action. In his haste, Lakshman swerved around a pair of red-faced children struggling to move a stubborn, braying donkey and came face to face with a bare-waisted man juggling half a dozen knives. He dodged the lethal display and almost stepped into a small cook-fire on which a dark-skinned Malayali couple were roasting rice dosa pancakes. The southerners glared up at him as he backed away, apologising. He bumped into a stark-naked long-bearded fakir and recoiled, doing a respectful namaskar as the holy man continued playing his wooden bow, drawing a piercing monotonous tone from the single-stringed instrument as he rolled his eyes back into his skull, lost in his ecstatic bhakti.

Still grinning, Rama pointed up ahead at the relatively clear grassy shoulder of the raj-marg. Lakshman nodded with relief and left the king's highway for a few yards before joining with Rama up ahead. Lakshman shook his head in bemusement. 'This bunch doesn't need to enter the city. They've got their own Holi mela right here!'

They reached the gate without further adventure or discussion. Here the crowd on the raj-marg had overflowed on to the grassy shoulders on either side for several dozen yards in both directions. Lakshman noticed a stick-thin goat-bearded man perched quite comfortably on the crook of a shepherd's short-stick, surrounded by a shaggy mountain horse, several northern-featured women and an astonishing number of children playing around them all. Gandaharis, he noted, from the northernmost Arya nation.

An ageing senapati stood at the head of the platoon of armed soldiers before the first gate. While his men were dressed in the traditional white and red of the gate-watch, he wore a distinctive saffron-and-black uniform with the Sanskrit letters corresponding to P and F stitched on his shoulders in decorative gold embroidery. Lakshman recognised him at once.

'Senapati Dheeraj Kumar, General of the Purana Wafadars, our battalion of veterans of the Last Asura War.'

The senapati saluted his princes smartly, his movements belying his age.

'Rajkumars. Quads of soldiers are already out seeking you and your brothers. I have orders.'

'Senapati Dheeraj Kumar,' Rama said, using the general's name out of genuine familiarity: the youngest of the senapati's sons had attended Guru Vashishta's gurukul in the same batch as the four princes. 'Why are these people not being allowed into the city?'

The grey-haired veteran shrugged unhappily. 'What can I say, my prince? Never before has Ayodhya turned away its own brothers and sisters. But this is a strange day. And I have my orders. I am to escort you directly to your father's palace, under my guard.'

'But what about these people? When will they be allowed in? They're not rakshasas and Asuras, they're just ordinary commoners wanting to attend the maharaja's Holi feast.'

Lakshman saw that the motley band clustered on the raj-marg were watching the discussion eagerly. Several had picked up their belongings or boarded their mounts and vehicles, expecting that the rajkumars would secure entry for them into the city.

The senapati pursed his lips. 'Rajkumar Rama, what you say is true. But the beast that entered earlier was able to change his bhes-bhav to resemble the great Brahmarishi Vishwamitra. His devilish deception fooled almost everyone, including the gate-watch and the maharaja's guard, and even the maharaja himself.'

He gestured at the crowd gathered along the highway, now occupying almost a quarter of a mile of the road and still absorbing newcomers who were arriving with increasing regularity as the sun rose higher. 'How are we to know that one of them isn't an Asura in disguise too? Or all of them?'

Rama smiled wryly. 'In that case, senapati, how do you know we aren't Asuras too, my brothers and me?'

Dheeraj Kumar's jaw slackened. Then he regained control of his dignity and nodded with a sharp smile. 'Well spoken, rajkumar. But I have my orders. Please.'

Rama sighed. There was no point arguing further. The senapati was only doing his job. Still, Lakshman felt his brother's embarrassment.

Several moments later, when the gate-watch soldiers cleared the raj-marg of commoners to allow the rajkumars' chariots and horses to pass through, Lakshman felt even more acutely embarrassed. Every pair of eyes was on the four princes as they rode with their armed escort. And as the commoners were kept at bay at spearpoint while he and his brothers rode across the lower drawbridge, he felt like dying of shame. Yet, he noted, not one of those poor folk spoke a single word against the rajkumars. Instead, they cheered and blessed their princes with long life, fruitful marriages and all the usual Arya blessings.

It is that damn rakshas's fault, he reminded himself as they rode through the seven gates, passing similar crowds of commoners who had been caught between gates when the full alert had been called. Not our fault or Father's fault. The fault of that rakshas, damn his soul to hell.

EIGHTEEN

Raising his hands to subdue the shocked murmurs that had met his announcement, the seer-mage Vishwamitra continued in a level tone. 'Pray, hear me out fully. As some of you may be aware . . .' his eyes met those of Guru Vashishta, 'for a while now, I have been absorbed in tapasya, a brief penance with a single goal.'

As if on cue, Guru Vashishta spoke up. 'Brahmarishi Vishwamitra,' he said, 'your dedicated lifelong pursuit of spiritual prowess is a model taught in every gurukul and ashram from the western borders of this great continent to the eastern extremities. It was through such rigorous tapasya—penance,' he conceded for those who did not follow Sanskrit highspeak, 'that you achieved your great deva-given prowess in the mastery of brahman. Pray, tell us then, what is this necessity which compelled you to interrupt your sacred meditation?'

Vishwamitra responded in the same idiom, using Sanskrit as pure as Dasaratha had ever heard. 'Many thanks for your gracious words, Guru Vashishta. Coming from you, those words are high praise indeed. For your prowess as a seer far exceeds my own humble achievements. It was you who was responsible for my conversion from a ruling kshatriya raja into a spiritual seeker, a rishi, then a maharishi, and eventually a brahmarishi. Yet my entire life spans barely three thousand years, while your own illustrious light has shone for fully seven thousand. I trust that the citizens of this kingdom of Kosala appreciate the gift of your wisdom, as well as the great sacrifice you made when you chose to devote your services as a guru to guiding the dynasty of Suryavansha in matters spiritual and moral rather than pursue further spiritual ascension.' Vishwamitra paused and looked around at the assembled Aryas, all of whom were listening with rapt attention. 'For had he chosen to continue that path of ascension, your Guru Vashishta would be no less than a deva himself by now, I warrant.'

'Brahmarishi Vishwamitra lavishes profuse praise on my simple piety.' The guru's voice was gruff. *So he is capable of feeling embarrassment*, Dasaratha noted with amusement. 'But enough about me. All of us are eager to hear you explain your alarming comment, my friend. What is this crisis that faces us?'

Vishwamitra nodded. 'To know that, you need only understand the motive of my present tapasya.' He turned once more to address the sabha. 'It was to ask that the reign of the demon lord of Lanka be ended and that he and his minions be flung back for all eternity to the lower world whence they came.'

A collective murmur of approval rippled through the audience.

'I see from your reaction, good citizens of Kosala, that you have knowledge of the one of whom I speak.'

Guru Vashishta responded instantly. 'Sadly, old friend, word of that dark villain's evildoing has travelled as far as blessed Ayodhya. We have some hearsay of the Lord of Lanka's excesses.'

'Be thankful then,' Vishwamitra cried, his voice ringing through the packed sabha hall, 'that you have only had word and hearsay of his doings. For if he has his way, that vile creature would invade your city and overrun your proud nation!'

A storm of consternation exploded in the assembly. Several pundits and brahmins called out anxious questions to the seer-mage.

'Maharaja Dasaratha has already witnessed first hand what the Lord of Lanka is capable of doing. The rakshas Kala-Nemi sought to impersonate me in order to get within the walls of the royal palace. Once inside, he would have embarked on a spree of murder and destruction like nothing ever seen before in Arya history.' He paused to let his words sink in. 'If a single rakshas is capable of infiltrating the most sacrosanct city in all the Arya nations, imagine what an entire army of rakshasas could accomplish.'

'And rakshasas are only one of the several vile species at the command of the Lord of Lanka,' Guru Vashishta added smoothly. 'Some of our brave veterans may recall the horrors of martial combat against those terrible legions in the Last Asura War.' He inclined his head respectfully towards the throne. 'Our noble maharaja himself fought at the helm of the united Arya armies in those last terrible conflicts. In fact, it was his extraordinary valour that stemmed the invasion and enabled mortal forces to drive back the Asura legions.'

Time. Dasaratha spoke with as much calm and regal dignity as he could muster. 'Guruji rewards me with rich praise for merely performing my duties.' He performed a formal namaskara of sincere gratitude. 'But since those terrible times, our intelligence has maintained a careful watch on the activities of Lanka.' A gesture at Sumantra, who nodded in agreement. 'It was my understanding that while Ravana continues to control Lanka and the gateway to the netherworld, he has not dared to attempt another ingress on mortal territories.'

Vishwamitra held his staff casually, the way a warrior might hold his battleaxe between clashes. 'You speak truly, raje. The Asura forces have not dared to encroach on mortal territories since you drove them back across the ocean to their island hell.'

Dasaratha wondered why Vishwamitra sounded as if he disagreed even when he was clearly conceding Dasaratha's point. 'Yes, that is what I just said. Ravana and his forces were pushed back to Lanka, and have not dared to cross the ocean and land on the shores of Prithvi again.' He added with deliberate casualness, not wanting to alarm those present who had little knowledge of such martial matters—it had been almost two decades since such matters had been discussed in open assembly, outside of the annual War Council of the Arya nations—'Except of course for the occasional stray rakshas, Naga, Uraga, Pisaca or other renegade Asuras who ventured into the inhospitable peninsula below the Southwoods. And of course, the Yaksa tribes have always been free of Ravana's command. Likewise the other species of creature that inhabits the jungles of Kiskindakhand and outlying areas.'

'Indeed. Your knowledge is admirable, great son of the Suryavanshas. Yet despite all your precautions, the hated Asuras have gained a foothold on the continent of Patal. A sizable one at that.'

Dasaratha leaned forward, his thick brows beetling. 'I hesitate to question your wisdom, mahadev. Parantu, what you suggest is quite impossible. As I said, our outposts and spies maintain a steady watch on all outlying regions.'

Vishwamitra sighed theatrically. 'And I say once again, the Asura races have made deep and wide inroads into the uncharted peninsula. How? you ask. In the same way that a new religion or creed spreads through a continent, raje. Not a pure, God-praising creed like the vedic Hindu faith, but the way a vile cancerous consumption creeps across the land. Or like a mist over the mangrove marshes of the eastern lands of Banglar.'

A mist? Cancerous consumption? New religions? What was the seer-mage talking about? Dasaratha was about to speak again when Vishwamitra raised a hand.

'Allow me to explain, raje. All these years while the Arya nations have enjoyed peace and prosperity, while your armies have grown soft and gentle with inactivity, while the pursuits of culture and civilisation have occupied you rather than the bloody arts of warfare and mayhem, your enemies have been marshalling their forces. Today, the Lord of Lanka has an army twenty times greater than the combined forces of all the Arya nations.'

A wave of unease rippled across the sabha hall. Even Dasaratha caught his breath. Twenty times? He couldn't fathom such figures, let alone visualise them. He shook his head. 'Mahadev, even if what you say is true—and I do not presume to debate your great wisdom—even so, the Asuras would not dare step on mortal lands again. Our outposts would instantly relay the word of any impending invasion well in advance and we would choke off their approach even before they broach the rebellious oceans. However vast their armies, they would never be allowed to land on the blessed soil of Prithvi, let alone advance a foot of the five thousand yojanas to the gates of Ayodhya.'

Vishwamitra nodded sagely. 'True, raje. Your knowledge of matters military is renowned through the seven nations.'

Dasaratha continued, emboldened by the unexpected praise. 'Nowhere near your own formidable store of

161

kshatriya vidya, mahadev.' Vishwamitra's legendary prowess as a warrior-king as well as a fighting seer in the armies of the devas was the stuff of legend. 'To continue: this Asura army you speak of. It is still in Lanka, am I right?'

'Indeed, raje.'

Dasaratha smiled. 'Then we have nothing to fear.' He extended his relief to the sabha. 'Even the largest ships existing today can carry no more than a thousand men. To carry an army that size, the Asuras would require a naval fleet of . . .' he glanced over at Sumantra, who was ready with the answer even before asked, 'two million ships? Yes, two million large ships!' He allowed himself a scornful laugh. 'There are probably not trees enough on Lanka to provide the makings of such a large fleet!'

Nervous laughter rumbled like distant thunder, but most eyes had stayed on Vishwamitra, awaiting his response.

The seer-mage nodded calmly. 'Dasaratha, you are indeed a great general. But even the greatest senapati cannot be in possession of all the facts. That is why I am here today, to bring to your notice first-hand these new developments and to show you the flaw in your perception.'

Dasaratha shifted in his seat. 'A flaw?'

'True, the construction of such a fleet would take decades.' Vishwamitra gestured. 'That is why the Lord of Lanka issued orders for work to be started the day he returned after his ignominious defeat at your hands, *twenty-two years ago*.'

He allowed that to sink in before continuing:

'Today, close to a million ships are ready and are moored in Lanka as well as at sea. It was on one such vessel that Kala-Nemi, the rakshas we faced down at your gate today, travelled to the western shores of Kutchha, whence he came on foot. If Ravana chooses, he can invade our world tomorrow, landing his forces all across the

162

continent, sweeping like a wave of blackness across the Arya nations.'

The seer-mage looked around at the stunned sabha. 'And invasion is his intention.'

NINETEEN

They reached the palace gates without incident. The
avenue was packed from end to end with people. Ordinary
citizens and titled gentry alike thronged the large square
before the palace gates. Both Raghuvamsa Avenue and
Harishchandra Avenue, the perpendicular concourses that
met precisely at the palace gates, were milling with
citizenry. More people kept arriving by foot, by horse or
on muleback; a tangle of chariots bearing the banners of
aristocratic families blocked Harishchandra West. The
usual festive mood was understandably dampened by
the awareness of the morning's intrusion. A quad of four
soldiers stood around a roughly circular spot where the
gravelled floor of the avenue was blackened and
scorched. From the excited conversations of the crowd,
the princes made out that the spot was where the two
seer-mages had consigned the rakshas. The excited crowd
cheered raggedly as the princes approached, some
belatedly recognising them and reacting with a flurry of
excitement. Several began calling out the names of their
favourite princes. There was no question whose name
was called most frequently. Rama's brothers exchanged
knowing glances: most of the callers were young women
of marriageable age, encouraged by their mothers!

A town crier began calling out a news update as they
approached the main palace gates. 'Maharaj Raghuvansha

164

Aja-putra Ikshvaku Suryavansha Dasaratha ki jai!' he cried. *Praise be to Maharaja Raghu-descended Aja's son Ikshvaku-clan Surya-dynasty-heir Dasaratha*. 'The royal sabha is still in attendance. The maharaja sends word to all of you to bear with him for a few more moments. He will join you the instant the sabha ends. He has good news to impart to you on this auspicious Holi day. The venerated sage Brahmarishi Vishwamitra will accompany him and grace our Holi celebrations today!'

The crowd's cheer was more enthusiastic this time, filling the large avenues with a boisterous roar. The princes exchanged quick smiles: there was no sound more reassuring than a few thousand Ayodhyans in one place together.

Senapati Dheeraj Kumar reined in his horse and had a word with the palace gate guards. He turned back to the princes while a pair of guards disappeared at a fast sprint, heading towards the palace. 'My son Drishti Kumar is in charge of the palace watch today. He was required to ensure the security of the sabha hall where the maharaja and sabha are in conference at this minute with the visiting sage. He has left word not to let anyone in without his personal accession. He will arrive in a moment. Please excuse the additional delay.'

Rama spoke for them all again. 'We understand, Senapati. These are part of the standard security procedures during a full alert. If you like, you may return to your post at the first gate.'

'If you please, rajkumar, I shall stay until you are within the gates.'

'Very well,' Rama replied. After a pause he added: 'I hope to speak to my father at the earliest and request him to give you leave to open the gates.'

The senapati hesitated. 'As you wish, rajkumar. However, I would advise against it.'

Rama looked at him curiously. 'Do you really fear that some of those commoners may be Asuras in disguise?'

'I wish that were all I feared.' The ageing warrior's steel-blue eyes went to the scorched spot marking the disappearance of the rakshas intruder. 'Nay, I suspect these occurrences happen not in isolation. I was a wrestler once as you mayhap recall and among wrestlers we have a game. In some parts of the kingdom it is called kho, in others kabbadi. You rajkumars have probably played it yourselves a thousand times.'

They nodded. Dheeraj Kumar was being politely modest. He had been both wrestling and kabbadi champion in the seven Arya nations, holding the titles virtually unbroken for over twenty years until his recent retirement. Even at his current age, some seventy-plus years, he was still a robust and towering specimen of akhada vidya, the ancient Arya regime of physical exercise based on natural training.

The senapati went on: 'In kabbadi, each team stays within its square and sends a single warrior into the enemy's square. The envoy has to continually chant "kabbadi-kabbadi-kabbadi" over and over without taking in fresh breath, and attempt to touch the farthest border of the enemy square. If he succeeds in touching it, the game is won by his team. If he cannot touch the border, he attempts to touch one or more of the enemy players, thereby removing them from the game. The enemy team's job is to grab hold of him at once and pin him to the ground until he is forced to take fresh breath, without letting him drag himself back to his own team's square.'

Rama noticed a small knot of darkly garbed men at the far end of the avenue. They seemed unusually agitated. Probably Holi revellers impatient for the celebration to begin. He tried to concentrate on the general's words but his eyes stayed on that growing knot of black.

The senapati looked around at the rajkumars to see if they had understood the significance of his description.

Bharat nodded first: 'You feel the rakshas Kala-Nemi was the first player sent by the enemy team to seek out our weaknesses and strengths, to see how far he could get before he was stopped, or even if he could go all the way and touch the goal-line of our chaukat.' Bharat indicated the towering spires of the palace. 'Perhaps take out some of our key players in the process. That is your analogy, is it not, Senapati?'

'Indeed, Rajkumar Bharat,' the veteran replied. 'And it's credit to our team for having safely ousted their first intruder without a single casualty on our side. But do you know what we must do next to follow their play?'

Shatrugan replied: 'Our turn. We send one of ours into their chaukat. Same strategy. Seek out strengths and weaknesses. Show them we're willing and able to fight back. Ideally, do more harm to them than they did to us. Otherwise, they'll just keep coming back.'

The senapati nodded. 'You have the lay of it, Rajkumar Shatrugan. I have watched you play with my grandsons in the akhada. You have great promise.'

At the unexpected praise, Shatrugan's face coloured rapidly. He managed to nod briefly and utter a short 'With your grace, sir.'

A voice called out from the far side of the gate. 'Enter and be welcome, princes of Ayodhya. Enter in the name of your father, Maharaja Dasaratha.'

The princes turned to see Captain Drishti Kumar supervising the opening of the gates. They rode in and dismounted, handing their horses and chariots to their grooms who had been waiting since before they had arrived back, watching eagerly and anxiously for their return.

Senapati Dheeraj Kumar saluted Captain Drishti Kumar smartly, giving no indication that the man he was addressing was his own son and heir. 'Captain, I hand over the four rajkumars Rama, Bharat, Shatrugan and Lakshman to your possession. Guard them with your life and honour. I bid you leave. Aagya.'

'Aagya,' responded the captain.

The senapati shot one last glance at the rajkumars as he rode out through the gates, straight-backed and as proud as any young kshatriya in his prime.

Bharat nodded in admiration as he watched the general leave. 'Now that is a kshatriya.'

'Rajkumars.' Drishti Kumar's handsome features were flushed and heated although his voice betrayed no emotion. 'My orders are to escort you directly into the palace and keep you within the protection of the palace guard until your father sends for you.'

Lakshman started to ask him what was being discussed in the sabha hall—it was obvious from the captain's face that something startling was going on up there—but before he could finish, a loud shout was raised by one of the gate watch, followed by several more yells of alarm.

They all turned to see what was going on. To their surprise, Rama was sprinting out of the gates. He slipped through a fraction of a second before the heavy wrought-iron monstrosities swung fully shut with a resounding clanging echo. The surprised gate-watch and gate-closers—it took eight men just to open or close the gates—yelled warnings in vain. The gates were shut and Rama was out on the crowded avenue, thronged now by thousands of people. In another second, he was lost in the crowd and had vanished from Lakshman's sight.

TWENTY

This time it was Dasaratha who held up his hand to invoke silence. The outcries of alarm and fear died down at once. Whatever their agitation, his people loved and respected him.

Dasaratha was angry now with the seer-mage although he fought hard not to show it. His entire world-view was being questioned. 'Even if this is indeed as you describe, great one, Ravana would not dare invade without provocation. Mortals have been at peace with the Asura races for twenty-two years. They would not dare take the first step towards their own annihilation.'

Vishwamitra permitted himself a smile. The sight of that unexpected expression on the legendary seer-mage's lined and scarred face was more infuriating than any show of anger. He responded grimly: 'Maharaja Dasaratha, you make the ancient mistake of judging the Asuras by human standards. Remember: *They are not human*! That is why they are Asuras!'

Dasaratha sat back, stung.

Vishwamitra went on relentlessly, gathering momentum and force now. The smile vanished from his face, leaving a craggy expression that promised fireworks. 'Let me say this without euphemisms or circumvention. Whether twenty days or twenty years from now, *the Asuras will invade*. It is the only goal of their existence. Every breath they take is dedicated to this purpose and this purpose alone. And they will not rest either until they have invaded the proud cities of the Arya nations and razed them to the ground, or until every last one of them is killed in violent combat. Their goal is total and uncompromising genocide. Either Asuras or mortals will remain to walk the earth, but both species will no longer co-exist.'

The silence that met this announcement was more frightening than any chaotic outburst. Dasaratha forced himself to speak again, realising that the seer-mage had cleverly drawn him into a debate that could only have one end. 'Mahadev, I do not presume to question your sources of information, but my outposts and spies—'

'*Your spies are sold! Your outposts are taken!*'

Vishwamitra's words struck Dasaratha's ailing heart like a pair of hammer blows. He gripped the armrests of his throne, struggling for composure.

'Hear me, raje,' the seer-mage went on sternly but respectfully. 'Hear me and know this for fact. The Lord of Lanka has corrupted your spies and every ally south of Ayodhya. None of them will ever bring you word of your enemies. This is why you have not heard anything to alarm you until this day. This is why Kala-Nemi was able to travel this far and enter Ayodhya undetected so easily.'

In a flash, Dasaratha knew the seer-mage was right and he was wrong. His heart fluttered now, and he suddenly felt the sabha hall grow dark around him. He clutched the armrests of his sunwood throne fiercely, his palms slippery with sweat. Still, instinct forced him to argue on.

'Perhaps,' he replied stubbornly. 'But it's one thing for a single rakshas in mortal guise to infiltrate our defences, and a completely different matter when you speak of tens of millions of Asuras crossing the oceans and invading the entire Arya nations. Even Ravana's black sorcery cannot cloak an army that large. We would be forewarned months before the first forces arrived. And,' he went on, asserting his convictions in the face of those devastating revelations, 'and even if this great host were to make the journey to Ayodhya unchallenged, then we shall not merely open our gates to them and say, "Come, bull, gore me".' The aphorism, an old colloquial one, brought nods of agreement from the more militant members of the sabha. 'It is not for nothing that Ayodhya is called Ayodhya the Unconquerable. Ayodhya Anashya! And as long as Ayodhya stands, the Arya nations will not yield, I tell you.'

Vishwamitra struck his staff on the ground. A small explosive sound issued, startling those closest to the seer-mage. A tiny cloud of purple smoke emerged from the top of the staff, spreading its tentacles across the heads of the nervous assembly. 'Behold, raje. Even as a cheap jadugar, a street magician, uses smoke and hypnosis to beguile his innocent audience, so has the Lord of Lanka used his god-granted powers to deceive and cloak your great mind.'

Dasaratha wondered if he had heard correctly. 'Maha-dev?'

Vishwamitra raised his staff. The purplish smoke rose to the high vaulted ceilings of the sabha hall, a thousand heads craning upwards to watch it. The smoke curled and spread surprisingly quickly, stretching long tendrils and tentacles in every direction. In moments the purple fingers covered the entire ceiling of the large hall.

Vishwamitra's voice continued as the awed assembly watched this unexpected display of his powers. 'Remember, raje. This is no ordinary rakshas king we speak of; this is Ravana himself. He whose thousand-year-long tapasya compelled mighty Brahma himself to grant him everlasting life and immunity from all destruction.'

171

'Still,' Dasaratha protested, hearing the uncertainty in his own voice, 'we have defeated him before. We shall do so again, if need be.' His eyes continued to follow the purple smoke as it spread across the white plaster ceiling.

Vishwamitra shook his head sadly. 'Even now, you protest, raje? Then I must reveal unto you and your court what I was reluctant to speak of until now. Know this, great citizens of Ayodhya, defenders of the Kosala kingdom and guardians of the southernmost borders of the Arya nations. Ravana's power is spreading amongst you even now, just as that purple mist is creeping through this assembly. He is here, in this very sabha hall, and is watching us even as we debate amongst ourselves.'

Dasaratha started to rise to his feet. This was beyond debate now; the mahaguru was clearly misinformed in this assumption. Spies in the court of Ayodhya? Impossible!

Before he could say another word, the purple mist fell on to the assembled courtiers with the suddenness of a clutch of hawks swooping on their prey. Ropes of purple smoke broke off from the main emission and sought out specific targets among the massed crowd. Dasaratha sank back and watched, amazed, as a moustached courtier far to the right of the sabha hall cried out. The purple smoke encircled him in the form of ropes, binding him fast. The courtier struggled as the ropes entwined themselves tightly around his flabby body, holding him as effectively as hemp cords.

Similar cries rose from across the hall. Dasaratha scanned the crowd of startled Ayodhyans. People were turning everywhere, pointing to one or another of their neighbours as the purple tendrils embraced and captured him. In moments, close to a dozen such courtiers were securely bound by the sorcerous smoke. Dasaratha recognised all of them by face, and several by name as well. One of them was court secretary to Jabali, minister

172

of administration. Jabali's perennially sour face had assumed an expression of disgust that would have made any portrait painter swear off his art for ever. He leaned as far back in his seat as he could, clearly unwilling to let himself be touched by the smoke binding his associate.

'Mahadev,' Dasaratha demanded. 'What is the meaning of this? What do you hope to prove by this demonstration?'

'Forgive me for resorting to this theatrical device, maharaj,' Vishwamitra replied calmly. 'It was necessary to demonstrate the extent to which the Lord of Lanka has corrupted the proud population of the Arya nations. The smoke you see is in fact the power of brahman made visible for your benefit. The mantra I spoke instructed it to seek out and expose those corrupted by the Lord of Lanka. These eleven mortals captured in its divine grasp are nothing more than acolytes and minions of Ravana himself.'

Dasaratha rose to his feet, the colour draining from his face. 'Impossible! These are old and trusted courtiers! I sit with these men every day and discuss matters of state and defence!'

'Do not blame yourself, raje,' Vishwamitra said in a voice tinged with sadness and anger. 'There was no way for you to know. This is the vile power of Ravana's sorcery. He has eyes and ears within your very court. His spies live beneath the same roof that you inhabit, in the very heart of Ayodhya. And for every one you see here, there are a thousand others throughout your proud kingdom. This is how Ravana has struck back at you for defeating him in the Last Asura Wars. He has corrupted your own people and converted them to his evil cause.'

TWENTY-ONE

Rama darted through the crowd like a swallow through a thicket. The crowd was dense and growing denser by the second, but there was still enough space between them to allow a slender youth to slip through if he was quick and agile. Rama heard the yells of dismay from the gate-watch behind him, followed by his brothers calling out to him, and sympathised with their concern, but he continued down the avenue. All through Senapati Dheeraj Kumar's kabbadi analogy, his attention had been diverted by that knot of black-clad figures at the far end of the lane, where Harishchandra Avenue was met by Jagganath Marg, the road leading to the sudra quarter of the city. As the senapati had continued speaking, Rama had watched that knot grow, more and more black-clad figures appearing from the Jagganath Marg turn-off until finally the knot had become an arrowhead. And then he had seen the unmistakable glint of sunlight reflecting off bright shiny objects. Weapons in use. He had known then that something was amiss down there, some aberration that was not a scheduled part of the Holi festivities. And because he had been preternaturally alert to precisely such signs as this, he had acted before speaking or thinking. The gates were about to slam shut. Getting Captain Drishti

Kumar to reopen them would take precious minutes, perhaps longer if the captain was adamant about following the maharaja's orders. So Rama had done the only thing he could do at once: slipped out before the gates shut, like a silvery mahseer slipping through a gap in a Banglar fisherman's net.

Now, he ran like his life depended on it. The crowds of bustling, excited people were too entranced with discussing the events of that morning to pay him any attention. Those that did glance his way saw merely a handsomely constructed young man in a hurry. He was on foot, running like a maniac, and carried no weapons or obvious marks of his princehood, just the simple whites he had worn that morning. Nobody recognised him instantly, and those that had a flutter of a doubt were unable to take a second look to check.

He ran like lives depended on it. In moments, he had crossed that swirling river of humanity that the avenue had become. Reaching the end of the concourse, he slowed, seeing the familiar glint of raised spears up ahead. A roadblock. The ever-watchful PFs had already cordoned off the trouble and contained it at the bottom of the avenue. The people down at this end were largely commoners more interested in moving up-avenue to goggle at the rich architecture of the palace rather than paying attention to the disturbance behind them. Rama made his way through a group of excited young vaisya girls, all clutching hands together and laughing excitedly, led by a trio of hefty daiimaas. Then he was at the cordon. He looked over the interlinked V of two PF spears to see a curious lack of activity at the end of the avenue. The turn-off where he had seen the black-clad figures accumulating was deserted now. But several black turbans lay unfurled on the ground, along with a PF scarf or two. And an entire regiment of PFs was forming under the orders of a lieutenant, preparing to march up Jagganath Marg.

Rama spoke to the PF closest to him, a wizened veteran with a small hole where his left ear had once been and a rash of shiny scars on the left side of his neck.

'What happened here?'

The PF spoke without turning back. 'On your way, citizen. The savoury stalls are up ahead and to the right, along Sarayu Marg, on the way to the parade grounds. This is PF business.'

Rama raised his right hand, formed a fist, and rapped his prince's seal-ring on the blade of the man's spear. It made a metallic sound that drew the man's attention. He swung around at once, spear lowering into a defensive stance. His partner, who had heard Rama as well, did likewise. Rama already had his hands raised, showing them he was unarmed.

'At ease, veterans. I only wish to know what happened. Do you recognise me?'

Both PFs glanced at each other and swallowed. 'Aye. You're Rajkumar Rama. Or a shockingly good imitation.'

Rama smiled. 'I'm Rama. Captain Drishti Kumar and my brothers are following after me. They'll confirm it. Now tell me quickly, what happened here?'

The younger man, a hefty fellow with no visible facial scars, looked suspiciously at Rama. But the older man said slowly: 'Some tantrics went berserk. Said one of the maharaja's queens had assassinated one of their number. They wanted to take a petition to the maharaja to protest the man's murder and demand he institute an inquiry at once.'

'And?'

The veteran shrugged. 'What's to say? The city's on full alert. Our orders are to let nobody through to the palace and to arrest any potential troublemakers. The lieutenant told them to put their protest through official channels. They became surly about it. Turned ugly fast.' The old man gestured at the platoon marching down Jagganath Marg even as he spoke. 'That's the clean-up now. While they were scuffling with our men, some brahmins came up and began screaming something about the tantrics stealing little boys from some orphanage, for sacrifices and suchlike. I don't know any more. We were only called in a moment ago to keep rubberneckers away from this end of the avenue.'

Rama nodded. 'Much appreciate the information, soldier . . . ?'

The veteran shrugged. 'Pai. S.T. Pai. I fought with your uncle Janak's regiment in the Mithila Brigade.'

'Thank you, Sipahi Pai. You'll have to let me through now.'

The PFs looked uncertain. Then the old one said, almost as if he was embarrassed, 'You'd know the names of Maharaja Janak's daughters then, of course. You being Rajkumar Rama, after all.'

Rama smiled. 'Of course. We played together as children before my brothers and I left for the gurukul.' He realised that the younger PF was watching him intently, as if alert to signs of horns sprouting or fangs popping out at any second. He said in a normal tone: 'Sita, Urmila, Mandavi and Kirti.' He added, 'My brother Lakshman has a soft spot for Urmila, most people do. But I've always thought Sita was the beauty of the lot.'

The old PF sighed and lowered his spear, gesturing to his companion to do the same. 'Aye, that she is. Forgive me, my rajkumar. This is a strange day.'

Rama patted the old man on his shoulder by way of gratitude as well as to show he didn't have any hard feelings. He passed through the cordon just as the regiment of PFs were given the order to march forward up

Jagganath Marg. He reached the turn-off and looked up the side road, barely a third as wide as Harishchandra Avenue but still broad enough to let the regiment march sixteen abreast easily. Further up the road, he could see the black robes of the tantric cultists intermingled with the saffron and green of the PFs. Several black-clad bodies lay sprawled on the marg, PF spears sticking out of them. A few saffron-and-green-clad bodies also lay beside them, trishuls embedded in them. There was also a white-clad tonsured brahmin body or two in there. Rama guessed the PFs had succeeded in moving the brahmins away and out of the riot. It seemed to be much harder to persuade the tantrics: after all, their faith was predicated on doom and the surrendering of all life to meet the coming apocalypse.

The regiment marching down the road was preparing to mount a fresh assault on the tantrics. The cultists looked sullen and white-eyed. Several of them were banging their trishuls, wickedly sharp three-pronged tridents, on tiny breast-shields engraved with the image of Kali, the dark devi who governed vengeance and the tantric cults.

As Rama watched, the officer commanding the regiment gave the order to prepare to charge. A bloodbath was about to take place.

Rama darted forward, sprinting around the PF line— there was room at either end of the marg—and into the no-man's-land between the two opposing groups.

He raised his hands. 'In the name of Maharaja Dasaratha, your king and ruler, I, Rajkumar Rama Chandra, command you all to lay down your arms at once.'

It took Captain Drishti Kumar several precious moments to get the gates reopened. That delay itself helped Lakshman understand Rama's unexpected action.

'He saw something happening and didn't want to get delayed waiting for the gates to open again,' he told his brothers. 'That's why he slipped through before they closed.'

'But what did he see happening?' Bharat grumbled. 'Irresponsible of him to just run off like that.'

Shatrugan clenched his empty fists in frustration. 'I wish I had time to go get my mace. I feel naked without a weapon.'

'No bearing weapons on feast days, Shatrugan. You know the law.'

'Come on, Lakshman. That rakshas didn't follow the law, did he? Whatever Rama saw happening, it wasn't any lover's fall-out, I can bet you that. He saw trouble. That's why he ran like that. And the best way to face trouble is with sharp steel.'

Lakshman shook his head. 'You're the limit, Shatrugan. Not every problem can be solved with violence.'

'Well, when you meet your first rakshas, you try kissing and cajoling, all right? Me, I'll settle for a good Gandahari mace any day.'

'I hear that, bhai,' Bharat replied, agreeing strongly.

The gates opened and they sprinted out, Captain Drishti Kumar leading the way. He had already given orders to his men outside, and twin lines of soldiers had formed a long clear corridor down the entire length of the avenue. They were all fast runners, and in moments they had reached the turn-off where Harishchandra Avenue met Jagganath Marg. The captain ordered the PFs to open the cordon and they passed through. Lakshman caught a glimpse of an old PF veteran with a scarred neck and a missing ear staring at him curiously, then he was at the turn-off and staring at a frightening sight.

Rama was standing between two opposing groups of armed men. On the far side was a mob of black-clad tantrics who looked as if they had nothing less than civil riot on their minds, while on the near side, backs to the approaching princes, were a force of PFs arranged into an attack phalanx, ready to charge.

'Rama,' he began. Then bit back the cry. He was afraid of setting off either group. Both looked hostile and ready to fight to the death. Lakshman couldn't see the faces of the PFs, but the tantrics looked white-eyed and wild, as if they were all intoxicated on ganja.

His brothers exclaimed beside him as they took in the situation. He knew what they were thinking; he was thinking the exact same thing: *What's Rama got himself into now? And how's he going to get out of it?*

Then Rama began to sing.

TWENTY-TWO

As the last stragglers left the sabha hall, Pradhan-Mantri Sumantra hurried to his maharaja's side. Dasaratha sat bowed on his throne, his face buried in his hands, elbows leaning on the armrests of his throne.

'Maharaj?' Sumantra's voice was soft and concerned. 'Are you well?'

'Aye.' Dasaratha raised his head with an effort that tugged at Sumantra's heart. 'I have no choice. I must be well to see our people through this great crisis.' He struggled to his feet, waving Sumantra away when he tried to offer his hand. 'What did we do wrong, old friend? I governed wisely and justly, did I not? I built on the works of my ancestors, raising Ayodhya and Kosala to new heights of prosperity and peaceful harmony, did I not? Then why am I plagued by these disasters in the twilight of my reign?'

'Maharaj, you are the greatest king of your line, the greatest to sit on the sunwood throne. Never before have the Arya peoples enjoyed this long a period of peace and security. Your works shall be remembered for millennia to come. Do not blame yourself for the evil wrought by Asuras.'

Dasaratha walked slowly across the empty sabha hall, nodding his head. 'Perhaps you are right, Sumantra. Yet

I cannot stand to leave this legacy to my sons. What else do we fight for in our youth and prime if not the future? And this is not the future I envisioned.'

'Maharaj,' Sumantra said, walking beside his king. 'The future may not be as bleak as you fear. Never before in the history of the Arya nations have we been so strong, so rich, so powerful. At the end of the Last Asura War, when you led that fateful foray against the Dark Lord of Lanka, all seemed lost. We were outnumbered and outmatched, exhausted and decrepit. Yet we won. And won triumphantly. Today, we are not only far stronger than then, we have the vidya gained from those martial encounters, our military strategists have had decades to study the strengths and weaknesses of the Asura races. Our population is almost twice as large as it was then. And you see how auspiciously things have begun for us. Instead of drawing first blood as they hoped, the Asuras have lost their chief spy and infiltrator—no ordinary rakshas but the dread Kala-Nemi himself, blood-kin of Ravana! Their spies in the royal court have been outed. Even now, they are being interrogated in the dungeons below the city jail. Soon, we shall root out every traitor and Asura sympathiser in the kingdom. Word has been dispatched to the other Arya nations to do the same. After this cleansing, the war council will convene in days here in Ayodhya. Take hope and courage, my beloved raje. We shall not only prevail, we shall triumph. And yours shall be the foot that descends to crush each one of Ravana's ten skulls.'

It was a long speech, from one who was not accustomed to speaking much, and Dasaratha knew it. He had paused before the sabha hall doors to look at his old gurukul partner, erstwhile charioteer, trusted adviser, then minister, and now prime minister. He laid a weary but still powerful hand on Sumantra's shoulder. 'The devas grant that it shall come to pass exactly as you say.'

Sumantra gripped his maharaja's wrist. 'It shall. I am willing to give my last breath to see it does. And so is every Arya citizen. Be not fearful, raje. Be proud. You have built a great nation, and now you shall see the fruits of your labour.'

Dasaratha nodded. 'I shall take a little rest now before speaking with Brahmarishi Vishwamitra on the other reason for his visit. He wishes to do so privately. Are my sons safely back in the palace?'

Sumantra frowned. 'They ought to be, your highness. Captain Drishti Kumar went to secure their entry into the palace gates several moments ago.'

Dasaratha caught the unsaid message in his tone. 'But?'

Sumantra shook his head slowly. 'The captain has not returned yet.' He managed a reassuring smile. 'I shall look into it myself, maharaj. As long as the rajkumars reached the palace gates, they will surely be safe. But I shall check personally. Depend on me.'

'I do, Sumantra. But do check. This is a strange day. And I expect stranger things yet. Make sure my sons are well and safe.'

It took Lakshman a moment to realise what he was hearing. At first he thought it was the death chant of the Kali cult. It was usually chanted by conscripts who were sent into a battle from which they would not return alive. To the tantrics, of course, it was an anthem of their dark faith that hinged on the belief that the coming Kali-Yuga would mark the end of human civilisation. He realised that the Kali chant was being sung by some of the cultists in the mob across the road. Then he heard the dhol-drum of the PFs, the steady four-beat they marched and

183

fought to, based on the traditional four-by-four beat to which all Arya rituals were conducted by vedic custom. He had failed to catch these two disparate rhythms, drowned out as they were by the cacophony from the crowded avenue behind.

But when Rama began to sing, Lakshman heard and understood what he was trying to achieve. Unable to appeal to the two clashing groups with logic and commands, Rama was resorting to patriotic emotion. After all, this was Holi feast-day. A day when all Aryas embraced their fellows and celebrated the completion of yet another year of their proud civilisation, while inaugurating the onset of yet another harvest year. Each Arya nation had its own special day, but Holi and Deepavali were special to all the Arya nations.

Rama was singing the traditional Arya farming song, 'Dharti Maa'. Literally, 'Earth Mother'. When he began, the rhythms of the PF martial beat and the tantrics' Kali chant had mingled to form a toll as deathlike as a funeral march, an ominous duet of doom.

Above this dark symphony, there now rose the melodious anthem of 'Dharti Maa'. Rama's voice was a clear tenor with perfect pitch and just enough bass to lend it depth. As he sang the opening sloka, Lakshman instantly felt the change in the atmosphere. The ancient anthem had great power, believed by some to turn desert lands fertile and calm the most ferocious predators of the wild. Even if those were exaggerations, the power of the anthem on Arya ears was undeniable. Lakshman could feel the hackles on his hands and neck rise as Rama sang the beautiful, stirring words that praised the mighty subcontinent that housed the seven nations of the Arya clans, addressing the land that nourished and provided for them, their mother, their devi.

Without stopping to think, Lakshman stepped out into Jagganath Marg, walking around the startled PF regiment and their commanding officer, and stood beside Rama, raising his own voice to join Rama's song. He didn't have to look behind to know that Bharat and Shatrugan were following as well. He ignored the prickle of fear that came when he found himself hemmed in by the trishul-wielding tantrics and spear-holding PFs, taking courage from his brother's lead. If it was Rama's fate to die here on a side street of his own capital city, killed by the hands of his own people, then Lakshman would die the same death.

As they approached the second verse Lakshman felt something strange and wonderful happen. It was as if a giant cloud had been pressing down on the whole concourse all this time, making everyone uneasy and restless, and some violent and agitated. With the singing of the anthem, Lakshman felt the cloud begin to lift.

And then he felt an even more wonderful thing. Others were singing too. Stray soldiers in the PF ranks. Voices rising uncertainly from the tantric mob. And further away, around the corner and up the avenue, past the cordon of PF veterans, the citizens were picking up the song too. Like all anthems, this one had a way of touching your heart no matter who you were, where you were, or what you were doing at the time. For those few moments that the ode to Mother Earth lasted, every Arya, young or old, male or female, high-caste or low, noble or impoverished, was united in a bond as ancient and undeniable as their mutual dependence on the gifts of food and life that the earth deity provided.

The anthem came to an end. Lakshman's voice died away, as did his brothers'. There was a brief moment of deafening emptiness.

And then, it was all over.

185

TWENTY-THREE

Manthara cried out with rage and threw the sacrificial trishul into the yagna fire, obliterating the image that had appeared there, an image of the happenings on the turn-off to Jagganath Marg. The trishul, identical to those carried by the tantrics in the scene she had just witnessed with the help of her Asura witchcraft, clattered into the chaukat, the sacred ceremonial square used for vedic rites, and was lost in the billowing flames of the fire. She screamed at once and leaped forward to try to retrieve it. Throwing the trishul might be interpreted as disrespectful, and she had taken too much care with the whole elaborate ritual to spoil everything now. She bent over the energetic flames, fuelled by prodigious amounts of ghee and the remains of the brahmin boy that she had sacrificed earlier. There. Between an almost denuded thigh bone and the skull with its contents still bubbling. She reached into the fire, burning her hands and losing her eyelashes and eyebrows as well, and retrieved the trishul.

It was flaming hot.

She clutched it firmly, enduring the unbelievable pain, and tried to understand what had gone wrong. She had thought it such a clever plan, to use the tantric's murder to incite a civil riot. Or at the very least a stampede. With several hundred thousand men, women, children and animals thronging the avenues, ringed in by armed and nervously alert soldiers, starting a riot had seemed easy enough. And things had been going so well. The tantrics and brahmins had fallen for the bait just as she'd known they would. And the PFs had done their job as usual. With the malevolent mantras she'd released into the avenue earlier, the minute the maharaja and those two seers had been cloistered away in the sabha hall, their minds should have been clouded by confusion and senseless rage long enough for them to engage in violence that would perpetuate its own cycle of retribution. It had been a brilliant plan. A major civil riot would have broken out over a tiny, irrelevant non-issue. And at the right time, she would have sent out a mantra to inflame the horses of the PFs on Raghuvamsa Avenue and cause a panicked stampede. A bloodbath should have resulted.

'Rama!'

Yes. Rama had come into the picture. And had spoiled everything. She still didn't understand how he had done it. By singing an anthem? That was ridiculous! How could people be moved by a stupid patriotic song? What was a country anyway? Just a land occupied by different people. What was there to get so emotional about?

Yet he had done it. Had broken her mantra's power. Dispelled the dark fugue she had tried to cast over the minds of the groups involved. Turned her plans to dust as easily as wiping out a sloka written in sand. True, her powers were still nascent, still growing. But she had tried so hard. And sacrificed so much. Just to have kept her worship of the Dark Lord of Lanka, Ravana, secret for so many years: that itself was a great feat in this holy deva-worshipping city of Ayodhya. Surrounded by an ocean of self-righteous Aryas, she had kept the tiny black flame of Asura faith alive here single-handed. Even Kaikeyi, her erstwhile ward and queen of this mighty kingdom, did not know the truth behind her power and influence. What it had cost Manthara to elevate her to this position. But all this was to change, starting today. And nobody, let alone a stripling of a boy, should have had the ability to thwart her dark designs.

'Rama!' she cried out again, waving the trident in a hand blackened by deep oozing burns.

Foolish hag!

The voice that boomed forth from the heart of the fire was as fiery as glacial ice applied directly to an exposed heart. It blazed with cold, nihilistic rage against her, enveloping her in black flames.

She gasped and struggled to bow her head, touching her forehead to the ground. 'My lord! I did not sense your arrival!'

How dare you speak that name in my sacred space? Have I not forbidden you before?

She searched her mind desperately, ignoring the agony of torture the flames inflicted on every inch of her being. It was like being whipped with fire and ice both at once. 'My lord? You mean, Rama?'

Do not speak it! Foolish creature!

'My lord, I . . .' She bowed again, repeatedly, striking her forehead on the floor until the skin broke and blood began to flow, bubbling instantly as it encountered the flames that enveloped her. 'Shama! Mercy, my lord. Shama!'

You would be wise not to underestimate that one. He is a creature of dharma, and they are not easily dissuaded from their path.

'My lord, never again. I beg your forgiveness.'

For your blasphemy, and for your failure this day, I should excommunicate you at once. This is how I ensure perfect discipline in my ranks. The soldier that falters, dies. You have done more than falter, Manthara. You

188

have failed me today. You were given tasks to perform; none were successful. You know how I deal with such failures.

Manthara cried out in naked terror: 'No, my lord! I beg you! Do not abandon me! I shall do penance to atone for my error. I shall never utter that filthy word again. I beg you!'

The fire raged around her still, as if relishing the taste of her fear. She was in a state beyond agony now. Her entire being was seared through with liquid heat, unbearable and inescapable.

Finally, the fist of fire released her, returning to the chaukat.

Only because I have need of you, wretched one. But make that error once more and excommunication will be the least of your fates.

Manthara trembled silently. Her head was bowed low enough that her forehead touched the rim of the chaukat itself. She could smell the stench of her hair burning. And somewhere through the mist of pain and mutilation she knew she had soiled herself in both ways. Still she abased and abused her tortured self. The Dark Lord was a greedy deity and it was better to give more than less. Finally, she felt his anger abate slightly.

I will withhold your penalty for the time being. But remember, it is only in abeyance, not erased. Now, pay attention, hag, for it is vital that we do not let this setback affect our greater plans.

'My lord,' she begged, her voice quivering with terror. 'Whatever you say, it will be done. I will not fail thee again.'

Even as we speak, both those old brahmins are working their insidious charm on Dasaratha. Soon, he will concede to Vishwamitra's demand.

Manthara raised her head slowly. Her eyes were bright red, blazing coals in her dark face. 'My lord, if you will it, I can go into that sabha hall and use my powers to destroy them all. In one act of terror, we will be rid of all the ruling heads of Ayodhya. The princes will have joined their father by now, and—'

Stupid, stupid woman. You would destroy yourself, use your shakti to explode like a human bomb, would you? That is not an act of courage, you twisted crone. It's utter idiocy. We want that sabha to end peacefully. We want Maharaja Dasaratha to agree to the seer-mage's demand. That is our plan. Do you understand now? Or do I have to scourge you again to get it into your thick head?

Manthara's mouth hung open, trailing a line of thick saliva. 'My lord . . .' She swallowed. 'Truly, you are magnificent.'

Enough. I tire of this discussion. When I have need of you again, I will call upon you. The Day is at hand.

The flame caressed her gently, insinuating itself into the sockets of her eyes, making the fluids bubble and stream down her face. Manthara quivered in ecstasy.

And when Ayodhya is in my clasp, you will be rewarded. Here is a token of my appreciation.

Manthara gasped and raised her head, staring at her arms, her body, feeling herself all over, unable to believe the power and ease of her master's sorcery. 'My injuries, my burns, they're all gone! Oh, master, you are magnificent and munificent beyond all measure! Your power is—'

The flame blazed one last time, shooting out in all directions, filling every square inch of the secret prayer room, enfolding Manthara in a sorcerous shroud that blazed without burning. She screamed with ecstasy and delight throwing out her repaired limbs to the unholy fire, embracing it with every fibre of her being. It was cold, like a cloak of ice rather than fire. As she knew her lord's naked body might feel against her own bare skin. She savoured the unholy ashirwaad of her dark deity.

As suddenly as it had blazed out, the fire withdrew, sucking itself back into the chaukat, then extinguishing itself in one last *whump* of flame. The chaukat was cold and empty, the last bones of the dead brahmin boy gone, the chamber dark and silent.

With a great sigh, Manthara got to her feet and went to fulfil her master's command. She looked exactly as she had done when she had entered the secret room; not a hair was out of place.

TWENTY-FOUR

They were almost at the royal bhojanshalya when a rather too shapely form emerged, sighing and belching at the same time, rubbing her bare midriff, looking like a cat that had eaten far too much fish and now regretted her gluttony. Lakshman and Shatrugan's playful banter stopped instantly, Shatrugan cutting himself short before the punchline of a particularly mischievous play on the Sanskrit and commonspeak words for 'nubile young girl'. Bharat's face lost its smile and he slowed his pace.

Kaikeyi turned and saw them approaching. She uttered a noise of exasperation.

'Where have you been?' Her voice was shrill and grating, flecks of paan visible between her teeth, the blood-red tobacco juice spraying out as she spoke. 'First you disappear all morning—and what a morning!—and then Manthara vanishes without telling me where she's going. And your father—let's not even start on him, I don't know what's got into him today. Nobody seems to care a damn about me in this palace any more.'

Lakshman and Shatrugan proffered the expected bows, their outstretched fingers barely brushing the hem of Kaikeyi's sari. She gestured vaguely, her ashirwaad—if she issued any—obscured by her mouthful of paan. Her lips were bright from the tobacco juice, a gory contrast to her pale northern complexion.

Lakshman observed that her eyes seemed bloodshot and wilder than usual, and the snappishness in her manner a bit more pronounced. If he didn't know better, he might have thought she was nursing a hangover: but Second Queen Kaikeyi always made it a point to announce proudly in public that she never touched alcohol as it was so *unladylike*. It was an odd boast, since neither his and Shatrugan's mother Third Queen Sumitra, nor First Queen Kausalya had ever touched alcohol in their lives, and never thought it necessary to remind the world of this fact. But then Kaikeyi did love to sing her own praises, even when nobody else seemed interested in singing along.

Bharat went with his mother, who was haranguing him about how nobody in the palace seemed to care about royal protocol any more, and how short-staffed she was, and how her seamstresses had utterly botched up her choli for the Holi parade, and how tiring such festivities were for a queen but nobody seemed to care, and so on. He glanced back briefly, giving his brothers a look of despair that Lakshman had seen often.

'Did you see that?' Shatrugan said. 'When she gets like that, it makes me so mad, I'd like to grab her fleshy shoulders and shake her until she just shuts up!'

Lakshman looked at his brother. Again he wondered at the cosmic irony that had bonded Shatrugan and Bharat so closely while he had formed an identical bond with Rama.

'You take one shoulder, I'll take the other,' he said aloud. 'She's too tough for you alone!'

Shatrugan looked at his brother, surprised. Then he saw the twinkle in Lakshman's eyes and let his scowl turn into a smile. 'Yeah, she is, isn't she? If only she'd use some of that kshatriya strength to fight rakshasas instead of taking it out on poor Bharat.'

Lakshman shrugged. 'I don't know. Maybe Bharat shouldn't be such a victim too. I mean, he could stand up to her once in a while. He's not a milk-drooling babe any more.'

'She's his mother, Lakshman. And never mind him, do you think either of us could raise our voice to her?'

Lakshman shook his head, acknowledging Shatrugan's point. The very thought of addressing an elder aggressively was anathema to any decent Arya. And though some parents could and did relax behaviour norms—Maharaja Janak of Mithila gave his daughters more freedom than most kings gave their sons, for instance—Ayodhya walked a line closer to rigid traditional formality than liberal individualism.

'Anyway, at least he's learned to deal with it. He doesn't let her feed him like a stuffed boar like when he was a kid.'

Shatrugan conceded that point. Before they had left for Guru Vashishta's forest academy, Bharat used to be the first one in the bhojanshalya and the last to leave, supervised closely by either Kaikeyi-maa or Manthara-daiimaa. Now, he was more watchful about his diet, more aware of his physical appearance.

'And thank God our maa isn't like that,' Lakshman added.

'Speaking of her,' Shatrugan said, 'shouldn't we see her first before having naashta?'

Lakshman caught a whiff of some fried savoury: samosas, he guessed. He adored samosas and jalebis. 'I guess we should,' he agreed reluctantly.

They turned away from the bhojanshalya with an effort and made their way to the third queen's palace through a connecting corridor. A chorus of cries went up as their

194

mother's serving girls saw them coming and conveyed the news with the speed of sparrows chittering at the arrival of sunrise. Their mother was waiting for them, the aarti thali beside her, ready for the Holi morning ritual.

'There you are,' she said, beaming up at them. Both her sons had at least a head of height on her. Confronted with them, her small, roundish face still youthful and childishly winsome, she looked like a younger sister rather than their mother. 'You boys must be hungry. Let's finish your aarti and you can have your naashta.' She sighed briefly as she hefted the thali on her little hands. 'I had to spend half the morning keeping Kaikeyi-maa company while she ate her breakfast. My stomach's grumbling too.'

'You mean Kaikeyi-maa's already eaten?' Lakshman frowned. 'But isn't she supposed to wait and do Bharat's aarti first?'

Sumitra gave her son a look that spoke volumes. 'Yes, she is. But you know Kaikeyi-maa.' She shook her head in bafflement. 'I don't understand that woman. Does she drink a cup of bile every night before sleeping? She's always so full of bitterness for everything and everybody. You won't believe the scene she made in Kausalya-maa's chambers this morning. I thought the rakshasas had invaded the palace! Anyway, let's not talk about such ashubh things before pooja. We all have a long day ahead.'

Lakshman and Shatrugan exchanged a last glance before bowing to touch their mother's feet. It was a glance of mutual relief that they weren't Kaikeyi-maa's sons.

TWENTY-FIVE

The moment Rama's face came into view, framed between two bougainvillea-twined marble arches, Kausalya was struck by a great urge to run and sweep her son into her arms, hugging him madly, the way she had done a year ago when he returned from Guru Vashishta's ashram. That day she had been standing ready from dawn on the steps of the palace, anxiously awaiting his return after a gap of seven unbearably long years. When she saw the slender young man walking up the avenue, she was startled at first: *this can't be my Rama.* Then she had recognised his delicately carved features, chiselled more finely than ever in adolescent masculinity. As he came closer, still absorbed in banter with his three brothers, she began to delineate the unmistakable silhouette of her father's aquiline profile in his face as well as reflections of her own nose, jawline and chin, mingled to form a strikingly handsome face and personality that was entirely his own—unlike Bharat walking beside him, a smaller and much less bulky but otherwise identical clay-cast model of Dasaratha—and Kausalya was struck with a shock of delicious realisation that her son had left as a boy and come back a man. Then he had glanced up while smiling at some comment by Shatrugan or Lakshman and met her astonished gaze, and she had seen the startled look of recognition in his own eyes. She had let all protocol fall by the wayside as she ran down the steps, past the surprised night-watch, and swept him up in her embrace, her tears leaving streaky trails down his dust-limned shoulder.

He was fourteen, almost fifteen, then. A whole year had passed since that emotional reunion. A year in which they had grown closer than ever despite the long separation, or perhaps because of it, and now not a day passed without Kausalya spending an hour or several in her son's company, making up for those lost years. But now, as she watched him enter the courtyard of her palace and walk through the arched entranceway, she felt a tearing at her heart and eyes that was as wrenching as the anticipation she had felt that day.

Then, it had been the realisation that her little boy had returned a man. Today, it was the knowledge that he was about to become crown prince of Ayodhya. Crown prince! Even the sadness that lay in her breast like a hard, cold lump, the awful certainty that his ascension would be as a result of his father's untimely demise, even that sad fact couldn't lessen the joy of this moment. Earlier this morning, in the akasa-chamber, Dasaratha had reproached her for thinking like a wife rather than a mother.

And so she had. But now that she had had a little time to absorb the unexpected news, to accept the inevitability of Dasaratha's mortality, she had begun to think like a mother again. And now, flushed with the pride and exhilaration of her thrilling secret, it took every ounce of her self-control to remain standing as she was in the proper dignified posture, and not to shout out Rama's name, run laughing to him, trumpet her message to the skies. She must behave immaculately. There would be eyes everywhere from now on, watching him as well as her. For if he was to become king, she would be queen mother, and there was a protocol to be followed. And jealous eyes would be watching constantly.

All this passed through her mind in the space of the moment it took Rama to step through the marble archway. His face softened in a shy smile as he caught sight of her across the twenty-metre length of the square aangan.

He raised his arm in greeting and was about to sprint to her when he saw the entourage of serving girls surrounding her and the pooja thali in her hands. He slowed his pace and strode in measured steps across the aangan, past the sacred tulsi that he had helped Kausalya plant when he was seven, past the greedily admiring doe eyes of the first queen's entirely female palace staff, each one admiring every nuance of his lithe, muscled frame with the avariciousness of a johari testing the purity of gold—although even a jeweller would not dwell as shamelessly on the intimate anatomical details of a piece of jewellery as did the palace nubiles admiring Rama's body. And after the announcement today, not just nubiles but every woman of the court would give her life for a single night in his embrace. Kausalya had no fear that Rama would give in to their temptations—she had brought him up too well for that, she knew—but she took some small pleasure from his popularity. It was a fine thing to be desired, as long as one never succumbed to desire.

To his credit, without even throwing a flirtatious glance in anyone's direction—he was his mother's darling after all, she told herself with a brief flash of pride—he climbed the seven steps to the threshold where Kausalya stood. As he had passed the tulsi plant, a trio of little butterflies twirling playfully in the air attached themselves to him, roiling and fluttering around his head. As he reached the seventh step, they hovered before his face, attracting his attention for an instant—he laughed delightedly, turning cross-eyed as he tried to look at the bold admirers—then danced away in the wind. *Prajapati*, she thought. Butterflies were an embodiment of the One God that had created all living creatures large and small. The other six million gods—including the holy trinity that were in fact varying aspects of the One God—were all avatars of Prajapati, and the butterflies gracing Rama at such a moment were nothing less than a supreme blessing. She sent up a silent prayer and vowed to offer a special yagna to Prajapati before the season was over.

'Maa, pranaam,' he said, bowing low to touch her feet. *Greetings, mother.*

'Ayushmaanbhav, Aryaputra,' she responded formally. *Live long, son of Arya.*

Touching his forehead with the tips of his mother-blessed fingers, he accepted her ashirwaad and straightened up. The maids beside Kausalya stepped up with the phool-mala and other tokens of the aarti, and she performed the simple ritual that every Arya mother and wife dutifully executed every day, praying for the long life, health, wealth and happiness of her husband and children. Traditionally, a wife performed the daily aarti for her husband before he left for his day's duties, be they farming or kingship. This morning, she had already performed it for Dasaratha, but through these many years of marital estrangement, she had satisfied herself by blessing her son every day. And so it was this little ritual that made her feel as though her day was now truly begun.

The aarti done, her oldest maid, Susama-daiimaa, the same midwife who had presided over Rama's birth, rang the brass bell that hung over the threshold. In response, the assembled serving girls and women sounded their little silver hand-bells, signalling the end of the aarti. As the last tinkling of the pooja bells filled the aangan, rising into the clear morning air with the twining smoke and sweet odour of agar, an identical tinkling rose from other aangans within hearing distance—the Second Queen's Palace, Third Queen's Palace, and the Palace of Concubines. Across the capital city, identical sounds and fragrances were rising from a hundred thousand aangans as mothers blessed their husbands and first-borns and prayed for an auspicious start to the sowing season.

'What a day this has been, maa,' Rama said as they seated themselves in her reception chamber. They had a few minutes before the royal parade began. He briskly recounted the events of that morning, from his encounter with the deer and the poachers to the near-riot on Jagganath Marg. Kausalya listened patiently, though her heart was filled to bursting with her own news. She was surprised and a little disturbed to hear of the near-escapes from violence he had experienced. She had long since made her peace with the fact that violence would always be a part and parcel of Rama's existence. She consoled herself with the knowledge that she had trained him well to seek peaceful solutions whenever possible. But it alarmed her that he had taken on both challenges unarmed. At times like this, she almost wished that Rama could be less truthful than he was, but immediately admonished herself for thinking such a thing.

Serving girls bustled to and fro excitedly, bringing refreshments for them. Freed from the formality of the religious rite, the nubile young girls couldn't take their eyes off Rama, and more than one brushed intimately against him as she bent to offer a platter of fruit or a cup of rose-water, offering him easy glimpses of her cleavage or 'accidentally' caressing his face or arms. After the second or third time, Rama cleared his throat and looked pointedly at Kausalya. She smiled wryly and clapped her hands, ordering the maids out of the room. They left reluctantly, and watched discreetly from the windows and doorways.

'Maybe later,' Rama said when she offered him food. He accepted only a clay cup of rose-flavoured water, sipping it slowly. Kausalya abjured eating too. There would be a feast later, and formality would require her to partake of some of that rich, heavy banquet. Rama had taken after her in his frugal eating habits, a stark contrast to his brother Bharat, whose appetites promised some day to rival even his father's legendary voluptuousness.

Kausalya remembered the time Rama had sat by his father's side, sipping rose-water as Dasaratha guzzled goblets of wine, looking up adoringly at his father from time to time and trying so fetchingly to imitate Dasaratha's peculiar habit of holding the goblet by the rim rather than the stem—until the cup slipped from his little fingers and shattered on the floor of the king's bhojanshalya. The look of sadness that came on his little face as he looked down at the broken cup and the shards of painted clay was not for the spilled rose-water, he told Kausalya in a soft voice later that night, but for the broken cup, which he had crafted with his own hands at a potter's wheel behind the palace. At the memory, Kausalya was struck by an impulse of motherly love so strong that it made her heart ache.

Rama glanced up at her, sensing her eyes on him, and smiled his familiar distracted half-smile. Even now, he was as patient, as calm as he had been as a boy. The stillness of steel, Guru Vashishta had once commented. Kausalya leaned forward, resisting the urge to clasp him to her breast and hug him until he laughed and ran away to hide among her silks—rolling in their fragrant folds while she pretended to search half the palace before 'luckily' happening to find him—and finally spoke the words that had been waiting for release.

'Your father came to me this morning.'

He lowered the clay cup. It was an identical replica of the one he had made as a child, but far more perfectly finished and shaped—he had made this one too. He waited for her to go on.

'He has decided that you are to be king on his passing. He wishes to crown you prince-heir on your sixteenth birthday this very month.'

She waited for him to respond.

But there was no response from Rama.

TWENTY-SIX

Rama remained silent, his eyes, fixed now on the granite-tiled floor, as dark and unfathomable as her own at such times. Like a well in the late afternoon, the water glinting far below in reflected sunlight, yet not directly visible no matter how hard you looked. Deep waters. She had been exactly the same in her youth, staying so silent that the elder women of her father's palace had offered critical opinions of a possible lack of intelligence.

'He wishes to make the announcement today,' she added. 'To prepare the kingdom for your coronation with great pomp and ceremony. He is very proud of you.'

Still Rama said nothing. Only listened, the clay cup now set on the floor between them, leaning forward, elbows resting on his crossed legs. From somewhere in the city, the sound of conch shells announced the formal start of the Holi festivities. A new flurry of excitement rippled through Kausalya's maids. They would be waiting impatiently for she and Rama to finish their refreshments and join the rest of the royal family. Kausalya briefly flashed on the memories of the many Holi festivals over the years that she had spent without Rama by her side, without the attentions of Dasaratha, feeling like a third wheel on a chariot that had long outlived its usefulness. She firmly put aside those painful images. This was a new beginning, time to create new memories and record happy images. She focused on conveying to Rama the importance of her message.

'It is your birthright, as you know. You are next in line to the throne. It is your place to be king after he is . . . gone.'

He raised his head. The change that had come over his features was small but frightful. She had some notion of how formidable he must have seemed to those trespassing poachers. So much rage in such a serene youthful face was terrifying to see.

His voice was soft as molten steel, the words smouldering with fury.

'And what of you? What of your place, the place you were denied? The humiliations you bore silently? The betrayal and the infidelity? The negligence? Will those be restored to you as well? Will his passing magically make everything all right?'

His eyes were filled now with an inner light that was a reflection of the threat lurking in those deep waters. There was a gharial beneath that deceptively calm surface. An ancient reptilian creature whose ferocity and ruthlessness belied the apparent calm. She guessed that even the encounters with the poachers and the rioting mob would not have awoken this sleeping beast; those were problems his kshatriya upbringing and training had more than prepared him to deal with, while this was something he had no defence against, no solution for, no means of dealing with. She had seen this same emotion surface in Rama once before, when he was very small, the first time he understood that despite her status as first queen, his mother was treated as an unwanted mistress while her usurper Kaikeyi reigned supreme with the king's assent. That was the day the gharial had been born; now, it was an almost fully grown creature, matured by his realisation on his return from the ashram that nothing had changed: his mother still lived with the daily humiliation of being a cast-aside wife in her own palace.

She paused, choosing her words carefully. She was not among those women who nursed their hurt and humiliation within their breasts and passed it to their children like sour milk, to curdle their stomachs and turn their hearts against their fathers.

'He is ailing, Rama,' she said gently. 'He does not have long to live. He wishes . . . to make amends. He has already . . . reconciled with me, and I have accepted.'

'Accepted?'

Softly spoken though it was, the word sprang from his lips like an arrow shot at her heart. Her head throbbed with sudden anxiety. She feared she would not be able to convince him, to make him forgive his father's past errors, to accept his legacy and wear the crown that had touched Dasaratha's scalp.

'What do you mean, accepted, Mother? How could you accept him back in the space of a single morning when his negligence has spanned a decade and a half?'

'He is still my husband,' she replied, keeping her voice level and as calm as she could manage. 'And I am still his wife. We walked seven pheras around the sacred fire. Nothing can undo that.'

He was silent, staring in rage at her for a moment. Then he saw something in her face that explained more than her words. He looked away, angry and ashamed, and she felt a flush burn her face. He had understood just how intimate the reconciliation had been.

'And where do you stand on this . . . this royal change of heart?' He said it without looking at her.

'I stand as his wife and your mother.' She tried to appeal to his softer side, to retreat to their unblemished bond as mother and son, free of the emotional baggage of her damaged relationship with his father. 'I want this for you, Rama. I want to see you crowned king. It's my life's greatest wish. Nothing would make me happier. Try to understand.'

'Don't say that.' His voice was hoarse with anguish. 'I understand everything. I understand that you're willing to forget all and forgive him for the sake of my future, to put aside your long, silent suffering just so that I can sit on the throne of Ayodhya.'

'No, Rama. That isn't entirely true. I am done with the anger and the suffering. I'm ready to put it behind me. I want to go forward now, to make a new beginning. I want to celebrate Holi today with my son and my husband, and begin a new season of happiness. I want to enjoy this blessing that God has given me once again, and be content with it for as long as it lasts. And we both know that nothing lasts for ever. Heed my words, son. Put aside your anger. I believe your father is sincere and genuinely repentant. Forget his past mistakes. Accept his ashirwaad, and the crown of Ayodhya.'

Rama made a gesture as scornful as flicking a bug off his shoulder. 'I don't want a crown as a consolation prize.'

She was shocked at his sarcasm. It was not usually his way to use verbal barbs. He was too good a boy for that. But she had underestimated his banked anger all these years. Perhaps she had passed on some curdled milk after all, without her knowledge. Perhaps simply being her son had soured the good milk in his belly. Like her, he kept his gharial caged so deep that by the time it emerged it was too late to prepare for its ferocity.

But she had banked emotions of her own. And this was one fight she had to fight, not against him, but for his sake.

'Be careful now, son,' she warned. 'Don't let your anger with your father cloud your judgement. You are a

Suryavansha prince, the rightful heir to the throne. Accept your place in the dynasty. Ascend the throne you were born to occupy. This is beyond any personal feelings. This is a matter of history and destiny.'

'History can be rewritten. Destiny can be changed.' He almost snarled the next words: 'If queens can be replaced at will, so can crown princes. Who knows what plans his other wife has in store for us in future?'

'Rama Chandra!' She spoke his full birth name for the first time in years. Not since he had left the palace for the ashram had she used his entire name aloud to his face. 'You go too far. Remember who you are. As your mother, I forbid you from speaking another word against your father.'

He looked at her. The fire in his eyes burned low and deep. But there was something else now. An awareness that she had changed. And bonded as he was to her, she prayed that he would understand and change with her. That he would cross over from the scorched lands of hate and bitterness and take that crucial first step on to the bridge of forgiveness. This was a test of everything she had taught him, things that were harder to learn than sword-art and archery. Lessons that must be learned so deeply that they became part of one's personality. *Please, Sri*, she prayed to her patron goddess, *let him see right and do right*.

She placed her palm on his cheek. His skin was hot. 'Listen to me,' she said in a tone that she might have used when he was a gurgling baby in her lap fifteen years ago. 'Put the past away. Make a new beginning today, Rama. This is no accidental reconciliation. It was meant to be. Whatever is done, is done. It no longer matters. The only thing that matters is what lies ahead. Face it with an open and free mind. Accept it. Accept your dharma.'

The glint in his eyes seemed to soften at that last word, grow less hostile. She pressed her advantage.

'It is your dharma to fulfil your father's wishes, to take his place on the throne of Ayodhya, to rule your people justly and wisely. These things you must do without doubt or question. These have nothing to do with his negligence of me, or our long estrangement. Those are insignificant in the larger context. Yes, I have forgiven and forgotten all lapses, just in the space of one morning. Yet I do not demand or even request that you do the same. It is your decision to make. What I do demand is that you honour your parents and ancestors and heritage. Your dharma calls out to you. Answer it wisely.'

A maid came to the door, looked in and started to speak. Kausalya dismissed her with a silent gesture. When she turned back to Rama, his face was still scarred with sorrow, but the rage was gone, she was relieved to see. The gharial had sunk beneath the surface again, descending into the depths.

'My dharma.' The words were soft, unaccented by anger. Yet Kausalya read an entire childhood of pain in them, the pain of a son who had seen his mother pining secretly in private while a younger woman took her place in public by her husband's side. There was nothing she could do to chase away that pain. All she could do was to give him a positive goal to look forward to, a target on which to focus his energies. And pray for the best.

'Your dharma,' she agreed.

He was silent for another long moment. Conch shells were sounding all across the city now. After a morning of surprises, Ayodhya had finally officially begun the celebration of the most rambunctious festival of the year. In moments, coloured rang powder would fly from a hundred thousand fists, painting the city in rainbow hues. But the mood in this chamber was still grey, the celebration outside kept at bay by a decision that could change the course of Arya history itself.

For several moments, as Kausalya waited for Rama's final choice, she thought that he would surely deny his father's desire. That despite his princely training and upbringing, Rama the son of Kausalya would prevail over Rama the prince and heir of Dasaratha.

Then she realised that she must not even think of such a possibility, that the mere fact of her thinking it might be communicated to Rama.

Yet she knew that Rama understood everything she felt. He always had. Even despite the barrier of protocol that prevented a Hindu mother from speaking to her son about his father's faults and lapses, Rama understood without being told. And in the end, he would do the right thing; he always did.

The sound of conch shells was everywhere now, an orchestra of celebration as overwhelming as a herd of elephants trumpeting on one's doorstep. The maids were beside themselves with excitement, running to and fro, fetching their rang and implements in anticipation of their mistress's permission to start playing.

After another moment of tense anticipation, Kausalya sensed that Rama had reached a decision. But instead of speaking, he rose directly to his feet, taking Kausalya by surprise.

He bowed and touched her feet, the tips of his fingers brushing her gold-ringed toes. Straightening up, he joined his palms in a respectful and affectionate pranaam. His face had lost all trace of anger or pique and was composed in its normal expression of peaceful serenity once more. Looking into his eyes, she saw that the wave of resentment had passed. He had somehow come to terms with this difficult and unexpected shock and was coping with it.

He even managed a tiny smile of tenderness as he said to her gently:

'It will be as you wish, Maa.'

Kausalya was weak with relief.

The female guard who entered the room was one of her oldest and most loyal.

'Rani, shama.' *Excuse me, my queen.* 'The king wishes to see Prince Rama in the sabha hall at once.'

TWENTY-SEVEN

As the towering doors of the sabha hall were unbarred and opened to admit the four princes, Rama heard the sound of loud booming voices from within. They were a faint counterpoint to the distant sounds of revelry and music that reverberated from the rest of the palace and the city. Celebrations without, solemnity within. Truly, this was a strange festival day. He entered first as protocol demanded, forcing himself to walk not run. The voices faded as soon as he entered, and he was uncertain whether he had heard or imagined them. Behind him, the sound of the doors being shut and bolted was very loud in the empty stillness of the enormous chamber. He began to walk down the long aisle to the royal dais at the far end, the sound of his brothers' sandalled feet following close behind.

Coming here brought back memories of the few formal occasions when the princes had been permitted to attend court. There had been many voices in those days, raised in incessant conflict. Why do maharajas always have to argue with people? Rama had asked his mother once. Why can't they just be nice to everyone? She had smiled and hugged him to her breast and told him that when he was king he could be as nice as he liked.

Whatever argument had been raging a moment ago, it seemed to have ended. The four princes walked up the long central aisle to the royal dais in absolute silence now, unusual in a place built for debates. Rama noted that his father looked older and wearier than usual; he looked soul-sick, his thickened jowls drooping, eyes ringed with dark circles of exhaustion, complexion pale from the cancerous attacks of his mystery ailment. He was seated on the throne but leaned forward with his elbows on his knees and his head in his hands, like a man exhausted from thinking. The three other men standing before him on the dais formed a triangular tableau of conflict and disagreement: Pradhan-Mantri Sumantra stood by the king's right hand, facing the two brahmins, while Guru Vashishta was shoulder to shoulder with the visitor, who had his back to the princes as they approached.

Yet even with his back turned, he was an imposing sight, a picture of radiant strength and virility contrasting sharply with Dasaratha's sickly exhaustion. It was difficult not to see the irony in the contrast.

He must be all of seven feet tall, if he's an inch, Rama thought. *And look at that musculature, and those scars. He still looks like a king even today.*

Rama reached the end of the crimson carpet and bent his knee. 'Pranaam, Ayodhya-naresh, pranaam pujya pitaaji.' His brothers mirrored his gesture and salutation. *Greetings, lord of Ayodhya; greetings, respected father.*

'My sons.' Dasaratha sounded strained. 'Come to me.'

The princes stepped on to the saffron carpeting of the royal dais and joined their father.

As Rama approached, he kept his hands clasped together to greet the others in the correct order that protocol demanded.

First, the honoured visitor.

212

'Pranaam, respected guest. You honour us with your visit. I pray, if you find this humble kshatriya worthy, grant me your ashirwaad. I shall be eternally blessed.'

Vishwamitra took a step sideways and turned slightly to offer more of his fore-side to Rama, while taking care not to turn his back on the king.

'Greetings, Prince Rama.'

As Rama bent to touch the seer-mage's feet in the traditional greeting to a respected elder, Vishwamitra simply said, 'Ayushmaan bhav, rajkumar.' *Live long, prince.*

The response was delivered without embellishment, and so curtly that Rama almost looked up at the seer's face before rising. He sensed Pradhan-Mantri Sumantra's eyes blinking briefly before returning to their contemplation of a spot in the middle distance. The maharaja said nothing. Rama stepped back to allow his brothers to repeat the showing of respect and granting of ashirwaad, taking care not to meet anyone's gaze directly. The tension on the dais was palpable. Rama guessed that the argument had reached a stalemate, not an end.

As his brothers bent to touch the visitor's feet, Rama sensed someone staring intently at him. It was the piercing gaze of a large and powerful animal in the deep forest, like a tiger watching him from a mangrove tree. The penetrating study of a fellow predator. But when he glanced cursorily around, both Guru Vashishta and Brahmarishi Vishwamitra were looking elsewhere. Still the sense of being watched persisted.

The visitor's ashirwaad to the other princes was less curt, and by the time he touched Lakshman's head, there was almost a trace of warmth in the deep voice.

The four princes stood in a row to the left of the throne. Now the tableau resembled an upturned V, with the maharaja at the conjunction of the two lines.

'My sons,' Dasaratha said, sounding tired and on edge. 'It is a strange and disturbing day in our history. The arrival of our exalted guest on the auspicious day of Holi Purnima would be an occasion to celebrate with twice the customary pomp, yet other events have occurred to cast a shadow over our great city.'

Dasaratha gestured to Sumantra. The prime minister quickly brought the princes up to speed on the events of that morning, from the arrival of the impostor to his exposure and dismissal by the two seers, right up to the discussion in the sabha hall and the unmasking of the spies.

'They are now in the city jail, being interrogated by Mantri Jabali, who has some expertise in these matters.' Sumantra gestured at the deserted expanse of the sabha hall. 'At the maharaja's order, the sabha was dismissed and a state of emergency declared in the city. It's believed that an entire network of Asura-sponsored spies exists throughout the kingdom, perhaps even throughout the Arya nations, and an emergency plenary session of the war council will be held a week from today to discuss how best to attack and destroy this network.'

Sumantra's voice and face betrayed his own disbelief at the things he was describing. Bharat and Shatrugan exchanged glances with each other before looking at Rama. This was far worse than any of them had thought.

Rama spoke up. 'Something strange happened to us a few minutes ago.' He briefly sketched the near-riot on the streets outside the palace gates. His brothers, clearly dissatisfied with his lack of detail, chipped in several times. Finally, Bharat took over the telling, praising Rama's swiftness of thought and action, and his ingenuity. 'If not for Rama,' he finished, 'the streets would be washed with innocent blood today.'

214

Sumantra and Dasaratha exchanged glances. Sumantra looked even more troubled than he had been before. 'Captain Drishti Kumar told us that something strange had happened but nobody seems to be sure exactly what it was.'

'There was sorcery at work,' Lakshman said. 'It was like a mist had descended to cloud everyone's mind.' He added proudly: 'Only Brother Rama was unaffected.'

Rama shifted uneasily as his father congratulated him with as much energy as he could muster. He saw the two seer-mages exchange a look, but couldn't see Vishwamitra's face clearly as he was being embraced by his father.

Sumantra added uncomfortably: 'We have been hearing strange rumours from the rakshaks for a while now.' He was speaking of the sub-caste of kshatriyas who were entrusted with the task of guarding the bridges and causeways of the kingdom. 'And last month there was a courier from Mithila who delivered a message from Maharaja Janak and left here safely but never reached Mithila.'

Rama spoke his mind. 'There is a conspiracy afoot, Father,' he said. 'And Ayodhya is the target. We have not seen the last of these unnatural events.'

Before Dasaratha could reply, the visitor spoke.

'Well said, Prince Rama. It is just as you say. The Lord of Lanka has spread his net far and wide all these years. Now, he begins to pull it in one patch at a time. If we do not act swiftly and decisively, we will live to see a reign of terror such as no Arya nation has ever witnessed.'

'What can we do to prevent this from happening?' Rama asked. 'Can't we attempt to parley.with Lanka?'

Vishwamitra's craggy face was softened by an unexpected smile. 'Would that it were possible. Sadly, young prince, Asuras do not parley. This war has too long and bloody a history for peace to be an option any longer.'

Rama looked at Dasaratha. 'My father taught me that peace is always an option.'

Vishwamitra raised his eyebrows, exchanging a look with Dasaratha. 'And he taught you well. But this is no ordinary adversary. These are Asuras, eternal enemies of the devas. And as long as we worship the devas as our gods, we can never be at peace with the Asuras.'

Bharat was about to speak up, but Rama went on, persisting: 'But there was a cessation of hostilities once. Before we mortals were created. The devas and Asuras came to an understanding and put down their weapons to negotiate peacefully.'

Vishwamitra nodded at his fellow seer-mage. 'And Guru Vashishta too has taught you well. You know your history. You speak of the Amrit Manthan. And so you must also know the outcome of those peaceful negotiations?'

Rama realised his mistake at once. 'The devas churned the ocean to produce the nectar of immortality. But when the time came to give an equal portion to the Asuras, the devas tried to cheat them because they feared that once the Asuras became immortal too, they would be unstoppable.'

'And so the war resumed, fiercer than ever.' Vishwamitra gave Rama the benefit of a smile. 'Still, it is good to find a kshatriya prince who speaks of peace, young Rama Chandra. If only there was a way to end this war without violence.' He sighed. 'Sadly, there isn't.'

Rama noticed that his father was favouring one leg slightly; Dasaratha had an old war injury on his left thigh that troubled him in times of illness and weakness. He looked at Guru Vashishta to see if he had noticed. Vashishta looked sorrowful and compassionate. His father's condition was worsening but nothing could be done about it.

Vishwamitra went on: 'Ever since I entered Ayodhya, I have sensed spirals and wisps of kala jaadu in the ether. It saddens me to see the presence of evil in the heart of such a noble city.'

'Brahmarishi Vishwamitra,' Bharat said respectfully, his taut expression betraying his inability to control his anger any longer, 'respected father, great Guru Vashishta, we must root out this evil at once. Let me lead the hunt for these treacherous rats. I will wash the gutters of the city with their black blood and cleanse our great capital of this evil intrusion.'

Guru Vashishta raised his palm. 'Shantam, my prince. Control your emotions. Angry haste is not the way to deal with this problem.' He gestured fluidly at Vishwamitra. 'Our illustrious visitor has interrupted his two-hundred-and-forty-year penance for the precise purpose of aiding us in this new war.'

Rama happened to be looking in his father's direction when the guru said the word 'war'. He saw Dasaratha blanch visibly. Rama's heart went out to his father. Maharaja Dasaratha had never recovered wholly from that final campaign. His most fervent prayer had always been that his sons would never have to experience similar horrors.

'I wish it were not so,' Rama said, speaking for his father. 'Better that this conflict had never begun.'

Vishwamitra looked at Rama. Their eyes met for a moment, and Rama could feel that it was the great seer-mage who had been scrutinising him moments ago, using his supernatural power of secret observation.

'Well spoken once again, young prince. Nevertheless, this conflict was begun, though not by your hand or ours. All that is within our power is the chance to end it.'

'End it?' Dasaratha said suddenly. 'Impossible! Even the gods could not end the Asura Wars. And not for want of trying. You have just said so yourself, great one. How can we mere mortals do what the gods cannot?'

'Nevertheless, Dasaratha, we cannot stop trying. Even the impossible must be attempted, if only in the hope of eventual success.' He chanted a Sanskrit sloka: 'Karmanye swahikaaraste mahaphaleshua.' *Perform your dharmic duty and do not think of the fruits of your labour*.

Bharat spoke up again, his anger still evident.

'Then as kshatriyas and defenders of the Arya peoples, we must act. That is our dharmic duty, is it not, mahadev?' He seemed to regard the question as rhetorical because he went on without waiting for a response. 'Besides, we have no choice in the matter. The Asuras made the first move. They violated the truce and infiltrated our city. We can't just stand by and wait for them to invade and destroy our kingdom. We must go to war now.'

'NO!'

Dasaratha's voice was cracked and hoarse, but there was power in it. Power which surely cost him much vital energy. Rama's earlier anger at his father's past mistakes had given way to a deep concern. He worried now about the toll this debate was taking on Dasaratha's dangerously weakened constitution.

'There will be no talk of war in my lifetime.' The maharaja's hand shook as he raised it to point at Kaikeyi's son. 'Bharat, my son, you know the price we paid—nay, are still paying—for the Last War. I swore a vow then that that was the last time we would pitch our war tents and go to battle against the Asuras. If you honour me, then respect and uphold that vow.'

'But Father, these demons—'

'These demons are demons. They will act as demons. We can still act as humans.'

'But these intrusions. The rakshas who infiltrated the city—'

Dasaratha rose to his feet, face red with anger. 'Enough! No more argument from you. There will be no talk of war here today or any day from this day onwards.'

Bharat fell sullenly silent. Shatrugan and Lakshman kept their eyes on the ground, knowing that there was no point in arguing with their father at such times. Only Rama kept his eyes on the maharaja, watching his father for any signs of an imminent collapse. Had Vishwamitra not been present, Rama would have asked Dasaratha to call an end to these discussions. But it would be insulting to tell his father to lie down and rest before a venerated guest.

Dasaratha resumed his seat, sinking heavily into the cushioned throne. He spoke hoarsely but passionately. 'I will not see those dark ages return to this land, not as long as there is still breath in my body.' He curled his hand into a fist, which he brought down heavily on the arm of his throne. 'I have said this to you a hundred times already, sage. Why do you not relent?'

Vishwamitra spoke into the uncomfortable silence that followed.

'Maharaja, you have made your views clear. Yet my dharma is as clearly defined as your own. As much as I dislike war and the horrors that attend its passing, I must repeat my request.'

'And I must deny it yet again!'

The seer's voice softened. 'Dasaratha, be reasonable. What I offer is an antidote to war. An end to the endless cycle of karmic violence and bloodshed that has plagued us since the beginning of time. A permanent peace in the three worlds of patal, prithvi and swarga-lok.'

Dasaratha uttered a sound that was half a laugh and half a cry. 'Your antidote is worse than the venom it seeks to cure, mahadev. I have told you already, it is unthinkable to give you what you demand. Ask anything else of me and you shall have it.'

'Ayodhya-naresh, your decision is not a wise one. I ask you yet again, reconsider. Or else you will commit the mortal sin of violating the sacred law of dharma!'

TWENTY-EIGHT

Dasaratha coughed harshly, hacking into his fist. He tried to speak, but choked on another fit of coughing. Sumantra quickly provided a spittoon for his use, then offered Dasaratha a goblet to sip on. The maharaja used both before replying in a voice hoarser than before. Beside him, Rama sensed his brothers exchanging worried glances—none of them had any illusions about their father's state of health, but none of them knew how to alleviate the current stress that he was under. As fascinating as the debate was, Rama felt anxious that it end for his father's sake.

Dasaratha's eyes gleamed in the torchlight. 'Honoured one, even another hundred years—were I blessed enough to live that long, which I doubt—would not make me reconsider my decision. What I said before is final and binding.'

Vishwamitra was silent for a moment. When he spoke again, his voice was deathly quiet. 'It is not in the nature of seers, let alone a brahmarishi, to repeat oneself. Nor should you deny your clan-oaths and defy the code of the kshatriya. But because the Suryavansha dynasty and the Ikshvaku clan whence you spring are so renowned for their service to the seers, I repeat my request one more time for the benefit of your sons, these fine and proud young princes of Ayodhya.'

He turned slightly, pitching his words slightly louder for the benefit of Rama and his brothers. 'Hear me, O Lord and Ruler of Ayodhya, seat of mighty Kosala, greatest of the Arya nations of the world. Grant me the dakshina I demand by right. And we may yet pull out the thorn before the bush grows beyond our reach.'

Dasaratha's head bowed wearily. 'Sage, I cannot sacrifice the life of my son at the altar of your faith.'

'You would rather sacrifice the lives of your people instead?' Vishwamitra's voice was sharp.

'If such be the will of the gods, so be it.' Dasaratha's voice was cantankerous, edgy with fatigue and brain-weariness. Rama knew that in the next instant, both men would be trading insults and then the fat would really hit the fire. If Brahmarishi Vishwamitra took offence at Dasaratha's comments, this debate would end with a curse rather than a decision.

'Father, mahaguru, shama.'

Both Dasaratha and the visitor stared in surprise at Rama as he stepped forward, kneeling before the throne while simultaneously bending his neck before the seer. The seer acknowledged Rama's apology for the interruption. Rama rose to his feet and looked up at his father, who was frowning down at him.

'Father, forgive my naivety. But may I ask what exactly is this dakshina that Brahmarishi Vishwamitra desires? And why do you break the code of the kshatriya by refusing to grant him his dakshina?'

Although his brothers didn't say a word, Rama felt their solidarity with him. What exactly was at stake here?

Maharaja Dasaratha bowed his head again, shutting his red-rimmed eyes. Sumantra stepped forward, peering at him anxiously, but Dasaratha waved him away weakly. After a moment, he opened his eyes once more, speaking hoarsely but clearly.

'He wishes to conduct a great yagna. This is the culmination of his two hundred and forty years of penance. But each time his purohits prepare the sacred altar for the yagna, rakshasas defile its sanctity and disrupt the preparations. Even as we speak, the propitious time for the completion of the yagna is wasting. He must complete the ritual within the next seven days in order to achieve his spiritual goal. To this end, he interrupted his penance and came to Ayodhya today to request protection against the rakshasas.'

Rama was baffled. 'But Father, this is the essence of the kshatriya code: to protect those who cannot, will not, or must not fight. We are sworn to protect the seers and brahmin classes with our lives, just as they are sworn to teach us all knowledge and guide us spiritually. Why do you refuse such a request?'

Dasaratha shook his head. 'You do not understand, Rama. I have already offered him the services of my best warriors, my Purana Wafadar battalion; my entire army is at his disposal if he desires its services . . . I can do no less, for as you say, it is our sacred duty to protect and to serve the holy men. Yet the brahmarishi rejects all my offers and insists on his own choice of protector.' Dasaratha shook his head in despair. 'He insists on having you, my son, even though he knows full well that even my mighty army was once routed by this king of demons. Indeed, I would not be sitting here before you today were it not for the intervention of your clan-mother Kaikeyi, who saved my life not once but twice on that same battlefield. This Ravana is no ordinary rakshas, Rama, as my own wounds testify.'

Second Queen Kaikeyi, then Princess Kaikeyi of the western kingdom of Kaikeya, had ridden in her father's stead at the head of his host, accompanied by Maharaja Dasaratha, Kaikeya's closest ally during the Asura Wars.

Dasaratha had faced Ravana himself in single combat, sustaining a wound that would have been mortal had Kaikeyi not intervened and spirited Dasaratha away to safety in her own chariot. Later, at the close of the battle, Dasaratha's chariot was destroyed by the Lord of Lanka. Kaikeyi put her own chariot between them and held out long enough for Sumantra to come to their rescue with reinforcements. Eventually the combined armies of Kosala and Kaikeya had pushed the Asuras back, and Dasaratha had always claimed that had Kaikeyi not saved his life twice, who knew what the outcome might have been.

Before Rama could speak aloud, Bharat stepped forward with his customary eagerness. 'Let me go then, Father. I shall protect the brahmarishi and see his yagna completed successfully. Offer him my sword and service.'

Dasaratha smiled indulgently at his second oldest. 'You are brave and bold as your namesake, Bharat. Well did I name you after the founder of the Arya nations, great Bharata himself. But alas, this is not acceptable to the brahmarishi either. He wants Rama, and Rama alone, to accompany him back to the forest.'

Rama felt everybody turn to look at him as he spoke. 'Then let me go with him. I will be blessed to perform such a great service.'

Vishwamitra wheeled around, his piercing eyes finding Rama and pinning him with an expression of ferocious pleasure. 'You see, Dasaratha? Even he is willing to go with me. Now, you have no argument left to oppose me!'

Dasaratha rose to his feet, his fist trembling. 'He does not understand, sage! He is young and inexperienced. You are one of the Seven Seers. The Asuras can no more harm you than they can harm the flow of brahman itself. You are virtually immortal and invulnerable, shielded by mandalas, mantras and dev-astras, divine weapons and shields given to you by the devas themselves. But my Rama is merely a mortal boy. He is no match for Asuras sent by the Lord of Lanka. He does not even have the full measure of these demons!'

Vishwamitra replied calmly: 'And they do not have his measure.'

'What can a fifteen-year-old boy do against such creatures? Rakshasas, no less! Rama is fresh from the gurukul, barely of marriageable age. He should be out right now playing Holi with his brothers and friends, enjoying the prime of his youth, celebrating the spring of his life. Not listening to this weary debate. He is too young for such matters. He is no more fit to fight Ravana's two strongest demons than I am to fight Ravana himself at my age and in this condition!'

'He may surprise you yet, raje. After all, he is your son.'

Dasaratha shook his head vehemently. 'Do not persist in this exorbitant demand, mahadev. I beg of you! Today, at the spring feast, I am to announce his succession. In less than one fortnight, on his sixteenth naming day, he will be crowned heir to the throne of Ayodhya. Have a care for his future if not for his youth.'

'I care a great deal about his future, Ayodhya-naresh. That is why I promised you that I would bring him back safe and sound before the date of the coronation. You have my word on it, the word of one of the Seven Seers.'

Dasaratha seemed on the verge of crying out. He controlled himself with an effort and said in a voice that was only one level above a broken-down sob: 'Shama, mahadev. Ask of me anything other than this. I cannot give you my first-born. Take anything you will from me, but not my Rama.'

This time the brahmarishi's response was a long time coming. Rama saw that the seer had reached the end of his patience. Vishwamitra's features had hardened into a mask of grim anger. At that moment, he looked more like the king he once was than a man of God. He took a step toward the dais and raised his staff.

'So be it then, Dasaratha. I have no more business here. I take my leave. Good day.'

Vishwamitra turned, carrying his raised staff, and proceeded up the hall with long, decisive strides. Nobody else moved or spoke. They all seemed frozen. *He's leaving,* Rama thought, *without his guru-dakshina.* It was a violation of everything he had been taught since childhood. Rama's brothers looked at each other nervously. Sumantra set down the goblet and spittoon he was holding, and fell to his knees, praying. Even without hearing the words, Rama knew that the pradhan-mantri was invoking the Holy Trinity to protect them all from the krodh of the great seer-mage. Entire nations had been wiped out by the holy curse of brahmarishis for less cause than Dasaratha had just given.

Guru Vashishta stepped forward, his eyes blazing at Dasaratha, before turning to call out to Vishwamitra. The departing seer-mage was almost at the doors when the guru spoke.

'Brahmarishi Vishwamitra,' he called. 'I entreat you, stay a moment. This matter is not done yet. There are still words left to be spoken.'

Vishwamitra paused, but didn't set his staff on the ground. Without turning around fully, he said over his shoulder: 'I have heard all the words that matter. Nothing more remains to be said.'

'In the name of our shared status as brahmarishis, I request you earnestly, come back to the dais. Give us but a moment to confer. To leave thus would be a great insult to the honour of the house Suryavansha and the clan Ikshvaku.'

'Any insult here was given by your maharaja. It was my honour that was sullied. Now he must live with the consequences of his decision.' Vishwamitra took another step toward the doors, but the guru's voice made him pause again.

'Then pray, give me but a moment to repair those insults and undo this mistake. For it is a mistake, I assure you. The house of Suryavansha is known for its munificence. Dasaratha's own ancestor Maharaja Harishchandra gave away his entire wealth as guru-dakshina. And noble Raghu had already bankrupted his royal treasury by gifting all he owned to one rishi when he was called upon by another to deliver a fabulous sum as guru-dakshina. Raghu obtained the amount from Kuber, Lord of Wealth, and fulfilled his sacred obligation for the second time. The seat of Ayodhya has ever been known for its adherence to dharma.'

Vishwamitra partly turned his body, his eyes diamond-bright in the shadow of an ornate marbled pillar. 'Your words contradict those of your king, great guru. Look! Even now he sits there silent while you implore me on his behalf.'

Guru Vashishta turned to look at the maharaja.

Dasaratha's face was filled with such despair and pain, Rama could hardly bear to look at his father.

'Ayodhya-naresh,' the guru said, 'and Brahmarishi Vishwamitra. Both of you have reached an impasse. One asserts the right of a brahmin to demand dakshina from a kshatriya. The other asserts the right of a father to preserve the life of his son. This debate could rage for ever without an end. Nor would I have you fling insults at one another.'

'What would you have us do, guruji?' asked Dasaratha in a sobered tone. Rama could empathise with his father's dilemma: he was torn between his concern for Rama and his desire to fulfil his dharma. 'Pray, give us the fruit of your wisdom.'

Vashishta spread his hands wide, indicating the empty sabha hall. 'When Manu Lawmaker, the first maharaja of Kosala, was crowned, in this very chamber, and on that very sunwood throne, he laid down two laws by which he would govern. Those two laws determine all life-and-death decisions in Ayodhya even today. Rajkumar Rama, would you tell us what those two laws are?'

'The first law is to obey dharma at all costs,' Rama said promptly. 'For dharma is the moral code by which the pillar of Arya character stands upright.' He paused, seeing the destination of the guru's argument even before he spoke the words. 'The second law is that the maharaja rules not for himself, his dynasty, clan, varna or family. He rules for the people. If he takes a decision that affects the people, then it must meet with the people's consent.'

There was silence for a moment as everyone absorbed the implications of the second rule.

When Guru Vashishta spoke again, it was in a lighter, almost mischievous tone. Rama thought he could see a playful twinkle in the ancient seer's eyes. 'Maharaja Dasaratha, do you deny the second law of Manu?'

Dasaratha looked puzzled. 'Of course not, gurudev. The maharajas of Ayodhya have always ruled only at the people's behest.'

'Then there is the solution to your vexing dilemma. Abjure any further discussion on this matter. Proceed with the Holi ritual prayers and festivities. When you stand before the citizens of Ayodhya on the mela grounds today, confront them with the question. Let them decide if Rajkumar Rama is to go with Vishwamitra or stay here in Ayodhya. Ask Ayodhya to decide!'

In the stunned silence that followed, Rama saw the unmistakable gleam of a smile in the eyes of Vishwamitra.

TWENTY-NINE

'Dashasu dikshu apratihatam ratham calayateeti
Dasharatha.'

The chanting rose from a thousand brahmins led by
the court purohit Rishi Vamadeva. Seated cross-legged
on a flat wagon drawn by a train of sixteen elephants,
the brahmins headed the procession winding its way
majestically down Harshavardhana Avenue, the traditional
starting point of the annual parade. A boy of not more
than seven years sat at the head of the chanting brahmins,
his shaven pate decorated with caste marks in the shape
of a Shiva lingam, an appeasement to the god of destruction
that he might allow this moving machine to pass unharmed.
The elephants trumpeted at varying intervals, punctuating
the chanting of the Sanskrit slokas praising Maharaja
Dasaratha. The wagon bearing the brahmins was a little
less than three yards wide and twenty yards long, rolling
on eighty wheels each a yard high. The crowd lined up
along the sides of the avenue were kept back safely by
silken ropes held by PFs in full battle regalia but unarmed.
The order to shelve weapons had been given by Pradhan-
Mantri Sumantra after hearing the story of the near-riot
on Raghuvamsa Avenue earlier that morning. Even so,
the PFs still made an imposing sight, and the children
watching from behind the ropes were as fascinated by

their battle scars and towering stature as by the royal parade. Among the thousands of children watching were two young vaisya girls, their packets of rangoli and pitchkarees still clutched in their hands, faces and clothes splattered and stained with a rainbow of hues. The taller of the pair, attractive in an honest, clean-featured way, seemed to have endured more rang-smearing than her partner. Her face was a bright crimson smudge relieved only by small patches of purple and indigo. From this quilt of gay colours, her bright blue eyes shone out eagerly, transfixed by the flat wagon.

'There must be lakhs of purohits,' her friend said excitedly. 'Look at how perfectly they're chanting together. That's how Maa Prema always tells us to chant and we can never do it so well!'

'How many times have I told you, Sreelata,' the taller girl said impatiently. 'A lakh is a hundred thousand. There aren't even ten thousand purohits there, let alone a lakh!'

'Oh,' Sreelata said. 'Well, I can never figure out number counting. But there certainly are a lot of bald heads on that wagon, aren't there, Nandini?'

'There sure are,' Nandini agreed, smiling at her friend's choice of words. 'And the parade hasn't even started yet. Just wait till you see the royal wheelhouse pass. It's a hundred yards long, divided into four sections of twenty-five yards each, which are joined by little bridges so you can walk from one end to the other without getting out of the chariot.'

'I thought you said it was a wheelhouse, not a chariot,' Sreelata said, chewing on the end of her sari anxiously.

'Yes, yes, wheelhouse,' Nandini said. 'And then you have to see the battle elephants. They're so beautiful! There are lakhs of them in the royal army, but of course they can't parade them all at once so they only bring out a few from each akshohini. That's a division of the army. One akshohini consists of 21,870 elephants, 21,870 chariots, 65,610 horsemen and 109,350 foot soldiers. The army of Ayodhya has twenty-five akshohini, while another fifteen are quartered around the kingdom at various places.'

'How do you know all this?' Sreelata asked wide-eyed. She was constantly in awe of Nandini's knowledge of numbers and things. It made her aware of how large and complex the world outside the temple walls really was.

'You have to keep your ears and eyes open,' Nandini replied mysteriously. Then she nudged her less well-informed friend affectionately, adding: 'And keep the guardsmen talking after they finish with you. Men can talk ten times as long as they can love. That's something you must know by now, Sreelata!'

Sreelata giggled. 'That I do. They really can talk, can't they? Oh, look, what's that big chariot coming up now? The one with all the gold carvings and conch-bearers getting ready to blow their conches? Is it the royal chariot? I mean, wheelhouse?'

'No, silly! That's just the conch-bearer chariot. It's the first of the royal procession. Look, they're blowing their conches now. That's to let us know the royal procession is coming up.'

Over the pervasive, city-filling sound of the conches, Sreelata said almost shyly, 'Do you think we'll see Prince Rama then?'

Nandini looked at her companion. 'Why? Do you want to ask him to visit us at the temple?'

Sreelata punched her friend in the stomach. 'Shut up!' Her cheeks and neck blazed with embarrassment.

Nandini laughed delightedly. 'So your heart is lost to Prince Rama, huh? Well, then you had better be that one-in-a-crore girl. Because he's sworn to take only one wife in his lifetime.' Nandini waved her hand excitedly.

231

'Look down there. The elephants! The elephants are coming!'

'What do you mean, one wife?' Sreelata nudged her friend curiously. 'He's the prince-heir. He can have a thousand wives if he wants.'

Nandini glanced at her friend fondly. 'That's the point. He can, but he won't. I hear he's sworn to find just one wife.' She shrugged. 'Maybe it has something to do with his father having too many wives! If you know what I mean.'

'Jai Mata Ki!' Sreelata's mind spun with the idea. A man who sought only one mate? What a romantic notion! Suddenly she adored Prince Rama all the more for being so unattainable, so principled. A man who would only love one woman? She instantly wanted to be that woman! Although she knew the odds of a mere temple prostitute catching the eye of a prince-heir were . . . what was that number? One in a crore? One in a hundred crores, more likely.

Nandini released a long, shrill scream, dropping her carefully cultivated upper-class air without a second's thought. 'Sreelata,' she shrieked. 'Look! There's the royal wheelhouse! And in the front, riding on those four horses, it's the princes! Look, the handsome one in front with the dark, almost bluish skin, that's Rama! Isn't he gorgeous! Oh, I could just eat him alive!'

Sreelata joined her friend, shrieking as loud as she could, echoed by every woman, man and child in the crowd. Never mind that he was sworn to take only one mate. A girl could dream, couldn't she?

The parade wound its way down Harshavardhana Avenue, tracing the heartline of the city in its slow, stately progress. The sounds of conches, elephants, dhol-drums, trumpets, flutes, brahmins chanting, people shouting, children crying with joy, all mingled in one enormous cloud of jubilation. The citizens crowding the streets were painted with rang and drenched with water. The soldiers riding the elephants and chariots, astride the war horses, marching in full battle armour, all strode proudly under the admiring gaze of their families, their friends, their people. This was Ayodhya's day for displaying her colours, in every sense of the word. From the sigils of the different noble houses to the banners of vaisya merchants and sudra traders, every varna, tribe and clan in the great Arya nation of Kosala participated in this grand spectacle.

As the parade reached its destination, the people migrated down-city to the rolling northern bank of the Sarayu. Here the royal procession parked and dismounted, flanked on three sides by the representatives of the army, administration and nobility. On the fourth, the south side, was the citizenry, seating itself cross-legged on the bank of the river. This enormous stretch of land was in fact well within city limits, between the third and fourth gates. Ayodhya was designed to include a microcosm of the entire landscape that surrounded her. Manu, the ancient king who had built the city, had planned well and with foresight. Ayodhya was not a city that walled out the world; the world was here, within its walls, as much a part of her structure as the river that wound its way literally beneath her greatest buildings.

It took the better part of an hour for the parade to wind down and the people to settle down. Finally, when the riverbank was carpeted for the better part of a mile with gaily stained white-clad kurtas and saris sitting in long neat rows, Rishi Vamadeva stood on a large hummock that served as a natural dais and led the people in the traditional chant.

'Yatha raja tatha praja.' *As is the king, so are his people.*

'Yatha raja tatha praja,' chanted the people.

Birds took flight in the thicket downstream, swooping across the river, veering away from the Southwoods—a few stragglers boldly going to the very edge of the dark, malignant forest—and returning in a wide arc to their original roosts.

The chanting was followed by the customary bhashans, speeches by various mantris and political representatives of the four castes and the several dozen varnas and gotras, efficient divisions of labour equivalent to the guilds of Western nations. Except for a few dozen house banners mounted on tall poles to mark out the leading noble families, the crowd was a mélange of varna, race, sex and community. The banners flapping in the warm westerly wind made a sound like faint applause. Brahmins sat beside sudras, vaisyas with kshatriyas, all intermingling freely.

Pradhan-Mantri Sumantra stood and made a speech that was hugely popular on account of its being blessedly short, and then invited the maharaja to speak.

Maharaja Dasaratha's weathered voice carried easily across the heads of lakhs of his citizens, all of whom had been waiting eagerly to hear their king speak. Even those well past drunk on bhaang or charas managed to settle down sufficiently to listen. Perhaps Guru Vashishta had magically enhanced their ability to hear him over the sounds of the river and the chirring of hummingbirds in the thicket downstream. Whatever the reason, the maharaja's voice was clearly audible even to the farthest citizen sitting several hundred yards downstream.

Dispensing with the ritual benedictions quickly—one of the advantages of being a kshatriya-king was that you could leave it to the brahmins to take care of the religious and ritualistic formalities—he came to the point.

'Today we have among us a legendary and illustrious guest. Guru Vashishta has already extolled the story of his ascension from a bold warrior king to the exalted brahmanic stature he holds today. Brahmarishi Vishwamitra needs no further introduction. But what most of you may not yet know is that he brings us disturbing tidings.'

THIRTY

Dasaratha held up a hand to still the murmurs of anxiety that greeted his introductory remarks.

'There is no reason to be alarmed. Even as you enjoy your Holi feast, the war council of the Arya nations is preparing to convene, and I promise you we will find ways to deal with and crush this possible threat without delay. Rest assured that your liege will seek the quickest and least violent solution to the problem. You will be kept informed of further developments as they happen.'

He paused, feeling sweat pop out on his upper lip as the sun rose higher in the spring sky.

'But there is another matter that is more pressing right now. The brahmarishi has come to me with the traditional demand for guru-dakshina. As you know, it is the sworn duty of any kshatriya to immediately and unhesitantly grant the guru-dakshina without question. The Aryaputra Suryavansha Ikshvaku kshatriya line has filled the chronicles of Bharat-varsha with such legendary tales of generosity and munificence. And yet, the brahmarishi's demand is so unusual that it behoves me to share it with you, my people. For his request is nothing more nor less than that I grant him the life of my son Rama!'

The silence that followed these words was so complete that it seemed for a moment that even the birds had stopped chirring, the river stopped gurgling, the grass stopped rustling in the breeze.

'I shall explain. The brahmarishi is performing a yagna at his ashram in the Southwoods. It is part of our greater attempt to protect ourself from the Asura menace. It is imperative that his yagna is performed successfully and according to vedic rites. But his ashram is threatened by rakshasas.'

An uneasy murmur rose from the crowd.

'Were these ordinary pooja-violaters, common outlaws or outcasts, I would not think twice. My son Rama is the pride of our race, a champion in every sport he lays a hand to, a master of weaponry and vedic knowledge, a superb specimen of Arya manhood. But the rakshasas the brahmarishi is plagued by are no ordinary Asuras. They are front-soldiers dispatched by the wretched Lord of Lanka himself, sent to the Southwoods for the express purpose of rooting out the brahmins and rishis. The Asuras have controlled those dark, evil forests for generations and now they fear that our rishis and maharishis will purify those unexplored regions and make them hospitable for civilised Aryas.

'Three of these rakshasas, dispatched by the rakshas king Ravana himself, and backed by untold numbers of accomplices, are breeding in the Bhayanak-van. They make impossible the completion of the brahmarishi's yagna, or any attempt to purify the woods. They are said to be desperate, vile beasts, capable of doing anything to ensure that the brahmarishi's yagna is not completed successfully. Against these deadly creatures, the brahmarishi wishes me to send my son Prince Rama, to stave them off while he and his purohits perform the sacred yagna before the sacred full moon of Holi Purnima waxes to awamas. This is the guru-dakshina he desires.'

Maharaja Dasaratha paused to take the measure of his listeners. The crowd was enraptured by his announcement. Even the royal family on the podium exchanged wary glances, although their anxiety was related more to what came next than the announcement itself.

'It is at the wise suggestion of our esteemed Guru Vashishta that I place this matter before you, beloved Ayodhya. For before I even knew of the brahmarishi's arrival or any of the other happenings in the Southwoods, I had arrived at the decision to declare before you all this morning my intention to crown my eldest heir, Prince Rama Chandra, the liege-heir of our kingdom.'

This statement was greeted by an uproar. People leaped to their feet, yelling, shouting and cheering. The pandemonium that broke out resembled the response to the outcome of a decisive battle in a hundred-year war. The air, so silent an instant earlier, was filled with the sound of a million throats crying out with joy. The birds in the thicket screeched, echoing the thrilled cries of the women and girls in the audience—in the devdasi group, Sreelata and Nandini were hopping up and down like mad rabbits—and a shower of butterflies descended from the sky to flit around the royal entourage like a fistful of rang flung by the devas from above. First Queen Kausalya's face creased in a smile of relief and pleasure. It was one thing to know that Rama was popular; quite another to witness this enormous display of support and joy, and these auspicious omens. Third Queen Sumitra leaned across and took Kausalya's hand, squeezing it warmly for a moment. Similar expressions of pleasure or approval were reflected on the faces of every member of the royal household present there, as well as those of the noble houses, whose young girls of marriageable age looked in the direction of the four princes like peacocks preening lustfully under a monsoon cloud. Even Mantri Jabali's normally pinched, sallow face softened for a moment in a quick, impatient smile of approval, before lapsing into deep contemplation of some new Platonic moral conundrum.

The only face that didn't resemble all others was that of Second Queen Kaikeyi. She seemed frozen in a posture of shock and rage so intense that a crow might have been tempted to peck at her face in hopes of getting a chip or two of bitterwood for his nest. Behind her, the hunchbacked Manthara, seated within her lady's palanquin, contorted her face in rage and frustration, her hands clenching into curled fists as twisted as the gnarled roots of the banyan tree that spread its ancient limbs over the royal entourage. The other wet nurses, Susama-daiimaa and Ahilya-daiimaa, were the only ones who heard the muffled grunts of anger that drifted out from the dollee, and shifted away nervously. They knew and feared Manthara-daiimaa's foul moods well enough to know when to keep their distance. It was obvious that the news of Rama's ascension hadn't been well received by the second queen or her aide.

Bharat, Lakshman and Shatrugan were all happily hugging their brother and slapping him on the back. It would have been obvious to even a casual observer— the Greek envoy perhaps, seated among the foreign delegates—that the young princes were not divided in their response as their mothers were. They looked like a team of archers who had just won first prize in the annual tourney thanks largely to the efforts of their best player. Even the small jabs and punches they showered on Rama were more affectionate than envious.

Maharaja Dasaratha held up a hand to ask for silence. It took a moment to be given, but finally the crowd managed to curb its exhilaration and heed his next words.

'Rama is to be crowned prince-heir on the tenth day of the new moon of Chaitra, the sixteenth anniversary of his birth. I promise you, friends, that before you have entirely cast off the hangover of today's Holi feast and celebration, you will be fasting to prepare for a jubilee unparalleled in the history of our kingdom. Mark the day well in your horoscopes; it is the day a new star will rise in the Suryavansha universe.'

A kshatriya girl, barely nine years of age and already marked with the scars and signs of a Mithila bowman, stood to ask the king if there would be pedas on that day.

The roar of laughter that greeted this question was deafening. Pedas were the simplest, most common sweetmeat, available daily in the mithaigalli of any part of the city for a few paisa a kilo. Asking the king about pedas at his son's coronation feast was akin to asking a wedding host if drinking water would be available at the banquet.

Dasaratha received the naïve question with good humour, smiling indulgently and taking a moment to respond politely to the solemn-faced young apprentice.

'Yes, indeed, young bowmaster,' he replied indulgently. 'There will be as many pedas as you can eat for a month! And much, much else besides!'

He allowed the brief humorous respite to roll its course, then continued in a more formal tone.

'But you will recall that I began by telling you about my samasya. On the one hand, I am a father and a king, eager to see my eldest son appointed to the throne in my stead. After all, I will not live for ever, despite the heartfelt wishes of you, my friends. On the other hand, I am bound by the honour of the Ikshvaku clan and the Suryavansha dynasty, by the tradition and heritage of the Arya forefathers who seeded this mighty nation before venturing northwards to foreign lands where they settled the Germanic wildwoods. I am compelled by the repositories of our knowledge—the shastras and vedas that guide us in all we do—and finally, by the code of the kshatriya that asserts the duty of every warrior, king or common foot-soldier to grant his guru's wish for guru-dakshina without question or hesitation. Above all, I am governed by dharma.'

At the last word, even the few sporadic whispered discussions faded away to utter silence. Once again, Ayodhya listened raptly.

'Dharma demands that I fulfil the seer-mage's wish and send my son Rama Chandra, now officially your crown-prince-in-waiting, into the Southwoods to face and combat God knows what danger. A father's heart cries out that I send my mighty army in his place, that I select my bravest warriors, that I go myself if need be, but at all costs keep my precious heir from this dire mission. But dharma,' a heavy sigh, echoing the weight of age, long illness, and the burden of kingship that rested on his tired shoulders, 'dharma is unrelenting and uncompromising. Dharma demands that I comply with the brahmarishi's demand without question or doubt, hesitation or negotiation.'

Dasaratha glanced at the two seers, standing apart from the royal entourage. Brahmarishi Vishwamitra had remained motionless through this long speech, his staff held upright in his right hand, his impassive weathered face and flowing beard revealing no hint of his inner thoughts or responses. Guru Vashishta looked just as stoic, although there was an air of sadness and empathy that could be sensed rather than seen on his lined face as he listened to the impassioned words of his old friend and shishya, Dasaratha. After all, the greatest living seer in the world had chosen to grant his spiritual guidance exclusively to the Suryavansha dynasty of the Ikshvaku clan a thousand years ago, and in a thousand years even the most austere penitent will start to feel some measure of attachment. He listened to Dasaratha's words attentively, tacitly indicating his approval of the maharaja's announcement without needing to say a single word.

Maharaja Dasaratha continued: 'I was greatly troubled by the brahmarishi's request, I admit this freely. What father would not be? Yet dharma demanded I obey. The quandary might have gone unresolved even now, except that Guru Vashishta, the venerable and infinitely wise mentor of my line, offered a brilliantly simple suggestion. It is on his advice that I do what I do now.'

Maharaja Dasaratha turned in his place, addressing his next words to Brahmarishi Vishwamitra directly.

'Pranaam, mahadev, you whose penance exalted our entire race and inspired us all. You whose devotion won the admiration of mighty Brahma himself, who saw fit to grant you the mastery of brahman, the force that created, sustains and nourishes the universe. I bow before you, great one.'

Dasaratha matched his words with actions, bending his head in a saprem namaskar. Straightening up with folded hands, he continued:

'My answer to your request for guru-dakshina is this, great one. You ask for Prince Rama. I say, Prince Rama is not mine to give. He belongs to Ayodhya. To every one of us assembled here today. Because of his seniority and birth, he is the natural and true heir to the throne of Ayodhya. Rama does not belong to me alone, nor to his mother or family. He belongs to the people whom he is birth-sworn to serve all his natural life. Dharma itself demands that a member of the ruling dynasty places his people's needs before his own. So even Rama himself cannot decide his actions purely for his own selfish benefit. He must act in the best interests of the people he serves. You ask me for the guru-dakshina of my son

242

Rama. But I do not have first right over Rama. Ayodhya does. If you wish to have the services of Prince Rama, you must ask those whom he truly belongs to. Ask Ayodhya.'

And Maharaja Dasaratha gestured with both hands outflung to encompass the vast crowd seated on the banks of the Sarayu, and the great city around them.

THIRTY-ONE

'Ayodhya!'

The voice of Brahmarishi Vishwamitra sliced through the pandemonium and uproar that had raged unabated for the past several minutes. If Maharaja Dasaratha's announcement had had the effect of a blazing mashaal tossed into a field of dry straw then the legendary seer-mage's single spoken word was a waterfall of icy water dousing the inferno. The crowd subdued itself with a great effort, remembered tales of the wrathful temper of seers impelling them to control their dismayed anxiety for the moment.

The brahmarishi gestured at Maharaja Dasaratha, who had seated himself on the palanquin throne once again and was draining a goblet of wine beneath the disapproving eyes of the royal vaids. 'Your maharaja is wise indeed and greatly versed in dharma. He speaks truly. Prince Rama Chandra belongs to you, the people he was born to serve. And it is you who must decide whether or not my demand for guru-dakshina should be fulfilled. But before you do so, you must know that he will not be risking his life for the successful fulfilment of my yagna alone. This mission that he will be called on to execute is for the greater good of all humankind at large, including Ayodhya.'

The seer-mage raised his towering staff over his head. 'But I am no statesman or liege. My meaning will be best conveyed by giving you a glimpse of what might unfold lest my words go unheeded. The images I am about to show you will speak for themselves. I give you, the invasion of Ayodhya.'

At the words, Rama started. Lakshman, standing beside his brother, noticed a change come over him. Rama stared transfixed at the brahmarishi, a haunted, desolate look on his face. It was as if his brooding wariness of this morning had been in anticipation of this very thing.

As the crowd muttered and shifted uneasily, Vishwamitra chanted aloud a mantra too arcane and complex for any brahmin to decipher. Dark thunderclouds appeared in the sky above, converging as suddenly as crows on a fallen fledgling. The day turned from bright morning to dusky twilight in the space of an eye-blink. The air grew thick and heavy, like the air during an electric thunderstorm. Lakshman's skin tingled with a peculiar stinging sensation, like the time he had brushed against poisonleaf as a small boy. From the way the mantris nearby were rubbing their arms and necks, he guessed everyone felt the same way. The scent of damp rotting earth filled his nostrils, clogging his nasal passages.

As Vishwamitra reached the end of his incantation, lightning exploded in the skies, accompanied immediately by the crashing of thunder so deafening that people cringed and cried out, covering their heads in fear. Children had begun to bawl across the field, dogs howled, elephants trumpeted in alarm and stomped their feet, camels rolled their eyes and foamed at the mouth, monkeys chittered madly and leaped from tree to tree in the thicket downstream. The easterners in the crowd—visitors from Banglar, and the other far-flung areas of the kingdom— looked around in stark terror, fearing one of the awful

245

natural calamities that plagued that part of India; a typhoon perhaps, or a tidal wave, even though Ayodhya was hundreds of yojanas away from any ocean.

Lakshman was startled by the sound of an agonised groan. He saw Rama drop to his knees like a man who had been clubbed on the back of the head, eyes tight shut, teeth clenched, hands bunched into fists, bending over until his forehead touched the swaying tips of the grass.

'Bhai?' Lakshman bent down beside Rama. He touched Rama's shoulder and was shocked to find it fever-hot and clammy with sweat. 'What's wrong? Are you—'

Rama's eyes opened wide, rolling up to the skies. Lakshman reared back in fright. A cry exploded from deep within Rama's belly, less a human scream than the anguished howl of some primitive animal. The cry was lost in the crashing of thunder, but Lakshman was too shaken by what he had seen in Rama's eyes to realise that his brother's startling behaviour was being mirrored in the ranks of the PFs and other kshatriya warriors throughout the field. Yet even these anguished howls went unnoticed in the mêlée of terrified panic that had erupted. In moments, a happy celebration had turned into a nightmare.

And above the chaos, the brahmarishi's voice rang out, reverberating amid the echoes of thunder that rolled down from the boiling ocean of clouds.

Vishwamitra reached the end of his second mantra, and as abruptly as the chaos had begun, it ended.

Every man, woman, child and animal in Ayodhya froze.

One moment they were a mob filled with fear and panic, on the verge of running amok and causing needless harm to one another and themselves, terrified by the nightmare illusions perpetuated by the seer's sorcery. The next they were still as statues, frozen in the attitudes in which they had been at the instant the mantra took effect.

Lakshman bending over to help Rama. Rama on his knees, fists raised to the sky, mouth open in a howl of anguish, eyes staring at some as yet unseen horror. Bharat and Shatrugan, standing together, one looking east, the other west, hands on their bows, ready to fight as always.

Brahmins frozen in the act of bending to kiss the ground in admiration and awe of Vishwamitra's mastery of brahman. Kshatriyas with faces contorted in fear and disgust at the sorcery unfolding around them. (Warriors always abhorred magic, Guru Vashishta had taught the young princes, because you cannot fight what you cannot understand. That was why it was so important for a kshatriya to learn much more than mere warcraft.) Vaisyas, sudras, ordinary citizens, mothers and babes in arms, aged couples leaning on the strong young shoulders of their grown offspring, large extended families of as many as a hundred members accustomed to living beneath a single roof, now joining hands in a human chain, taking comfort from the presence of their parivar at this terrifying moment, devdasis and purohits, mochees and dhobis, sutaars and sitar players, kavees and carvers, archers and fletchers, blacksmiths and forgers, masons and philosophers, architects and money-lenders, halwais and hawaldars . . . all stood, sat or lay frozen in place, protected now from riot or panic-driven accidents by the seer-mage's magic, able to do nothing but watch as the brahmarishi's enormous sound-and-light show unfolded before them.

First came the darkness. Pitch-black as a crow's feather. As a lock of Rama's hair. With the darkness, a complete absence of sound, more terrible than any normal human silence.

Then, with the mellifluous artistry of a stage musician producing a taal for a Sanskrit drama—an epic tragedy perhaps, the doomed love story of Dushyanta and Sakuntala or the blood-drenched romance of Vasavadatta, or some

247

older, more arcane and pagan tale of blood and terror and love gone wrong—the wind began to keen. It was a nerve-racking sound, like the noise of a stone being scraped across glass very hard and slowly. Yet it had its own arcane rhythm, as though the invisible stage musician was pounding his tabla to a frenzied climax.

And then, rising above the intolerable keening of the wind, a strange, unnatural sound like nothing heard before by any of the citizens gathered on the riverbank. Only the warriors and veterans present understood what this new sound meant. And it was good that they were frozen immobile, or else they would have rushed to arms.

It was the sound of an invading army.

Like an enraged wild boar breaking free of a thorn bush, the Asura army emerged from the Southwoods.

They crawled, ran, leaped, flew, rode, slithered and seeped out of the black forest, exploding on to the south bank of the Sarayu like a plague.

Their numbers were beyond counting. An army of ants would not have been more numerous. Vishwamitra's earlier estimates, given in the sabha hall, were modest if anything. There were enough creatures of the netherworld assembling on the far bank to turn the earth black for a dozen yojanas in every direction, an area of a hundred square western miles. Even if viewed from Chand, the earth's moon, the Asura army's progress would be visible, like a seething carpet creeping amoeba-like across the land, a gigantic primordial force that consumed everything in its path.

For a moment the Asuras stood on the south bank and viewed the great prize they had come so far in search of: Ayodhya the Unconquerable. Rakshasas, Danavs, Daityas, Pisacas, Yaksas, and every crossbreed thereof feasted their alien eyes on the goal that had eluded every invading army for a millennium.

248

And then, with one bone-rattling, blood-boiling cry, they charged down the hill.

And the rape of Ayodhya began.

THIRTY-TWO

Rama recovered the use of his limbs with an exhalation of breath that threatened to drain him of life itself. He sucked in fresh air as needily as a disoriented infant taking its first independent breath. The cool winter-spring air was as blessed as a mother's touch. The warmth of the sun on his bare shoulders and face was a benediction by a kindly god. Across the field, lakhs of Ayodhyans were recovering too. All kept glancing up and around to make sure the sorcery was truly over and they were back in the real, normal world once more. Babies and immature children had been shielded from the experience, and now they blinked and gaped dumbly, as if woken from a brief nap. The smell of wet grass and damp earth remained like a pall over all.

After giving his audience time to recover and reassure itself that the nightmare show was really over, Vishwamitra spoke again, his pervasive voice rolling out across the field, commanding rapt attention. He was the puppet-master, they were his puppets as well as his audience. Never before had such a display of brahman sorcery ever been witnessed or heard of by any of those present. Rishis and self-styled seers were mouthing mantras of praise for the brahmarishi, praying that some vestige of his incomprehensible power might rub off on them. Power alms for the powerless. The kshatriyas, especially those

250

warriors who had been stricken to their core the way Rama had—if not as intensely, for none had felt quite what he had felt—looked around with haunted expressions, unable to believe that those terrible sights of death and destruction had been only an illusion. The seer's magic had not spared the viewers the horrific details, but his mantra did guard their minds from the total breakdown that could afflict anyone confronted by such horrors. Sudras and vaisyas, commoners and soldiers, nobility and their servants, all bore the same shocked and stunned expressions as they realised the implications of what they had just seen. Even Maharaja Dasaratha, rubbing his own bleary eyes and silently cursing seers and their sorcery, was shaken out of his complacency. In that moment, he realised as he looked around at his bewildered people, Ayodhya was totally united, all caste, class and other petty differences forgotten as they turned their eyes up to stare in hushed awe at the seer-mage.

Vishwamitra's voice was a calming balm.

'Fear not, Ayodhya. This was but an illusion. A vision of what might be. One possible future that lies in store for you. If the Dark Lord of Lanka has his way, then this vision will become reality within the year, just before winter falls, when Ayodhya is most vulnerable to siege. He has prepared for this day for years, even centuries, for he whom the gods named Ravana is no ordinary rakshas, as you know. He is destined to become ruler of the three worlds one day.'

He cut off the startled protests with an upraised hand.

'Hold steady, brave Ayodhya. The wisdom of the devas is infinite. For every Ravana they allow to seep into creation like a pus-boil on a diseased animal, they also create an antidote. This is why we proud inhabitants of the land of the Aryas have been blessed with an infinite number of avatars of the One True God. The progeny of the

251

devas are limitless in number and power. Ravana can and must be defeated. As your noble maharaja has said, he and your kingdom's rulers will find a way to combat the Asura menace before it reaches the banks of the Sarayu and threatens the Arya nations. This too has been prophesied.'

A ripple of relief passed across the crowd. Vishwamitra continued without pause.

'But before we can even address that issue of Ravana, we must first show him that he has met a foe more formidable than any he has ever fought before. Today, he issued a challenge to your honour. He sent one of his most trusted aides, his own uncle no less, into the heart of this great city. His mission, it can only be surmised, was to wreak havoc and slaughter in the royal family.'

Angry murmurs now. Feelings ran strong about the morning's intrusion. Feelings strengthened now by the sorcerous vision.

'This was no mere intrusion. It was a test and a challenge. Ravana wishes to know if we are prepared to withstand him. Or to simply roll over like a meek pup and beg his mercy. What do you think, Ayodhya? What would be your response to the Lord of Lanka? Fright or fight?'

The answer boomed like thunder across the assembled hordes. 'FIGHT!'

The seer-mage nodded, pleased. 'I thought no less. And yet it is important to give Ravana this answer in a manner that befits his asking of the question. To gather up an army and march to Lanka would be an overreaction. Perhaps that is even what he hopes for, because then he would have the upper hand, as he had before during the Last Asura War. No, that would be too strong and premature a response. He sent a single champion into our midst. We must do the same.'

252

There was silence now as everyone contemplated his meaning. A single champion? Into the midst of Lanka? Was that what the brahmarishi meant?

'Not into Lanka,' he said, as if reading their collective consciousness as easily as chalk letters on a child's slate. 'Into the Southwoods, the dread Bhayanak-van, which he has created and maintained as a barrier between the Arya nations and the great southern sub-continent. For millennia he has curbed the progress of the Aryas at this geographical barrier, by creating an environment so hostile and threatening to mortals that even the greatest warriors of lore have rarely returned alive from its depths.'

He paused, scanning their silent upturned faces. 'You wonder, then, if the Bhayanak-van is so dangerous, how would our champion survive it? But this is precisely my point. If one of our kshatriyas can enter the Bhayanak-van and wreak damage on the ranks of Ravana's vile hordes, then we will have sent a powerful message to the Lord of Lanka. We will have shown him that not only do we not fear him, we are stronger than he believes. Behold, we shall say, just one of our kshatriyas, a young and untried warrior at that, can inflict such destruction upon your numbers. Imagine, then, you vile creature of hell, what an entire army of Arya kshatriyas could do.'

The crowd began to nod, whispering, understanding his point at last. Several began to break out into exclamations of agreement and support. Lakshman observed that these were mainly kshatriyas rather than brahmins. He was impressing even the warriors with his war strategy, the old seer. After all, he was once a great warrior-king.

'Now, you ask, who then shall we send? Which young, untested warrior do I speak of? Who can undertake this deadly mission and accomplish it successfully? I ask you in turn, Ayodhya, if Ravana could risk his own blood-uncle, can we do any less? You must send no less than your greatest son of all. Your prince and just titled prince-heir. Rama Chandra.'

The silence was deafening. Lakshman could hear the wind whispering through the ranks of Ayodhyans for hundreds of yards around. He could hear the distant calling of cuckoos and parrots in the mango grove downriver. He could smell the odour of food roasting in the pavilions, waiting for the feast to begin.

Then a flurry of arguments and queries broke out. Vishwamitra answered each one painstakingly but briefly, with devastating logic and unshakeable conviction.

Senapati Maheshwari asked why it would not be better to send a full akshohini contingent into the Southwoods rather than a single warrior. That would be less than an army, yet more capable of victory than a single kshatriya.

Vishwamitra replied patiently:

'Maharaja Dasaratha has already offered me his entire army, his greatest warriors, his most accomplished champions. But I say nay to all these. What will Ravana think if we send a whole army to fight his small force of berserkers? Or even our best champions? The rakshasas of Bhayanak-van are dangerous, true, but Ravana has other champions far greater and deadlier. His own eldest son is not named Indrajit without reason: the boy earned the title when he defeated mighty Indra, king of the devas, during the Asura invasion of Indraprastha, the capital city of the gods. Nay, only a single warrior can send the message we wish to give Ravana.'

Mantri Ashok asked reasonably how a single warrior could be expected to face an entire forest filled with demoniac Asuras.

Vishwamitra nodded sagely. 'Young Rama will not be alone. I will be beside him every step of the way. I shall prepare him en route to face the perils ahead. I shall gift him the most potent maha-mantras ever created for martial combat. When he enters the Bhayanak-van, he will be alone, true, but he will have the power of a thousand kshatriya veterans. When we have cleared the Bhayanak-van of Ravana's vile filth, the rajkumar and I shall proceed to my ashram, where he shall defend my purohits and myself as we conduct the yagna of which I spoke earlier. Thereby we shall sanctify that forbidden land and make it hospitable at long last for Arya habitation. Bear in mind, people, I do not ask you this favour idly. I know well of what I speak. It is a seemingly impossible task, I admit. Yet sometimes, a single man can do what vast nations cannot.'

Finally, the arguments wound down, and the brahmarishi reached his conclusion.

'And so I ask you, as is my right according to the code of the kshatriyas and brahmins: give me Prince Rama Chandra as my guru-dakshina, and I will give you a champion. Give me your crown-heir for this mission, and I will help strike an important first blow in this new war against the Asuras. Give me this boy-warrior to wield as a weapon against the berserkers who threaten my yagna, and I will prove to you as well as to Ravana that under the guidance and tutelage of a brahmarishi such as myself, even a single inexperienced kshatriya can defeat a horde of rakshasas. Grant me this guru-dakshina, for Ayodhya's future, and humankind's sake.'

And the brahmarishi joined his palms together and bowed his head before the people, waiting for their reply.

It was not long in coming.

Later, there would be much debate about the finer points of the matter. People would ask: 'But can a young stripling truly face a force of berserker rakshasas?' And others would answer indignantly: 'Under the tutelage of Brahmarishi Vishwamitra, even a carpenter could face them.' And they would add, sniffing: 'Not just any young stripling, mind. It's Prince Rama he speaks of.'

A dhobi seated with his wife and six children, his head covered in the white roughcloth turban of his class, heard his wife say anxiously from beneath her sari's head-cover, 'God forbid that the prince should come to any harm. But even if he were to die fighting the demons, it would be a noble sacrifice for a good cause.'

The dhobi turned and glared at his wife, reflexively raising his palm, withered and creased by years of washing, and threatened her with a slap that would rock her head. But slowly, he lowered his hand, acknowledging the truth of what she said, then rose and spoke, expressing what all the gathered assemblage had only been able to think nervously until now.

'If a son of Ayodhya must go, better it should be our proudest son. If Maharaja Dasaratha agrees to send his own scion, then no father in the Arya nations will hesitate to send his own heirs into battle against the Asuras.'

As the dhobi sat down, Lakshman glanced at his father. Dasaratha's face was drained of all colour. The dhobi's simple logic was unassailable. If the maharaja refused the seer now, every parent would have a ready excuse to refuse to draft his children into the coming war.

'Yatha raja tatha praja.'

The dhobi was the first to take up the chant. In moments, the entire crowd was thundering the words.

'Yatha raja tatha praja, yatha raja tatha praja, yatha raja tatha praja!'

Dasaratha came to his feet, unable to ignore the call of his own people. The people whom he was sworn to rule and govern, by the second law of Manu and by his own conscience.

The people's answer was crystal clear.

As does the king, so shall the people.

Rama must go.

256

THIRTY-THREE

On Guru Vashishta's advice, they rode discreetly to the palace, using simple chariots rather than the elaborate royal entourage. It was the guru who suggested they do their leave-taking at the rear gate of the palace rather than the parade grounds. After that, the brahmarishi and the rajkumar could take the old road out of the city, thereby bypassing the crowds of exuberant Holi revellers. It was not that they wished to avoid the people, but if they took their leave of all of Ayodhya, it would be days before they left the city. Kausalya would have liked to see Rama to the first gate, but the guru as well as Sumantra advised against it—security was still a concern. Only after they reached the palace and were behind barred gates did Captain Drishti Kumar withdraw his men to a discreet distance to allow the royal family space for a private moment.

Kaikeyi was conspicuous by her absence, as was Manthara: Bharat had seen both the second queen and her aide leave the parade abruptly after the brahmarishi's amazing demonstration, hurrying angrily back to the palace. They were probably within the Second Queen's Palace even now, seething with anger over the coronation announcement.

But Bharat was there, as were Shatrugan and Sumitra-maa. The third queen was already in tears, less in control of her emotions than the more stoic Kausalya, even though it was Kausalya's son who was leaving.

Everyone stood around for a moment, uncomfortable and nervous, except for the two seers, who remained as impassive as ever.

Lakshman was the first to end the awkward pause.

'Father,' he said, kneeling before Dasaratha. 'I beg your leave to go with my brother on his sacred mission.'

Dasaratha blanched.

'My son, how can you even ask such a thing of me? It is Rama's karma to go, I understand and accept that now, as I have accepted the will of the people and the desire of the great brahmarishi. But do not ask me to sacrifice another son to this terrible task! It is perilous enough for one kshatriya, yet with the blessings of the devas, I pray that he shall return victorious. But with two of you, the chances of mortal harm increase twofold. I cannot brook such a thought. Please, Lakshman, don't ask this of me.'

Lakshman looked up at his father with an expression filled with all the sorrow and longing of youth.

'Father, I have never asked you for anything. But you know that from the time I could stand, I stood beside Rama. When he would not eat, I starved. When he laughed, I was happy. We have never been separated for a moment, by any force. Do not separate us now.'

Dasaratha's face was a mask of conflicting emotions. He passed a hand wearily across his brow, trying to find a way to convince his son.

Rama spoke quietly. 'Father, forgive me for speaking out of turn. But I wish to say something to Lakshman. My brother, stay. The shadow of the Asura threat hangs over Ayodhya still. Your bow will be needed here should any more intruders come. You saw the brahmarishi's warning of what might come to pass.'

Lakshman turned his head. 'But Rama, you heard him yourself. The reason he wishes to take you into the Bhayanak-van is to prevent that invasion from taking place! By going with you, I will help prevent it more effectively than staying here. Besides, one bow more or less in Ayodhya will not matter much. While in the forest, it would double the chances of success.'

Dasaratha looked at the brahmarishi in despair. 'Mahadev, what is your esteemed opinion on this matter?'

Vishwamitra leaned on his staff. 'Maharaj, I have no opinion in this matter. This is a father's and a mother's decision to make, not a guru's. If Rajkumar Lakshman wishes to accompany his brother, so be it. If he stays, that is acceptable to me as well.'

He moved away after saying these words, distancing himself from the family debate. Dasaratha looked around, searching for someone to aid him in his argument against Lakshman. His eyes flicked across Kausalya, who wisely remained silent, and were passing on to Guru Vashishta when Sumitra-maa spoke, struggling through her tears.

'Send Lakshman with Rama.'

Everyone turned to stare in surprise at the third queen. Sumitra's delicate small features were smeared with damp kajal and a streak of sindhoor. She stepped forward, wiping her face with the pallo of her sari. 'He speaks the truth. He and Rama share a bond that is beyond this mortal plane. If he were to stay back, he would pine and waste away. In the woods, at least they will look out for each other.'

'Sumitra?' Dasaratha replied, astonished. 'Do you know what you're saying? You would risk the life of your own son even when not required? Rama is honour-bound to go now. Lakshman does not have to take this great risk. Think before you speak your mind, my gentle queen!'

'I'm saying what's right,' she said with surprising determination. 'Do you think it doesn't hurt me to say it?' She held the pallo to the corner of her mouth, her eyes misting over again. 'It's like pulling a piece of my heart from my breast. But then I say, if I can endure the pain of sending Rama, then I can endure the pain of sending Lakshman as well. That way, double the pain will halve the risk at least.' She looked around defiantly, challenging anyone to prove her wrong. 'I cannot speak for Bharat, but I would send Shatrugan as well. Because—'

Both Bharat and Shatrugan stepped forward, speaking hotly. 'Father, send us too!'

Dasaratha waved them to silence, gesturing to Sumitra to go on.

'Because,' she went on, 'Rama is a son of my heart if not of my body. To lose him would be as unbearable as to lose my own birth-sons. So I say, if Lakshman's going gives him satisfaction, if the presence of one more bow improves the chances of success, then why should I not send my son as well?'

All eyes watched Dasaratha, waiting for his verdict. He looked at Sumitra's tearful, defiant face, at Lakshman's desperate pleading eyes, and his tired shoulders slumped. He released a great sigh. 'Very well, then. So be it. Lakshman shall go with Rama.'

Both Bharat and Shatrugan began to protest.

Dasaratha waved them wearily into silence again. They quietened instantly. 'But none other than Lakshman. Leave me at least half my sons in this time of crisis!' He seemed to address the plea to some invisible deva rather than to anyone present.

Rama spoke to his brothers. 'Bharat, Shatrugan. Heed Father's words. He is ailing. If for any reason imaginable we should fail in our mission, Ayodhya will need your axe and your mace. Stay and defend our mothers and our city.'

Bharat and Shatrugan bowed their heads reluctantly, agreeing. Lakshman rose and stood beside Rama.

Guru Vashishta cleared his throat. 'You must make haste. The brahmarishi desires to reach Ananga-ashrama before sunfall. You have a great walk ahead.'

The rajkumars glanced at each other, then, moving as one, went forward and bowed before their guru together. They touched his feet in the ritual plea for blessings.

'Guruji, ashirwaad dijiye.'

The guru laid his hands on both their heads gently. 'Ayushmaanbhav, Ayodhya ke rajkumaron. Hum tumhari safalta ke liya prarthana karenge.' *Live long, princes of Ayodhya. We shall pray for your success.*

Next they turned to the maharaja. Dasaratha's eyes were red and swollen even though he hadn't shed a tear. His face was blotchy and flushed with strain. Rama's heart twinged as he raised himself after touching his father's feet. 'Father, have faith in us. We shall bring you triumph.'

'I expect nothing less, my sons.' Dasaratha's voice was hoarse and cracked. Suddenly, as Rama and Lakshman started to turn away, he lurched forward and put his arms around them both, enfolding and crushing them in a massive bear-hug. 'Oh, my sons, my sons. What have I done? Can I never do right by you? What have I done to deserve this cursed karma?'

Rama hugged and kissed his father gently. The maharaja's greying stubble was rough against his smooth, hairless cheek. 'You have always done right by us, Father. It's not your karma but our dharma that leads us where we go.'

Dasaratha looked at his son, fat opaque tears spilling from his anguished eyes. 'So young and yet so wise. If I have ever done anything to deserve a boon from the devas, I pray for your safe return. Both of you.' He clutched their arms one last time, his meaty fists twice the size of their slender shoulders, and released them, turning away with a choked cry.

They went next to Kausalya-maa. She had tears in her eyes when they bent to take her ashirwaad, and made no attempt to conceal them, but her voice was steady and clear. 'Heed the words of your new guru carefully and obediently. Care for one another as well as for yourselves. Guard each other's backs night and day. Do as your gurus have taught you and as your duty demands. Fulfil your dharma.'

The boys took their leave of Sumitra-maa, Bharat and Shatrugan next and turned to Guru Vashishta once more. He nodded, acknowledging the momentary disorientation that was visible on their faces. 'Be brave, young rajkumars. It is a great thing you go to do today. A noble undertaking. Your names shall be writ large in the chronicles of your dynasty and your line. Go now, with the grace of the devas. I shall use every power at my disposal to pray for your speedy and safe return.'

Vishwamitra tapped his staff on the ground, indicating to the captain that they were ready to leave. The brahmarishi looked back once at Maharaja Dasaratha and the rest of the royal family.

'I give you my word, Ayodhya-naresh. Either I shall return both your sons safely to you once my mission is accomplished; or I shall not return at all.'

Dasaratha felt a chill in his heart at the brahmarishi's words. *Not return at all?* Was the seer admitting there was some chance of failure? But of course he was, he chided himself. Even the most powerful of seers couldn't guarantee the future. What he meant was that he had pledged not just his honour but his life on ensuring their safe return. Either they would all return safely, or none would return.

Dasaratha couldn't deal with the implications of the latter possibility.

As the rear gates of the palace swung open, Drishti Kumar and his guards gave the departing trio a royal salute. Then, turning smartly, they began to shut the gates, following their security procedures without lapse. Bharat and Shatrugan ran forward, clutching at the bars of the gates and calling words of farewell and encouragement to their brothers.

Rama and Lakshman walked behind the seer, following the customary three paces to the rear of their new guru, without looking back once. A way had been cleared specially for their passing right through to the first gate, and the raj-marg was deserted as far as the eye could see, with soldiers standing alert at regular ten-metre intervals along the way.

The three travellers reached the end of the avenue and turned the bend, passing out of sight.

More Than Human

ONE

From a window in the Second Queen's Palace, Manthara and Kaikeyi watched the three figures walk down the avenue and disappear round a bend in the road.

The minute they were out of sight, Kaikeyi turned her tear-streaked eyes on Manthara.

'My son was to be crowned maharaja. My son, Bharat. Not Rama! Bharat!'

The daiimaa let the drapes fall back into place. She replied calmly: 'Before he can be crowned maharaja, he must be crowned prince-heir. And then he must wait for his father to resign the throne or die. That is the law of ascension.'

'I don't care about the law,' Kaikeyi shrieked. 'I want my son to be king! You said it would happen! You said his kundalee is that of a king, not a mere lord or thakur. You promised me he would become maharaja!'

'So I did,' Manthara replied levelly. Kaikeyi's shriek still echoed in the corridors. The palace was deserted. Everybody was at the parade grounds, celebrating the feast. The rest of the royal family would hardly care to enter these chambers. 'And so he will.'

Kaikeyi bent down and clutched Manthara's bony shoulders tight enough to hurt the daiimaa. 'Then why was Rama declared crown prince today? Answer that, you witch!'

Manthara hissed. A flash of greenish-yellow flame, like the tongue of some enormous lizard, snaked out from deep within her throat. The sorcerous fire shot out and struck Kaikeyi between the eyes, crackling at the impact. The second queen's eyes rolled up, astonished, and like a rag doll being tossed aside by a playground bully, she was flung back bodily across the chamber. She struck a chaupat on the way, knocking it over and sending crystal jal-bartans and greasy dishes from her afternoon snack crashing, and landed with a bone-jarring impact on the bolsters and well-padded mattresses of her own baithak-sthan. She lay there like a crumpled toy, breathing noisily through her open mouth, nostrils flared in shock, eyes wide and round.

Manthara crooked one finger and Kaikeyi sat up abruptly, her head lolling forward like a dog's wagging tail. She gasped, as startled by the involuntary movement as she had been by the flight across the room.

Manthara took three steps towards her, raising one long, gnarled finger in warning. 'Never lay a hand on me again, my queen. Next time your fall will not be cushioned.'

Kaikeyi rose slowly to her feet, checking her limbs. Her hands shook with fear and conflicting emotions. 'How . . . how . . . did you do that?'

Manthara shrugged. 'What difference does it make? I can do it. That's all that matters to you. Just remember, you snivelling, spoilt Arya she-whelp, you've grown much too old to slap and spank. And I don't have the patience I used to.'

Kaikeyi blinked, puzzled. What did the daiimaa mean? She had never had any patience to begin with. She realised belatedly that Manthara was being ironic. That was somehow even scarier than the sudden display of power. 'I'm . . . sorry . . . I touched you.' She stammered out the words.

Manthara ignored the apology. 'You mentioned Bharat's kundalee. Yes, his horoscope clearly says he will be maharaja. And he will be. All in good time.'

She paced the room thoughtfully. Kaikeyi watched her like a child watching a puppet prance across a kathputhli stage. 'But there is work to be done to make that come to pass.' She looked at Kaikeyi. 'Instead of playing with your over-muscled wrestlers in gloomy inns at night, you will have to do as I say. Time is short and every moment counts in this game.'

Game? What kind of game? Kaikeyi managed to hold her tongue, something that was almost as difficult for her as controlling her diet. She watched the daiimaa pace.

Finally, the hunchback paused, her eyes gleaming.

'Yes. That is exactly what she must do. Your genius knows no bounds, my lord.'

Kaikeyi looked around the chamber, wondering whom Manthara was addressing. Had Dasaratha come unexpectedly into her chambers? But there was nobody else here. She shivered suddenly. She had frequently called Manthara a witch, in her mind and behind the daiimaa's back. But that was only in the figurative sense. Now she began to realise that the hunchbacked crone's abilities did indeed lie in that forbidden realm of dark sorcery. What Manthara had just done to her, merely by crooking a finger, that had been the work of sorcery. And not brahman sorcery either. What other secrets had Manthara kept from her all these years? What else was the woman capable of?

Manthara turned her eyes to Kaikeyi. It was as if she knew every thought and emotion racing through Kaikeyi's confused brain. 'Don't pretend that you want Bharat's ascension for his sake. You haven't a selfless bone in your body, Kaikeyi. If you ever did have one, then I must have broken it years ago. No, all you care about is your own status as second queen. You fear that if Rama were to ascend the throne, Kausalya would cut you down to size quickly enough, taking revenge on you for warming Dasaratha's bed these many years. You fear the loss of your unlimited allowance, your river of silks and trinkets that the maharaja's generosity keeps in spate. You fear that with Dasaratha's passing, you will be relegated to the status of a widow, banished to some remote corner of the kingdom, there to spend the rest of your days in nameless ignominy. This is your true motivation in wanting Bharat to be crowned prince of Ayodhya.'

Kaikeyi stared up at Manthara wordlessly. She was speechless because Manthara had said everything there was to be said. These very fears kept Kaikeyi awake at night, these were the demons she sought to drown when she downed her endless goblets of wine and gorged like a feasting brahmin each morning, noon and sundown. Even so, hearing them spoken aloud brought home the selfish crudeness of her innermost concerns with the bracing impact of a blow to the face.

Manthara smiled grimly. 'Have no fear. It shall be as you desire. Your son shall be crowned prince-heir, to become maharaja on his father's passing. And you shall retain your status as the first queen in all but title for many a year to come. The keys to the kingdom's coffers shall be in your fleshy fists, and not even Kausalya will dare to question you on any account.'

Kaikeyi's eyes narrowed. 'You taunt and tease me, Manthara. I already apologised for laying hands on you. Don't humiliate me now. I'm a grown woman, not a girl any more.'

'Taunt you? Tease you?' Manthara's laughter was like the sound of a monkey gibbering. 'My poor fat Kaikeyi. I am only telling you what is written in *your* kundalee.

Don't you recall? I have told you these very things before, when I read your horoscope on your sixteenth naming day!'

Kaikeyi's mouth fell open. She *did* recall the daiimaa reading her kundalee when she was sixteen, and the hunchback had reeled off a list of wonderful things that would transpire in Kaikeyi's future. 'You mean . . . all the things you said . . . they will really come to pass?'

Manthara's mouth continued to smile, but her eyes hardened, the wrinkled skin around them tightening. 'Every word. You do wish them to come to pass, don't you, my little girl-whelp?'

Kaikeyi was so excited, she could only nod her head vigorously, unable to form any words.

Manthara bent her head forward and crooked her finger.

'Then come to me and let me tell you how you can help bring these things about.'

The maharaja's highway ran alongside the bank of the river Sarayu for a full yojana. Vishwamitra and the two princes walked the distance without speaking, the seer leading at a pace that soon had both boys sweating freely. The only sound was the clicking of their wooden sandals and the steady roar of the Sarayu.

It was late afternoon, perhaps two hours from sunset, yet the day seemed warmer than usual, a sign of the seasonal change and a good omen. Rama and Lakshman were still in their whites, each wearing a simple dhoti, with an ang-vastra draped loosely around their shoulders. Despite the bracing coolness of the air, their new duty as oathsworn kshatriyas required them to abjure all comforts. Vishwamitra had politely declined Dasaratha's offer of a chariot and a platoon of PFs to see them to Mithila Bridge. It was said the brahmarishi had not ridden a chariot or sat on a horse for over seventeen hundred years. Even Vashishta, despite his status as royal guru, walked the distance to and from his ashram every day, a distance of one and a half yojana each way. And Rishi Vamadeva, who perforce lived in the palace to supervise the small army of purohits the sunwood throne employed, slept on a mat of rushes and ate simple fare from an earthen bowl. As the saying went, 'The Greater the Seer, the Fewer His Needs.'

Nor could Rama and Lakshman be permitted to accept any of the comforts of their princely heritage. The moment they had sworn their oaths to the brahmarishi, they had given up all claim to their worldly titles, possessions and comforts. They were bound to follow Vishwamitra and do his bidding implicitly until he released them from their obligation to him. Such was the tradition of the guru-shishya contract.

As the city fell further behind, the sounds of revelry and games and the parade fading with every step, Rama felt a pinprick of wonder at the twist of fate that had put him upon this path. Not doubt or fear, no. Just a tiny little question mark curling inside his belly, its tip pricking his gut.

We knew what we were getting into when we accepted the sage as guru, Rama thought. *Or at least I knew.* He stole a quick glance at his brother, matching him pace for pace in perfect step. *But I should have known that Lakshman would want to follow me. I should have done something, pre-empted him somehow, made him stay back. It was my responsibility as his older brother.* A thread of sweat trickled down Lakshman's face. Rama reached out and dabbed at it with the end of his ang-vastra. Lakshman nodded. At that exact moment, a drop of sweat rolled down Rama's own forehead, stealing into his left eye. Lakshman tried to use his own ang-vastra to wipe it away but was too late. It stung mildly.

Rama blinked it away, grinning. Lakshman grinned back. They walked.

The sun passed behind a stray cloud shaped like a wineskin filled to bursting with buttermilk—a mental association that was probably the result of his unfed stomach—and when it reappeared, it seemed to have grown fiercer. Rama felt as if he was holding a blazing mashaal at arm's length. Sweat ran freely down their faces and bodies; their ang-vastras were soon soaked through. Winter certainly is through with us, he thought.

He glanced at the cool, welcoming white waters of the Sarayu. *A dip in the river would be heaven right now.* He caught Lakshman sneaking a glance leftwards too and knew he was wishing the same thing.

Sarayu's cool breath carried a fine mist redolent of the iron tang of glacial ice-melt. It was a scent of mountains and flower-vales; the scent of their ancestral homesteads. A drove of dragonflies as large as pigeons whirred over the water, travelling upstream. Deep within the shaded glade where Rama had sat only a few hours earlier, a pair of koyals called insistently.

I would love to sit with you awhile, my friends, but duty calls. Squirrels leaped along branches overhanging the river, racing deftly from tree to tree, leaving a row of swinging limbs behind them as they dashed downriver. The silver flanks of enormous mahseer and rawas gleamed in the river, silver and lean from the long hard winter. Soon they would grow fat and slow, fit for the cookfire.

I should have eaten some of Susama-daiimaa's naashta after all. A stag slurping water near the same rock where Rama had found the wounded doe cornered by the poachers looked up and stared at them fearlessly. He was a young black buck, also lean from the winter, but his fur was sleek and glossy. Soon it would be mating season and he would dash his proud horns against a brother buck to decide their mate; only one of them would survive the ritual. Fruitlessly Rama scanned the bank for a sign of the doe, hoping she had survived the arrow wound, although it didn't seem likely.

The sun fell steadily in the western sky as they walked on, and soon even the faraway sounds of conches blowing and elephants trumpeting faded behind them. The river's sound dimmed as the raj-marg rose steadily above its banks. They passed mango groves, orange orchards, apple groves, grape vineyards, and sugarcane patches rife with scorpion-birds that hovered above the high stalks, their carapaced bellies swollen with the sweet treacly juice. The welcome shadow of jackfruit trees shielded them from the slanting sun. Rama and Lakshman had sat beneath the shade of these very trees, eating their stomachs' fill of the chewy gum-like fruit, carrying the rest back to Susama-daiimaa, who cooked a delicious sweet-sour phanas curry in the Marathi style. Now they only looked wistfully up at the swollen ripe fruit, and walked on.

As the raj-marg rose steadily higher, the day seemed to grow even hotter despite the shade of the wayside trees: too hot for winter, too hot even for spring. *Hot on Holi day means monsoon's not far away*, the daiimaas always said. Rama licked his dry lips, missing the moist air of the Sarayu riverbank, the refreshing cool spray on his face, the delicate scents of the lotus and jasmine blooms that drifted downriver. Wiping the side of his face with the tip of his ang-vastra, he remembered suddenly that he hadn't even anointed himself with rang. He couldn't recall a Holi when he and Lakshman had failed to colour each other. Yet here they were, without even a dab of powder on their faces, clothes unmarked. Then he remembered the kumkum that his mother had

274

pressed on his forehead after her aarti; he did have colour on his face after all. Maa had seen to that.

A small pebble caught between his toes and he paused to remove it. Lakshman paused as well but Rama motioned him forward. As Lakshman walked on behind the sage, Rama saw that his brother's rig was arranged in such a way that the tip of his curved bow pointed east, the quiverful of arrows west; his head and feet already marked north and south. *He lit up the cardinal directions as he rode into battle on his flaming chariot.* Now, where was that from? Some old poem about one of Rama's ancestors, Surya probably, who gave the Suryavansha dynasty his name when he took the only daughter of tribal chieftain Ikshvaku the Settler. Rama stood and followed the others, catching up quickly, unaware that his own rig mirrored Lakshman's perfectly, their hair as black as crows' wings, their posture identical.

The sun was a little more than an hour from sunset when they reached Mithila Bridge.

One of only three such bridges spanning the Sarayu, Mithila Bridge was built at the highest point on both banks, an awe-inspiring seven hundred yards above the river. Far below its carved span, the Sarayu ran rough and fast over a half-mile of enormous grey boulders that had fallen in some avalanche a few thousand years ago. The river boiled and seethed as it roared over the boulders.

Precisely one and a half yojana or fourteen western miles from the outermost gate of Ayodhya, Mithila Bridge also marked the end of the royal protectorate. As they approached the bridge, Rama made out the forms of several men mounted on elephants, guarding both the north and south ends of the structure. Even the elephants were dwarfed by the enormous proportions of the bridge.

Hewn from the sturdy timber of a single massive shagun tree, which the Greeks called 'teak' after the Greek word *tekton*, for 'carpenter', the bridge was broad enough to allow not two but three royal wheelhouses to pass at a time, or seven elephants ambling abreast. Even at this considerable height, much of its span was obscured by a cloud of spray-mist from the river.

Vishwamitra stopped at the point where the raj-marg curved slowly to present good access to the bridge for wheelhouses and other large vehicles.

He turned to Rama and Lakshman. 'Do not reveal yourselves, rajkumars. There are enemy eyes everywhere, and it would be best if our mission goes unreported. Act the part of my acolytes and leave the talking to me.'

Without waiting for an answer, he gestured and spoke a brief mantra. Rama and Lakshman found themselves transformed into the spitting likeness of two shaven-pate chotti-sprouting brahmin acolytes, while Vishwamitra had become a paunchy, jolly-looking red-faced pundit dressed in ritual saffron.

The seer nodded approvingly and turned back to face the two outriders who had ridden to meet them.

TWO

They came quickly but cautiously, their bodies glistening with the wet mist of river spray. They were all but naked in the style of all rakshaks, the kshatriya clan designated as the guardians of life and property, clad only in white cotton langots that covered their maleness. Slabs of muscle rippled on their oiled torsos and thighs, gleaming in the afternoon sun. Their faces were broad and fleshy, their skin as dark as Rama's hair, heads glistening darkly, unprotected from the harsh sun. They were so similar in appearance, Rama could hardly tell them apart at first.

'Punditji,' the first one said curtly to the seer. 'Are you lost? The way to Ayodhya lies behind you.'

'Well met, rakshaks,' Vishwamitra replied cheerfully in his new role as pundit. 'And greetings to you on this feast day. Regretfully, my holy business takes me in the opposite direction of the Holi mela at our great capital city. My young apprentices were quite sullen about not being permitted to partake of Maharaja Dasaratha's munificent hospitality. I admit I too would not have been averse to enjoying the exotic sights and sounds of the celebration. However, I am bound to Ananga-ashrama on a holy errand and must reach there before nightfall.'

The two rakshaks exchanged a troubled glance. 'Ananga-ashrama? This very day? Can't your business wait a day or three, pundit? Our advice is to return to the capital and take advantage of the maharaja's hospitality for the duration of the seven-day celebration. Nightfall is not long coming. You will be safer within the walls of Ayodhya. Come this way again next Somvar, and we will wish you good journey and let you pass without question.'

Rama saw a frown crinkle the brow of the brahmarishi. He tried hard to keep a straight face: the sight of Vishwamitra posing as a plump pundit was incongruous to the point of hilarity. Yet it was an impressively effective disguise. He touched his own face and felt a weaker jaw and fleshier cheeks, a bulbous nose. The inclination to smile faded at once as he realised how foolish he too must look. *But what exactly does the brahmarishi fear? The bridge-guard can't be spies too, can they?* Come to think of it, why couldn't they be spies? With a shock he realised that all his assumptions might have to be altered to suit the new reality they were facing.

'Alas, brave protectors, my journey must be completed this day itself, or my karya will be bhung. What lies ahead that makes the way so perilous? We are at peace yet with all our neighbours, are we not?'

The rakshak snorted. 'Not for long, if Maharaja Dasaratha stays as docile as he has been for so long.'

His companion shot him a warning glance. Rama thought the second rakshak was an older man, although it was hard to tell without hair. He spoke less curtly than his partner, with some modicum of respect, and seemed apologetic about his young companion. *Father and son*, Rama realised with yet another flash of insight. 'My fellow rakshak means no disrespect to our great maharaja, punditji. This has been an odd day, with many wild rumours abroad. Talk of strange happenings across

278

the kingdom. We who watch and protect Mithila Bridge meet travellers from all parts of the land, and hear much that Ayodhya itself may not hear at all, or only days later.'

'And what do your ears hear today, good man?' Vishwamitra's tone was cheerful but puzzled, as befitted a brahmin ritualist seeking to return to his ashram with his apprentices in tow. 'What scares you so that you seek to bar the raj-marg to righteous pilgrims?'

The first rakshak bristled. 'Scares? You'd do well not to use that word when speaking of rakshaks, holy man! Nothing scares a rakshak.'

His companion put a hand on his arm, quieting him. 'As I said, there are strange rumours abroad. It is difficult to know how much is truth and how much idle speculation or malicious gossip. We who guard the ways hear much but know little for certain.'

He continued before the first rakshak could speak again. 'We had news of a team of rakshasas breaking into the royal palace and ravishing two queens and killing several dozen palace guards before being cut down by a volley of thunderbolts flung by the mighty seer-mage Vishwamitra, resurrected by the mantras of Guru Vashishta.'

'Two queens ravished?' Lakshman blurted in startled surprise. Rama poked him in the ribs, admonishing him into silence, but he was not amused at the inaccuracy of the so-called 'news'.

'Untitled queens,' the rakshak replied. 'And another rumour spoke of an army of Asuras amassing in the Southwoods at the behest of the Lord of Lanka. At the height of the feasting and celebration, when the army and PFs are all heady with wine and the gate-watch is least manned, accomplices of the Asuras within the walls will open the gates and let them into the city, to pillage and run amok.' He added belatedly: 'Or so the rumours say.'

Ridiculous! Rama almost broke his silence too, startled at the malicious incorrectness of the rumours. *Do you think Ayodhya's entire army and guard will be reeling around drunkenly just because it's Holi? Fool!* He was on the verge of countering indignantly that his father had ordered the gate-watch tripled, and the army kept on full alert. The orders had been issued by Dasaratha to Sumantra, who in turn had informed the senapatis of each akshohini in a private briefing. The army would patrol the city in plainclothes with weapons concealed so as not to alarm the citizenry. No soldier on duty would take a drop of soma today, and six-hour duty shifts had been allotted, ensuring that three-quarters of the full force would be on duty at all times, day or night. But an ordinary brahmin acolyte could hardly speak of such things, so he held his tongue, seething.

Vishwamitra seemed unruffled. 'Even if this gossipy chatter contains a smidgen of truth, my good man—and mind you, I do not grant it even that much licence— what does it have to do with us? Why bar the road to Ananga-ashrama? Surely the Asuras do not seek to waylay simple men of God such as us?'

He leavened the questions with a good-natured chuckle that matched his portly appearance. 'What would they hope to gain after all? Vishnu's blessings?'

The first rakshak, the one Rama thought of as the son, looked down darkly at the seer. 'How do we know that you aren't Asuras yourselves? There's been word—'

He broke off, glanced around, and swallowed before continuing gruffly: 'There's been word of Asuras who alter their bhes-bhav and appear as common travellers, or even as nobility and royalty to deceive us protectors. They say three rakshak wardens have been murdered in the woods by such deceivers.'

He hawked and spat angrily, missing Rama's foot by inches. 'I'd give my right arm to get one chance, just one, to put my lance through one of them khottey-sikkey! I'll show them how we deal with Asuras here in Kosala!'

He's scared, Rama realised. *That's why he's so belligerent and rude. He doesn't know whom to trust.*

Vishwamitra replied calmly: 'And you may get your chance sooner than you think, young man. But now let us pass and go about our holy business. The great Lord Shiva will not be pleased if we do not reach Ananga-ashrama in time to complete our ishta.'

The older rakshak looked down at his halter for a moment. 'I wish I could be of help, old one. But our order has decided that until we receive orders directly from a king's envoy, we are not to permit anyone to pass over Mithila Bridge.'

He backed his horse away a few paces, preparing to turn around and ride back to his post. 'Carry out your ishta on another auspicious day. Now, return to Ayodhya before sunset. There will be a curfew outside the city and throughout the kingdom, and all travellers without authorisation scrolls will be dealt with on the spot. These are our orders.'

He turned his horse around, and the younger rakshak did the same.

'Halt, rakshak!'

Vishwamitra's voice rang out sharp and clear, his nasal twang and chuckling tone gone. 'Look at me.'

The two rakshaks turned their horses back again, peering suspiciously at the seer. The younger man already had his lance in hand, and the older was reaching for his sword.

Rama glanced at the brahmarishi and saw a faint haze surrounding him, like a cloak that fluttered inches from his skin, sheathing him loosely all over. It shimmered in the bright sunlight, flecked with gold and blue tones. Brahman power. Vishwamitra's appearance had reverted to its original form.

'I knew there was something not right with this lot,' the younger rakshak began, spurring his horse to ride the travellers down.

A bulb of brightness popped out of the brahmarishi's aura and travelled to the rakshak, stopping him and his horse dead in their tracks. An identical bulb struck his older partner. The bulbs hit the faces of the two rakshaks with a wet plopping sound, and enveloped their heads, like translucent balloons filled with a treacly fluid. The substance of the bulbs began to seep into their eyes, ears, nostrils and mouths. The rakshaks' eyes widened in alarm, their nostrils flaring with panic; then, abruptly, twin expressions of perfect calm descended on them. They smiled, and their smiles were so goofy and unlike themselves that Rama almost laughed out loud in amazement. *They look happily high on ganja!*

'What's with them?' Lakshman whispered, nudging him.

'Those things the brahmarishi shot at them, they've acted as some kind of tranquilliser.'

Lakshman stared at him perplexed. 'What things?'

Rama glanced at his brother curiously. 'The things on their heads. Don't you see them?'

Lakshman looked. 'All I see are those goofy grins on their faces.'

Why am I able to see them when he can't? The answer that sprang unbidden to Rama's mind was as vexing as the question itself: *For the same reason that you had the dream of Ayodhya's rape and he didn't. Your karma and his are intertwined, yet separate. Do not forget: you are blood-brothers, so close you feel like two halves of the same person, yet even two halves must differ in some*

282

ways. This is one such way. Accept it, move on. With an effort he cleared his mind of these distracting thoughts.

Vishwamitra raised his staff and strode forward. For a moment, he continued speaking in the voice of the portly brahmin.

'Thank you for your concern and for sharing your news, good rakshaks. Lord Shiva strengthen your arm and protect you from harm.'

In mid-sentence his voice changed back to its normal bass, but of course the rakshaks were long past noticing such incongruities.

Rama and Lakshman followed Vishwamitra as he walked to the bridge. An entire platoon of rakshaks were spread out across the northern end, backed by elephants that swung their trunks to and fro restlessly. A single barked command from their ebony-skinned captain, and the elephants would line up to make any passage impossible, the rakshaks joining shields to attack. Rama had never seen rakshaks fight but he had watched them train. They were clan-sworn to protect and guard the way-stations, bridges and forest ranges of the Arya nations: *gate-keepers of the Arya world* was how they described themselves. Infant rakshaks were given weapons to hold even before they were weaned. These men on Mithila Bridge would die without surrendering or retreating. And if their orders were to let nobody pass, then nobody would pass.

But they weren't equipped to deal with the brahman powers of Brahmarishi Vishwamitra.

'Rakshaks!' the seer called out, raising his longstaff. His aura flowed thick and fast around his body, alive with swirling motes of gold, blue and bright jade green. A dozen, then another dozen bulbs of luminescence broke free from the translucent flow and shot towards the rakshaks and their pachyderm reinforcements.

It was all over in moments.

THREE

They emerged on the south side of Mithila Bridge, a light sheen of river mist spray on their bodies the only thing they had to show for the crossing. *Toll-free crossing*, Rama amended, still smiling to himself at the goofy expressions on the faces of the rakshaks. Even the elephants had gone cross-eyed and rolled their trunks around in spirals before slumping to their knees. One had defecated copiously as he passed, following the release with a deep sigh of contentment. He had patted the wrinkled grey flank of the mare for good luck, wrinkling his nose at the stench. *Perfume of the road*, his father always called it. He was glad the encounter with the rakshaks had gone so easily. A fight would have resulted in spilt blood. A lot of it. It was one thing to defend oneself against violent poachers or marauding Asuras, but the idea of taking Arya lives sat uneasily on his conscience.

Lakshman expelled a sharp breath as they emerged from the cool shadow of the bridge's overhang and stepped on to the dusty surface of the raj-marg once more. 'Amazing! Bhai, if we knew that trick, we could get into any place we wanted!' He dug an elbow into Rama's ribs. 'Even the princesses' quarters at Uncle Maharaja Janak's palace!'

Rama grinned at the thought of Lakshman loose in their uncle's palace at Mithila. 'You need to get married soon, brother. Before you become a father!'

Lakshman winked slyly. 'And you need to get married before you become a monk!'

Rama shrugged good-naturedly. His self-control regarding matters sexual was notorious. 'I'll marry when the right girl comes along.'

'You mean you'll marry Sita when she comes of age! Don't deny it, bhai. You've always had a soft spot for Maharaja Janak's eldest.'

Rama felt a tiny pinprick of irritation. He didn't like Lakshman speaking of Sita that way. *Although I haven't seen her in years, so why should I care?* 'You're probably thinking of her younger sisters. Urmila, was it? The one with whom you were caught swimming nanga in the fountain?'

It was Lakshman's turn to be embarrassed. He punched his brother in the shoulder hard enough to hurt. 'She talked me into it. Besides, we were just babes. Barely weaned.'

Rama replied with deceptive innocence: 'So when we meet her next, you'll be sure to tell her that you've been fully weaned now, right?'

He dodged his brother's fist this time.

Lakshman raised his hands in surrender. 'All right, you got me. I always did like Urmi. Why deny it? In fact, I can't count the number of times I've heard Susama-daiimaa and my mother talk about making a match with Janak-chacha's four daughters and the four of us. Always when Shatrugan or I were within hearing distance.'

It was a logical match. Ayodhya and Mithila were sister cities, identical in architectural planning and most other ways. Both the clans were descendants of Ikshvaku, with the Ayodhyan Ikshvakus tracing their descent through Surya and the Mithilans through Chandra: lunar to

285

Ayodhya's solar. A marital alliance between the sunwood and silvermoon thrones would cement the already healthy relationship between the two powerful kingdoms and almost double the size of Ayodhya's fighting forces. An alliance that strong could make the difference between success and failure when faced with an imminent Asura invasion.

Rama was about to say this aloud when the seer-mage slowed ahead of them. For a moment he thought Vishwamitra was stopping to admonish them for their mischievous banter. Both Rama and Lakshman prepared themselves for a tongue-lashing.

But the brahmarishi spoke with surprising gentleness.

'Rajkumars Rama and Lakshmana, on the south bank of the Sarayu the very hills and trees have ears. We are in hostile territory now. Your innocent banter may be heard by spies of the Lord of Lanka. Keep your tongues in check unless something important needs saying.'

Rama and Lakshman lowered their eyes respectfully. The seer-mage looked at each of them in turn, his white beard stirring slowly in a gentle breeze.

He added in a faintly amused tone: 'Impossible as it may seem to you now, I was young once too. But keep your chatter for some more suitable time. Now, you need to conserve your energy. We still have a fair way to go to Ananga-ashrama and the daylight fades swiftly.'

He seemed to want to say something further, but turned away without speaking again. He resumed his powerful strides, as precise as the fourstep of a kshatriya army on the march. Rama and Lakshman glanced at each other briefly, exchanging an identical look of 'well, that wasn't so bad after all', and followed their new guru without speaking another word.

Sarayu's voice formed a pleasing backdrop to the sounds of their footfalls and the quiet inner sounds of breathing and heartbeats. The perfume of the river enveloped them, keeping at bay the stench of the Southwoods that loomed on the cliffs to their right. *Like an army host lined up ready and waiting . . . but for what?*

The only thing Rama knew about the Bhayanak-van was that it was a forbidden forest, segregating the mapped Arya territories from the vast unexplored wilderness of the southern sub-continent. No Arya truly knew what lay beyond the dark dense Forest of Fear, which was the literal translation of Bhayanak-van. Even the Arya outposts along the coastline were always visited by ship, the outpost kshatriyas seldom daring to venture too far into the interior regions. Those who had done so over the centuries had never been seen again.

The fauna was sparser here on this side of the river, the ground rocky and pebbled, unlike its lush northern counterpart. That was strange since the silt should have been as rich, as fertile. Up ahead, Rama saw a solitary tall tree growing out of the smooth red clay of the riverbank. A maharuk, which the common folk called the Tree of Heaven. It was tall for its species, well over twenty yards high. More unusual, it was in full bloom already, its pale trunk capped by a closely woven foliage ablaze with little golden-yellow flowers. Normally the maharuk bloomed well after spring began. *So it's just another sign of early spring, another good omen.* The tree's tall trunk, thick foliage and delicately scented flowers provided shade as blessed to a sun-weary traveller as the hand of a deva offering ashirwaad.

As Rama passed beneath the fragrant canopy, a gust of wind rustled the maharuk's upper branches. With a sound like crisp silks rubbed together, the tree showered the three of them with gaily coloured flowers. At the same moment, a cluster of butterflies—so similar in colouring to the flowers that he mistook them at first—appeared before him, hovered momentarily above his head and danced away gaily.

The road turned to avoid a heap of large boulders which effectively obscured the view of the river and of Mithila Bridge. The terrain began to change almost at once. To their left a steady line of anjan trees rose ominously, effectively obscuring any view of the Sarayu valley. Patches of colour were starting to appear on the anjan trees—colloquially dubbed 'ironwood' for their sturdy blackish timber, as dark as the anjan grease used to line one's eyes—and soon they would burst with a profusion of hues. But right now their dark green foliage and sombre trunks, some as much as eight yards high, made for a grim hedge that loomed over the road, overcasting the bright day with a monsoon gloom. After a moment, Rama realised what else was eerie about this natural avenue: there was no birdsong or insect sounds at all.

Humps of reddish-black boulders began to sprout from the cliff face to their right, like boils on the face of some diseased animal. As they climbed steadily upwards, the boulders grew more profuse until the entire cliff wall seethed with the gnarled dark protrusions. The rusty streaks and gashes in the black stone were signs of raw iron ore, Rama knew, but in the dimness of the ironwood avenue they resembled suppurating pus oozing from the dark boils. He'd heard it said that when the makers of this raj-marg had carted the iron-rich fragments of these boulders down to the city, the Lohars of Ayodhya refused to smelt them in their smithies, believing that Southbank iron was cursed and would not cut Asura flesh. He wondered now if this were true or just a superstition, one of the many that centred on all things south of the

Sarayu. He resisted the urge to reach out and touch one of the ugly lumps; even the sage was clearly walking in the middle of the raj-marg, staying well away from the anjans at the left as well as the cliff face to the right.

As they reached the top of the raj-marg, Rama's attention was caught by one particularly large boulder overhanging the road. It was so big it completely shut out the sun for a moment, so when the sage passed into its ponderous shadow, he was swallowed by darkness as smoky as dusk. From this angle it was difficult to be sure, but Rama thought he saw scores running along the top and the sides of the rock. Something crunched underfoot and he looked down to see scrapings of red and black, curled exactly like shavings left by a sutaar's planing of a wooden plank. What creature or force of nature could have scraped ironstone hard enough to produce *shavings*? Nothing he had ever encountered in his short life, he was certain.

Just when he thought they were approaching the peak of the cliff, the marg grew darker still. The anjan trees huddled in closer, reaching across the avenue in an attempt to touch the protruding boulders of the cliff face. The boulders were larger and more unruly here, even though Rama knew that the marg-makers who maintained the king's highway must have cut and planed them smooth. *Maybe they keep growing after they're cut.* That was ridiculous—boulders couldn't grow! But he stopped smiling when he saw a swatch of torn cloth caught between a jagged spur of rock and a clawing leafless branch, as if the two had come together like pincers to catch some hapless traveller.

Looking up as he passed below the dangling strip of cloth, he could vaguely make out the sigil of the House of Janaka, belonging to his uncle the Maharaja of Mithila. *There was that Mithila courier who disappeared last month with a message undelivered, Sumantra said.* He could only just make out a faint dark stain below the stag-against-a-full-moon crest and forced himself to look at the road again. He felt a buzzing in his ears and swatted instinctively before he realised that there were no insects. *Must be the damn iron in the rocks; the royal vaids say it affects our individual magnetic force and its harmony with the polarity of the planet.*

One final slow curve around a boulder that was far too large for even the tireless marg-makers to shape, and they were suddenly blessedly blinking at soft but still warm sunlight, out of the wretched anjan avenue.

'Om Shiv Hari Swaha, *Praised be the Name of Shiva*,' Lakshman said in a whisper beside him, and Rama sent up a brief prayer of his own. It felt as though they had just emerged from some dark tunnel filled with a thousand watching wild beasts. *But all we did was walk up a byroad of the king's highway in broad daylight!*

The raj-marg broadened considerably here, providing a respite for wagons and wheelhouses before they attempted the more dangerous downward journey. It brought back memories of his father's old charioteer Santosha yelling orders to the horse-boys as they scurried about hitching horses to the back of the royal wheelhouse to help control the downward passage of the monstrous luxury cabin, and he was faintly disappointed at the absence of neighing horses, laughing soldiers and his father's hoarse loud voice, and the overpowering stench of that familiar road perfume, freshly dropped horse dung! All that met them was the tracks of the countless wagons and horses that had passed this way before, and a few dried droppings. To the right, the looming periphery of the woods was kept at bay by a field of kusalavya grass that grew from dark scorched earth. *They have to keep burning the woods as they try to come closer to the road*. Even so, the skulking darkness of the thicket instilled a sense of foreboding that was strong enough to make his head ache. *Like a beast that just sits there, biding its time*. He wondered if the sage would take them into the woods from here. The faint line of a footpath cut across the desolate field, entering the woods through a narrow mouth between two crouching trunks. A fresh mark caught his eye and he knelt to examine a small round impression in the dry earth. Another seer with a wooden staff about the size of Vishwamitra's had passed this way only hours earlier. Perhaps it was Vishwamitra himself. After all, he had come out of the Southwoods. The knowledge that the brahmarishi had endured centuries in the dreaded woods and had emerged alive and unharmed gave Rama a sense of reassurance, until he remembered that the seer had mastery of brahman. *While all I have is my bow and a shortsword*.

He had expected the seer to lead them directly into the woods, across the burnt field. But Vishwamitra was looking the other way, out at the valley, standing on the lip of a jutting promontory that stuck out over the cliff face to provide a scenic view of the Sarayu valley. The spot was popularly known as Ayodhya-darshan or Sarayu-darshan, all important things in Arya having at least two names. Rama and Lakshman stood alongside their new guru and looked down.

The view was breathtaking. The Sarayu valley lay below them, stretching as far as the eye could see in either direction. To the north, the mountains of the Garhwal Himalayas rose steadily, vanishing into the mists of late winter. A thick carpeting of palas trees gave the north bank a rich red texture, like the intricate dense weave of the deep-pile Gandahari dhurries his mother loved to collect. The Sarayu's white line formed an undulating border at the bottom of this roughly rectangular deep-pile rug. Rama could trace the point at which the river entered the valley, far to the distant left. It then passed out of sight beneath the shooting towers and vaulting arches of Ayodhya, roared down sharply over the twenty-yard drop of Aja-putra Rapids, turning into a foaming, seething bundle of cold white fire that calmed down only slightly as it expanded its width and worked its way steadily to the extreme far right of the panorama, beneath spray-shrouded Mithila Bridge, down the ragged boulder-strewn rapids, finally disappearing into a thicket of mangrove on its way to Mithila.

When next I look upon you, my river-mother, I will have earned the right to be called Rama Rakshas-slayer. Or I will not look upon you again. This I swear.

He looked at Lakshman and saw his brother's eyes gleaming a little more brightly than before. Moving at the same time, both placed their hands on each other's shoulders and squeezed tightly.

When they turned, Vishwamitra was waiting.

The seer-mage raised his staff and pointed silently.

They followed him across the burnt field and into the thicket, turning their backs on their last sight of Ayodhya.

FOUR

Maharaja Dasaratha reached the last turn and paused to catch his breath. It had been a long day and a hard one, and he had eaten and drunk too much, as usual. *Well, it's Holi*, he thought, trying to shrug it off. *A little extra wine and meat on a feast day never hurt anyone.*

But the leaden weight in his distended belly, the piercing ache in his lower back, the crushing pressure in his neck and the back of his head, all disagreed fiercely. After a moment it dawned on him that he was not going to feel much better any time soon, and with a weary sigh and a muttered curse he climbed the last few steps.

He stood on the red-marble floor of the Seers' Eye, the star-chamber at the peak of the Seers' Tower. Seen from without, it was a needle-like protuberance that spiralled upwards, like a talon touching the belly of the sky; from within, it was a circular platform open to the skies, its seven inward-curving pillars shaped like lances representing the Seven Seers who had raised and infused the tower with brahman power. It was windy here, and the powerful currents yanked urgently at his clothes and hair, calling him to the edge and into the arms of oblivion.

It would be so easy to simply let it carry me over. To float like a bird for a few moments until Prithvi Maa rushes up to embrace me. It would be an end to all his troubles and ailments, to this long, slow climb up the waterfall of time. He knew he should feel ashamed for even contemplating such a thought; perhaps it was the soma talking. Perhaps.

He lowered his aching bulk to the stone floor, expecting to find it cold from exposure to the long winter nights; it was surprisingly warm. *Brahman magic. Always, I am surrounded by the sorcerous power of mages.* But for once, his ageing bones were grateful for the sorcery.

He had come here to get away from the inevitable rush of questions and debate after the tribulations of this morning and post-noon. Vishwamitra had got his guru-dakshina. Rama and Lakshman were on their way to fulfil their dharma. Kausalya would be content, or as content as could be expected. The citizens had their prince-apparent, and their feast. The sportsmen their games. The vaisya book-keepers a whole new set of odds to manipulate now that the four biggest favourites were out of the games—Bharat and Shatrugan had opted out in the absence of their brothers.

Even the lawbreakers in the city prison had their freedom, in keeping with ancient tradition. The city would celebrate this Holi like never before, the games and revelry continuing for the rest of the seven-day. Somewhere in that week, the war council would convene, and the warmongers would have their day as well, lobbying furiously for increases in weapons manufacture, siege defences, war machines, soldiers' pay-scales, senapatis' fiefs, rakshak deployment, and the devas knew what else. Everybody had what they wished for, or close enough.

And what did Maharaja Dasaratha have? Nothing but a body that was falling apart faster than a mud wall in a flood, and a heart heavy with fear and anticipation. The setting sun dipped further, turning the silver thread of the Sarayu into gold, and he sighed as he instinctively muttered the sandhyavandana mantra: *Soon I will run my course like all rivers must, and I will sleep in the breast of the ocean and dream no more nightmares.* And Rama would rule in his stead. He felt a pang of guilt; was it fair to lay such a burden on so young and untried a boy? Ah, but king-rule was never fair, only necessary. *It is his dharma to rule, just as it was mine in my time. His time has come.*

And yet. And yet.

The instant the three figures had vanished over the last rise, Dasaratha had felt his belly turn to ice. He had wanted nothing more than to get on his chariot and ride, ride, ride, the way he had so often in younger days, except that this time he would ride not to take his mind off his troubles, but to leave them behind once and for all. It had been hard going through the complex formalities of the parade, the pooja, the yagna and havan, the speeches and entertainments, the feasting and games. As for the hours after Rama's departure, they were all a blur, a sunsmeared line of endless smirking faces and fake smiles—or so they had seemed to his cynically despairing mind.

Finally, he had been able to take it no more. Borrowing Sumantra's chariot—his own chariot was too lavishly bedecked to ride quickly—he had returned to the palace without a word to anyone, leaving the feast moments after it had begun, escaping it all.

It had been strangely disquieting, that ride back to the palace grounds. The city roads were oddly silent and deserted—everybody was at the parade grounds, celebrating and feasting. Approaching the palace stairs, he had veered away at the last moment, distracted by a glance of sunlight off the towering Seers' Eye, driven by some inexplicable urge to go up there.

Now, he intended to sit here in blessed privacy while the city feasted. He could see the threads of smoke from the hundreds of tandoors set up specially for the feast, slender plumes rising into the ocean-blue sky that would be visible for a dozen yojanas. *Like smoke from a burning city.* There was enough meat roasting down there to feed every belly in the city for seven days; the royal huntsmen would be busy day and night, supplying fresh meat daily. His stomach churned in memory of the quickly and angrily eaten joints he had consumed while downing copious quantities of soma.

Even at this height, the sounds of merriment and jubilation were faintly audible. Ten thousand serving girls. Thousands of dance performers, jugglers, sword-swallowers, rope-climbers, snake-charmers, knife-throwers, tightrope-walkers, body-piercers, glass-eaters, mujra dancers, musicians, puppet shows, nautanki performers and several dozens of others that Dasaratha could hardly recall the names of, imported from every corner of the kingdom to provide the people with unparalleled entertainment while also educating them on the variety of cultures in their great nation. Every imaginable entertainment, cuisine and skill was on display, and the people fell on it all with the ravenous appetite of a child woken from a nightmare. The morning's rakshas intrusion had been easily forgotten, a minor aberration on a day of great jubilation, dealt with decisively by Brahmarishi Vishwamitra's plan to launch a counter-strike against the Asuras. Dasaratha smiled as he recalled the brain-numbing thunder of applause and cheers that had greeted his announcement of Rama's ascension and forthcoming coronation.

It didn't take much to make Ayodhya dance, and she was dancing with joy now, celebrating the good omens of an early spring—which invariably meant a fertile seeding—and a new crown-prince. Even if that newly announced crown-prince had been dispatched to the dreaded Bhayanak-van to risk his life in service to his nation; he had heard the confident words of every second citizen and noble alike: 'Rama will return safe. He has the power of right on his side.'

It was a sentiment that Dasaratha could hardly contradict, no matter how dark his secret fears and anxieties might be. He envied his city her ability to hang her cares and dance. *Dance now, my love, for who knows when the music will end and the screaming begin?*

Then he sighed, realising he was being uncharitable and unfair. *They deserve their jubilee. It's these fine people that have made Ayodhya the pride of all the Arya nations and made it possible for you to wear your crown with such pride, Dasa, don't forget that.* He rubbed his aching thighs, feeling the weight of his sixty years and a lifetime of kingship. Soon he would have to turn his mind to the matter of the intrusion, and the interrogation of the spies in the city dungeons, and to addressing the concerns of those who feared an all-out Asura invasion. The war council would convene soon, and all would look to him, Dasaratha, He Who Fought In Ten Directions At Once, to propose a typically brilliant military strategy.

How could he explain to them that he was weary of battles and warmongering. That all he desired was to spend his last waking hours in the soft perfumed arms of his first queen, his first love, and in the company of his sons. All those ten directions for which he was named seemed to have been shut off now, leaving only one way for him to go: down the long dark corridor into oblivion.

'Dasa?'

The voice was soft and concerned. Dasaratha knew the speaker's identity even before he turned his head.

'Kausalya?' he said, surprised but secretly pleased. 'You climbed all the way up here?'

'You climbed, didn't you?' She smiled cautiously as she reached the uppermost stair. 'Why did you leave so suddenly? I called after you but you rode like you were in a chariot race! I had to borrow Mantri Jabali's two-horse to chase you here. He looked sour-faced as usual, and suspicious, and the Greek envoy goggled as if suspecting some royal intrigue.'

Dasaratha shook his head, grinning. 'Good. We'll give the court something more interesting to talk about than Asura intrusions. Come to me, my speedy one.'

She came to him across the breadth of the Eye, bright parrot-green silk sari rustling sensuously as the wind caught at its folds, jewellery tinkling. A horizontal bar of sunlight struck her midway, illuminating her hair and flawless skin, making her shimmer in a green-gold haze, and he was filled with an emotion so pure and strong, he thought his heart would burst.

She looked at him closely. 'Should you be climbing up here in your condition?'

He shrugged. 'The vaids would like me in my bed all day and night. Would you rather have that?'

She smiled fondly, sitting beside him, her hand on his thigh, lightly placed. 'I would have you live a thousand years.'

'Even after I sent your son into the Southwoods to fight rakshasas?' He looked at her, trying not to show his anxiety. She was not one of those he had sought to run from, but he was still unsure how she felt deep within her heart. But there was no reproach in her eyes, no sullenness in her tone. Only a quiet acceptance.

'You had no choice, Dasa. The sage demanded his guru-dakshina, the people's choice was unanimous. You could only say aye, never nay. Besides, if Rama is to be king, he must learn to fulfil his dharma without question.'

He nodded, hiding his relief just as adroitly as he had hidden his anxiety. 'It was not he who protested. I was the one who could not bear to fulfil the sage's demand. Even in the sabha hall I had rejected it, and Rama all but dropped to his knees and pledged his sword then and there.' He shook his head, recalling Rama's eagerness to accede to the seer's request as well as to please his father. 'It was a blessed day that made me the father of that boy.' He touched Kausalya's hands, lying clasped in her lap; her bangles clinked softly. 'And when he left with the sage, so calm and dignified, I tell you truly, Kausalya, at that moment I was never so proud to be his father nor so wretched at being a king.'

'He will enhance your pride and make you forget your wretchedness,' she said with complete conviction. 'And will make you prouder yet. Wait and see.'

He looked at her closely. 'You have grown so much, Kausalya. My God. You were always strong as burnished bronze, but now you are forged and tempered steel.'

She looked away, her eyes brimming with sunlight. 'Steel that has been hammered, beaten, folded upon itself countless times, and dipped into the icy heart of a glacier.' She looked at him, twin suns blazing. 'Fifteen years in the forging.'

A searing dagger of pain pierced his exhaustion. 'Tempered, yes, forged, yes. But never beaten. I have wronged you, my queen. But you have grown stronger as a result. And in your strength I see Rama's strength. My kingdom will rest in able hands. Crowning him will be the best thing I have ever done as a maharaja.'

She softened. 'You judge yourself too harshly. You are a man as well as a maharaja. Men make mistakes.'

He nodded, more sober than when he had woken that morning. 'You believe that my sending Rama and Lakshman to the Southwoods was not one such mistake?'

'Why do you seek new ways to torture yourself, Dasaratha? You did what you had to. He will do what he must.'

He sighed. 'Well said, but hard words. I feel as if I have sent my son to his death.'

She shushed him loudly, placing her fingers on his lips. 'Ashubh! Rama will return. And he will be crowned. The stars foretell it. It was in his kundalee at birth, you must remember that.'

He did. He remembered his son's horoscope far too well. 'His kundalee also predicted that he would be crowned king when he is thirty years of age. Yet I propose to crown him heir in the next fourteen days, not fourteen years.'

She looked away. 'Being crowned prince-heir is not the same as being crowned king. You will rule for another fourteen years, if not twice as long. That was what was meant in our son's kundalee.'

He smiled. 'If a dutiful wife's karma could be joined to an undutiful husband's karma, then perhaps it would be so. But I think you ask the devas for too much, Kausalya!'

Her jaw tightened. 'They owe me as much. Do you deny that?'

He saw the resolve in her eyes and stopped smiling. 'You speak true. There are reparations to be made. You have suffered greatly.'

She shook her head. 'Not reparations. The devas owe us nothing. This is all a vast game played by the wheel of time. But this I believe: Rama will return from the Southwoods safe and triumphant, his reputation established and his prestige enhanced. And in due course, he will ascend the sunwood throne and join the illustrious ranks of the great Suryavansha monarchs.'

He took her hand, kissing it. 'My queen, you speak with a golden tongue. The devas grant your every wish.'

They were distracted momentarily by a great roar of excitement from below. The last game of the evening was reaching a close. The chariot race. A line of two-horse one-rider chariots had left the city on a circuitous route, and were now returning to the starting point. The line of dust curling up from their wake rose slowly into the sky, reminding Dasaratha of days when he would have been there on the royal palanquin, watching and roaring as loudly as the crowd, and still older days when he would have been there on a chariot, riding with the best and besting them all.

He was absorbed in trying to identify the chariot in the lead—his eyes were failing him as rapidly as the rest of his weary physique—when a voice rang out harshly above the sound of the wind and distant cheering.

'The deceitful husband and his harlot. Caught together at last by the betrayed wife. Someone run and fetch the royal kalakaar quick. This will make a portrait worth hanging on my bedchamber wall. Or perhaps my bath-chamber wall.'

Dasaratha started up at the sight of Kaikeyi, flushed from the climb, eyes burning with feverish hatred and fury.

As if her barbed tongue wasn't enough, the second queen carried a shortspear in her hand, and wore a sword at her waist. She was dressed in full battle armour and looked every inch a warrior-queen.

She raised the shortspear in her right hand, squinting against the setting sun as she prepared to cast it.

FIVE

They were at the lip of the woods, yards away from the first gnarled trees, when they heard the thunder. At first Rama thought it was coming from the thicket, but almost immediately he realised that was an auditory illusion created by the close-growing foliage: the woods were bouncing the sound back at them, which meant the source was actually—

'Behind us,' he said, turning and dropping to his knees, pulling his bow and and stringing his arrow in a single smooth motion. A peculiar fetor rose from the ground, a stench as if some beast had died, rotted, and then been roasted to ash. It crept into his nostrils, threatening to nauseate him. He suppressed the urge and scanned the periphery of the cliff edge, searching for the origin of the rumbling. Beside him, Lakshman had fallen into the same defensive stance, arrow strung and ready. Through the knee that was pressed to the ground, Rama could make out the cause of the sound more easily; what had sounded like a distant rumbling from a monsoon cloud was in fact the approaching thunder of hoofbeats, the rumbling of chariots, and a deeper, heavier sound.

'Bigfoot,' Lakshman said, voicing Rama's thoughts. 'Ten or more in battle armour.'

'Horse, a hundred or more,' Rama added. 'Wheel, about twenty, lightly armoured.'

Vishwamitra, still behind them, said calmly, 'Sixteen elephants. Battle-armoured and shielded. With eight horseback warriors and one chariot apiece.' He added what all three of them knew by now. 'Vajra.'

Rama and Lakshman both smiled and relaxed their aim. Rama started to rise, returning the arrow to his quiver as he did so. The brahmarishi's voice stopped him.

'String your dhanush-baans and keep your aim steady, rajkumars.'

Lakshman looked at Rama, perplexed. 'But these are Ayodhyans approaching. Surely they cannot mean us any harm, gurudev?'

'From the time you left Ayodhya, you are no longer merely Ayodhyans. You are pilgrims on a holy mission. Anyone and anything that stands in our path must be treated as a potential enemy.'

Seeing their confusion, the brahmarishi added more gently: 'I am sure this issue can be resolved with a few words. But even so, it is required that we support our words with strong actions. I ask you once again, string your bows and do not hesitate to unleash them if these approaching kshatriyas should happen to disregard my requests. Do not forget, you are now oathsworn to me, and I command this action. Whatever happens from this point on, you yourselves shall be blameless. I take full responsibility for all consequences.'

Rama had already restrung his bow. Lakshman followed a brief instant later. Both their faces had lost their smiles of anticipation and were tense and grim now, intent on following their guru's orders. Rama refused to allow the slightest shred of doubt to enter his mind: what the guru said was the same as any commander would expect of his troops. Without total obedience no military unit could survive long. He waited calmly, his entire concentration focused on the space at the end of his arrow's projected trajectory, as the sounds of the approaching Vajra grew louder and closer.

A Vajra attack force was a small elite squad of mounted and wheeled warriors supported by a retreat line of elephants, divided into sections of one elephant, eight horsemen and one chariot each. Four additional chariots acted as scouts. Typically, the chariot and horse units rode deep into enemy territory to launch quick stabbing forays, inflicting as much damage as they could in the shortest time, then pulling out before the enemy could recover and retaliate. When the enemy did rally and give chase, the elephants provided effective dissuasion.

During a large battle, the Vajra were sent to make repeated short attacks at the flanks of the enemy's main force while the main battle was being fought in the vanguard; the Vajra soon became an irritating and costly distraction which provoked the enemy into chasing them away from the main body, thus splitting their resources and stretching them thin. Stripped for speed, the Vajra's swift chariots and light horse would lead the enemy on a merry chase—all the way into a cul-de-sac of armoured battle elephants waiting at a predetermined location. The horse and chariots would then loop back smartly, fan out behind the pursuing forces and drive them directly towards the elephants, boxing them in. Then the slaughter would begin. Each akshohini of the army had its own Vajra squad, named after the mythical thunderbolt of Lord Indra, ruler of the devas.

The Vajra that appeared at the rim of the cliff, the first horses snorting as they breasted the top of the rise, was the best of all its brother-squads in the maharaja's army. *Father's personal Vajra, led by his best captain.*

The chariots rolled smartly across the burnt field, fanning out. That instantly told Rama that they weren't planning to attack. A Vajra always attacked in straight-arrow formation, presenting the enemy with a single chariot as target. *And they haven't strung arrows.* The horses that followed also fanned out behind the chariots, and he could see that their riders had no flailing maces and ball-chains at the ready. He picked out the lead chariot and targeted the Vajra captain standing at the helm, hands by his sides despite the lurching motion of the fast-moving chariot.

A Vajra bowman's hands are for holding his bow or his bride, not for clutching the sides of a chariot like a milksop toddler.

He had heard the words spoken when he was barely a boy of six, watching the Vajra captain yell them at a ragged line of new recruits struggling to learn the art of firing a bow from the helm of a rattling chariot. Now, his arrowtip marked the throat of the same man. The sound of a hundred and twenty horses ought to have been deafening, but the immaculately trained riders and charioteers—and their equally disciplined mounts— moved with surprisingly little sound across the grass-matted field. *The only reason we heard them coming was because they came by the raj-marg and weren't trying to be quiet.* The lines of gleaming chariots and sleek Kambhoja stallions filled his field of vision, looming larger in his heightened window of perception, the approach made more ominous by the relative lack of noise.

They'll run us into the ground if they don't stop . . . now.

As if hearing his thoughts, the Vajra captain raised his arm. The bowstring tightened between Rama's thumb and forefinger, the taut cord thrumming in the soft breeze from the valley.

'Halt!' called the captain. The chariots and horse came to a halt, their line filling the field to either side of Rama and Lakshman. If the approach had been relatively lowkey, then in contrast the silence that followed was deafening. Rama's attenuated hearing picked up the unmistakable sound of elephants honking and plodding ponderously up the steep gradient of the cliff-road. *They'll take a few moments to catch up*. His arrow followed the Vajra captain as he unhelmed himself and stepped down from the chariot, his magnificent black horses snickering before the charioteer quietened them with a gentle tug of the reins. The head of the maharaja's own Vajra squad strode towards Rama and Lakshman, face creased in a cross between a frown and a smile. He was a squat, heavyset man, making up in muscle what he lacked in height. A face as ugly as the hog badger after which he was nicknamed was mostly covered by a bushy moustache and burns and a beard as brown and bristly as a hog badger's fur. Bejoo. Or Bejoo-chacha, as Rama and his brothers had always called him, using the ubiquitous Arya 'uncle' for endearment, giggling amongst themselves at the notion of calling someone Hog-Badger-uncle. He carried no weapon or shield, but even so Rama's voice rang out in warning.

'Come no further, captain, or my arrow flies to your breast.'

In fact, Rama's arrow was aimed at the squad-leader's throat, rather than his breast, which was protected by a close-woven chainmail coat. Although he had instinctively picked a needle arrow, whose sharp and unbarbed tip could easily penetrate the chainmail, the unhelmed man's throat made a much more attractive and comfortable target. Except that this wasn't just a target, it was Bejoo-chacha, a kshatriya he had hero-worshipped growing up.

306

Captain Bejoo raised his eyebrows. 'You would put metal in my breast? This same breast on which you played as a babe, bouncing on my knee, tugging at my beard until my eyes watered? Come now, Rajkumar Rama Chandra. You would no sooner shoot me than I would raise an open sword to your bare neck. Put that shortbow away and let me have words with the sage.'

Rama kept his arrow strung and his bow taut. 'Mahadev,' he said, addressing the brahmarishi without turning around. 'What is your desire?'

Vishwamitra addressed Captain Bejoo directly.

'I have no business with you, kshatriya. Return to Ayodhya and let us proceed on our journey. We have much ground yet to cover and the sun waits for no man.'

Captain Bejoo's face grew stormy. 'I do not ride out for my health, mahadev. My liege's orders bring me here. Maharaja Dasaratha himself ordered me to follow after Rajkumars Rama Chandra and Lakshman and join with them in their mission.' He gestured proudly at the row of mounted horsemen and armoured chariots. 'He sends his very own Vajra to assist them in their fight against the Asura intruders.'

Vishwamitra sounded unimpressed. 'Nevertheless, we do not require your services. Turn your chariot around and go back the way you came. We have no time to stand here and waste breath.'

Bejoo took a step forward, his thick hairy hands bunching into fists. Like most high-ranking kshatriyas, he wasn't accustomed to taking orders from anyone except his supreme commander, the maharaja. Had the brahmarishi been any ordinary brahmin or purohit, his head would lie at his feet by now, never mind the sin of killing a brahmin. Rama understood and sympathised with Bejoo's frustration at being spoken to so curtly. But his sympathies didn't loosen his bowstring by so much as a fraction of a millimetre.

Bejoo looked at Rama, his bushy brows beetling with anger. 'Rajkumar, make the sadhu understand that I have direct orders from your father. I cannot disobey the maharaja's command and return without my duty discharged.'

Rama's aim never wavered for an instant. 'Captain Bejoo, my sword and my brother's swords are oathsworn to *Brahmarishi* Vishwamitra now. I urge you to do as he suggests. I am sure my father would understand your position.'

Bejoo scowled at the emphasis on the sage's title. He shook his head, emphasising a word as well in response. 'Your *father* the maharaja's orders were explicit and left no room for interpretation. To return with my mission unfulfilled would be to openly disobey Maharaja Dasaratha. I cannot do such a thing.'

'And I will not permit you to accompany us. Heed your young prince's wise words, kshatriya. Return to Ayodhya. Do not delay us further.'

Captain Bejoo studiously ignored the sage and kept his eyes on Rama. 'Oathsworn you may be, rajkumar. Yet you are prince to the sunwood throne. Your father named you liege-heir today, to be crowned on your sixteenth name-day this very month. Your first duty is to the seat and people of Ayodhya and the kingdom of Kosala. You must understand why the maharaja sent me to accompany you. Two young boys . . . princes . . . can hardly face wild Asuras in the Bhayanak-van alone. You need our support to accomplish this perilous mission.'

Perilous? You mean suicidal, dearest Uncle Hog-Badger.

Aloud he said: 'I understand my father's reasons for sending you, captain. But my oath leaves no room for interpretation either. The brahmarishi has rejected your request and asked you to leave us be. Pray, heed his word and mine as well. Return to Ayodhya.'

Bejoo scratched his beard, looking perplexed and put out. He was torn between disobeying his maharaja's orders and flouting the will of his crown-prince-in-waiting. Behind him, the Vajra waited as quietly as it could, the well-oiled chariot wheels barely creaking, the horses keeping their heads down and snorts to a minimum: a careless snicker or a squeaky wheel could mean disaster in an ambush. As Rama waited for Bejoo's decision, the first of the Vajra's elephants crested the top of the cliff-road, raising its trunk triumphantly but silently, its discipline forbidding it from issuing its habitual honk of glee on accomplishing the difficult ascent. It was followed closely by its companions, all beautifully decked out in burnished armour, their gold-ringed tusks blazing in the afternoon sun. The ground beneath Rama's knee shivered under their weight.

Finally, Captain Bejoo nodded curtly to Rama, still ignoring the brahmarishi, and strode back to his chariot without saying another word. Climbing aboard in two quick steps, he signalled a silent order. At once, the entire line of chariots began turning their horses around; the mounted riders behind them did the same. The mahout of the lead elephant patted the side of his mount, bringing the giant beast to a surprised halt. *Sorry, old bigfoot, your climb was for nothing.* At least the way back was downhill, Rama reflected as he loosened his bowstring a fraction, still keeping the arrow in the bow.

Behind him, the sage spoke with surprising gentleness, in sharp contrast to the harshness he had used with the Vajra captain. 'Come, rajkumars. We have some way yet to travel before sunset, and the way ahead is not as easy as the raj-marg. Let us make haste.'

309

Rama rose to his feet and backed away, keeping his eyes on the retreating Vajra. The chariots and horse had stopped to wait for the last of the elephants to reach the top and turn around. Rama noticed fresh scratches scored along the backs of more than one elephant, blood welling up in some of the cuts. *From those low-hanging ironwood branches no doubt, wretched anjans. I bet they're bewitched.* He knew Lakshman would be concerned: his brother adored elephants even more than horses. But there was no time to feel sorry; these were only minor cuts, and he expected to see much more blood spilled before this journey was done. *And not just elephant blood.*

He backed up until he could feel a branch inches behind his head, the hairs on the back of his neck prickling in anticipation, then turned and ducked beneath an overhanging eave, entering the sullen gloom of the thicket.

Captain Bejoo waited until the princes and the sage had disappeared into the thick shadow of the woods. Then he beckoned to his second-in-command, a tall, handsome kshatriya mounted on a bronze horse. Like all Vajra kshatriyas, the young man was nicknamed after his patron animal. Because his long jaw, milky-fair Arya skin, dark-blond hair and almost white grey eyes resembled the fawn-stippled-with-black appearance of the plainswolf, he was named Bheriya.

'Bheriya.' Bejoo's eyes stayed on the place where the three foot-travellers had entered the forest. 'Tell Gaja to keep his bigfoots here for another hour then follow slowly and silently. And I mean slow and silent, samjhe? Not crashing through the forest like a pack of timber-elephants.'

Bheriya's handsome fair face frowned as he tried to absorb his captain's order. 'Captain, if we are to ride back to Ayodhya, then why the need for stealth?' He

310

blinked several times, understanding suddenly. 'Wait, did you say forest, captain?'

Captain Bejoo grimaced.

'Bheriya, it's a relief your beautiful new bride didn't suck your brains out along with your seed.' Bheriya was just married; had in fact enjoyed his suhaag raat just the night before. 'Wait a few minutes, then send three scouts on foot after the rajkumars and the brahmin. When they have determined the route they're taking, one will return to show us the closest cart-path fit to carry our wheel and horse through that cursed bunch of darkwood. A second scout will return another hour later, guiding us the rest of the way. By then it will be nightfall and we shall camp within easy reach of their camp if possible. We shall take up the pursuit at daybreak, using the same system to follow them to their destination, and fulfil our mission as commanded.'

Bheriya nodded, his expression revealing that he understood but didn't care much for his captain's plan: the Vajra kshatriyas permitted a far greater degree of informality and individuality than other kshatriya corps. 'Assuming we find a suitable cart-path even part of the way, and assuming the rajkumars stay close enough to it to be followed. Which would be unlikely, don't you think, Bejoo?'

Bejoo turned and spat on the ground. 'I don't want to hear unlikely and impossible, Bheriya.' He shook his fist in the air. 'Whatever happens, I will follow my orders. We must be close behind the crown prince when he encounters any threat.'

Bheriya glanced up at the brooding thicket. 'That would be every minute of the way.'

'The rajkumars can handle wild beasts and the like. I've seen them hunt and they're both as good with their

311

bows as any Mithila bowman. It's the rakshasas I'm talking about. Young Rajkumar Rama Chandra has no idea what it means to face such creatures.' He spat again. 'Stubborn brahmins. Vishnu-avatar Parasurama had the right idea, hewing down kshatriyas with his axe, except he should have taken his blade to brahmin necks instead. One good purge like that and we'd all be better off.'

Bheriya was inured to his captain's pet peeve. He spoke with grim bravado. 'Don't worry, Captain. We'll be between them and any Asura scum before those wretches can open their mouths to snarl.' He added quickly: 'I mean the rakshasas, not the rajkumars.'

'Bheriya, have you ever fought rakshasas before?'

'No, sir, can't say I've had the pleasure yet.'

'Then shut your slavering jaws and see to my orders.'

Bheriya saluted his captain quickly and wheeled his horse about. Bejoo suppressed a grin as he watched his second-in-command ride across the field. Bheriya was a very good man, perhaps the best lieutenant he had ever commanded, but Bejoo would die before he admitted as much to the younger man. If anything, his captain's fondness for him earned Bheriya harsher treatment from Bejoo, who expected nothing less than perfection from the man he fully expected to succeed him in the command of his unit. Why, if Shakun and he had been able to have children, he would have wanted nothing more than a son like Bheriya.

Thinking of his wife brought back the familiar knife-twist of regret and pain. For an Arya kshatriya not to have progeny was painful beyond description. For a man of Bejoo's stature to remain childless was unbearable.

And yet, having Bheriya almost made it bearable. After all, a fighting kshatriya's unit was his extended family. Bejoo's Vajra was his home away from home.

Shakun even joked drily that he spent more time with his sautan—his second wife—than with her. And, she added invariably, he seemed to enjoy the sautan's company more. He sighed. It was true that as the years had turned his hair greyer, and he had come to terms with the cruel fact of his childlessness, he had begun to seek more pleasure in his work with the Vajra than from his wife's company. There were times when he had to resist the urge to hug Bheriya tightly and call him putra. Hence his gruff harshness with the lieutenant. He was only concealing the feelings he feared would betray the soft kernel within his hard exterior.

He watched now as Bheriya rode across the field, giving quick, precise commands to the mounted soldiers, charioteers and elephant-warriors, using a carefully perfected sequence of hand gestures to communicate it all. Vajras were used to communicating thus while deep in enemy territory where conversation could be overheard. Moments later, three charioteers handed the reins of their two-horse teams to their bowmen and stepped down. Bejoo nodded approvingly. As navigators, the charioteers would make the best scouts, and the bowmen were all capable of leading their chariots and firing at the same time. Already, the three bowmen were attaching the reins of their chariots to clasps in their chainmail. Now they could direct their horse-teams simply by twisting their bodies; not the most efficient way to manoeuvre a chariot, but it would do.

The Vajra kshatriyas had developed their unique skills over centuries of stealth-fighting. Bejoo had heard that there were clan warriors in that island-kingdom far to the north-east who used similar silent-attack tactics. *And no doubt they learned our techniques from some Nipponese envoy who carried home news of our Vajras.* Like the

Arya hand-to-hand fighting technique of kalarappa, which was rumoured to be the most popular new martial art in the Mandarin kingdoms north and east of Myanmar.

He squinted up at the sun, still high above in the azure-blue sky. There was a good four or five hours of daylight left. He had no idea how far the sage intended to lead the two rajkumars before sunset, but stop they must before it grew dark. The Southwoods were treacherous enough as it was; to move in there after dark would be madness.

As is this whole mission.

The three scouts awaited his command to leave. He made a hand gesture, pointing three joined fingers at the spot where the three travellers had entered the woods, thumb kept down on the palm. Then he shot his forefinger up, followed by his middle finger. The scouts signalled back their confirmation silently: message understood. Three to follow, one to return, then a second one to return. Moving in perfect rhythm, the three scouts jogged forward, sprinting to the edge of the woods. They entered the close thicket and were lost to sight.

We'll be right behind you, Rajkumar Rama Chandra. No rakshas will harm a hair on the head of an Ikshvaku Suryavansha. Not while Bejoo Vajra-rakshak still draws breath.

He waited impatiently for the return of the first scout.

SIX

'Maa!'

Bharat's hand shot out as he broached the top of the stairs. He caught the shortspear to wrest it away from his mother. She struggled momentarily, her face contorting with fury, and for a moment Dasaratha thought that his son would lose the contest. *She's a strong one, as strong as Kausalya in her own way, and a warrior.*

But Bharat had the advantage of gravity on his side: reaching up, he had grabbed the hilt of the spear just as Kaikeyi had drawn it back to throw. All Bharat had to do was pull down and Kaikeyi was knocked off balance. She swung around, still holding on with one hand, snarling at her son. Then something passed across her face, some pale shadow of a maternal instinct, and she released her grip on the weapon. Bharat took the spear and broke it across his knee, his face rippling with anger and shock.

'You were about to throw this at *Father*,' he cried, holding up the broken halves of the spear. 'How could you?'

Kaikeyi adjusted her coronet, her face grim with sullen rage. Dasaratha realised she was dressed for the women's mêlée. Her armour grew a little tighter each year, but she always won the shield. She must have seen him leaving, with Kausalya close behind, and followed them both on her horse. Bharat must have been her second man; they had been practising together for a few weeks.

'I wasn't aiming for your father, you idio—my son. I was aiming at his harlot.'

'Kaikeyi!' Dasaratha's voice rang out across the wind-blasted space. 'Be careful how you use your tongue! Kausalya is my queen and deserves your respect.'

Kaikeyi stared at the first queen, her head bent low, her eyes gleaming with the reddish fire of the setting sun. 'She behaves like a harlot; she *is* a harlot.'

Dasaratha strode across the Seers' Eye, his hand raised. 'Take back your words.'

She raised her face to meet his blow. 'Go on. Smash my face. You've done it often enough to know where best to strike.'

He stayed his hand with an effort that took more energy than any ten blows. 'You are not in your senses. Apologise to Kausalya and leave my presence at once.'

'Why? So you can continue conspiring against my son and me in secret?'

'Your son?' He faltered, confused, glancing at Bharat. The look of abject misery on the face of his second-oldest was heart-breaking.

'Don't think I don't know what that chudail is doing! From the moment I heard that she had lured you into her chambers, I knew that she was casting her spells again. By what black art did she seduce you into depriving my son of his birthright, raje? Or did she achieve her ends by the use of her vile womanly wiles?'

Kaikeyi sniffed disparagingly. 'Although I fail to see what you could find attractive in that bag of bones. Any one of your concubines would serve you better in the bedchamber.'

316

Kausalya's voice was devoid of the venom that infected Kaikeyi's tone. The first queen spoke surprisingly calmly, but beneath her words was a blade of steel, barely sheathed. 'You're confusing your own methods with mine, Kaikeyi. You were the one who lured my husband away from my marital bed into your illicit arms, or have you forgotten that, *Second* Queen?'

Kaikeyi snarled. 'You witch! Don't deny you used sorcery to corrupt the maharaja's mind. He would never have consented to deny my Bharat his kingship otherwise. It was all your doing!'

She spat across the open space, and had the wind not been so strong, her spittle would have spattered against Kausalya's face. The first queen stood her ground calmly.

'Kaikeyi!' Dasaratha's voice was hoarse with exhaustion, but he summoned up the last vestige of his strength with a superhuman effort. 'You have overstepped your bounds. I command you to apologise to Kausalya at once.'

She turned to him, and for a moment he thought she was about to spit on him as well. But her words were as galling. 'You betrayed me, Dasa. I heard palace gossip but didn't believe it. All these months, you neglected me and avoided my bed, feigning illness and weakness, spurning my affections, and all the while you were falling under the spell of this—'

The word she used was one that he had never heard her speak aloud before—except in the heat of passion. He recoiled at the sound of it, shocked that she would use it in her own son's presence. How had he shared his bed with this woman for so many years? How had he abandoned gentle, beautiful Kausalya for this hysterical shrew? *Because she did such wild things as no other woman ever did for you, you fool, you fool, and you were young and foolish enough to think with your manhood rather than your head.*

317

He strained to control his hand, still quivering with rage and eager to strike the filthy words from her gaudily rouged lips. 'You go too far now, woman. Remember your place. Behave like a queen of Ayodhya.'

He gestured to Bharat, standing miserably behind her, head bowed in embarrassment. 'Behave like a queen mother.'

'A queen mother, am I? Funny. After the announcement earlier today, I thought I must be just another untitled concubine. Why else would you pass my son over for that witch's whelp and make me feel like a cast-aside mistress?'

He tried to keep his voice from rising to a shout.

'Rama is my eldest son and the rightful heir to the throne. You know that as well as Bharat does. Ask your son if he begrudges his brother his birthright. Go on, ask him.'

She didn't even turn to look at Bharat, whose eyes were filled with such pain that Dasaratha's heart went out to him. *Forgive me, my son, for letting such a day come to pass. May you never have to witness such a scene ever again.*

Kaikeyi shook her head, sneering. 'Don't drag him into this mess, you brute. This is between you and me. You made a promise once. Now live up to your words! Or do I have to remind you what happened on the field of Kaikeya, when you lay unconscious and mortally injured, your host smashed and fleeing before the might of Ravana's Asura hordes? Does your precious *first* queen know about that day? About how I swooped down into the heart of the battle in my chariot, picked you up in my own arms and carried you to safety, then returned and led my father's forces as well as yours in a regroup that held the Asura hordes back long enough to give you time to recover and lead your army once more? Have you forgotten that day, Dasaratha?'

'I remember it as if it were yesterday,' he said quietly, his anger suddenly fled. And he did. *A terrible, dark yesterday.*

Kaikeyi's chin rose proudly. 'Then tell Kausalya what you promised me when we returned to my father's palace.'

He was filled with a sense of dread so acute he thought for a moment that the whole world was turning dark. Then he realised it was only the setting sun, dipping down below the western mountains.

'I will listen to no more, Kaikeyi,' he said. 'Leave me now. Bharat, my son, escort your mother to her chambers. She needs to recover her wits.'

Kaikeyi shook off her son's hand. 'Don't lay a hand on me! You may be fooled by your father's deceit, but I won't let him get away with this. The only thing I need to recover is your birthright. And I promise you, son, I'll get it back even if it takes me until my last breath.'

She pointed a clawing finger at Kausalya. 'Hear my words, First *Witch*. Even if your precious whelp returns alive from his trip to the Southwoods, which I honestly doubt, he will not be crowned prince-heir of Ayodhya. Not on his name-day or on any other day in his entire lifetime. This is my curse as a wronged mother and betrayed wife. Hear my shraap and tremble!'

Dasaratha experienced a moment of such pure, white-hot anger, he thought his head would burst with the intensity. His hand moved of its own accord and the next thing he knew, he had Kaikeyi's throat in his grip, the pads of his fingers and thumb pressing against the most tender part of her spine. An ounce more pressure and he could snap her neck as easily as Bharat had snapped the shortspear. He still had that much strength. *Do it,* a deathly-quiet voice said in his feverish brain, *do it and put the ghost of your sins to rest once and for all. Do it, or after you are gone this woman will become your son's worst enemy; have no doubt that she will do everything in her power to cut Rama down, clan-mother or not. Do it, Dasaratha. Kill her now.*

But Bharat's face was before him, staring up at him with an expression that said that never in his wildest dreams could he have foreseen such a day or event. Those sorrowful tear-filled eyes wrenched at his heart, staying his hand. *My son, oh my son, you should not have to see this day.* The strength went out of Dasaratha's arm. A white wave came roaring down from the skies and bore him away and he saw and heard no more.

They emerged from the woods into the direct light of the setting sun. Rama's eyes, accustomed to the dimness of the thicket for the past hour, were momentarily dazzled.

That moment was all it took for him to take a step too far. The ground crumbled underfoot and then there was nothing left to hold his weight. He stepped out into the void, his other senses seeing instantly what had eluded his light-blinded eyes. *It's a sheer cliff and I've stepped over the edge!* He started to fall, mouth opening to yell a warning to Lakshman and the seer, and his guts rose up to fill his throat.

A hand caught his rig, another his left shoulder. For a fraction of a heart-stopping instant, he hung suspended in mid-air, the wind howling around his head, sun filling his eyes like a mashaal thrust into his face, and knew what a bird must feel at the moment when it ceases to flap its wings and starts to plummet back to earth. Then he was yanked up and fell on his back, feet scrambling over the crumbly dry soil, struggling to anchor himself.

Lakshman fell on his knees beside him, grasping his arm with a sweaty palm. 'Bhai? Bhai! Bhai!'

'I'm all right,' he said, not feeling all right at all. He glanced up at the sage, standing calmly beside them. The brahmarishi looked as impassive as ever.

'Mahadev, aapka lakh-lakh shukar hai. Aapne meri jaan bachaii.' *Great one, a hundred thousand thanks. You saved my life.*

Vishwamitra seemed not to hear. Rather than acknowledge Rama's gratitude, he gestured at the void before them. 'There are far greater dangers in store for us than the natural pitfalls of geography, rajkumar. You would do well to remember that. Next time, I may not be at hand to protect you from your own clumsiness.'

Clumsiness? Rama blinked and bit back a response. He saw Lakshman start to rise and speak, and caught his hand, holding him down. *The seer-mage is right: I ought to have sensed the thicket was ending and slowed.* Yet he knew that he had been neither clumsy nor distracted. The thicket had simply ended and given way to a sheer drop with startling abruptness. *One instant we were in the heart of the heart of the woods, barely able to see a yard ahead; the next we were on the tip of a precipice. Nobody could have seen it coming.* Although clearly the seer-mage had seen, and had slowed in time. *Then why didn't he warn us?* Rama got to his feet, brushing off the dirt without a word. Lakshman shot a sullen glance at their new guru but held his tongue as well. Rama turned and looked down at the void that had nearly claimed his life.

They were standing at the edge of a sheer fall at least two hundred yards high. To either side the woods clustered thickly, crowding the very edge of the rocky cliff for as far as the eye could see in either direction. At the edge of the cliff, the thickly growing forest ended in a crumbly mud-covered lip less than a yard broad.

No wonder I went over the rim; even a Ladakhi goat would barely be able to hold its footing on this terrain. Why, my two-horse has a wider running ramp on either side! A step back and his head would bump against the last tree, its dense shrub-like overgrowth reaching over his head.

A leaf fell from above, drifting directly down despite the strong breeze, falling like a stone into the void, turning round and round but never once turning over. The setting sun was almost parallel with them at this height, glaring directly into their faces. Peering down between his feet, Rama saw the familiar silver-gold gleam of water at the foot of the precipice. *A river? Here?* It was only a thin rivulet really, perhaps a tenth of the width of Sarayu, but it was a surprise to see any flowing water in this cursed place. More surprising was the apparently peaceful flower-studded glade in the valley below. It looked almost . . . idyllic.

'These are the Southwoods?' Lakshman's voice reflected the incredulity that Rama felt.

The seer sounded distant and aloof. 'It is Kama's Grove, our destination.'

Kama's Grove? But that was a holy place. What had happened to the dreaded Southwoods? The so-called Bhayanak-van, the forest so terrible that even Asuras feared to enter? So far he had seen little more than the dense thicket of anjan trees through which they had just come, sister to the same ironwoods that lined the raj-marg on the far side of the plateau. Difficult to negotiate, rife with dagger-long thorns and clawing limbs, but not quite the horrific forest he had grown up hearing terror tales of. The only unusual thing about the thicket had been the complete absence of any fauna. Not a bird, not a squirrel, not a living thing apart from the closely crowded trees. And the only danger they had encountered thus far had been his narrow escape just now. *If this is what the whole trip's going to be like, it's not much of a challenge.* But he knew there had to be more to it.

'Come,' said the seer. 'We have to reach the river before sunset. You must perform your sandhyavandana.'

Vishwamitra turned and made as if to step sideways over the lip of the precipice, like a man getting off a horse. To Rama's surprise, the seer seemed to find firm footing easily, and he went over the edge, his matted white hair ruffled by the wind as he descended step by step, disappearing from sight. Lakshman and Rama leaned over, peering down. The sage was directly below them, only his head and broad shoulders visible from this angle. At first it looked as though he was walking on thin air, but then Rama saw that he was treading a narrow in-ledge cut directly into the side of the sheer cliff face. Judging from the comfortable speed at which he was descending, Vishwamitra had come this way before. *Which means it shouldn't be too hard for us to follow.* The realisation did nothing to reassure him. He looked at Lakshman, who was waiting for him to decide what to do next, then he shrugged and imitated the seer's action. He fully expected his foot to flail in mid-air, his weight carrying him over the lip, this time to plummet straight down to the bottom. He had a wild vision of himself falling, passing the still drifting ironwood leaf, and reaching for it as if in a dream. Then his foot found the cleverly cut step and took a firm purchase. To his surprise, the ledge was easier to walk on than he had thought. It took him several heart-stopping moments to get used to the unusual posture—practically hugging the face of the cliff—but once he got going, it was doable. He heard Lakshman's sharp intake of breath as he followed his example. In moments, they were both descending the precipice, Rama resisting the urge to peer down to see how far Vishwamitra had gone. Somehow he had a feeling that if he fell again, the seer wouldn't be able to catch him in time. Rather than scaring him into freezing still, the thought made him more determined to make it safely down. He moved with growing confidence and precision, increasing his pace steadily until it felt as if he'd been doing this all his life.

SEVEN

They reached the foot of the cliff without any mishap. The sun was very low by then, minutes away from setting. Vishwamitra stood by the bank of the stream, waiting. The angular light of the sun had turned the water into a mirror and Rama could see two Vishwamitras as he approached, one facing away from him, the other looking up from the water. The Vishwamitra in the water looked like a white-wax statue on fire. Except for the soft gurgling the water made as it flowed past, it could well have been a mirror, so still and quiet did it glide. *It's as pure and clear as Sarayu herself. It even smells like Sarayu. That mix of glacier and lotus and herbweed that nothing else on earth smells like; yes, it is Sarayu herself or her twin sister, I'd wager.*

'What is the name and source of this stream, mahadev?' Lakshman asked.

The seer continued to stare at the horizon, his white beard and hair ablaze with the fiery shades of sunset. 'It is a diversion of the Sarayu, Rajkumar Lakshman. I diverted it myself some six hundred years past, in order to provide sustenance for the rishis who inhabit this grove.'

He turned, casting a keen appraising eye over them. Rama felt himself straighten his back and keep his face moulded in a respectful expression. It wasn't hard; he had walked many times this distance before. But his stomach growled with anger, a creature beyond his control. He hoped the seer hadn't heard the growl.

The mage finished appraising them, gesturing at the river. 'You are sullied by your journey. Cleanse yourselves in the purifying waters of Sarayu, and perform your sandhyavandana with complete sincerity. After that, I will convey to you the twin maha-mantras of Bala and Atibala. Come, waste no more time; your ancestor Surya grows impatient to leave this part of the land and visit his dominions on the far side of Prithvi.'

Rama joined his palms together. 'Jaise aagya, gurudev.' *As you command, great guru.*

The two princes waded out into the stream. It was surprisingly cool and fragrant, and as he washed the dirt of the road from his face, Rama felt instantly refreshed. Thus far, the journey hadn't been half as bad as he had anticipated. And if the guru meant what he said, he would be receiving two of the greatest mantras any kshatriya could aspire to know. *What do you mean, if he meant what he said? Of course he meant what he said; a seer doesn't make false promises.* He took his acamana the three prescribed times, softly chanting the mantras of the sandhyavandana or evening worship, thanking the sun-god for nourishing the world this past day and expressing his eagerness to see Surya at the dawning once more. When he was done, he found himself hoping the seer had plans for them to eat before long.

From the riverbank, Vishwamitra watched the two princes perform their evening ritual. He admired the way they moved with perfect synchronicity, Lakshman's actions mirroring his elder brother's. They had kept their weapons on their backs as was the custom during forays into hostile territory. He could have told them to leave the rigs and swords on the bank; no enemy would attack them here. But it was better to let them follow their kshatriya training. Guru Vashishta's teachings at his gurukul were the basis of their world view. Soon, the young rajkumars would be flung headlong into events beyond the ken of their wildest imaginings, and it was important that they be allowed to cling to some of their childhood beliefs.

A part of him thought differently. There were limits to even Guru Vashishta's knowledge after all; the great seer still clung to the ancient ways. To face and survive the challenges that lay ahead, the ancient ways would not be nearly sufficient. They would merely be the basis on which he must build a new, more effective defence.

As he watched them perform their ablutions, Vishwamitra felt the faintest twinge of sadness at the obstacles and challenges these two young boys would soon face. They were barely out of boyhood; they deserved a few more years of youthful carelessness. Why, he himself had enjoyed these very years to the hilt, squeezing out every last pleasure to be had in his adolescent days. The rajkumars did not deserve the harsh burden that he was about to lay on their smooth shoulders. But he had no other recourse. There were forces at work now that were far greater than any seer could hope to control. Vashishta had understood that and supported him explicitly. This was not just a matter of two young princes of Ayodhya; it was a crisis of history itself. And desperate times called for desperate methods. Samay had decreed that two young boys would undertake a task that even the greatest champions of yore would have feared to attempt.

The rajkumars emerged from the river, their bodies shedding golden beads in the dusky light. Without needing to be told, they prostrated themselves at Vishwamitra's feet to receive his ashirwaad, then sat facing him in the cross-legged lotus posture, the traditional yogic stance of shishyas receiving vidya from their guru.

They waited, their faces shining in the reflected light. He wasted no time on lectures and introductions; it was not his way. Unlike Vashishta, who used eloquence as a lubricant for the knowledge he imparted, Vishwamitra preferred to let his vidya speak for itself.

'Empty your mind and become one with brahman,' he commanded. 'The maha-mantras I am about to impart to you are the mothers of all martial knowledge. When you have received them, you will feel neither hunger nor thirst, heat nor cold, weariness nor drowsiness, pain nor discomfort. You will no longer fear any foe, neither the nameless ancient spirits that walk abroad in the ungodly hours before dawn, nor the hideous Asuras that will seek your destruction in the days to come. As long as you respect and use these gifts wisely and sparingly, neither disease nor age will touch you. No enemy can attack you unawares when you are asleep or off guard, no bodily urges will overcome your wits or allow you to be seduced. Even the most ravishing apsaras of Indra's court and the most sensuous gandharvas of the forest will not succeed in arousing your desires. The strength of your limbs will be unmatched on this earth, and none other in the three worlds will equal your vidya, your shakti and your chaturta. You will have no equal on or off the field of battle. Accept the gift of these great scientific formulae, master the use of them, deploy them wisely and sparingly, and you will be warriors among warriors, kshatriyas from whom other kshatriyas may learn, gurus to your varna.'

He paused, seeking their minds with his own inner eye. All it took was a deep, relaxing breath—the opposite of concentration—and the bluish-white glow of his brahman aura sprang ablaze. The force flowed through him with an intensity that was uplifting, intoxicating. He flowed with it, probing around the much fainter but strong young auras of the two rajkumars.

He was pleased to see how receptive and ready they were. *Guru Vashishta taught these boys well, their discipline is admirable. They desire learning fiercely, these two.* Just as the great Brahma was filled with desire at the dawn of creation—not the desire to procreate, but the desire for knowledge. The desire to be one with the universe. That was the essence of brahman, and it was strong in these two young boys.

Opening the doorway to the innermost kernel of his consciousness, that part of himself which was no more human than any deva or Asura, the gateway to brahman, the force that was everything and nothing at once, the essence of all creation and the absence of it, the soul of all matter and the opposite of matter both at once . . . opening that sacred passage, he released the maha-mantras. The searing blue light of brahman blazed around the three of them, burning like a giant sapphire triangle in the dim light of dusk, consuming the two young rajkumars in an explosion of light and energy that made a thunderclap seem mild.

It was done.

From this moment on, these two young men are more than mortal. Brahma be praised.

From the top of the cliff, three pairs of eyes watched the two princes and their new guru seated below on the riverbank. Only one pair of eyes possessed the ability to see the frighteningly beautiful burst of brahman power that accompanied the transference of the two maha-mantras. Even though the owner of this pair of eyes did not know exactly what had caused the show of power, she could hazard a few good guesses. *Brahman sorcery. The seer's preparing them to face my cousins in the Bhayanak-van. Foolish sage. You do not know what you do to these innocent boys. If my cousins don't kill them, your mantras will.* Like all rakshasas, Supanakha had no great respect for the force of brahman or its practitioners.

She raised her head and issued a cry that was part-deer and part-rakshasi. On her left shoulder, a fresh scar marked a recently healed injury; the spot where the poacher's arrow had struck her that morning. She lowered her head again, crept over the lip of the cliff, and began working her way downwards on all fours. In the fading dimness of the dusky twilight, her reddish-black fur blended perfectly with the rusty veins of the lohit stone.

Not forty yards to the left of the Yaksa, the two scouts of the maharaja's Vajra looked around curiously. They were Geedhar and Doda, named after their respective totems, the jackal and the raven.

'What in Kali's name was that?' Geedhar asked, his neck prickling at the loud animal cry.

Doda shrugged. 'No idea, but don't speak Kali's name in these dark places, brother. You never know, she might hear and come searching to see who uses her name in vain.'

Geedhar snorted derisively, but felt a secret twinge of fear. He had heard less likely stories of the Southwoods. Although thus far he and his companions hadn't seen much to fear, he had no doubt that great dangers lay lurking in wait in these dread forests.

'Dhole should have reached the captain by now,' he said, in the hope of changing the topic. Doda had a morbid turn of mind and Geedhar was in no mood to hear further dire pronouncements. Not with night falling as rapidly as a white sheet over a corpse.

'And what will he tell him? That there's no cart-path through the thicket? And even if there were, how would our horse and wheel go down this slope? Or for that matter, how will we?'

'The seer and the rajkumars went down easily enough,' said Geedhar.

''Twas still light then. In a few minutes it will be as dark as your mother's womb. How are we to do it then?'

'We wait until dawn. Ananga-ashrama is across the stream, in Kama's Grove. The seer and the rajkumars must mean to camp the night there. We wait here until dawn. At first light, we go down.'

Doda mumbled something incomprehensible, then chewed his betel-leaf-and-tobacco silently for a moment. He spat a mouthful of tobacco juice to one side and nodded.

'First light, then,' he agreed reluctantly. 'You take first watch while I get some shut-eye.'

Geedhar didn't argue. He wouldn't have objected if his companion had asked him to stand watch all night. He didn't think he was going to get much sleep tonight. Not after that last animal cry. What was that anyway? Some kind of vixen? Somehow, he didn't think so.

The princes tried wading across the stream in the fading twilight. It was their third attempt to find a crossing point. Once again, they were forced to turn back. Though shallow and weak, the rivulet was still twice the depth of a man's height. They emerged dripping and bowed to the brahmarishi.

'Gurudev, the only way across is to swim.' Lakshman indicated the width of the stream. 'It is only a few yards across.'

331

The brahmarishi remained immobile, staring up at the western sky, now streaked with the hues of sunset. 'It is after sundown, Rajkumar Lakshman. I prefer not to immerse myself in running water after Surya's last kiran leaves the prithvi.'

Lakshman looked at Rama, confused. 'Kintu, gurudev, it is the only way across.'

The brahmarishi turned his attention to Rama, staring silently at him. Rama's eyes met his and something passed between them. Lakshman saw it and sensed a glimmer of what had happened. *The guru just showed him another way we can cross the river.* He had no idea how he had understood this, but he had.

Rama turned silently and walked to the edge of the cliff. A tree-trunk lay fallen there, battered from its long descent down the craggy cliffside. Its roots and lower branches were withered and cracked, sticking up into the air like the limbs of some overturned insect. Lakshman frowned as he watched Rama climb up to the large boulder on which the trunk lay at a diagonal angle. Rama glanced up and down the length of the tree briefly. It was perhaps seven or eight yards long at the trunk, and about a yard thick.

'Bhai? What do you . . .'

His voice died away.

Rama had bent down and was grasping hold of the trunk. He put his arms around it, grappling it firmly. Then, as Lakshman watched in astonishment, he heaved and stood upright again.

Holding the tree in his arms. The way a hay-farmer might hold up a bale of threshed straw.

Rama leaped off the boulder, landing on the ground with a thump that Lakshman felt reverberate through his own bones. The tree stuck out for yards to either side of his slender form: it was at least ten times his mass, and as many times his weight. *It must weigh half a ton if it weighs a kilo*, Lakshman thought, unable to believe what he was seeing.

Rama carried the dead tree over to the rivulet. He braced himself on some submerged stones at the stream's edge, the water splashing lightly around his ankles. Then he raised the tree in his arms, like a weightlifter jerking his ironrod above his head. For a moment, he stood silhouetted against the darkening dusk sky, an impossibly small ant bearing an incredibly large splinter of sugarcane. He threw the tree into the river. It landed with a noisy splash, splattering water fifteen yards to every side, a few drops falling on Lakshman's head like a blessing.

Rama surveyed his work for a moment, then he turned and walked back to where they stood. He bowed to the brahmarishi. 'Gurudev,' he said, indicating the stream. 'You may now cross without immersing yourself.'

Lakshman followed the brahmarishi's gaze. The tree-trunk lay where Rama had tossed it—*like a bale of straw*!—forming a perfect makeshift bridge across the stream.

The guru put a hand on Rama's shoulder. 'Well done, Rajkumar Rama.'

He turned to Lakshman, and even in the growing darkness Lakshman could see the twinkle in the seer's eyes. 'You are wondering how your brother has suddenly gained the strength of a bull elephant, Rajkumar Lakshman.'

Lakshman shut his mouth abruptly. 'I am, gurudev.'

Vishwamitra nodded. 'This is the result of the maha-mantras Bala and Atibala. Already they have begun to transform your physiognomy, altering the very cellular structure of your bodies, enhancing your abilities and empowering you in numerous immeasurable ways. This little display of raw strength was only a small taste of the full effect of the maha-mantras. Soon you two will be able to do much more than simply pick up and toss dead trees.'

'We two?' Lakshman's voice caught in his throat. 'Even I, mahadev?'

The seer smiled. 'Of course, young Lakshman. The maha-mantras act differently on different individuals, it is true. They may enhance some aspects of Rama's mind and body while altering other aspects in your own makeup. But alter they will, beyond the shadow of a doubt. Already you can see the effect of their miraculous empowerment. Look at your brother and at yourself. Look closely.'

Lakshman looked at Rama. It took him a moment to adjust, the way one had to refocus one's vision when gazing suddenly across a vast distance after staring at a close object for too long. Then he saw it.

The tips of Rama's fingers, the corners of his eyes, the orifices of his nostrils, his mouth, all exuded a faintly glowing bluish light. Rama glanced down at the palm of his right hand, plucking out a splinter from the tree-trunk, and tossing it away. Lakshman saw the point at which the splinter had imbedded itself shallowly in Rama's flesh glowing brighter, deeper blue, as if his blood itself had been infused with the power of brahman.

Lakshman looked down at himself. The same phenomenon was happening to him. *I'm filled with brahman power. We both are.* And as the realisation came upon him, so did the awareness of the transformation working within his cells. He could feel his power and strength growing with every breath he inhaled.

'And in time,' the brahmarishi went on, 'after the maha-mantras have fully empowered both of you, I may induct you in the use of dev-astras, the divine weapons of the devas themselves. Imbibing Bala and Atibala are an essential foundation before taking that step.'

Lakshman was impressed. *Dev-astras? The mythic weapons of the great wars between the devas and the Asuras? Given to me and Rama!* 'Gurudev,' he said, folding his hands. 'Truly, your vidya is immense and mighty.'

The brahmarishi gestured with his staff. 'Come now, rajkumars. It grows dark. Let us make our way to Ananga-ashrama.'

They crossed the rivulet easily over the tree, its squat broad trunk quite comfortable to walk on. As boys, Lakshman and his brothers had played at walking over small ravines on saplings barely the thickness of a wrist-width. This fat trunk he could have walked blindfolded. He leaped down on the far side behind the brahmarishi and Rama, stopping to look back at the dead tree.

'Gurudev, should we leave the tree as it lies?'

The brahmarishi glanced back. 'It might be better to remove it.' He paused. 'Perhaps you might like to take care of the chore, Rajkumar Lakshman?'

Lakshman grinned. He had been hoping the guru would say just that.

Supanakha watched from the face of the cliff. She was suspended barely ten yards from the foot of the rise. She had stopped in her downward descent to watch Rama pick up the tree and toss it across the rivulet. Now, she watched as Lakshman picked up the same tree and threw it to one side on the far bank. Lakshman dusted off his palms, looking as pleased with himself as a child who had won his first race, and turned to follow his brother and his guru into the thicket. In a moment, the three of them had vanished into the fruit grove.

Supanakha completed her descent, pondering the meaning of this new development. So the brahmarishi had administered some form of brahman magic to the two rajkumars, something which made them much stronger, and presumably faster and more tireless as well. This was something she would have to report back to her master. Her cousin.

She gnashed her teeth at the thought of facing Ravana again. For a while, she had dwelt in the fantasy that she would just follow her saviour Rama and observe him on his journey south. She could bear to do just that for a while longer; he was immensely watchable. And she still wanted to try to understand this human youth who had risked his own life to save the life of an anonymous doe. But she couldn't deny the fact that she was, after all was said and done, a rakshasi. And not just any rakshasi, but the cousin of Ravana. And she had a mission to execute. No matter how much she hated the idea.

She snarled her displeasure, the sound echoing in the sleepy stillness of dusk.

EIGHT

They blinked in surprise at the soft warm glow of oil lanterns glimpsed through the trees. As they approached the clearing, the outline of a large plain hut came into view, limned by the illumination from a pair of lanterns. It was a simple thatch-wood hut, put together with mud, straw and dung. The most basic building unit of Arya common architecture.

The hut was made in the familiar rectangular shape of an ashram, a simple straw awning over the doorless doorway, and seemed large enough to house fifteen or twenty men at best. Two cows and a calf were tethered to a bamboo pillar, munching steadily on freshly plucked darbha grass. They lowed sleepily as the visitors approached the aangan of the hut. Rama noticed that the aangan had been freshly swept with a thrashbroom, judging by the faint parallel lines in the flat ground.

A head emerged from the doorway, hair tied in a neat bun on top of the head in the style of hermits. A young rishi with a smile as wide as his waist was narrow came out, beaming warmly.

Shaivites, Rama thought. No other order would starve themselves so. The Shiva-worshippers were slowly gaining in numbers; although nowhere near equal the ubiquitous Vishnu and Brahma cults, Shaivism was starting to grow in respectability as well as popularity.

Several more rishis poured out of the hut, most of them young acolytes—brahmacharyas sworn to twenty-five years of celibate meditation. All of them fell to their feet and tekoed their foreheads to the ground before the seer-mage Vishwamitra. Shaivites or brahmins, all deva-fearing souls revered a brahmarishi.

'Ashirwaad, gurudev,' they chanted in unison, their harmony honed to perfection by years of daily practice. 'Aadharniya samman. Padhariyen.' *Blessings, great guru. With honour and respect, we invite you to enter and be welcome.*

'Ayushmaanbhav, rishiyon.' *Long life, monks.* 'May your prayers be fruitful.'

A very tall rishi, his bun whiter and face more lined than all the others, hurried forward, prostrating himself before the seer and kissing his feet reverentially.

'Mahadev, you honour our humble hermitage a thousandfold with your presence. We welcome you and your noble companions to Ananga-ashrama. Blessed are all who enter here.'

'Well met again, Rishi Adhranga. I accept your generous invitation on behalf of my companions and myself.'

Vishwamitra touched the flank of the mother cow as he stepped up to the doorway. 'Forgive me yet again, wise one. I have learned the error of my ways.' He presented his feet for the customary arghya, and was washed by Rishi Adhranga himself. The other rishis performed the arghya for Rama and Lakshman.

Rama wondered why the brahmarishi had apologised to the cow. He vaguely recalled some legend from Vishwamitra's past—relating to the seer's first encounter with Guru Vashishta, if he remembered correctly. He would have to ask the sage about it at some appropriate time.

338

The interior of the hermitage was just as plain as the exterior. Four windowless walls washed white with limechalk. Not a stick of furniture on the bare floors, only a pile of straw pallets at one corner. A very young brahmacharya acolyte, interrupted in the midst of setting out the pallets for the night's rest, turned and stared dumbstruck at the sight of the sage and the two rajkumars. Uttering a gasp of amazed wonder, he fell to his feet, thumping his shaven pate on the floor.

'Brahmarishi, mahadev, ashirwaad,' he gasped in a voice choked with adoration.

Rama and Lakshman exchanged amused glances. *Now there's an eager brahmin.*

The odour of fresh dung hung over everything, competing for their olfactory attention with the acrid aroma of fresh cow urine. Two of the five gifts of Mother Cow: dung, urine, milk, leather and meat. Though Rama didn't expect to find the last two under a Shaivite's roof: the cult was notorious for its self-deprivation and austerities, as their skeletally thin figures proved.

Even before his eyes adjusted to the dimness of the interior, lit within by a single lantern, Rama could tell that the floor was made of recently hardened straw-and-dung, and had been freshly swabbed with cow urine. He had to resist the urge to wrinkle his nose, reminding himself that cow-dung and urine were known for their antiseptic qualities. Actually, he didn't even mind the dung very much; once dried, it tended to fade to a nondescript muddy odour that wasn't wholly unpleasant. It was the pungent stench of fresh urine that he had never been able to love.

If only the sage's maha-mantra gave me the ability to make cow urine smell like rose petals, he thought. *Now that would really make me feel no discomfort here.*

Rishi Adhranga looked up, peering around his ashram in bewilderment. 'What is that smell?'

'It smells like. . .like a woman just passed through here, guruji,' said one of his acolytes, as puzzled as his teacher.

'Not a woman, young brahmachari, more like . . . a basket of flowers,' said another brahmacharya, looking just as puzzled as his companions.

Lakshman was looking around too, sniffing for the source of the fragrance. Rama realised that Vishwamitra was the only one who was looking at him directly. The sage seemed to be unconcerned about the source of the smell. The other rishis had begun riffling through the straw pallets on the floor, clucking to themselves in incomprehension.

Rama realised he had been holding his breath. He sucked in air and was amazed to find it smelling as sweet as that of his mother's akasa-chamber. *I did it with the blink of a thought, by wishing that cow urine could smell like rose petals. Holy Vishnu, I never meant to actually change the smell!*

He glanced up nervously at the sage, expecting to be admonished. *He should have warned us that we could make things like this happen just by willing it.* Already, the older rishis were looking at Vishwamitra and muttering comments about brahman power.

Rama was about to confess his innocent error when one of the young acolytes held up a rose in full bloom. 'It was in the north-east corner, with the agarbattis. Dumma must have brought it in.'

'I did not!' cried the young boy who had been alone in the hut when they had all entered. Rama guessed him to be not more than seven years of age. He was clearly the youngest acolyte. 'Just because I brought in a Queen's Blessing once doesn't mean I'm always bringing flowers!'

Rishi Adhranga held out his hand for the rose. 'Powerful scent from a single rose.'

He glanced up at Vishwamitra with a knowing expression. 'But no harm done. We of the order of Shiva usually eschew luxuries of any kind, including scent-giving blossoms. But we must consider this unexpected offering an auspicious greeting for our honoured guests.'

'Indeed,' Vishwamitra replied, his face inscrutable.

Rama realised he could now smell the pungent odour of cow urine again. *He changed the smell back to its natural form, and made that rose appear to justify the fragrance.*

He avoided looking directly at Vishwamitra but later, while seated on the ground, eating the simple repast of the hermits, he happened to glance up and thought he saw a twinkle of amusement in the sage's eyes.

He decided he would be very careful about controlling his thoughts and actions. It would not do to show off his newly developing abilities before these humble brahmacharyas. They were obsequious enough because of the presence of Vishwamitra and their awareness of his and Lakshman's royal status. Besides, he was hardly aware what his new abilities entailed. Tossing dead tree-trunks and making roses appear was all very well; but there had to be much more to the maha-mantras than these tricks.

He glanced sideways at Lakshman and saw from his brother's expression that much the same thoughts were passing through his mind as well. They nodded subtly, a tacit agreement passing between them. *Let's just be normal boys tonight.*

Their meal consisted of a piece of johar ka roti and a little rock salt. Rishi Adhranga had a fire built outside in their honour and invited them to sit awhile and sip a little berry juice. The juice tasted sour to Rama, as if it had been kept standing too long, but to see the brahmacharyas

341

drink it, you would have thought it was the finest soma nectar in the kingdom!

Rama caught sight of the youngest one, Dumma, holding his empty mud-cup and staring longingly at the single jug from which they had all been served—barely a mouthful each. Nudging Lakshman surreptitiously, Rama conveyed his intention; a few moments later, Lakshman slipped the young acolyte both their portions of berry juice. Rama enjoyed watching the brahmacharya novice relish the sour juice with the satisfaction of a palace brahmin finishing his tenth glass of bhaang at a Holi feast.

The night had turned cold after sundown, and Rishi Adhranga enquired if they would prefer to sleep out of doors beside the fire or indoors without a fire.

To Rama's relief Vishwamitra chose the former option: he would rather have slept in a blizzard than endure the odour of cow's urine all night.

'Yesterday my young companions slept on beds of satin and silk; tonight they sleep on darbha grass mats,' Vishwamitra told the assembled rishis. They nodded approvingly, glancing shyly at Rama and Lakshman. Several of them were still nervous in the presence of such exalted company.

'Austerity is the first step toward embracing Shiva,' Rishi Adhranga said solemnly. 'That is the only shiksha we teach our brahmacharyas for the first five years. How to do without, in order to grow within.'

The rishis spoke of matters spiritual, the virtue of penance, the importance of abstinence, the correct way to invoke the Lord Shiva's name during a long fast and meditation. They evidently sat every evening discussing such questions, the only time in the day when they took a pause from their grinding routine of work and meditation. They seemed to be pleased to have visitors to share their thoughts with, and for Rama, it was refreshing to be with men of religion after a year of attending banquets, diplomatic convocations, war councils and a hundred other lavish events on Ayodhya's crowded royal calendar.

He was surprised at how nostalgic it made him for Guru Vashishta's gurukul. *Those were the best years of our lives,* he thought with a small shock of insight. *But I had to go away from the gurukul to realise it.* He smiled at the irony: *why is it that we always have to leave the people and places we love in order to understand just how much we love them?*

He felt a strange affinity with his surroundings. Even though south of Sarayu, the place seemed more like his favourite northern grove than the fabled Southwood forest of terror. Except for the faint chirring of nightbirds and the occasional insect, there was none of the clicking of crickets or roars of predatory beasts he had expected to hear. The air was pleasantly perfumed with the scent of wild flowers and berries. And somewhere in the darkness, perhaps a hundred yards from the hermitage, the gentle gurgle of the Sarayu was audible. As always, the sound of flowing water soon lulled him into a state neither fully awake nor asleep. But when the sage spoke quietly, he snapped back to full alertness instantly.

'Rajkumar Rama, do you have a thought you'd like to share with us?'

Rama looked up at the sage, resisting the urge to blink against the bright blaze of the fire. His pupils must have dilated as he drifted off, because although the flames were no higher than they had been before—the rishis only used as much wood as was absolutely necessary— they seemed to glow with much greater intensity. Did Vishwamitra's voice carry a faint inflection of irony? The sage seemed to know everything he was thinking. Rama was fairly certain by now that the mantras formed some kind of link between himself, Lakshman and Vishwamitra,

343

giving the brahmarishi access to their innermost thoughts and feelings. Oddly, he didn't mind it very much. After all, he had nothing to hide. Least of all from his new guru.

'Mahadev, my brothers and I were weaned on such terrifying stories of the Southwoods. The so-called Bhayanak-van. The forbidden forest, domain of the Asuras. The desolate place, lair of demons and darkness.'

He gestured at the rishis gathered around the fire. 'This grove is on the periphery of that same dreaded Southwoods, within reach of its evil influence. Yet the rishis of this ashram don't seem troubled by rakshasas or other Asuras. Here they live outside the protection of Ayodhya and of the rakshak rangers, beyond the boundaries of the Arya nations, unmolested and unharmed. I don't understand it. For hundreds of generations, our people have believed these Southwoods inhospitable and uninhabitable. We have travelled unchecked as far north as the Norselands and the frozen wastelands of Siber, yet our supremacy has never been able to extend south of the Sarayu. And yet, here we are, in this beautiful glade that is as tranquil and fragrant as any flower grove of Ayodhya. An idyllic grove, a heavenly grove, apparently safe and free of all evil influence. It flies in the face of everything known about the Southwoods. How is this possible?'

Vishwamitra was seated directly across from Rama, his face barely visible through the heat-haze from the fire. 'Well asked, rajkumar. A puzzling conundrum that deserves a satisfying reply. And you shall have it. Rishi Adhranga, I believe you would be the best one to respond to Rajkumar Rama Chandra's question. Please, would you grace us with your knowledge?'

The rishi nodded sagely, bowing his head and folding his hands to the seer. 'It would honour me to share my vidya with these proud princes of Ayodhya, mahadev. I am fortunate that you deem me worthy.'

He stroked his beard steadily for several minutes, evidently a favourite gesture when preparing to speak. Rama noticed that the rishi's pepper-and-salt growth was shiny with spilled berry juice but it didn't seem polite to mention it.

Adhranga's dark eyes glistened in the light of the fire. He seemed able to stare directly into the flames for any length of time without blinking. Rama could imagine him staring at the sun until his pupils turned white: he had that hardened look of the pure penitent about him. A man who welcomed the blasting heat of the desert or the bone-numbing chill of winter merely as notches on an endless sugarcane rod, to be marked off without care for how many were done or how many more lay ahead. What little flesh he had on his bones was all sinew and gristle, so tightly stretched that his limbs appeared to curve slightly, in the way that a great longbow carved from stubbornly hard wood bent with great difficulty.

When he spoke, his voice was clear and soft, with the tone of one who believes in conserving every breath to offer in the service of his deity. *A word spoken needlessly is a missed opportunity to say the name of the Lord*. The voice that spoke the words in Rama's head was Adhranga's, but the rishi himself was still silent, stroking his beard in the same steady rhythm, rocking slightly on his folded legs.

Rama was suddenly flooded with flickering images of Rishi Adhranga seated before his pupils, in the shade of an enormous banyan tree, the same tree beneath which they now sat. Except it was early morning, almost sunrise, and the rishi was younger, his hair completely black, as was his beard. But the rhythm and manner in which he stroked his beard were identical. *He does it when delivering his morning pravachan, and when he sits with his fellow rishis and shishyas every night at their prashna-uttar sessions, and every time he's posed a particularly difficult philological query. He strokes it like this for a long time, and all the rishis wait patiently, knowing that he's about to deliver some special wisdom.*

With an effort, Rama struggled to empty his brain of the sensations flooding through like a river in spate. He silently spoke the first mantra that came to mind. It happened to be the Gayatri mantra, that most sublime of all verses, the sloka that paved the way for all auspicious beginnings. He sensed another consciousness doing exactly the same thing, like an echo. Opening his eyes, he saw that Lakshman was moving his lips silently as well. *We are both struggling with the change wrought by the maha-mantras. Becoming something other than human.* As suddenly as the sensations had flooded his mind, they drained away, like water vanishing down a gutter. He sighed, relieved.

At that moment, Rishi Adhranga began speaking aloud.

NINE

Shatrugan and Bharat waited restlessly outside their father's chambers. There seemed to be an endless coming and going of serving girls and vaids, all of whom walked past with quick anxious steps. Finally, after some hours, the traffic slowed, and everyone else had left the maharaja's chambers except for Guru Vashishta, Kausalya-maa and the royal vaid. Susama-daiimaa came thrice to ask them to come to the bhojanshalya for their evening meal, and thrice they refused. They understood from her nervous entreaties that nobody else had eaten either, except for Kaikeyi-maa. The hour grew very late, but even so, they could hear sounds outside the palace walls. Sumantra came by at one point and told them that the sounds were from a crowd collected outside the gates. Although no official word had been given to the people, the news of Dasaratha's collapse had spread throughout the city and many Holi revellers had left the celebrations to gather at the palace gates where they waited for news of their maharaja.

The princes leaped to their feet as the royal vaid emerged from their father's chambers. He was a tall, fair-skinned northerner with a long face lined with age, and bushy white eyebrows.

'Vaidji? How is he?'

He looked at the faces of the two princes, his brows knitting together anxiously.

'Rajkumars,' he said gently. 'I will not give you false hope. Your father's condition is precarious.'

Shatrugan asked with unexpected belligerence: 'Can't you give him something? A neem potion maybe? We learned in Ayurveda that a weakness of the heart can be treated with—'

'Rajkumar Shatrugan,' the vaid said patiently. 'I appreciate your knowledge. But there are some conditions that are beyond the scope of Ayurveda. Even the great body of Arya medical science has limits when issues of life and death are concerned.'

'What are you saying, vaidji? That our father—' Bharat struggled to finish. 'That he may not have long to live?'

The vaid looked at him sympathetically. 'That is what I was trying to avoid saying, but yes, it is true. He may last a week, a month, or even more than one month. But I am afraid his time is coming.'

Shatrugan's face darkened with anger. 'There must be something you can do. Guru Vashishta can do something. He has lived seven thousand years! He must know how to prolong Father's life.'

The vaid sighed. 'I can't speak for the mahaguru. All I can tell you is that our medical knowledge has exhausted itself. Now, whatever happens, it is out of our hands. Aagya, Rajkumars.'

Shatrugan watched the vaid leave, his face tight with anger. 'What good are they then? If they can't help him at a time like this? What good is all that knowledge and learning?'

Bharat put his arm around his brother. 'Shatrugan, calm down. This is not a mace-fight. You won't help Father by getting angry.'

Shatrugan struggled with his anger. Finally he nodded. 'I know you're right, bhai. But I can't seem to make myself understand it.' He thumped his chest with a clenched fist. 'It's as if something inside me refuses to accept that Father is . . . mortal.'

'Only his body, young prince. His atma is immortal.'

They looked up at the imposing figure of Guru Vashishta.

'Pranaam, guruji,' they said in unison, folding their hands before the guru.

'I understand your anger, Rajkumar Shatrugan,' he said kindly. 'When faced with something as omnipotent as mortality, our first reaction is fear. And in a healthy being, fear always manifests itself first as anger. You are right to feel angry. But you must learn not to vent that anger. Instead, channel it into a more useful emotion. Turn it into prayer.'

'Prayer?' Shatrugan's voice expressed his disbelief. 'Forgive my asking, gurudev. But will prayer truly help Father now? If I pray long and hard enough, will Yamaraj, Lord of Death, spare his life for another twenty years? Or forty?'

The guru looked sharply at Shatrugan. Bharat saw a spark of fire blaze in the brahmarishi's eyes. 'I will permit your lapse this time, young Shatrugan, because I empathise with the turmoil you are experiencing. But never again question so fundamental a practice as prayer. If every Arya, swayed by a momentary personal crisis, lost sight of his faith, this entire nation and all the Arya nations with it would be condemned to eternal damnation. You consider yourself strong, do you, Shatrugan? Then prove your strength of spirit as well as body, mann as well as tann. Keep control of your emotions and your tongue. You cannot put out a fire by adding the oil of your own anger into the flames.'

Shatrugan's rage melted away, washed clean by the guru's verbal lashing. Bharat resisted the urge to move away, to avoid being included in the guru's reprimanding. Instead, he stood closer to his brother, supporting Shatrugan with his presence.

Shatrugan relented. He folded his hands and bowed his head to the guru. 'Shama, gurudev. Forgive me. I forgot myself.'

The guru nodded brusquely, acknowledging the apology. 'You asked about prayer, young Shatrugan. About how it can help your father. I did not propose you pray for his recovery. His condition is beyond reprieve. Whatever is happening to him now is his own karma manifesting itself. Nay, I asked you to pray for your own sake.'

Shatrugan looked perplexed. 'For my sake?'

'Yes. Prayer cleanses the soul at a time of crisis and prepares us to meet and face any challenge. Turn your harmful negative energy into the positive power of prarthana. Pray not for your father, rajkumar. Pray that you may accept the inevitability of his passing with grace and fortitude.'

The guru whisked away down the long empty corridor, his words hanging in the air like echoes in a cavern.

Bharat and Shatrugan exchanged a glance. Shatrugan looked down, embarrassed. Bharat squeezed his shoulder.

'Let's go see Father now.'

Shatrugan shook his head. 'You go ahead, bhai. I . . . I need some time to come to terms with this.'

He touched his naming thread, rolling it between his thumb and forefinger as if it were a rudraksh mala and he was counting off prayers. 'I think I'll take guruji's advice. I'll be at the mandir praying if you need me.'

Bharat watched Shatrugan walk slowly down the corridor. *We each have to deal with life in our own*

individual ways. Brothers we may be, but we are separate
individuals too. Even seemingly identical sections of an
apple contain different numbers of seeds. Each of us has
a different course ahead. We must find our own separate
ways, wherever they may lead.

He turned and went into his father's chambers. Serving
girls stood about whispering nervously. They leaped to
alertness as he passed by. He reached the innermost
chamber, his father's sleeping room. As he parted the drapes,
he paused. It occurred to him that the guru had spoken
as wisely as always. His own first reaction had been
anger too. But his anger had passed much more quickly
than Shatrugan's. Now, he was only afraid. Very afraid.

The room was surprisingly bright, illuminated by
hundreds of little clay diyas. They were arrayed in rows
around the room, covering every available surface. It
was the precise opposite of the dimly lit sickroom Bharat
had expected. He blinked, surprised.

'He fears the dark. His vision is dimming and he wants
it to be as bright as possible.'

Kausalya-maa smiled at him from the bedside, sensing
his confusion. She was sitting beside the head of the maharaja's
bed, on a simple padded stool, a daubing cloth in her
hand. Dasaratha seemed to be fast asleep, his face ashen
and strained, but at rest.

Bharat nodded. Kausalya-maa was still dressed in
the sari she had worn to the Holi parade. She had not
had an opportunity to change all day, choosing to spend
every minute by the maharaja's bedside. It made him
feel guilty, not for himself, but for his mother, who had
stormed angrily back to her own chambers and hadn't
shown her face since the encounter in the Seers' Tower.
Although, he remembered unhappily, Susama-daiimaa
had commented on the huge dinner the second queen

351

had ordered to her private chambers. Evidently his father's condition hadn't affected his mother's appetite in the slightest. And here was Kausalya-maa, whom he knew hadn't touched a morsel or sipped so much as water since his father's collapse.

He knelt by her side, touching her feet. 'Maa, shama.' *Forgive me, Mother.*

Kausalya didn't click her tongue or make any false protestations as most elders customarily did. Instead, she placed her arms on Bharat's shoulders and said gently, 'You have done nothing that needs forgiving, my son.'

He looked up at her. She looked so gentle, so calm. He wished suddenly that he had been born as Kausalya's son rather than Kaikeyi's. 'I heard her calling out to Father, shouting at the servants. I had seen him go up to the Tower minutes before, he does that sometimes when he needs to be alone. I told her he was up there. Only after she ran up the stairs did I realise she was carrying the spear. I followed her thinking she might not be in her full senses.' He shook his head. 'I didn't know she would go so far, say such awful things.' He averted his eyes. 'I can't believe she threatened Father and you with violence.'

Again, Kausalya didn't sigh, make noises of commiseration or otherwise dilute the intensity of Bharat's words. He understood and appreciated that greatly; it had been hard for him to say that much. It still felt like betrayal, to speak about his mother when she wasn't present. But he had felt compelled to explain, to try and make Kausalya-maa see that he hadn't known what was going to happen. If he had, he would have never told his mother where the maharaja had gone. Especially after he had seen Kausalya go up to the Tower as well.

'We cannot control the actions of others, Bharat. Each of us makes our own choices, creates our own karma.

You are not responsible for your mother's actions. Don't carry her burden of guilt on your shoulders.'

He nodded. He knew what she said was wise and true. Yet the pain in his chest remained, like a chip of wood he had swallowed and which was now lodged in the space between his heart and his ribs. It throbbed with every beat of his life-blood, sending needles of anguish through his being. He clenched his fist, squeezing his father's bedspread.

Kausalya laid her hand on his fist. 'Be strong, Bharat. Your father needs you. Kosala needs you. All will be well as long as you remember who you are and what your dharma is. The rest is beyond any mortal's grasp. Free your mind of all guilt or regret. You have done nothing but honour your father and your line. Dasaratha and I have nothing but pride and love for you, putra.'

At the last word, his heart caught in his chest. He felt the chip of wood burst into flame, searing his insides, turning his blood to lava.

She called me putra. Son. My mother treats me like a contemptible stranger, treats Kausalya-maa with such loathing and disrespect, and yet she calls me putra. She regards me as a son. This is my true mother. She must be. Who else would show such love and kindness to the son of her arch-enemy? She is the one I must turn to for guidance through this time of crisis.

He bent down and caught hold of her feet again, clasping them tightly, holding on to her as if he would never let go.

'Maa,' he said, his voice cracking with emotion. 'Maa.'

Mother.

In the depths of his fever-sleep, Dasaratha stirred briefly, eyes fluttering without opening. He subsided again in an instant. His face was more restful, as if his soul had found some little peace in the midst of his suffering.

Guru Vashishta and Sumantra were in the seal room when Mantri Jabali burst in. The minister's usually immaculately groomed hair and dress were dishevelled and splattered with stains. He was out of breath and gasping as if he had run a mile or two.

'Mahadev, Pradhan-Mantriji, forgive the intrusion . . .' He broke down, sobbing. 'Something is happening in the dungeons! Please come. Now!'

TEN

'Ananga-ashrama is the last peaceful place you will find on your southward journey, rajkumar. Alas, you will find none of these gentle attractions as you proceed south of this point. Beds of darbha grass and sour berry juice will seem like palace comforts after tonight. My heart aches to imagine what trials and tribulations may lie in store for you two young rajkumars in the next few days. Especially—' He broke off, glancing up at the sage. 'But it is not my business to speak of those matters. By Shiva's grace, you are in the hands of the venerable Brahmarishi Vishwamitra. He is your guru now. And you should count yourselves blessed that after being raised on the infinite wisdom of Guru Vashishta, one of the oldest and most venerated of the Seven Seers, you are now being tutored by yet another of the same septet, the youngest and most powerful seer in this age, Vishwamitra himself. May his infinite wisdom guide you well on your perilous journey. For none have gone the way you go and returned this way alive before.'

Rishi Adhranga shuddered briefly, although there was no wind and it was warm by the fire. 'None who were mortal.'

He was silent after that, staring into the fire for several more moments, stroking his beard. When more time had passed than seemed intended, and the youngest brahmacharya, Dumma, had begun to shift impatiently, one of the older brahmacharyas spoke quietly in his guru's ear. Rishi Adhranga blinked and looked up at Rama again. 'Excuse my lack of manners. We of Ananga-ashrama are unaccustomed to the social niceties befitting such honourable company. You asked me how is it possible that this grove remains so idyllic and tranquil even though it borders on the dread Bhayanak-van, or to use its modern name, the Southwoods. To know this, you must first know the history of Ananga-ashrama and the grove in which it stands. By your grace, I will tell this tale. It is a short one.'

He permitted himself a small smile. 'Short, that is, by our standards.' The smile was mirrored all around the fire. 'And one you might perhaps have heard in brief from your Guru Vashishta. For this grove is more widely known as Kama-ashrama and the tale is often told as that of Kama's Folly.'

Lakshman spoke up, sounding surprised. 'But Kama's Folly is the place where Shiva destroyed Lord Kama. That's a myth.'

'Indeed, Rajkumar Lakshman. Over time, truth becomes fact, fact is rewritten as history, history fades to legend, and eventually, legend remains as myth. Yet you are blessed. For you live in the Treta-Yuga, the Age of Reason. Not as blessed as the Satya-Yuga or Age of Truth, but close enough that you may still tread the same sites where devas once lived and loved and fought, and those tales you call myths were once living events as real as your own actions. Over time even these tales will fade from memory, and by the coming of the Kali-Yuga or Age of Darkness, they will be mere race-memories, dismissed as mythology or fantasy by those who believe themselves rational and scientific. Yet to us who live here and now, these *are* scientific and rational tales. For they obey the scientific rules of our world without exception. All you need is a proper knowledge of our science. Or, as we Aryas name it, vidya.'

He smiled sadly, looking into the fire. 'But I digress once again. Forgive these little wanderings of mine. We rishis of the order of Shiva have vowed our lives to the worship and contemplation of the Destroyer. Katha-vidya, or the science of tale-telling, is an important and precious part of our calling. You might even say it is our only wealth, and if stories are treasure, why, then we are rich men, every one of us here. Are we not, my good rishis?'

'Rich men!' they responded with one voice. It was evidently a favourite call and response.

'To return to my katha, then. As I said, this hermitage which we call Ananga-ashrama is one and the same as the mythic place you know as Kama-ashrama. We call it Ananga-ashrama for a very good reason which you will know by the time I am finished. My katha dates back to the time after the creation, when devas lived on Prithvi, back in the morning of the first day of Brahma, also known as the Satya-Yuga, for all was innocent and uncorrupted then. Brahmacharyas, do you know how long is a day of Brahma?'

Dumma, the youngest, was the first to speak, his lips still glistening with drying berry juice.

'Pranaam, guruji. Each day of Brahma consists of 2,160,000,000 of our solar years. When Brahma has created the world, it remains unaltered for this entire period. At the end of a single day of Brahma, the world and all it contains is consumed by fire, only the brahmarishis, devas and elements surviving. Brahma then sleeps for an unknown period of time. When he awakens once more, he again creates the world, and a new day of Brahma begins. When he completes a hundred of his years in this manner, Brahma's own existence ends, and he, the universe, the devas and sages and all else are resolved into their constituent elements.'

The young brahmacharya's face broke into a triumphant grin, exulting in his rote-learning and obviously pleased at having shown off his vidya before his older fellows.

'Well said, young Dumma. But I only asked you for the duration of a single day of Brahma. The rest of your explanation was not called for. It expended breath and energy that could have been better utilised in your invocation of Shiva, rather than in a childish attempt to generate envy in the breasts of your fellow brahmacharyas.'

Dumma's grin vanished, reminding Rama of Bharat in younger days, when he always tried to compete with his oldest brother in Guru Vashishta's gurukul. It brought a pleasing twinge of nostalgia to his heart. *Those were great years, when the four of us were like one. Even our fights brought us closer together.*

'As I was saying,' Rishi Adhranga went on in his measured, patient way, 'these events happened in the first part of the first day of Brahma. The devas lived their lives unburdened by the responsibilities of governing creation. Only a few mortals had been created, and not all Asuras had yet declared their hostility against the gods. It was in this period that Rudra, whom we now speak of as Lord Shiva, a simple mendicant who took pleasure in meditating in cremation grounds and in passing his time in the company of spirits, ghouls, goblins and the like, took into his heart a desire to wed the beautiful Sati, daughter of Lord Daksha, Seed Spreader. I use the terms Seed Spreader or Seed Caster in the sense of Prajapati, or He Who Procreates His Own Kind, not in the agricultural sense of one who literally flings seeds into furrowed soil. For Lord Daksha was one of only a few chosen mortals who had evolved from their simian ancestors and had been given the task of multiplying the numbers of their race upon this Prithvi. Like your own ancestor Lord Manu, rajkumars, who composed the laws by which civilised humans would govern themselves, descended from the deva Surya himself, who was likewise a Seed Spreader and one of the founders of the Arya race.'

He paused in his beard-stroking for a moment, then continued. The silence that met his pause was testimony to the attentiveness of his listeners. 'So young Rudra— for even Lord Shiva was young once—became greatly enamoured with Lord Daksha's daughter Sati and desired to wed her, and beautiful and virtuous Sati herself desired to become mate to the young mendicant Rudra. At first, she was somewhat put off by Rudra's supernatural companions and wild antics in the netherworld, but she was confident she would rid him of his bachelor habits once they were conjugally united.'

He allowed himself a wisp of a smile. 'She would not be the first woman to believe that she could change our Lord Shiva through the use of feminine devices.'

Little Dumma flashed a grin at the rishi's aside, treating Rama to a glimpse of several missing teeth in his upper line. Rama resisted the urge to grin back.

'Prajapati Daksha did not share his daughter Sati's affection for the wild-eyed young wanderer. He had raised his daughter on silks and satins, gold and silver, pearls and diamonds. He was appalled at her desire to wed this unruly, dishevelled, homeless young mendicant who rode the black buffalo of the Lord of Death, Yamaraj, wore a serpent as a necklace entwined around his neck, drank poison as an intoxicant and went around clad in a chain of human skulls and a barely modest swatch of uncured leopard's skin. Lord Daksha took his responsibility

359

as a Seed Spreader very seriously and he wanted his daughter to mate with much better stock than this strange mendicant.

'So he rejected Rudra and refused his daughter's wish. But Sati's love for Rudra was too strong by then. Defying her father, she went ahead and married her chosen mate. Once Rudra became his son-in-law, Daksha was compelled by deva tradition to include him in all family rituals and affairs. But Daksha was proud and uncompromising. He knew that despite his wild appearance and peculiar habits, Rudra had a great sense of dignity. Daksha thought that if he insulted his new son-in-law publicly, Rudra would be so offended he would leave Sati alone and return to his wild bachelor ways.

'So, to slight his new son-in-law, Daksha staged a great yagna and deliberately neglected to invite Rudra, while making sure that Sati herself was present. Sati soon realised what her father had done as all the assembled guests began commenting critically on Rudra's absence.

'But Daksha's scheme flew back in his own face, like an ill-shot arrow returned by a powerful wind. More than Rudra himself, it was Sati who was devastated by her father's insult. Blaming her father for dishonouring her husband, she threw herself bodily into the very same yagna havan, calling out to the fire god Agni to accept her sacrifice. Before any of her family could stop her, she was consumed by the flames of the sacred fire. Her name became a synonym for self-sacrifice. Even today, any widowed wife who chooses to follow her husband to the afterlife may voluntarily consign herself to his funeral pyre in an act of sati.

'Lord Daksha was stricken by the outcome of his actions, but it was too late to undo what had been done. News of Sati's sacrifice reached Rudra. At first, the dark-skinned deva was consumed by anger as fierce as the agni that had consumed his wife, but he grew heartsick when he realised that he could not spill the blood of his beloved Sati's father. Unable to avenge her death and cleanse his grief through violence, he vowed to retire from life itself. Since he was a deva and immortal, he could not take his own life. Instead, he sat beneath a banyan tree and began the epic meditations which we attempt to emulate even today in humble mortal form as the asanas of yoga.'

Rishi Adhranga raised one hand, indicating the wild webbing of the tree above his head. 'This same ancient tree beneath which we sit tonight. As you can see, its vines and limbs are matted in empathy with our Lord Shiva's own matted hair, reminding us of his great grief at the loss of his beloved.'

Rama saw Dumma release a silent sigh. The young brahmacharya was enraptured, lost in the katha. As he glanced away from the boy, something flickered at the very edge of his vision. He glanced sharply at the far side of the clearing, at the place where the light of the flames dimmed and faded into the impenetrable moonless darkness of the grove. There it was again: two tiny red pinpoints briefly glimpsed. *Like the reflection of the firelight off a pair of eyes.* It was probably just a rabbit. Although those eyes had seemed too high and too large to be a ground-hugging rabbit. A doe then. He concentrated his attention on the rishi's katha.

'Now, as you all know, when Shiva meditates, the world could end and he would not be aware of it. So it was that in his grief he lost all consciousness of what took place around him. Aeons passed. The morning of the first day of Brahma grew closer to noon. Civilisations rose and fell. Great empires were raised and collapsed.

361

The eternal battle between the devas and Asuras began in earnest and raged on relentlessly. Millennia flowed by like the waters of the sacred Ganges.

'Our Lord Shiva would have maintained his yogic trance until the sun itself grew red and weak and the planets crumbled away to dust. Even the devas themselves dared not disturb his samabhavimudra, that sacred state where the eyes seem partially open but in fact the being sees nothing of this world with his physical vision. Shiva had accomplished this supreme state of existence, remaining barely alive enough to maintain his body in this world, yet achieving a perfect union with the inner self, or brahman. He had passed beyond karma or the need for good actions, and had transcended the material realm completely.

'But one day, an event came to pass in the material world that would result in his return to this physical plane of karma and rebirth. A powerful Yaksi named Tataka had began to torment the inhabitants of a forest near the site where Shiva meditated.'

'Gurudev, shama. Forgive me for interrupting.'

The rishi paused, and turned his gaze on Lakshman. 'Aagya, shishya. Speak your mind.' He addressed Lakshman as he would any student in his ashram. Here, there were no rajkumars or maharajas.

'Pranaam, guruji,' Lakshman said, joining his hands together and showing the customary respect accorded to any guru in his ashram. 'You said a powerful Yaksi was tormenting people. By Yaksi, I take it you mean a female Yaksa, guruji. But the Yaksa race is benign and friendly to mortals as well as to the devas.' He shrugged self-consciously. 'Of course, that is what we learned at our guruji Vashishta's gurukul. I don't actually know if Yaksas really exist any more. My mother Sumitra-maa says they were only created to scare naughty young boys to sleep.'

362

There were a few surprised titters at that. Rama smiled too. So Shaivites did have a sense of humour after all.

Rishi Adhranga stroked his beard. 'What you say is not wholly incorrect, Rajkumar Lakshman. Once the Yaksas, like several other Asura races, *were* benign and even friendly to mortals and devas. It was only a few thousand years ago that they became our bitter enemies. But to tell the story of how that came to pass would take many nights.'

He hesitated, glancing at Vishwamitra. 'To answer your question briefly, it was the Dark Lord of Lanka himself who turned the Yaksa race against mortals. Just as it was none other than Ravana who was secretly responsible for Tataka becoming the menace of her age. But that is another katha in itself. I am sure the esteemed brahmarishi will impart it to you at some appropriate time.'

Vishwamitra acknowledged the reference with a slight bow of his head.

Rishi Adhranga exhaled, his breath fogging as it escaped his lips, marking how much colder the evening had become. 'To return to our katha. This Yaksi was a scourge on the face of Prithvi. Her ravages had turned the entire region around her into a haunted and cursed forest. Literally, Bhayanak-van. What we now call the South-woods.'

Rama felt a chill spread through his chest. It had nothing to do with the gathering cold and the fading fire.

ELEVEN

The palace grounds were dark and silent, but there were quads of guards everywhere, watching every square yard of the property with hawkish scrutiny. Outside the gates, a surprisingly large crowd of citizens waited, several of them seated cross-legged on the street, talking in soft whispers or praying to lit diyas. A flurry of hope swept through them as they saw the familiar faces of the guru and the prime minister approach. Several of them rose and came forward, enquiring eagerly after the maharaja's condition.

'He is much the same,' Sumantra said. 'He counts on your prayers.'

They subsided at once, disappointed.

Sumantra and the guru left the palace, escorted by a whole platoon of PFs. Captain Drishti Kumar, back on duty after a brief respite, was taking no chances. They walked the two miles to the city jail, situated flush against the seventh wall on the north-east corner of the city. A series of gates, heavily guarded and barred, provided the jail with direct access to the outside world, effectively segregating the prison and dungeons from the city proper.

Even so, the prison was heavily guarded. It had been decades since spies had been apprehended in Ayodhya, and most of the current breed of kshatriyas had grown up unaware that such treachery could even be possible. Entire platoons had volunteered themselves for guard duty at the city jail. And had the palace permitted it, a crowd would have been gathered here as well, waiting eagerly to hear what treacherous revelations were forced from the tongues of the conspirators.

The guard acknowledged the three visitors and allowed them to pass unquestioned. They entered the compound, which was as heavily patrolled, and passed through the several gates that made escape an impossibility. Finally they were in the main prison building. They passed rows of empty cells filled with nothing more than bales of hay and chamber pots. Despite his misgivings, Sumantra had given the order to release all lesser prisoners that afternoon. It had felt strange to proclaim such a step in celebration of Rama's forthcoming ascension when Rama himself was not present to join in. But tradition demanded it, and tradition was everything in Arya society.

The warden of the prison, a man with a massive build that was well suited to his profession, was waiting for them at the portal to the dungeon stairwell. 'Masters,' he said. 'I beseech you. Go no further. Great evil is at work down in those dungeons.'

'And our job is to root out evil and send it fleeing,' Guru Vashishta said calmly. 'Let us pass, good warden.'

He looked at the guru, then at Sumantra.

Sumantra said firmly but without raising his voice, 'In the name of the maharaja, let us through.'

The warden nodded slowly, his face drained of colour. His hands trembled slightly as he inserted the key into the portal lock. The lock snapped smoothly into place, and he swung the iron-barred door open. Sumantra followed the guru in, then turned to see Mantri Jabali still standing outside the portal. He had begun shaking again. He clutched the bars of the portal gate, teeth clacking together.

'I cannot go on,' he said. 'The warden knows as much as I do. I was only questioning them when . . . when they changed.'

Guru Vashishta said kindly, 'Go home, good Jabali. Brew yourself some hot broth and cover yourself well. You are suffering from shock. We will deal with this matter. Tomorrow, in the light of day, we shall speak again.'

Jabali bowed, his head striking the bars inadvertently. 'Thank you, gurudev. I shall pray for your safe return.'

As they went through the second portal gate, the one that opened directly on to the stairwell, and began their descent, Sumantra looked back. Jabali was clinging to the bars of the first portal with the desperate look of a man imprisoned for life. Or a man watching his best friend being imprisoned for life. The bars created a curiously confusing image: it was difficult to tell if they were keeping the prisoners within or barring those who lay without.

The stairwell was barely large enough for a single man to pass through at a time. The warden, the tallest of them, led the way with a small diya in his hand to provide some light. The ceiling was so low, they had to bow their heads, and even so, Sumantra could feel the stones rasping against the back of his head all the way down. It was a safety feature typical of Arya military architecture: in the event of an outbreak, a single armed guard could contain an entire dungeon filled with criminals. It was impossible to fight one's way upwards with one's head bent over and arms clasped on one's chest. But under the circumstances, it felt even more unsettling, like a descent in some nightmare.

After what seemed like a small aeon, they reached the dungeon level. Another door opened directly on to the stairwell, providing yet another point of defence.

The warden unlocked this door and paused, glancing back at the guru and Sumantra, his face lit eerily from below by the flickering diya held in his palm.

'I have vacated the guards from this level. After the first two were killed, I did not deem it necessary to risk the lives of any more. In any case, the prisoners . . . whatever that thing is . . . it does not seem to seek to escape.'

Sumantra frowned. *Whatever that thing is.* There were eleven spies taken prisoner that morning. What was this thing he spoke of? And what did he mean, *it does not seem to seek to escape?* What other problem could one have with a prisoner?

He held his questions back as the warden led them out of the constricting stairwell and into a slightly broader and higher passageway. Still it was barely wide enough for two men to walk abreast—shoulder to shoulder— and the ceiling was a shade under seven feet high. The warden's bulk almost filled the entire passageway as he led them down a sloping corridor that continued to descend in stages, like very long steps in some unending staircase.

Sumantra tried to recall how low the dungeon was. About fifty yards below street level, if he remembered correctly. The architects had had to burrow this low to get well beneath the river's bed. Even so, the ceiling dripped in places, and centuries of constant seepage had formed a permanent patina of moss on most walls. The place smelled dank and wet. The small mashaals that hung on the walls at intervals sputtered in the drips from the ceiling. For a moment, Sumantra forgot what had brought them here and began to worry about the possibility of the whole place collapsing and the river coming roaring through.

Gradually the passage broadened enough to allow them to walk slightly more comfortably two abreast.

367

The seepage reduced. The walls seemed almost dry, although fingers of lichenous growth still poked their way through between stones at places.

Finally they came to a barred door that hung open. The inside of the door was spattered with more of the same dark stains that had discoloured Mantri Jabali's clothes. The floor was streaked with blood too, as if a bleeding carcass had been dragged across it.

The warden stopped and turned to them, his face pale. 'My second man dragged himself as far as this point. The key snapped off in the lock, as you can see here, so I had no choice but to leave this door open. That one, though,' he pointed ahead, 'is barred, bolted and locked shut. Not that it would do much good if that thing in there put its mind to getting through. I don't think locks and doors would stop what's in there.'

'Thank you, good warden. You may leave us now and return to your post. We shall proceed on our own now.'

The warden looked at the guru silently. Then he nodded. 'As you please, masters. Vishnu bless you for allowing me to save myself from entering that hell-hole again.'

He moved past them to return up the passageway they had come down. He handed his key-ring to Sumantra as he brushed past. 'That will open the last door. Now when you come back,' he added, his voice suggesting that the possibility was a remote one, 'I'll be waiting for you at the top of the stairwell. If you need any help—'

'Do you think you could help us if we get into trouble in there?' the guru asked quietly, indicating the dungeon.

The warden shook his head slowly. 'I warrant not. But even so—'

'We shall send for you if required. Go now, good warden. Leave us.'

Sumantra stepped forward. 'One moment. Are all the eleven prisoners in there together?'

'Aye, Pradhan-Mantri. But you may have difficulty counting them off.'

And with that cryptic reply, the warden shuffled up the passageway, fading out of sight.

Sumantra flinched as Guru Vashishta's hand fell on his shoulder. 'Courage, Sumantra. Remember this before we go in. The power of brahman is the essence of all supernatural and natural energy in the universe. Even those who seek to do evil deeds must use and pervert the same flow of brahman to serve their heinous ends. Therefore, they can never be a match for we who serve the good side of brahman. Good will always triumph over evil in this war.'

Sumantra nodded, unable to get any words past the lump in his throat.

'Now, open the door and let us face whatever awaits us within this dungeon,' said the guru.

Sumantra moved forward to unlock the dungeon door. His hands shook a little as he turned the oversized key in the massive lock.

The door swung open slowly on smoothly oiled hinges, exposing a dark maw as inviting as the open jaws of a gargantuan worm.

The guru raised his staff, reciting a mantra under his breath. He struck the staff on the floor twice. With a puff, the top of the staff began to emit a dull but surprisingly effective blue light. Holding it before him like a mashaal, the guru stepped into the dungeon chamber.

Taking a deep breath, Pradhan-Mantri Sumantra followed.

369

TWELVE

The rishi's voice was as soothing as the distant gurgle of the rivulet. Rama turned to it thankfully, immersing himself in the katha to shut out the chorus of thoughts, anxieties and emotions that were crowding the back of his mind. It had been a long and difficult day and it felt good to simply sit here and listen.

'Tataka's ravages were so terrible, the very land itself was blighted permanently by her forays. In time, she would have withered even the grove in which Lord Rudra sat meditating. Only his presence preserved this plot of land. On one occasion, she ventured as far as that cluster of cherry trees on the eastern edge of the grove, and—'

Vishwamitra spoke up, his voice quiet but firm. 'I will tell them the tale of Tataka some other time, Rishi Adhranga. Pray, continue your tale of how Ananga-ashrama earned its name.'

The rishi inclined his head to the brahmarishi. 'Shama, mahadev. I will try not to wander from my katha-path again.'

He stroked his beard a few more times, finding his rhythm once more. 'As I was saying, Tataka's atrocities soon grew too terrible for the devas to ignore. A day came when the extent of her devastation compelled an outcry on Prithvi and mortals began to appeal to the devas to intervene and put an end to her reign of terror. The devas sent the oldest and greatest of the Seven Seers, the great sage Narada himself, to investigate Tataka's misdeeds. He returned quickly with a terrifying report. When the devas heard it, they unanimously decided that Tataka must be stopped.

'But before anyone could take action, the devas were besieged by hordes of Asura armies led by the Lord of Lanka, Ravana himself. After many wars and battles in which the Asuras lost as much ground as they gained, their disparate races had finally united under the banner of Ravana. And his ambition was as great as the Asura host he led. He sought to invade the very cities of the gods. The shining cities of Amravati and Vaikunta were both besieged, and mighty Indra, leader of the devas, as well as Kartikeya and Ganesha, senapatis of the armies of the devas, were hard-pressed to defend those mighty domains. Not a single deva could be spared to go down to the realm of Prithvi and deal with the intolerable menace of Tataka.'

The rishi paused for effect. 'Except one.'

Young Dumma chirped up at once: 'Rudra athwa Shiva.'

'Yes, young brahmacharya. Rudra also known as Shiva. Only Shiva himself possessed the power to face the fierce Yaksi. For he had tasted the poison of Sagara and survived. In doing so, he alone of the devas had experienced the corruption of an-atma, the opposite of brahman, that darkest of darknesses that exist in the absence of the light of atma or the eternal soul. Shiva could use his power of destruction to cleanse evil things, preparing the way for their re-creation by Brahma. He had only to open his third eye and Tataka would exist no more in her present form.

'Jai jai Shiv Shankar,' chanted the assembled brahmacharyas in unison. Lakshman blinked at the

371

unexpectedly loud chanting, but Rama had seen it coming. He was still focused as much on the being in the grove as on the rishi's katha. He wondered how Lakshman had failed to notice it. It was evident that the maha-mantras Bala and Atibala were having different effects on him and Lakshman. A twinge of an insight flashed in his mind, a glimmer of an idea why this should be so. But it was gone before he could catch it and examine it clearly.

'However, as you will recall, Shiva was deeply engrossed in his meditation and was determined to remain engrossed thus for the duration of all the remaining days of Brahma, until the end of existence itself. Such was his self-discipline. So it was decided by the devas that an emissary be sent to awaken him from his meditation. Sage Narada declined the mission, for reasons unknown. The devas then sent the beauteous Parvati, an incarnation of Sati herself, Shiva's lost wife. Sati had chosen to be reborn once again in order to reconsummate her relationship with her beloved mate. This time, she made sure she picked a father and mother who would honour her husband, unlike the wretched Daksha, whose name was forever linked with his shameful misdeed. Sati in her new avatar as Parvati waited patiently for many thousands of our years in the grove where her lord sat meditating, gathering his favourite flowers and dressing her hair with their scented blossoms, and doing all she could to rouse him from his yogic trance. But even her sensual presence could not interrupt his samabhavimudra. So the devas resolved to send the god of desire, Kama, to help rouse Shiva.'

Rishi Adhranga paused, searching the far side of the circle for the face of his youngest acolyte. 'Dumma, can you tell us what human quality Kama is the god of?'

'Pranaam, guruji,' replied the boy, struggling to speak calmly. 'Kama is desire for good in any form. Be it love, procreation, or simply goodness on earth in all forms.'

The rishi nodded, satisfied with the response. 'Well spoken. And yet, being the lord of sexual desire as well as all other desires, Kama was prone to some mischievous ways. When he saw Parvati clad so sensuously in anticipation of her husband's amorous reawakening, he thought he could sling down two partridges with one throw. He would rouse Shiva by instilling in him sexual desire for Parvati, thus reuniting the lost lovers as well as fulfilling his mission. With this end in mind, Kama danced and frolicked in the grove around the tree beneath which Shiva sat.'

The rishi paused and gestured around at the clearing, giving them a moment to reflect and imagine the god of desire dancing in the very spot where they now sat.

As they glanced around, casting back to that mythic time in their mind's eye, several of them looked deep into the dark shadows of the grove itself, trying to recreate the events and time of which their guru spoke. *Now someone will see the being in the grove. Or at least Lakshman will.* But not a single one of them seemed to glimpse what Rama had seen. The two red eyes glowed as warmly as coals in a bed of ash. *Only I*, he thought grimly. *It is my karma to see and deal with the being that awaits me in there.*

The others had turned back to the rishi, who was continuing his katha.

'When Kama's first frolics went unnoticed by Shiva, the god of desire grew bolder. He strung his bow, made of a sugarcane stalk and a living cord of honeybees, dipped an arrow into the centre of a red rose, and loosed it at Shiva's heart. Pierced by the benign missile, Shiva awoke at last. But stirred as he was from deep meditation on his lost mate, he was angered to find the god of desire attempting to arrange what he thought was a new mating for him. Had Shiva only taken an instant to look closely at Parvati, he would have seen that Kama was only trying to reunite him with his own sweet Sati. But Shiva is not known for his patience. He opened his third eye and blasted Lord Kama into ashes. *Bhasam kar diya Kamadev ko.*'

Young Dumma shuddered and looked around fearfully, as if expecting Shiva to appear right there and then and blast them all to nothingness.

'Kama was left bodiless. An-anga. He Who Has No Physical Body. From which word our hermitage is named Ananga-ashrama. Then Rati the wife of Kama ran to Brahma tearing her hair, beating her breast, and moaning inconsolably over the loss of her husband. Brahma, creator of all creatures great and small, promised Rati that when Shiva and Parvati were married, Kama would be restored to his body. Now the task of rousing Shiva fell to Parvati, who had to do so not only in order to regain her lost mate, but also to restore Kama, and to defeat the Yaksi Tataka. More determined than ever to succeed, Parvati began a severe penance abiding by the laws laid down by Shiva himself, the father of austerity. These ten laws, of course, are the cornerstone of our life here at Ananga-ashrama.'

Rishi Adhranga glanced at Vishwamitra, and Rama knew that he was tempted to spell out Shiva's ten laws of penitential meditation. He was relieved when the rishi continued the tale instead.

'After millennia of self-inflicted austerity, the lovely Parvati had lost much of her beauty. Her spirit was as lean and withered as her body in the wake of such great tapasya. Yet still she toiled on in her attempt to rouse her beloved. And still Shiva failed to heed her prayers.

'Finally, when it seemed that Parvati must surely waste away to nothingness, a handsome young ascetic came to her and asked her why she inflicted such suffering on herself. When she told him the object of her penance, he laughed in disbelief and wondered if the strange and terrifying Shiva deserved the love of a woman so beautiful. The young ascetic then sought to arouse her desire for himself, promising to be a better husband to her than Shiva could ever be. Parvati was shocked to find herself responding to his caresses as she experienced an overpowering attraction to the handsome stranger. Disgusted at her own disloyalty, she resolved to take her own life once more rather than succumb to his advances. But just as she was about to reprise the self-immolation of her earlier avatar Sati, the ascetic revealed himself to be none other than Shiva, awoken at long last and only seeking to tease Parvati as she had teased and taunted him with her sexuality for so long in Kama's Grove. The two of them then danced the tandav, the great and terrible dance of procreation, awakening the entire universe with their tantric sexuality, and at the moment of their joining, by using the formidable energies unleashed by their union, Lord Brahma was able to restore Kama to his body.'

Young Dumma heaved a great sigh of contentment. His fellows grinned and exchanged amused glances at his evident relief. Rishi Adhranga nodded indulgently and continued.

'Shiva and Parvati were lost for aeons in love-making on the peak of Mount Kailasa, where they made their home. Eventually the devas began despairing of what they had done, for it seemed that Shiva would never leave Parvati's arms long enough to slay Tataka. But Parvati was mindful of their need, and bore Shiva a young son, Kartikeya. It was Kartikeya who went forth to put an end to the scourge of Tataka. Later, as we all know, Shiva and Parvati's blessed

375

union would yield another equally illustrious son, the mighty Ganesha. He who had his head lopped off by his own father and had to make do with the head of a baby elephant.'

'But that is another story, for another time,' said Vishwamitra hastily. 'Thank you, Rishi Adhranga. Seldom have I heard the tale of Kama's Folly told with such simple precision and accuracy. Truly, we are most pleased and honoured to have received the fruits of your katha-vidya.'

After Rama and Lakshman had added their own gratitude to the rishi, Vishwamitra steered the conversation back to the matter of their departure the next morning. 'We shall require a raft to sail downriver. I am aware of the skill of your ashram in making balsa wood rafts. Perhaps your brahmacharyas could show my young companions how to make one tonight. We leave at daybreak.'

'Even better,' the rishi said, 'my brahmacharyas will be happy to make such a vessel for your use. Of course, the young shishyas are welcome to watch and learn. We keep a supply of ready-cut balsa logs expressly for this purpose, and we are accustomed to lashing rafts together in an hour or two. My boys are quite happy to build one simply for the distraction it provides from their usual chores. I will see to it.'

From the ripple of excitement that spread through the brahmacharyas, it was evident that his acolytes agreed with this view.

'We are indebted to you for your grace and hospitality, rishiji,' Vishwamitra said.

Lakshman spoke up. 'Mahadev, may I ask the rishi one last question?'

Vishwamitra nodded. 'Go ahead, rajkumar.'

'The katha you narrated so eloquently was mainly about Shiva and his epic meditation on the loss of his consort. Kamadev hardly plays much part in the whole story. Then why is this spot named after Kama?'

Rishi Adhranga smiled, turning his face to his shishyas, all of whom were smiling as well.

Lakshman looked around, puzzled. 'Did I say something unseemly?'

'Not at all, shishya,' the rishi replied. 'It's just that every time the katha of Kama's Grove is narrated, the listener always asks this very same question. Who will answer this time?'

Dumma's hand had shot up even before the rishi asked the question, Rama noted with amusement. Adhranga beamed at the young acolyte.

'Tonight seems to be your night to speak, young Dumma. Very well, perform this last service to our guests.'

Dumma spoke rapidly, his words tumbling one over the other like a series of child-acrobats at a country mela. It was obvious he had this answer down pat. 'The story is not just about Lord Shiva and Devi Parvati, but about their great love for one another. A love that neither samay nor karma could tear asunder. It was for this reason that the devas sent Kama, god of love, to try to awaken Shiva from his deep meditation. Hence this spot is named in honour not just of the god of love but for the epic love of Shiva and Parvati. Kama's Folly, Kama's Grove, this is the most sacred lovers' rendezvous in all the three worlds.'

He stopped to catch his breath, glanced at his teacher, then went on unexpectedly: 'And good sirs, some day when you find your own life's true love, then you would be well advised to visit this grove with your beloved and seal your bond in this most romantic of spots!'

Rishi Adhranga's face lost its beatific smile and he sputtered indignantly: 'How many times have I told you, Dumma! That is not part of our katha-vidya. You are not to repeat that last part ever again! Am I understood?'

Young Dumma's face fell. 'But guruji, they said you had changed your mind and I should make sure to tell our esteemed guests about this romantic side of our sacred shrine.'

Rishi Adhranga's face turned dark. 'Who said that? Show him to me!'

Young Dumma looked around at his fellows. They were all standing around with completely innocent expressions, as if they had no idea what had just transpired. He shifted uncomfortably, then hung his head, his babyish features curled into an appropriately contrite expression.

'Perhaps I mistook their words, guruji. I'm sorry. It won't happen again.'

Rishi Adhranga scanned the faces of his acolytes intently.

'What are you all staring at? Go on and start fetching the material for the raft. You heard the brahmarishi. That raft has to be ready before daybreak. Get to work then, Shaivites. Om Namah Shiva. *Praised be the name of Shiva.*'

'Om Namah Shiva,' they repeated, and scuttled about busily.

Adhranga caught sight of Dumma standing alone, waiting to be chastised further. 'You too, Dumma. Go on and make yourself useful.'

Dumma grinned with relief and sprinted to join his fellows. Rama had the distinct impression that the young acolyte wasn't quite as contrite about his lapse as he had looked earlier.

Rishi Adhranga scowled and turned back to the princes and the brahmarishi. Vishwamitra seemed to be staring at a point high up on the trunk of a nearby jackfruit tree. Rama couldn't tell if he was offended or amused by the young acolyte's outburst.

'My apologies, brahmarishi,' Adhranga said, looking irritated. 'I have told him several times before that it would not be in our best interests to spread that legend once again.'

378

'Once again, rishidev?' Rama tried to keep his face straight and suitably serious. It took some effort.

Rishi Adhranga sighed. 'Until recently, perhaps just a hundred or so years ago, this place was a notorious lovers' rendezvous. It was believed, you see, that couples who . . . um . . . consummated their relationship in this sacred grove would experience a bonding as eternal as the love of Shiva and Parvati.' He cleared his throat uncomfortably. 'It made things quite awkward for our order, as you can well imagine.'

'Yes, indeed,' Vishwamitra said, still keeping his eyes on the distant point. 'We can well imagine.'

Rama and Lakshman looked at the brahmarishi curiously.

Vishwamitra glanced at them, then added quickly: 'We can imagine how awkward it must have been. Very, very awkward, no doubt.'

Adhranga nodded unhappily. 'Couples sneaking through the grove all night, indulging in . . . grossly inappropriate behaviour . . . often while we were busy with our katha-vidya. And it would . . . distract some of our younger brahmacharyas while engrossed in their celibate studies. It's hard maintaining celibacy when half the kingdom's love-besotted couples are rolling about and squealing all around you.' He shook his head, sighing. 'Thank Shiva we don't suffer those distractions any more.'

'Yes, thanks be to Shiva.' The brahmarishi was staring at the jackfruit tree, Rama realised suddenly, with a touch more concentration than was needed. Rama and Lakshman glanced at each other and turned their faces away, to avoid the rishi seeing the gouts of laughter that threatened to burst free.

Rishi Adhranga shook his head. 'I can tell you one thing, my friends. One hundred and twenty years old I am, and for almost that entire duration I have known only this ashram as home, devoted to the service of Shiva.

But in all these many years, one thing that never seems to change is the shamelessness of young lovers in heat. Why, on one occasion, I was walking through the grove at dawn in search of some berries for our ritual—'

'Excuse me, Rishiji,' Vishwamitra cut in hastily. 'But perhaps my companions could join your brahmacharyas and assist in preparing the vessel for our journey. And as we have to leave early, I have a few spiritual obligations of my own to perform before this night of Holi Purnima passes.'

'Of course,' Rishi Adhranga said. He beckoned to a passing acolyte. 'Shambhu, our guests wish to observe how we make our rafts. Take them and treat them with respect. Brahmarishi, if you will follow me, I will escort you to the mandir we maintain on the north wall of the ashram. That would be the most appropriate place for you to offer your prayers.'

Rama and Lakshman nudged each other as they followed Shambhu to the far side of the clearing. 'Was the brahmarishi suppressing his laughter or was that just my imagination?' Lakshman asked.

'I think he was straining to hold back the loudest guffaw ever heard in the seven nations!' Rama replied.

Both of them laughed as they were led to where a group of brahmacharyas sat amidst a pile of freshly cut balsa wood logs, a pot of tar slowly melting over a cookfire, and vines and creepers they were weaving into ropes to use as lashings. They looked up as Rama and Lakshman approached. All of them rose suddenly, bowing deferentially to the princes.

'Be welcome, rajkumars of Ayodhya. We are honoured by your presence.'

Rama and Lakshman looked around, surprised. 'I thought Shaivites renounced all worldly titles and hierarchies when they took their oaths,' Rama said.

380

The brahmacharyas looked at each other, grinning awkwardly. 'That is so, rajkumar. But how can we ignore your royal stature?'

Rama went over and caught hold of the brahmacharya's arm, taking him by surprise. 'What is your name, my friend?'

'Shankar, my lord,' the surprised boy replied.

'Shankar,' Rama said. 'Feel my arm.'

'Rajkumar?'

'Go on, feel my arm. Squeeze it, bend it, pinch it if you like.'

Shankar looked around at his fellows as if wondering if he was being made the butt of some practical joke. Finally he turned back to Rama and looked at the prince's hand. He reached out hesitantly and touched it.

Rama nodded. 'Go on, don't be afraid. Squeeze it.'

Shankar squeezed Rama's hand.

'Does it feel any different from your own?'

Shankar shook his head.

'You see then? I am flesh and blood, same as you are. A boy, same as you are. Mortal, same as you all. Treat me as any other mortal flesh-and-blood boy, then, please. Not as a prince or a lord or a deva. Just a boy. Is that understood?'

'The same goes for me,' Lakshman said. 'The next one to call me rajkumar or lord gets a whack on the back of the head. Samjhe?'

'Samjhe!' they all chorused, looking surprised but happy.

Rama nodded. 'Now sit down and show us how you make your famous rafts.'

Dumma came and sat cross-legged beside the rajkumars. 'I'll show you, Prince Rama!' He made a face, catching himself. 'I mean, brother Rama!'

'That's better,' Rama said. 'But I thought you, brother Dumma, were the expert on naughty stories rather than making rafts. That was quite a shock you gave your guru back there! I think he's still recovering from the surprise.'

Dumma grinned cheekily, all pretence of contrition gone. He leaned forward, speaking softly lest his guru should happen to overhear—even though the rishi was nowhere in sight. 'If you like, I can tell you some more naughty stories. About Kama's Grove. And the things that happened in there.'

'Watch out, brothers,' the brahmacharya named Shankar called out. 'Dumma's stories will turn your ears red with embarrassment! Don't be fooled by his cherubic looks. He's a rascal of the first order when it comes to jokes and pranks!'

Rama looked at Lakshman. 'Well, I think my brother and I wouldn't mind our ears turning a wee bit red. Not purple, mind you, just a little pink, and maybe a bit darker too!'

Dumma grinned. 'Then prepare yourselves, brothers. Because I'm going to start with the story of one of your very own ancestors and how he crept into Kama's Grove one Shivratri with his new bride. It was a moonless night and your ancestor was amorous to the point of priapism . . .'

THIRTEEN

It was a sizable chamber, perhaps ten yards by fifteen. But after a moment, as Sumantra's eyes adjusted to the bluish glow from the guru's staff, he began to discern another level, lower down. And beyond it, faintly outlined in the shadows, yet another level. He remembered from the rare past visits he had made to the dungeon that it had three levels in lengthwise sequence. The entire chamber was perhaps forty-five yards long and ten yards wide. Every fifteen yards, it fell by two full yards. The harder the criminal, the lower the level to which he was banished. The lowest level was usually waterlogged from seepage, he recalled. And the water tended to be cold, especially in winter, when the Sarayu's temperature fell to a degree or two short of freezing.

By the bluish light of the staff, he could see the chains and manacles bolted to the walls on this first level. They were all empty. There was nobody here.

The guru walked slowly to the end of the first level and started down the stairs cut out of the rock. Sumantra paused a moment at the top of the stairs, peering ahead in a vain attempt to penetrate the darkness ahead. All he could see clearly was that the second level was also deserted. But there were dark patches and streaks everywhere, and he thought he could see something caught in the manacles. They look like hands, severed hands.

Even as the realisation came to him, he caught the first whiff of the smell. The dungeon's unforgettable rankness had reached him even before they had come through the second door. A combination of mildew, rot, old stone and earth, and the various bodily emissions of generations of unfortunate traitors and criminals. But this smell was something new, something unlike anything he had smelled before. It was the smell of the deep forest, of animal sweat and fur, of leather and blood, ash and ghee. He couldn't think of any single thing that smelt like this. Yet it aroused a churning in his guts that made his bowels turn to liquid fire.

I should have stayed up there with Jabali. Why in Vishnu's name did I come down here? Fool that I am! I'll never see daylight again now.

'Steady, Pradhan-Mantri. Keep your mind free of negative thoughts. Here, take my hand.'

The guru's hand reached up to Sumantra. He stared at it dumbly for a second, then ventured down the steps. One, two, three . . . six. He stood at the second level and touched the guru's hand, thanking him.

'I can manage, gurudev. Pray, go on.'

Vashishta turned and began the descent to the third and lowest level. Halfway down the steps, he paused abruptly. Sumantra was forced to stop as well. The guru raised the staff as high as he could reach, and flexed his arm. The light blazed brighter than ever, turning almost pure white in intensity.

Sumantra was straining to see beyond the guru's head and shoulders when the door of the dungeon suddenly slammed itself shut with a clanging impact that hung in the air like the echoes of a temple bell. He turned to stare up through the darkness. The door was barely visible at the top of the stone steps, only the iron bars gleaming faintly in the light of the staff. But the sounds coming from the far side were unmistakable. *The door was being bolted and barred shut!*

He was starting up the steps when the guru's voice stopped him. 'Keys will not work on that door now, Sumantra. The force that bolted it shut wishes us to remain here until its work is done.'

Sumantra turned back, staring at the back of the guru's head. From this height, three steps up, he could see a little of the third level now. The seepage that had accumulated at the bottom of the pit over the years was now a slime-covered pool of dark fluid. That was all he could see. Just black water. Nothing else. And nobody. The stench he had smelled was coming from that pit. From something within it.

As if sensing his thoughts, a voice spoke from within the foul-smelling black water.

Come, brahmin. Come to me and see what gifts I have in store for you and your mortal companion.

And with a sputter of sparks like a mashaal being extinguished, the blue light of the guru's staff winked out, leaving them in pitch darkness.

In the darkness of Kama's Grove, the doe's downy fur glowed golden as a gilded idol. Supanakha moved slowly between the close-growing trees, stepping nimbly and delicately. Her wound of that morning was fully healed and she moved with an almost dainty gait, fully immersed in her role as a naïve forest-dwelling herbivore. She nuzzled the ground, as if searching for food or seeking the trail of her fellows. At times, she paused to raise her head, seeming to hear sounds inaudible to human ears, and shuddered briefly before moving on, away from the clearing.

The light from the ashram lanterns faded gradually, and the sound of the brahmacharyas chanting Shaivite bhajans as they worked at the raft fell slowly behind, until they were mere murmurs on the wind, ghostly hints of human presence felt rather than actually heard. The floor of the grove was soft and mulchy beneath her hooved pads, as if it had drizzled lightly in the past evening. The scent of freshly dampened earth was rich in her nostrils, as were the smells of the berries of the grove and the overall pungent effervescence of botanical growth. The leaf-carpeted ground was pleasant and cool to walk on and she found several choice tidbits to munch on as she strolled leisurely.

She had changed back into deer form before entering the grove. She had considered darkening her fur to blend in with her surroundings but the thought of changing her golden sheen to a dull, lacklustre brown or even a matted black offended her sense of aesthetics. What if she should come across Rama and he should see her in that unattractive form? Why, he wouldn't even recognise her. It occurred to her that if he came across her in her natural rakshasi form he would hardly recognise her either, but she dismissed that thought impatiently. Rama would see her as she chose to be seen. She owed him that much at least for having saved her life.

She slunk slowly through the grove, moving from tree to tree cautiously. She had moved away from the clearing when the katha-vidya session ended. The minute Rama had risen and joined the other Shaivites, she had wished him good night silently, sighing as she watched his slender form move away.

There had been many moments during the fireside tale-telling when she had feared being caught. After all, the brahmarishi had potent magic; surely he could sense

386

the presence of one rakshasi so close by? Then again, her disguise had always proved quite effective. In this garb, she *was* a doe. Even a brahmarishi would be hard pressed to perceive her as anything but.

Still, she had shivered deliciously, thrilled by the magnititude of the risk she was undertaking. And yet nothing had happened. Not only had Vishwamitra failed to notice her, even Rama, who had been preternaturally alert and on guard the whole evening, hadn't sensed her presence. Now that had been disappointing. At times, she had almost wished he would see her. Perhaps even leave those other mortals and come visit her in the grove. After all, this was Kama's Grove and this was Holi Purnima, a beautiful full-moon night in the most romantic lovers' rendezvous. And if he had come, she would have taken on the most gorgeous feminine form imaginable, more alluring than any of Indra's apsaras, and she would have thanked him for saving her life. She would have spent all night thanking him, in fact.

But that was expecting too much.

Now, miles away from the clearing, she shivered again. She had wandered aimlessly with her fantasies, hardly aware of where she was going. She was deep in the heart of the grove, in a place where the trees grew so thickly, the moonlight could barely reach the forest floor. As she moved on, lost in her reverie, the trees parted and opened out into a small clearing evidently created by lightning striking a tree and burning away a few dozen square yards of the grove. The smell of burnt timber and leaves still hung in the air, and as she moved across the clearing, the moonlight shone down as bright as silvery daylight, catching the motes of ash that were churned up by her hoofs. She was so absorbed in her reverie that she failed to notice the strange disturbance taking place only yards away.

The trees were shuddering violently. Twisting and bending apart. One particular tree, the same gnarled dead trunk that had been struck by lightning at some point in the recent past, was the centre of the disruption. Its bark rippled like the surface of a lake in which fish thrashed about just beneath the surface, unseen. The wind grew stronger in the windless grove, raising micro-tornadoes that caught up leaves and loose soil and spun them like dervishes up to several yards high.

A miniature storm cloud clustered into existence above the stump of the blasted tree, little bolts of lightning snaking out from its depths to strike at the stump. It was only when the lightning was followed by a deep ominous growl of thunder that Supanakha became aware of what was happening.

As she stared at the unnatural storm-in-the-clearing, her eyes widened, her nostrils flared, and her heartbeat quickened to flight speed. A red eye began to grow in the centre of the storm cloud, and she tried to back away slowly, her hind legs stumbling against the roots of a tree, her rear end striking the trunk of another. She shuddered violently, nostrils flaring, snout raised in that characteristic posture of a beast-of-prey confronted by a feared predator.

The trunk of the blasted tree began to uproot itself with a groaning vibration that reverberated through her body. The dust dervishes grew fiercer and faster and rose higher into the air, cutting cylindrical passages through the leaves of the overhanging fruit trees. With a shower of red sparks and a flurry of lightning bolts, the stunted tree-trunk separated from the ground, its dead but deep roots clogged with clods of soil, and began to alter form. As it grew greater in height and slimmer in shape, Supanakha herself began to change back into her natural rakshasi form. With a snort she fought the change, unwilling to return to the world of her own kind. *Let me stay a while longer*, she pleaded silently, her eyes wide and round with desperation. Just long enough to meet him again, just once.

The tree-trunk had become something obscenely unlike any natural tree-trunk. Unlike anything that could possibly grow organically from the rich belly of Prithvi Maa.

It was a being almost nine feet in height, with its heads adding perhaps two feet more. The being's body was surprisingly proportional, much like that of a human. It could have belonged to any Arya kshatriya, one who had spent a fair amount of time in rigorous physical activities. It was a superbly formed masculine body, muscled and toned to perfection. The skin was the colour of dark honey, almost blackish when seen in the darkness of the moonless grove, but glowing with a golden inner sheen on closer inspection. It reeked of good health and conditioning. This superbly formed body was clad in the minimum of clothing, just a warrior's leather langot modestly concealing its maleness. Metal-worked leather straps were lashed across the chest and shoulders and waist and thighs in a puzzling pattern that made sense only when you perceived that their purpose was to carry weapons, not clothe the body. And weapons they did carry, a dozen or more, sheathed or clasped on every limb of the magnificent body. Each an exotic artefact of a different, alien design, some clearly intended for combat against creatures not human, others capable of inflicting brutal wounds on mortal bodies, yet others of no discernible purpose. Supanakha knew that they were weapons designed to be used against all the three species: Asuras, mortals and devas. This creature had only natural enemies, no natural associates. The ultimate predator, fighting everyone, trusting no one.

Above the impressively constructed body was a massively thickened neck, easily thrice the size of a normal

389

adult Arya's neck. Veins and muscles stood out on it in bas-relief, testifying to the weight it was required to bear. Yet the unnatural girth of this part of the being's anatomy seemed oddly proportionate to the exquisitely shaped body below.

The neck had to be that strong to support the ten heads of Ravana, Lord of Lanka.

Each of these heads were about half the size of a human male head, with all the normal features in the usual places. The heads were arranged side by side, four extending beyond the creature's right shoulder to about the point at which its right elbow would reach if that arm were held out. Five more heads extended over the creature's left shoulder, just short of the left elbow if that arm were similarly held out. Each head grew out of the side of the previous one, joined at the place where the neck should have been, and joined at the ears as well. There was almost no gap between each head. Only those on either end had perfectly formed ears on their open sides. These were the auditory organs the creature used to achieve the task of hearing.

In the centre of this row of nine smaller-than-normal heads, placed directly above the massive squat neck, was the creature's primary head. This one was larger than normal size, as if to compensate for the relative smallness of its companions. Almost twice the size of a normal male head, it was unexpectedly striking. Though not exactly handsome by human standards, it had a masculine appeal that was unmistakable. This was a powerful person, its features insisted, a being accustomed to wielding and maintaining great forces. It had the arrogant, relaxed look of a being that had never known defeat and brooked no possibility of it.

Each of the ten heads had a completely different face, none bearing the slightest resemblance to the others. Yet it was clearly the one in the middle that dominated the bizarre menagerie. It was evident from the glances of fear and hatred that the others shot at their central brother, and from the supreme indifference with which the central head regarded the world, ignoring its lesser associates to either side.

Supanakha looked upon that massive central head of her cousin Ravana and felt her insides turn to mulch. With a snort of terror, she released urine involuntarily, the hot, acrid emission spattering on the leaf-carpeted floor of the grove. The rancid odour filled the little clearing at once. The ten-headed being, now fully formed from the mass of the uprooted tree-trunk, sniffed the air with his ten pairs of nostrils and snorted derisively.

Cousin. You don't seem pleased to see me.

FOURTEEN

The man with ten heads took a step toward the doe.

Cousin, you have been in that wretched form so long, you have begun thinking and acting like a deer. Transform into your natural form.

Supanakha shuddered as the last drops of urine squeezed their way out, but remained in her animal form.

You defy me? I see that you have been corrupted by your contact with mortals. How many times have I warned you about this, foolish one? Why did you not report to me earlier as ordered?

—I was injured, she replied, using the only language she could use, a kind of mental voicing that she shared with her cousin. —Some mortals attacked me while in this form. I was not prepared.

She showed him the fast-fading scar of her wound.

A scratch. I have seen you fight mortals. You can tear a dozen apart without thinking. Why did you not follow through on our plan when Kala-Nemi failed in his mission?

—You know about that? She was surprised and guilty both at once. It had been her task to report back to him. Yet as always, somehow he had known everything that was going on. —I . . . I . . . was too disoriented. There were too many mortals about. They barred the gates. There was no way to enter the city.

The creature with ten heads walked a few steps away, bowing to avoid touching the overhanging branches. His heads, displaying varying expressions, argued amongst themselves. Each offered a different set of opinions, different suggestions, ideas, orders. The majority seemed to be advising killing Supanakha. She had been tainted from contact with mortals. Had been tamed somehow. Her lapse bordered on treachery. She must be destroyed. She shuddered again, wanting desperately to flee yet knowing that there was no corner of the three worlds where she could escape the wrath of the ten-headed one. She stood her ground, legs still splayed in that defeatist attitude of the cornered animal.

When Ravana swung back to face her, his central head was smiling.

You have slipped, cousin dear. But not fallen. I see a way in which you may fulfil your obligations yet. A brief pause, a flickering of disagreement and doubt across the ten bickering faces. *You do wish to continue serving me, do you not?*

—Of course, my lord. You know my allegiance is to you alone.

A flash of a smile on several faces. Scowls on the remaining ones. *Good, I knew you would see reason. You are not the first of our kind to be seduced by the gentle glamour of these soft-skinned animals. They have a certain . . . how would you put it? . . . charm?*

—Nobility, she said, excited. Then caught herself. —I mean, not the same nobility that you possess, my lord. But a kind of crude, animal grace that is quite attractive. In a primitive, un-Asura fashion.

The central head was watching her closely. Other heads were speaking to each other or looking elsewhere, disgusted by the conversation.

393

Yes, I see. Another long pause, but all the heads were silent this time, contemplating the words issuing from the lips of the central one. *You have grown fond of them, in quite short a time. That is interesting.*

—Not all of them, my lord. Just one. She struggled to express herself in a way that would explain her inner turmoil without winning her a punishment from one of those gruesome weapons. —He was . . . good to me. I find it pleasing to be near him.

Again, that continued silence among all ten. A deceptive sense of casualness, almost indifference. The opposite of the rage and fury she would have expected.

In that case, go on. Pursue this mortal. Stay as near him as you can. Indulge your desire.

—Cousin? she said, too surprised to remember to use the more formal form of address. —You do not object to this?

He waved a muscled arm derisively. The ears on either end-head twitched.

As long as you do not seek to consummate this obsession. Not until I give you leave. Do you understand? That is a strict condition. Follow, observe, but no direct contact. And this time, I will brook no dereliction. Are we clear on this?

—Yes, my lord. Her posture had changed to that of a doe in the throes of excitement, leaping in place, thrilling with shudders of delight. —You have my word. I shall not fail you again. I am to follow discreetly, observe, and report back to you.

And when I order you to step in, you will do exactly as I command, no questions asked. No matter how much you dislike the command I issue. I have no time to waste. Even now, another pressing matter calls me. You understand? I can say this only one last time. When I command, you must obey!

—I understand perfectly. Cousin, thank you. Thank you so much! I promise you, this time—

But he was already turning away, finished. The ten heads were muttering agitatedly to one another again, speaking of other things, other matters. He stepped towards the spot where the trunk had risen, the exposed undersoil still gaping copper-red. The storm began again, the dervishes and cloud and lightning, and in moments he had morphed back into the tree-trunk and it in turn had settled back in its original location, the roots groaning as they found their places in the subterranean soil.

Then the night was dark and silent again, and Supanakha was alone in the grove once more.

'Ravana. Show yourself.'

The guru's voice was quiet, but in the deep silence of the lowermost dungeon, it reverberated like a temple bell in a stone tower.

You wish to gaze upon me. Very well. Here I am.

A red flame grew in the depths of the pit. Within the black water. It grew more intense until the water itself seemed to have turned the colour of the flame. Then it rose from the water and hung suspended in mid air, several yards above the pit. The ceiling of the dungeon was high at this point, perhaps twenty yards above. The red flame hung halfway to the ceiling, illuminating not just the pit but the entire dungeon.

Within the pit, the water began to churn. It boiled and seethed, roiling and circling faster and faster. Like a dervish, the water rose up into the air, still spinning madly. In the garish crimson glow, the dark water glowed like a spout of blood. Suddenly, the spout rose to the ceiling, then exploded into a million fragments, splattering across the dungeon. It cascaded across Sumantra and the guru, the liquid rubies shattering like manic raindrops against their faces, their limbs, their bodies. Sumantra cried out in horror and disgust as the foul stench of the pit-water coated him, clung to him, cloying, nauseating. *This was how Jabali's clothes were stained*.

In the pit, a figure had risen out of the water, raised by the dervish.

Sumantra stared at it goggle-eyed and bit down on his fist to keep himself from screaming. His mind struggled to comprehend what he was seeing. It defied human logic, the logic of anatomy and wholeness. Once he had been unfortunate enough to see the offspring of a woman raped by a rakshas. The snarling, clawing infant that had lain in that crib, grinning through a mouthful of its dying mother's life-blood, had not been half as monstrous as the creature he now faced.

The beast before him was made up of the eleven spies who had been consigned to the dungeon. Somehow, through what dark sorcery he knew not, the wretches had been torn apart, limb from limb. And their separate parts had been reassembled to form this . . . this . . . abomination!

The body was that of a single man, with an extra pair of arms grafted on below the wretch's natural pair. The rest of the body was more or less normal, if you could overlook the horrible gashes and wounds inflicted on its barely clothed flesh.

The truly horrible part was the heads. All eleven of them. Somehow the obscene sorcerous power of the Dark Lord of Lanka had welded the flesh of the ears together, fusing the eleven heads of the doomed spies into one long line, arranged side to side atop the neck of the dead man. It was an impossible sight to behold, and one that made Sumantra's mind reel in shock and disbelief. He understood now why Jabali and the warden had been so shaken. They must have seen this . . . thing being shaped before their very eyes. The spies being torn apart, then re-made in the unspeakable image of their master.

The eleven heads opened their eyes, leering up at the guru and Sumantra.

Does my flesh sculpture please you?

'Obscenity.' The guru's voice was calm but hard. 'You murder your own followers and defile their bodies.'

Murder? Defilement? These are mortal concepts, brahmin. They have no meaning in the world of Asuras.

'Even Asuras must obey the laws of nature. Such misuse of the power of brahman will not go unchecked by the devas, Ravana. Your excesses go beyond endurance.'

The devas! I met their host on the battlefield and my colours ruled the day. Now they hide their heads in shame from me. No, brahmin. This war is between me and these feeble mortals you seek to protect. And as you can see, mortal flesh is so easy to destroy. Or to corrupt.

'Do your worst, rakshas. You will not triumph. This transgression marks the beginning of your end. You hasten your own downfall with every evil act you perpetrate.'

You speak boldly now, old one. But you will not speak so when I ravage your mortal cities and lay waste to the civilisation of which you puny two-legged insects are so proud. I will triumph this time, and you will be the one to fall. I will crush you so low you will never rise again. The days of the Seers are past. The days of mortals are coming to an end. My time is just beginning.

The guru's voice thundered, echoing through the large chamber. 'Speak no more to me, Ravana! I have no wish to hear your ill-thought boasts and see your cheap antics. Begone from this place. Begone before I cast you back into that furnace of agony where you truly belong. Back into patal, that lowest level of narak. And this time, even a thousand years of penance will not get you Brahma's attention. Nor Shiva's. The devas are wise to your ways now. Begone before I send you fleeing like a pariah dog!'

Watch your tongue, old one. Do not make threats you cannot carry out. Your days of threatening me are done. Now my sun rises in the blood-red sky of the west. You seek to banish me to the lowest level of hell again? Watch as I turn this mortal plane of Prithvi itself into Patal. Watch as I undo in a few mortal years all that you have done these past seven thousand. Watch and weep, brahmin. For weep is all you will be able to do when I come to take Ayodhya.

'Your threats do not scare me, rakshas! Already, your assassin has been exposed and dispatched. Your spies have been uprooted. And soon we shall strike a mortal blow at the heart of your forces. Your grandiose dreams are merely that, dreams. Your cloven feet shall never step on the proud avenues of Ayodhya.'

The creature laughed. It began as a low chuckle from the head in the centre, but soon spread to all the other heads as well. All eleven laughed together, each in his own individual way. The sound clashed and echoed through the dungeon, reverberating off the stone walls, booming through the corridors and stairwell of the subterranean prison, wafting all the way up the stairs to where the warden stood sweating and praying for the safe return of the visitors.

Fool! Brahmin, you believe these are victories? They are as flea bites on the rump of a dying mule. Merely nips to get your attention. You believe you rooted out all my spies? I have eyes and ears in the palace itself. My followers include the highest and mightiest in your puny Arya nations. To root out all my spies you will have to cut out the heart and lungs from the diseased body of mortal civilisation itself. And even if you have the courage to do so, it will start a civil war among your mortal nations. My uncle Kala-Nemi is alive and well and here by my side already, unharmed by your charlatan mantras. As for Ayodhya. . .

The laughter went on longer this time, until Sumantra felt he would go insane at the sound.

I am already in Ayodhya!

The monstrosity reared back, all eleven heads still laughing manically. The red flame overhead grew brighter, dazzling white in its intensity.

Guru Vashishta raised his eyes, shielding them with his hand as he peered up at the light. 'Sumantra,' he cried. 'Leave this place! At once! Flee!'

Sumantra didn't need to be told twice. He turned and stumbled up the slippery damp stone steps. He reached the second level and resisted the urge to look back.

'Go, Sumantra!'

The creature's laughter built in a crescendo, now as multifarious as eleven hundred separate voices, then eleven thousand . . . It was as if every dead atma roving nearby had been drawn into the dungeon by the charisma of the Lord of Lanka's demonic presence. The laughter pierced Sumantra's ears, searing his brain, threatening to immobilise him with its sheer intensity.

He reached the uppermost level, then the door. But the door was locked and bolted! From outside!

From below, the guru's voice rang out, counterpointing the screeching hordes of laughing atmas, calling a mantra. With a burst of blue light, the dungeon door blew open, right off its hinges, tumbling over and over itself with a crashing and ripping. Sumantra blessed the devas and ran into the passageway, towards the stairwell. Then up, up he climbed, his legs pumping desperately, scraping his shoulders and head and hands innumerable times, shedding skin, breaking a fingernail, drawing blood, as he fought his way up the narrow stairwell. The laughter and the mantras followed him all the way. Finally he burst into the torchlight of the upper prison building, into the waiting arms of the warden.

'Vishnu be praised!' the warden said, grasping hold of Sumantra.

The pradhan-mantri turned. 'Gurudev?' The seer was not behind him. Then he heard the sounds bubbling up from the bowels of the dungeons below. The guru's voice was barely audible over the deafening cacophony of demonic laughter. But it was audible nevertheless.

A deafening impact shook the jail to its very foundations. A roaring red and blue flame—the colours intertwining like battling serpents, Sumantra saw—came racing up the stairwell, billowing out into the hallway.

The warden cried out and was thrown back on to the floor. Sumantra was knocked off his feet by an impact like the hot breath of a furious dragon. Then, as suddenly as it had occurred, the explosion ended. And there was nothing but silence.

FIFTEEN

The light in the eastern sky above the cliff was still soft and pink when the brahmacharyas carried the raft to the river. Rama and Lakshman were to the fore, marching in step with the Shaivites and joining in their cheerful working chant. In honour of the princes, the brahmacharyas substituted their customary 'Om Namah Shiva' with the traditional Kosala chant: 'Dasa naam satya hai.' Literally, *Dasaratha's name is truth*, or more liberally, *Praise to the true king, Dasaratha*.

It was a short distance from the ashram to the riverbank, but the vigour and enthusiasm of the brahmacharyas once again made Rama feel suddenly nostalgic for his gurukul days. There had been a strong bond between his brothers and the other shishyas of the kul, regardless of their caste, varna, gotra, birth-rank or wealth-stature. Even now, he would still be willing to risk his life for any one of those friends; but where were they now? All scattered across the kingdom, some across the seven nations.

As they emerged from the grove on to the gravelly bank of the river, Rama called a halt, eight pairs of bare feet crunching as they stopped as one person, then gave the order to lower the raft to the bank. All eight moved as one, and the raft settled without a whisper on the silt-slippery lip.

401

Brahmarishi Vishwamitra had followed with Rishi Adhranga and the older rishis, and they said their farewells now, speaking the customary ritual blessings and mantras. Rama and Lakshman had already said their goodbyes to the other brahmacharyas when they had gone down to the river together for their morning ablutions.

As he had recited the Gayatri mantra, standing waist-deep in the icy flowing water, taking his acamana, Rama had been aware of eyes on his back. It was little Dumma, more intent on watching the prince-heir of Ayodhya than on performing his own morning prayer.

'I am not the sun-God, Dumma,' Rama had said softly when he had finished his mantras. 'Just a shishya who enjoys a good joke as much as you do. Always remember that. Respect all men, but worship none. Adoration is for the devas.'

He had heard the little brahmacharya's sharp intake of breath and hissed whisper: 'He has eyes in the back of his head! I told you, a prince of Ayodhya has *powers!*'

It had made him smile and wish yet again that Lakshman and he could linger here a while longer. *Better still, if we could fetch Bharat and Shatrugan here too, it would be like old times again.* He winced at the irony of how, when they had been at the gurukul, they had dreamed of nothing more than becoming active kshatriyas, risking their lives, having adventures, fighting enemies and Asuras. And now, when he was embarking on the most amazing adventure of his life, here he was, wishing for those gurukul days again.

Guru Vashishta had said it best: *To want what you have not, that is the eternal longing of the mortal heart.*

Now, as Lakshman and he checked the raft's riggings one last time—only because the senior brahmacharyas insisted, proud of their craftsmanship—and waited for the brahmarishi to board, he felt someone watching him again. He turned instinctively, a smile ready for Dumma. But there was nobody there, only the empty grove, its perfectly spaced fruit trees casting long shadows in the slanting light of dawn.

He glanced around. Dumma was over there, up in a tree, tossing fruit down to his fellow brahmacharyas.

Rama turned back to the grove. He had distinctly sensed someone watching from this direction. Even now, he was aware of a consciousness somewhere deep within the grove observing him intently. He shut his eyes, letting his mind travel where his vision could not reach. Behind the trunks of fruit trees; amongst the grapevines, swollen green bunches hanging pendulously, ripe for the picking; up in the leafy branches of a mango tree, its fruit still small and green, a month or two away from ripening— the sour-sweet taste of the kairees palpable on his tongue, filling his mouth with saliva; into a small open field of watermelon, dark green and growing fatter by the day; across a patch of tomatoes left to ripen in the sun; behind a cluster of—

'Bhai?'

He opened his eyes, blinking in the brightening light as his pupils adjusted. It had been dark in the grove. Lakshman was staring at him. 'Are you all right?'

He nodded brusquely. 'I'm fine, Lakshman. Just saying one last mantra.'

Lakshman grinned. 'Staying with Shaivites has made you suddenly pious. I hope you won't try to shoot down the rakshasas with mantras instead of arrows!'

Rama grinned. 'Actually, I thought I might try tossing tree-trunks at them!'

Lakshman raised his eyebrows. 'Speaking of that, I've been wanting to ask you since last night. Have you felt anything else? Anything different?'

Rama shrugged. 'Not really. Just better, stronger, healthier. But I thought it was because we had such a good time with the brahmacharyas last night.'

Lakshman grinned. 'It was fun, wasn't it? Wish we could stay a week or two! We never did get to celebrate Holi after all.'

'Well, maybe after we finish off the rakshasas and the brahmarishi completes his yagna, we can make a detour and stop by at Mithila.'

Lakshman frowned. 'Why Mithila?'

'So you can smear a little Holi rang on your Urmila's pretty face.' Rama looked thoughtful. 'Or maybe not just on her pretty face.'

Lakshman punched him on the shoulder. Rama punched him back. Lakshman fell off the raft, landing with a loud splash in the shallows. Mud splattered the other brahmacharyas standing around, staining their spotless white dhotis. Shambu got mud on his face. He wiped it off with a finger and put the finger in his mouth, sucking off the mud.

Rama wiped mud and water from his own face, laughing at his brother. 'You don't have to be so touchy about her, little brother. I'll ask the brahmarishi to speak to her father about your match, if you like. Chacha Janak will be glad to have you as his son-in-law, I'm sure!'

'Shut up,' Lakshman warned.

'Okay, okay, peace,' Rama said. He held out his hand.

Lakshman hesitated, suspecting a prank, then took it. Rama heaved him up a little too fast, and Lakshman shot to his feet and stumbled towards the other side of the raft. Rama caught him with his other hand, balancing him. 'See? You've fallen head over heels for that girl!'

Lakshman grinned back at him. 'Not as much as you've fallen for her sister Sita.'

Rama was about to respond when Vishwamitra's voice cut through their horseplay. 'If you have finished your tomfoolery, rajkumars, we might consider departing. We have other things to do besides pushing one another around in muddy riverbanks, if you recall.'

'Ji guruji,' they said at once, turning serious.

They picked up the three-yard-long balsa wood poles the brahmacharyas had carved for them. The brahmacharyas bent together and began shoving. The raft resisted for a moment, then broke free of the bank, floating out on to the water, bobbing from the shove-off. Rama and Lakshman stuck their poles into the river, and easily touched bottom. They needed to push the raft out into the middle, but Rama's first push was much too hard, swinging them around in a complete west-east circle. Lakshman tottered and started to fall back on the raft, his pole rising out of the water with a whoosh of splattered drops. The seer's powerful hand gripped his shoulder and held him steady.

'Sorry,' Rama said, raising his free hand in apology. Lakshman shot him a warning look and stuck his pole back in the river. Rama used his own pole to stop their swinging momentum and slowly the sluggish current caught them and began pulling them downstream.

Rishi Adhranga and the other rishis raised their hands, bidding them goodbye and wishing them Shiva's protection on their mission. The raft began to drift slowly downriver, the fresh logs still settling in the water with popping and cracking sounds. The brahmacharya acolytes ran alongside them, waving and yelling out words of encouragement. A small figure came sprinting down from the grove, barrelled through the watching rishis, weaved through his fellow acolytes, and ran along the lip of the bank beside them. His feet began to sink into the loam at once, almost tripping him up. His hands clutched something to his bare chest.

'Rajkumar Rama! Rajkumar Lakshman! I have fruits here for you, to nourish you on your journey!'

Rama and Lakshman exchanged a grin. Rama called out across the few yards of river that separated his side of the raft from the young acolyte: 'You are a wise brahmacharya, Dumma. Warriors must eat to gain strength. Toss them across one at a time, and mind that you do not fall into the river.'

'Prepare to catch,' Dumma called back breathlessly, struggling to keep abreast of the raft. The current was slowly picking up their pace and his first throw went astray, the small ripe papaya rising high above Rama's head to smash across the cliff-side bank, bursting open on a rock and startling a jal murghi that rose squawking angrily into the air.

Rama laughed, just as the little brahmacharya's next throw caught him full on the neck, a sitaphal striking him wetly and bursting open to release its milky-white innards across his chest. Lakshman roared with laughter at that, while the young brahmacharya cried out in horror.

'I'm so sorry, Rajkumar Rama! So sorry!'

Rama smiled encouragingly. 'It's okay. Just don't throw any more sitaphal.'

The boy's next throw was deadly accurate, the fruit flying straight to Rama's outstretched hand. He snatched it out of the air without missing a beat in his steady poling. He caught the rest of the fruit one-handed too, using the other hand to continue poling to keep them in mid-river, away from the rocks on the north side and the silt on the south. Dumma managed to toss him three oranges, two pears, an apple and three small kairees in quick succession before the raft picked up speed.

'Watch out!' Rama cried.

Dumma looked ahead just in time to see the fallen tree-trunk barring his way, and with a whoop leaped over the obstacle and landed in a pool of muddy water. His dhoti unwound itself at the impact, leaving him stark naked.

He clutched at his sacred thread as if it could cover his nakedness. The other brahmacharyas running behind him on the firmer earth of the upper bank broke into hysterical laughter at the sight of poor Dumma scrambling for his dhoti while belatedly trying to keep his groin covered with his other hand.

Rama and Lakshman laughed too, and Rama thought he even glimpsed a flicker of a smile pass briefly across Vishwamitra's face. Dumma cried out in frustration as his dhoti floated out of his reach into the river, and splashed furiously in a futile attempt to grab it. The dhoti dodged his hand and went drifting slowly downstream, racing the raft. He spat out a most unbrahmacharya-like string of curses at the escaping garment, driving his fellow acolytes to another paroxysm of laughter. He realised that the raft was about to turn a bend and waved frantically to Rama, forgetting for a moment to keep his nascent manhood covered.

'Visit us again on your way back, Lord Rama! I'll keep more fruit ready for you! Sitaphals!'

Lakshman giggled as the brahmacharya stepped back, lost his footing, and splashed down on his bare bottom in the mud of the bank. The raft went around the bend, and that was their last sight of the little acolyte.

'Shaivites,' Rama said, shaking his head.

He lifted his pole out of the water and looked at the sage. Vishwamitra was standing with his legs apart, at a slight angle to the river, arms crossed across his chest. His eyes were open, yet he seemed to be looking at worlds beyond the one they were in right now. In the growing light of the new day, he made an impressive sight, his statuesque muscled body dappled by the shadows of overhanging boughs. A bird cry distracted him then and he looked across the river again, past Rama.

'Look,' Lakshman called. 'Chini kulang.'

They were passing a marshy pond close by the river. The pond was filled with a number of immaculate white cranes with bright red beaks. They shuffled together, shoulder to shoulder in the water, plucking greedily at tubers and stalks.

'Burmuch,' Rama corrected, using the name he had heard his mother call the birds on a journey a long time ago.

'Same thing,' Lakshman replied. 'They're known as kare kare west of the Indus, tunhi up north, and in Kausalya-maa's desh, burmuch. But Father and Guru Vashishta always call them chini kulang, because they fly south to our land every year from North Chinn, to escape the harsh winter snows.'

Vishwamitra said: 'From the frozen tundraland of Siber, to be accurate. Much further north of Chinn. There the Russis name them whitecrane or sibercrane. Mostly they seek out the warmer climes of Marwar and Gujjar, but some grow weary of the long flight and settle here. They will return home to their snowlands in a few days.'

Lakshman raised his hand, cupping his mouth, and emitted a loud piercing bird call. Thousands of red beaks rose in unison, seeking out the source of the sound. But not a bird took wing.

Rama nodded in admiration at the immobility of the birds. *They have never known danger before; they live fearlessly under Shiva's protection.*

Lakshman grinned, proud of his imitation. 'How was that, bhai?'

'Pretty good,' Rama replied, trying to keep a straight face. 'Of course, it happened to be a jhilli's mating call,

408

rather than the chini kulang's natural cry, but I'm sure they didn't mind.'

Lakshman's face fell. 'A jhilli's mating call?'

'Yes. Right now, those snowcranes are probably wondering since when marsh crakes grew so tall and poled rafts downriver.'

'Go catch long fish with your short beak,' Lakshman retorted, then glanced at Vishwamitra. The seer seemed absorbed in his contemplation. They poled along in silence for a while.

The current flowed gently, just strong enough to keep them moving at a steady pace. After a while, the river grew much broader, wide enough for the raft to float smoothly along without needing constant correction. They sat then, keeping their poles ready beside them, with not much more to do than watch the countryside scrolling past. To their left the cliff face rolled by relentlessly, a blurring blackish-grey wall scarred by jagged red veins of ore. It blocked the rising sun for the first few yojanas, keeping it from falling directly on them, and the cool wind and moist spray from the river kept them refreshed and alert. To their right, the fruit thickets of Kama's Grove fell behind after less than an hour, giving way to fertile marshlands, which in turn gave way to a succession of wood-thickets. These were populated by common animals who watched them boldly from the trees or banks without any sign of nervousness.

Rama and Lakshman called out the names of trees, birds and animals as they came into view, arguing over the varied nicknames used for the species in different parts of the continent. When they fell silent, unable to identify a bird or a plant, the seer supplied its name, reeling off a succession of alternatives in a multitude of languages.

409

After several yojanas, Rama began to realise that they hadn't spotted a single predatory beast or heard any of the dreaded cries of the notorious forest hunters. *No wonder the herbivores are so numerous and so bold; even their natural predators aren't around to hunt them. Shiva's umbrella of protection must extend right up to here.*

The sage remained standing the whole time, like a ship's captain on his vessel's prow, watching for signs of land. *Or dangerous reefs.* After the rajkumars tired of identifying species he fell silent too, and only the sounds of the river and the wildlife on its banks marked their passing.

As the sun rose and found the centre of the river, the day grew warmer, losing its dawn chill. The water was warmer too, when they trailed their hands in it, and flowed much faster. The sound of the river, the calling of the birds and animals in the woods, and the placid calm of the whole landscape began to lull them.

Finally, the landscape began to change. First to go were the woods, giving way to a strange semi-denuded habitat, neither wholly swamp, nor wholly forest. The trees here seemed malformed rather than destroyed, their trunks stunted, branches and leaves withered, flowers and fruit absent. The ground became marshland, but oddly brownish marshland, with no lichen or moss or reeds. As they rushed along, even these stunted waterlogged half-woods ended, followed by vast open patches where the aborted trunks of dead trees struggled to rise above an unnatural purplish-blackish undergrowth. The stink of these patches was awful, reminding Rama somewhat of the organic stench of fields filled with compost, but much worse. After another few yojanas, even these stench-patches gave way and a new phase began.

The riverbank became stony, jagged black lohit-stone boulders lining either side, some looming so high they obscured any view of the forest beyond.

The forest itself was dense, dark, impenetrable, the direct opposite of the benign profusion and fragrant calm of Kama's Grove. The trees were enormously tall, their twisted, writhing shapes lunging out at one another like snarling beasts. Deep within their thick undergrowth, the glittering dark eyes of unseen creatures watched them pass, reminding Rama of a rksa he had once seen caught in a trapper's pit. The great black bear had stared up at him with eyes as dark and fathomless as these hidden creatures.

He was so busy watching the woods that he didn't see when the cliff ended. One moment it was there to their left, towering above them, capped by the late morning sun, then it was gone, falling rapidly behind. He looked back and glimpsed the fast-disappearing cliff between the clawing limbs. It veered away sharply then vanished from sight, their last link with the normal mortal world.

The river slowed to a seeping sludge-flow, sluggish with thick undergrowth, covered with rotting logs, wormriddled limbs and mossy scum. The surface seethed with swarms of insects. The unnaturally sharp-edged boulders crowded in on either bank, and as the river grew narrower, they seemed to reach out to try and snag the travellers on the raft, looming above them like sullen elephants. The cries of predatory animals grew louder and more profuse around them: roars, howls, screams, maddened shouts and bestial yells. Angry screeches were countered by plaintive sounds of pain or fury; it was hard to tell which.

Somewhere, a lone wolf howled mournfully, and was drowned out by a pack of completely different beasts, threatening savagely rather than answering his solitary plea. A terrified animal screamed and thrashed around in a futile attempt at escape, its cries fading to a desolate whimper as its hunter caught up with it and ripped it apart with liquid shredding noises. There were stranger cries too, unknown species calling out questioningly to one another, as if communicating or seeking out their fellows.

The sky had vanished almost completely, glimpsed only in slices and sections viewed through the panoply of clawing limbs. They were enveloped in a twilight that was not quite night-dark; here and there, greenish-yellowish patches glowed faintly on the ground and on the bark of trees.

The raft ground to a halt with a grating that set their teeth on edge. Rama stopped poling at once, but Lakshman was slightly slower in following suit and the vessel's momentum carried it a half-yard further. Rama felt the underside scraping over something yielding and fleshy, and a gut-churning stench rose from beneath the lashed logs: the water-swollen corpse of some unidentifiable creature.

Lakshman turned his head and spat several times into the water, clearing his throat hoarsely. Rama resisted the urge to retch. Vishwamitra bent and picked up his staff. Rama noticed for the first time that the seer had wound a succession of coloured threads around the top of the staff, at the place where it was gripped: they were red ochre, parrot green and lemon yellow, wound tightly enough to form a knob. The colours seemed to glow faintly in the gloom of the forest as he raised the staff. The forest sounds died down slowly, as if aware of their presence, waiting to see their next move.

In the stillness, the seer spoke softly, using the same calm tone with which he had named birds and trees earlier.

'Rajkumars, welcome to Bhayanak-van.'

SIXTEEN

'*Rama!*'

Dasaratha's voice was hoarse but the panic in his tone was unmistakable. The maharaja sat up in bed, sweat pouring down his face, hands stretching out desperately as if trying to grasp someone just out of reach. '*Rama, be careful! The Bhayanak-van—*'

Kausalya was the first to reach his side, simply because she was closer. Bharat had snapped awake the instant Dasaratha uttered the first cry, but he was reclining in the baithak-sthan across the room and the comfortable nook had lulled him into a fitful doze. He blinked himself awake as he joined Kausalya-maa beside the maharaja's bedside.

'*Rama!*'

Dasaratha's face contorted in a look of utter futility and despair. He clenched his fists tight and slammed them down weakly on his thighs. His body shuddered and he bent over, weeping. Kausalya offered a cloth to catch his tears, and was shocked to find them searing hot. The maharaja was still burning with fever.

'It was just a dream,' she said, caressing his shoulder, trying to soothe him. 'Just a bad dream.'

He turned jaundiced eyes on her. 'A dream?'

'Yes, Father.' Bharat sat by Dasaratha's feet, massaging them gently. 'Just a fever dream.'

Dasaratha looked down at himself, then at his surroundings, as if becoming aware for the first time of where he was. 'A dream,' he repeated dully, then pressed the heels of his palms into his eyes.

A cluster of serving girls appeared in a flurry at the doorway, alerted by the sound of the maharaja's voice. Kausalya ordered one of them to fetch some freshly squeezed juice and fruits in case the maharaja was able to take some nourishment, and dismissed the rest. The room fell still and silent again, but after a moment or two, Bharat heard the distant sound of cheering from the avenue outside the palace. Word had reached the crowd: the maharaja had regained consciousness.

'A dream,' Dasaratha repeated for the third time. He looked up at Bharat, who was still massaging his feet. He reached out and touched his son's hand, as if unsure whether he was real or a figment of his nightmare.

'Bharat,' he said slowly, wonderingly. 'My son.'

'Yes, Father, I'm right here.'

Dasaratha raised his eyes to Kausalya. A light of hope shone in his pupils. 'It was all a dream. Rama and Lakshman are still in the palace. Playing Holi. They never went to the Bhayanak-van. They aren't gone to fight Asuras. They're right here, safe and sound, in their beds, asleep.'

Bharat saw Kausalya-maa stiffen. He couldn't see her face from where he sat but he could sense the pain in her heart. He didn't know what he might have said had the question been posed to him. Might he have lied rather than tell his father the bitter truth? It was obvious that the maharaja was delirious and intensely troubled.

Kausalya spoke softly. 'No, my lord. They have indeed gone to the Southwoods. To fight Asuras. They are under

414

the protection of Brahmarishi Vishwamitra and are well armed and equipped. They will return home soon, safely.'

Dasaratha cried out and put a hand up to his face, as if to ward off a blow. As he cringed in misery, Bharat's eyes grew moist. He couldn't bear to see his father like this.

'Father,' he said. 'Rama is the best bowman in the kingdom. He's better than even Shatrugan and I. He'll come back safely. I know he will.'

Dasaratha stopped crying. He uncovered his face, his hands clutching his chest instead, and looked at his son. 'Yes, yes,' he said faintly. 'He is the best.'

Kausalya watched Dasaratha for a moment longer. The serving girl brought in some pomegranate juice and diced fruit. Kausalya told her to set it all down by the bedside, then dismissed her. She went out backwards, staring in dismay at the maharaja.

After a moment, Kausalya turned to Bharat. 'Putra. Your father needs to be alone for some time. Why don't you retire to your bedchamber and take some rest. You can come see him first thing in the morning.'

'And you, Maa?'

'I will stay with him a little while longer. To tend to his needs.'

Bharat wanted to protest, to stay and try to nurse his father back to health, but he understood that Kausalya-maa wanted to be alone with his father for some reason. It was her right and privilege. He nodded and bent to touch her feet, taking her ashirwaad one more time before he left the room.

She touched his head affectionately. 'Ayushmaanbhav, bete.'

Kausalya waited until Bharat had passed out of hearing range before she leaned forward. 'Dasa?'

He was staring dully at the far wall. Unseeing.

'Dasa, what is it? What was the dream you just had? Why did it trouble you so?'

He turned slowly towards her. Still unseeing.

She reached out and touched his cheek. His stubbled skin was fever hot and damp with sweat. 'Look at me, Dasa. It's me, Kausalya.'

He looked at her, focusing for the first time since he had awoken. 'My beloved Kausalya.' Tears welled up in his eyes again.

'Tell me about it. It will make it easier to forget. Tell me your dream.'

He stared at her for a long moment, then looked over her shoulder at the tray the serving girl had brought in. She saw his line of vision and turned, picking up the juice and offering it to him. He took it and sipped, barely wetting his lips. It seemed to make him feel better. She waited for him to speak.

'Satyakaam,' he said at last.

She looked at him.

'The curse of Satyakaam.'

She scanned her memory. Who was Satyakaam? An Asura whom Dasaratha had fought in the Last War? A mortal enemy? Some would-be usurper? A challenger to the throne? A noble who had betrayed him? But she couldn't connect the name to any memory. She had no recollection of any Satyakaam.

'Who was he?' she asked gently.

He looked at the juice as if surprised to find himself holding it. He gave her the bowl and she put it aside carefully. Perhaps later, when he had unburdened his mind, she would get him to take some nourishment. For now, he seemed to need to talk, to relieve his mind of this ugly dream, or memory, or mixture of the two.

'I loved to hunt,' he began. 'Before I met you, when I was young and strong and brainless. I loved to hunt more than anything else in the world. Except maybe women.'

He remembered to whom he was speaking and hesitated.

She shook her head, smiling. 'I'm a woman too. You love me, that's true.'

He smiled back tentatively. But the smile barely moved his lips. He went on after a moment, more rapidly now, as if eager to get the telling over with. 'Once I was deep in the forest. Hot on the trail of a Nilgiri stag. A big one. I had been after it for the better part of a full day. It was evening, almost sundown. I was tired and exasperated at not having downed it yet. My companions were searching for me; I could hear them calling faintly in the distance, miles away. There was a princess, I think. A beauty. I wanted to return with a trophy. Not empty-handed.'

She listened. She saw how involved he was in the telling. As if the story was more than just a story. How his hands, face and body moved and jerked spasmodically, trying to participate in the telling. This incident meant something to him. Something very important. She had never heard him speak of it before.

'Just when I thought I had lost it, I heard a sound up ahead. I went carefully through the bushes. It was thick and close there, the undergrowth. Tiger territory. I was on edge, my bow strung, my arrow ready to be loosed if I so much as breathed on the string. There was a waterhole up ahead. I could smell the water, and the odours of the animals that came to drink there. Many different animals. I heard an animal drinking, the wet slapping sounds, like a large stag's tongue might make when slurping up water thirstily.'

He clenched a fist, drawing back his right hand, raising his left. 'I judged its position, behind a berry bush. And loosed my arrow.'

He dropped his hands, his head falling forward. When he raised his face again, he was crying once more. 'I went down to the waterhole, knowing I had hit it squarely. I found him there, his earthen pot fallen by his side, shattered into two halves. The arrow was in his throat, a mortal wound. He was clutching it, gasping for breath, for life. Life that I had stolen. Because I wanted a trophy. For a princess.'

He stopped. Kausalya felt her own tears welling now. She could see how much anguish it cost him to tell the tale. She suspected he had never spoken of it before to anyone, ever. Had bottled the knowledge in his chest all these many years where it had festered and seethed. Until today, when it had burst free, loosed like an ill-timed arrow in search of a victim.

'He tried to tell me something. I tried to beg his forgiveness. He pointed, unable to speak. Gestured at the water, at the broken pot. I held him until he died. He was a strong, handsome young man. In the prime of life. Like myself.

'After he had passed away, I tried to understand what he had been trying to show me. I went the way he had pointed. I found a small path, worn from use. From his daily trips to the waterhole and back. At the end of the path, I found a tiny shack. Barely a cottage. A hut. Inside the hut were an old couple, weak and ailing. Both were blind.'

Dasaratha passed a hand across his eyes. It came away dry, but he squeezed his eyes intensely, as if trying to release more tears, unable to understand why more would not come. He shook his head, still grieving for the death of that young man he had shot, forty or more years ago.

'I told them what I had done. I tried to explain that I was a rajkumar of Ayodhya, heir to the sunwood throne.

418

Money was no object. I would see to it that they were taken care of for the rest of their lives. They cursed me.'

Kausalya reared back, like a child stung by a snake. Dasaratha nodded, understanding her reaction.

'Cursed. They said that they had little time left to live. The only thing that kept them alive was the knowledge that they had such a fine young son. That he would go on after their passing away, would take a wife some day, would continue their line. Now, with him gone, they had nothing left to live for. What good was my money? They wanted their son back.'

Dasaratha hung his head in shame. 'I left there in mortal fear. Their curse rang in my ears. I found my hunting party. Returned to the hut, intending to take the old couple back to the palace with me, ask my father Aja to decide what to do next.'

He raised his eyes to the ceiling, desolate. 'When I returned, they were both dead. They had taken their own lives by chewing on a poisonroot plant.'

Kausalya placed her hand on his. He gripped it tightly, taking comfort in the contact.

Then he shrugged. 'And that was the end of it.'

She shook her head. 'Not the end. The curse. That was what gave you that bad dream, wasn't it? What was the curse they laid upon you. What was it, Dasa?'

He looked at her levelly. A strange kind of calm had descended upon him, as if the telling of the tale had burned out his anxiety and anguish the way a fever burned out a disease.

'They said that one day I too would lose a son the way they had lost theirs.'

Kausalya's hand flew to her mouth.

'That it would happen when I was old and ailing like they were. When I needed him most. That he would

419

be brutally murdered the way I had murdered Satyakaam, not even knowing or seeing the face of his enemy.'

Kausalya rose from the bedside. 'No! NO!'

Dasaratha spread his hands helplessly. 'My dream was of Rama in the Bhayanak-van. He was alone, separated from Lakshman and the brahmarishi. And that was when the Asuras attacked him from behind, from above, from all around. He was surrounded, and torn apart by the beasts. Torn to shreds.'

'No, Dasa! That is not Rama's fate! Rama will come back to us safe and sound. Alive!'

Dasaratha bowed his head. 'I pray that you are right.' He looked at her beseechingly. 'But if you are right, then what of the curse of Satyakaam? What about my karma?'

Manthara offered Kaikeyi a thali full of paans. Kaikeyi looked at the little betelnut-leaf squares stuffed with an assortment of spices, and squealed: 'Paan! I love paan!'

She took the largest, plumpest one and stuffed it into her mouth. Sticky sweet juices spilled out of the corner of her mouth, dripping on to the blouse of her sari. She wiped it away carelessly, spreading the stain further.

'Umm, this is wonderful, Manthara. What's in it?'

Manthara smiled. If she told Kaikeyi what was in these paans, the second queen would vomit out the entire mouthful. She replied cryptically: 'Everything you like. And a little special something of my own.'

Yes, my dearest. A little brahmin boy's blood. Sanctified by our Lord of Lanka at my last yagna. Does that taste better now?

She took a paan too. The smallest one, made specially for her. She hated having to eat a morsel more than was absolutely essential to survive, as her bony arms and limbs testified so eloquently. Kaikeyi watched her eat the miniature paan with wide, surprised eyes.

420

'Manthara? You eating a paan? What's the occasion? There must be an occasion if you're eating paan!'

Manthara waited until she had chewed most of the paan. She resisted the urge to spit out the betelnut juice. If she spat, she would spit out the sanctified blood too. She forced herself to swallow the whole thing down, juice and all. Then she answered Kaikeyi's question.

'It's been a very good day for us, my queen. A very good day indeed. And an even more fruitful night.'

She had just heard from her informants about the tamasha in the dungeons. It had been the perfect nightcap to an almost perfect day.

Kaikeyi mistook Manthara's meaning. 'Yes, it went just as you said. I did as you told me to do. Confronted Dasaratha and Kausalya and gave them both a piece of my mind. And I told them what you said to say, that Bharat would be the next king of Ayodhya, not Rama.' She smiled, displaying a mouthful of red-stained teeth. 'You should have seen Kausalya's face. She thought I was going to spear her!' She chuckled, spraying flecks of paan leaf. 'I almost did too!'

'A little more control next time,' Manthara warned. 'You must not use physical violence against anyone. You saw how much more effective it was to threaten the maharaja emotionally? It brought him to his knees more effectively than even a spear throw. And this way, nobody can blame you for what was after all just a family squabble. You were only venting your natural, inevitable reaction to your son being passed over for the coronation.'

'Yes,' Kaikeyi admitted. 'But I hope Dasa won't really die. I mean, I was angry with him. But if he dies . . .'

Manthara's voice was as sharp as a whip cracking across the flank of a wayward horse. 'If he dies, then his successor will become maharaja at once. And that successor will be Bharat.'

At the mention of Bharat, Kaikeyi's face lit up. 'Yes! I understand that. But how exactly will it happen? I mean, as of now Rama is still crown-prince-in-waiting. And if Dasa passes away without changing his decision . . .'

'Dasa will live a while yet. Long enough to change his decision.' Manthara smiled, her lips curling up slowly in contempt. 'And long enough to see the bloody, broken corpse of Rama laid before his eyes.'

Kaikeyi's eyes widened. 'Rama? Dead? But how? You don't mean that we will—' Then understanding dawned on her face. 'Of course! The Bhayanak-van. The Asuras will kill him. That's what you mean, isn't it?' She frowned. 'But what if he survives? What if he returns home safe and claims the crown? He'll be a hero then. The people will support him over Bharat. So will the court.'

'The people and the court will support their maharaja. And as I said before, the maharaja will rescind his decision and declare Bharat his successor. Less than two weeks from today.'

Kaikeyi reached for another large paan, glancing questioningly at Manthara first. Manthara gestured. Kaikeyi thankfully stuffed the delicacy into her mouth, chewing steadily as she pondered Manthara's words.

'But,' she said through the mouthful of spices and betelnut, 'how can you be so sure? I mean, how can you guarantee that Dasaratha will rescind and declare Bharat?'

Manthara leaned forward. 'Because we will make him.'

Kaikeyi stopped chewing. 'How?'

Manthara told her.

Kaikeyi choked on her paan. She went into a paroxysm of coughing, spewing out pieces of paan and juice and assorted flecks and bits of various things. Manthara watched her, wrinkling her nose in disgust yet keenly aware that it was weaknesses such as Kaikeyi's gluttony that gave Manthara greater control over her.

Finally, Kaikeyi regained control of her voice again. 'Manthara,' she said, hoarsely. 'You're a genius. You think the time is right to do it now?'

'Not yet,' Manthara said. 'But soon. Very soon.'

SEVENTEEN

Vishwamitra raised his arms over his head, gripped his staff in both fists, and leaped off the raft. He landed in a flurry of dried leaves and dust that rose like a nest of agitated serpents.

Rama and Lakshman followed his example, leaping together. At the instant their feet were about to leave the raft, it issued a groaning noise and shifted uneasily. Rama corrected himself in mid-leap, landing upright, but Lakshman lost his balance and landed on one foot, stumbling forward. Rama caught him just in time to avoid him striking his chin on his bended knee. Lakshman recovered and stood, darting a suspicious look back at the raft. Rama turned to find the seer staring in a south-westerly direction. Dust motes swirled around him, caught in a solitary thin shaft of sunlight that had somehow managed to penetrate the thickly webbed foliage.

'Our presence has been sensed already. Soon she will get word of our arrival. At first, she will not deign to come herself, believing her minions to be more than capable of dealing with us. Only when they fail will she take serious note. Even then, we may have to go to her rather than wait for her to approach. Her power grows strongest at midnight, and is weakest at noonday, when the sun reaches its zenith. That is the time you must attack, and cleanse the earth of Tataka forever.'

Rama sensed Lakshman's surprise before his brother spoke aloud. 'Tataka? Parantu mahadev, just last night Rishi Adhranga told us the story of how Kartikeya killed her.'

Vishwamitra glanced at Lakshman. 'The story he told was of the history of Kama's Grove, Rajkumar Lakshman. Of how Kamadev and Parvati-devi interrupted Lord Shiva's grief-stricken meditation to tempt him into creating a son who would be able to destroy the evil Yaksi. That son was Kartikeya and he was indeed created to kill Tataka, which duty he fulfilled to his great honour.'

Lakshman looked even more confused. 'But if Tataka was killed . . .'

Vishwamitra held up a hand, motioning for silence. He listened carefully for a moment. Rama attuned his senses to the seer's pitch, a level slightly below the normal range of human hearing, and heard what the sage heard: a distant thumping, like a giant hammer being struck on some unimaginably large anvil. But the sound was many dozens of yojanas distant, and was growing fainter rather than louder. Whatever was causing it was clearly travelling away from them. The seer returned his attention to Lakshman's question.

'Tataka is dead. Killed by Kartikeya. But as you know, matter can never truly be destroyed, only transformed. So when she died, she only left this mortal plane and was sent to the next plane, where she now belonged. Where would that be, Rajkumar Rama?'

'To the netherworld,' Rama replied. 'Narak. The third and lowest of the three worlds. Otherwise called Hell.'

The seer indicated the forest around them. 'Behold. Hell.'

Lakshman and Rama looked around, baffled.

'But, mahadev, we are still on prithvi, are we not? How can hell be here?' Lakshman pointed upstream in the direction from which they had just come. 'This is very much our own world, the mortal plane of prithvi.'

The seer nodded. 'This is the sorcerous power of Ravana, king of the Asuras, young Lakshman. Listen.' He leaned on his staff as he spoke. 'After he was banished by the devas to patal, the lowest level of hell, Ravana the Terrible spent many thousands of years performing bhor tapasya so austere and awful to contemplate that even the devas were compelled to grant him many boons. Among those boons was his elevation to the stature of a master of brahmanical power, a level of shakti comparable only to that which is wielded by the Seven Seers, the brahmarishis like myself who have been ordained by Brahma himself to oversee the smooth functioning and harmony of the three worlds.

'But Ravana misused his shakti, performing terrible, barbaric sacrificial yagnas to achieve evil ends. One result of his efforts was the tearing of a hole between the realms of prithvi and patal. This was the very reason why he chose to build his capital, the Black Fortress, over the then submerged island of Lanka. Lanka was in fact not a piece of dry land at all, but a giant extinct volcano used by the devas to plug the entrance to patal deep beneath the Great Ocean. Ravana's sorcery raised the island, resurrecting the volcano, with whose molten lava he built his impregnable fortress, creating a passageway through the heart of the volcano into patal. Through this, he raises a constant stream of Asuras, recruiting them directly from hell itself, to create the largest Asura host ever assembled.'

The seer pursed his lips tightly. 'As long as that portal remains open, Ravana has access to unlimited hordes to fling at the Arya nations.'

Rama felt rather than saw the seer's fist clench the threaded knob at the head of the staff. The motes of dust caught in the shaft of sunlight swirled faster, rising in a flurry like a dust dervish although there was not a mite of wind in the still, unnaturally silent forest.

Lakshman shook his head, bewildered. 'That is shocking, mahadev. But, pardon my asking, what does it have to do with Tataka and this Bhayanak-van? Lanka is hundreds of yojanas distant from here.' He corrected himself uncertainly. 'Or at least, it should be, by the normal laws of geography.'

Vishwamitra was patient despite the deep anger that Rama sensed within the seer. 'What you say is true, Rajkumar Lakshman. But Ravana's ill-gotten brahman shakti has grown powerful enough to enable him to punch holes in the fabric that separates realms. He has made another such hole here, releasing Tataka and her berserker sons into this beautiful land, and giving the evil Yaksi dominion over it.'

Lakshman looked around, his throat bobbing as he swallowed. 'Beautiful land, mahadev? This accursed forest?'

Vishwamitra leaned on his staff. 'This accursed forest you see was once the site of two great twin cities, named Malada and Karusha.'

'Malada, Karusha,' Lakshman repeated. 'Dirt and Impurity?'

'Indeed. So named because it was at this place that Lord Indra was washed clean of the terrible sin of brahmin-hatya by the devas using the pure cleansing waters of the holy Ganga. The two places where his dirt and impurities fell to earth he named Malada and Karusha,

427

blessing them with eternal fertility and prosperity for absorbing the detritus of his sin. In time they became two of the most prosperous cities in mortal history, great storehouses of wealth renowned for the fertility of their farmlands. But then Ravana released Tataka and her bloodthirsty sons from Patal and gave them this country to roam and dominate.

'The Lord of Lanka did this with shrewd intent. Once, before even Lord Indra washed his sins here, this was the place where the great sage Agastya made his home and hermitage. It was here that originally Tataka was cursed by the sage and transformed by his shraap into the ugly wretched Yaksi she is now. By releasing Tataka into these same lands, Ravana could be certain of controlling her. For she can never leave this tract of forest to enter the world of Prithvi herself. This is her curse, to eternally haunt the Bhayanak-van, which, as you now know, was in fact once the blessed land Malada-Karusha.'

The seer pointed at the scummy stream behind them. 'And that is all that remains of the sacred waters of the holy Ganga which fell to earth when Lord Indra washed his sins.'

Lakshman glanced in amazement at the filthy, choked stream. 'The Ganga? That gutter of filth? It looks more like a Patalganga, the river of hell!'

'Indeed, young prince. That is why the Patalganga is so named, because it is that stage of the holy Ganga that traverses the netherworld. Once that sickly stream you see there was also pure and clear as the Ganga itself. Tataka's foul presence has made it unclean.'

The sage raised his staff and pointed south-west, in the direction he had been staring earlier. 'That way lies my ashram, where my fellow rishis await my swift return. Once we have purified this haunted forest and restored it to its earlier glory, it will become a place of the Prithvi

428

once more, reclaimed from patal. The Ganga will flow clear and pure again, and this land will regain its former flowering beauty which it enjoyed after Indra's blessings were showered upon it.'

Lakshman asked his next question in a tone that suggested he suspected what the seer's answer might be. 'How will we achieve this great and holy task, Gurudev? How will we convert Bhayanak-van back into a part of Prithvi once more?'

The seer looked at him impassively, then glanced at Rama. 'By killing Tataka, of course. That is why we are here.'

Before Lakshman could give voice to his reaction, the sage stiffened, gesturing for silence. He turned his head this way, then that, listening intently. With his new powers, Rama could easily see what the seer saw, hear what he heard.

'They're coming,' Rama said quietly to his brother, reaching for his bow and stringing an arrow.

Lakshman dropped to his knee in a shooting stance, drawing bow and arrow in the same action. 'Tataka and her sons?'

'If it was them attacking all at once,' the seer-mage replied grimly, 'this fight would be over in moments, one way or another.'

He glanced up at the faint slices of sky visible through the intertwined branches high above. 'It will be noonday in a few hours. We would do well to wait and face Tataka when the sun is at its highest point.'

He tilted his head, listening once more.

'In the meanwhile, we must contend with Tataka's horde of minions.'

'What are these creatures, mahadev? Rakshasas? Yaksas? Pisacas? Daityas?' Lakshman licked his lips, his eyes flicking from side to side, bowstring stretched to its maximum.

'None of the Asuras you name, young Lakshman. Tataka was too proud to ask Ravana for reinforcements to maintain her dominion. Or perhaps she feared that the Lord of Lanka might station a great force here and usurp her power to command. So she created her own fighting force.'

'Created?'

'By crossing the animals of these woods with her own rakshas sons. Mutant beings, neither wholly animal, rakshas or human, but with characteristics of all three. She has been breeding these cross-species monstrosities for a long time now, and only recently, Ravana has commanded her to multiply her stocks as rapidly as possible. He wishes to send them as berserkers and reavers north of the Sarayu to terrorise the farmers in the outlying regions of Kosala and other border kingdoms. In less than a week, he will issue the command for these terror forays to begin. So we are here just in time to foil his plans.'

'What exactly do these creatures look like, gurudev?' Lakshman asked. 'How will we know them when they attack?'

Rama could see the grim smile on the seer's face without taking his eyes off the dim shadows between the thickly growing trees.

'You will know them, rajkumar. Do not be fooled by their somewhat familiar shapes and forms, or even their speech, for some are part-human and retain a vestige of their human qualities. These things are abominations of nature and creation, mules synthesised by a corruption of brahman power and dark tantric acts of cross-species breeding. Destroy them all. Once they are decimated,

430

we can get on with our main purpose: finding Tataka and her sons and killing them. Only then can I go on to my ashram and complete the yagna in time.'

A sound like a gust of wind through leafy branches rose slowly, gathering momentum and volume. But no wind rustled their hair or clothes. As it grew steadily louder, the sound resembled the moaning of some titanic beast. It raised the hackles on their arms and every pore on Rama's body itched maddeningly as if the air had turned poisonous. He kept his hands on his bow.

Rama said quietly in Lakshman's ear: 'Bear scratches back against tree.'

Lakshman immediately put his back to Rama's, assuming the classic two-warrior defensive stance. Now, their outward-facing bows covered all four directions of the compass.

The seer used his staff to draw a mandala pattern in the forest floor at the exact spot where the shaft of sunlight touched the ground. Leaves and dust swirled angrily at the staff's touch, spiralling upwards like agitated cobras to disappear high above in a translucent golden column. The seer stepped on to the magic circle he had drawn. The mandala would protect him from any attack, physical or sorcerous, and would keep aggressors at bay as effectively as an impenetrable invisible wall. The Seven Seers were said to be indestructible, protected by the omnipotent hand of Brahma, divine ambassadors granted total immunity. The mandala was merely to remind those foolish enough to try that they were impotent to harm this man. It didn't escape Rama's notice that the seer had drawn no mandala to protect Lakshman and himself. They would have to fend for themselves.

'Mahadev,' Lakshman said in a voice that was steady but not entirely free of anxiety. 'If I may ask one last question. How many of these mutant berserkers might there be in the Bhayanak-van?'

The sage took a moment to respond. 'Thus far,' he said with deceptive casualness, 'Tataka has been able to create no more than a few hundred. Perhaps half a thousand at best. Surely no more than that.'

In the stunned silence that followed, the moaning sound grew louder, filling every molecule of air around the two princes, leaving no space to breathe. Now, it sounded not like wind but oncoming rain. The rattle of a sudden downpour on a tin roof.

Blood rain, Rama thought. And then the forest erupted around them.

EIGHTEEN

Bejoo's men waited for his order. The chariot and horse stood in two neat rows, horses steaming from their rapid descent. He had never known that path existed before. But Bheriya had managed to sniff it out somehow. Bheriya always found a way. When they returned to Ayodhya, Bejoo decided, he would officially declare Bheriya as his successor. It was about time.

Bheriya's only failing, if you could call it that, was his obsession with his wife. Of course, she was beautiful. But that was beside the point. Along with soma, gambling and indebtedness, the fairer sex was one of the banes of the warrior's existence. He'd seen many grown men hopelessly besotted with those soft chests and painted lips. Though Bheriya's wife was probably just an honest woman seeking what everyone craved—affection and attention—Bheriya would have to be careful that he didn't grow so attached to those slender arms and all that lay between that he forgot he was a kshatriya, oathsworn to defend and die for his maharaja, clan and varna, in that order.

Bejoo sighed. As he grew older, he found more to worry about. It was a condition of age, he knew, to fear that one's legacy was insufficient. He had fought long and hard in the Last Asura War, he could barely count his battles on both hands—and both feet—yet he remained relatively unscarred (except for that nasty white curved mark across his right breast and shoulder) and still had the use of all his organs and limbs.

He had a good wife, an enviable reputation, a fine house in a decent part of the city, and enough wealth to sustain his family for another generation should he die today. And he had won more than praise and honour for his military service; he had earned what the sages called yash. A shining name. The problem was, he had nobody to leave it all to. No one who would carry on that shining name.

And now Shakun had finally passed the age of productivity. She had told him the news just the night before last, on the eve of Holi, as they watched the effigies representing evil spirits burning on the parade grounds. Her monthly cycles had ceased, and with them, their last hope of producing an heir had burned away, like the towering wax-and-cloth effigies they were watching.

'Bejoo,' said Bheriya's voice, cutting through his reverie. 'The bigfoot are approaching. Should we ask them to keep their usual distance or close with us?'

Bejoo pursed his lips thoughtfully. 'What do you think, Bheriya? Look at the thickness of those woods. Do you think even the horse can get in there, let alone our wheel? I don't fancy the notion of walking in either.'

Bheriya looked at him, surprised. 'Are you asking my advice, sir?'

'Your professional opinion. Sooner or later you'll have to start making command decisions. Might as well attempt a few while I'm around to catch you if you stumble.'

Bheriya shot him a look that said, *Are you sure you didn't hit your head on a low branch?* Aloud, he said, 'Well, if you want my honest opinion, I think we should bring the bigfoot up forward and use them to punch a hole through those woods. It's the only way we'll get in

434

there apart from walking.' He cleared his throat. 'Or crawling. Which seems more likely if we attempt to get in there on our own.'

Now why couldn't I have had a son or a daughter as quick-witted and upright as this young man? Was it too much to ask the devas for just one heir? 'Very good, Bheriya. The same method we used in the Charaka-van during the Kaikaya dasya uprising?'

'Exactly, sir. Except . . .' The young lieutenant frowned, warming to his task. 'Maybe we could send a chariot or two ahead with those scimitars we got from the Moorish delegates as a gift last year. They might help to clear away some of that thornbush lurking between the trees. The trees themselves look reedy enough. I daresay our bigfoot could knock them down like shortstalks in a chaupat game.'

'Good, good. Make that three chariot though. Abreast. Give the order.'

'Yes, sir, Bejoo!' Bheriya looked pleased with himself. He wheeled his horse around, then turned back again. 'Bejoo?'

'Make it quick, boy. Our scouts haven't seen sight of the rajkumars since dawn today. They could be halfway to Lanka by now for all we know.'

'I just wanted to say that it's been a pleasure to serve under you these past four years. You're the best, sir!' Bheriya looked uncomfortable offering the compliment, but his sincerity was unmistakable.

Bejoo snorted. 'Your tongue drips honey sweeter than a bees' hive! Now get out of here before I whip you for insubordination!'

But as Bheriya rode back to the elephant in a cloud of dust, he whispered: 'It's been a pleasure to lead you too, my son.'

Bejoo fell back to musing on how lucky they had been to find that path down the side of the cliff; an ancient wheelpath disused since the days of Aja, apparently. Disused because it led only to one place: the Bhayanak-van. If they hadn't found that path, they would never have caught up with the rajkumars and the seer once they went downriver on that raft. The scouts had done their job well enough; their sighting the raft being built the night before had given Bejoo enough time to figure out the seer's plan and take action accordingly.

Still, he worried now that the river might not go very far into the woods—it seemed barely a trickle as it entered the thicket, a few hundred yards from where he sat. Tracking within the Southwoods might not be as easy as tracking elsewhere. As it was, his men were more than a little spooked about the prospect of entering the dreaded Forest of Fear. The last thing he needed was a bigger challenge.

His mind was just starting to turn back to the possibility of talking his wife into adoption, something she'd been averse to all these years, when the chariot nearest to the edge of the forest vanished in an explosion of shattered fragments.

At first Lakshman thought the ground itself was heaving and spitting up debris, like the tales he had heard of earthquakes. He realised his mistake when what seemed to be a large clod of earth unravelled in mid air to reveal long yellow talons, spotted flanks, and a face out of a daiimaa's horror tale.

'Shiva!' he cried, loosing an arrow by sheer instinct.

The missile struck the creature in the face, shattering its fragile cheekbones, and it dropped inches from his feet.

It thrashed, screaming in a voice that was neither bird call nor cat howl. Before Lakshman could shut it up with another arrow, three other shapes exploded from the forest floor, flying at him with claws outstretched and jaws bared to reveal slobbering fangs. He loosed three arrows in a blur of movement that was faster than thought, bringing down two and shearing the top of the other's head. He ducked as it flew, dying, over his left shoulder, judged correctly that it would miss Rama by a hand's breadth, and was stringing another arrow before he heard the thud of its fall.

Then he was loosing arrows with the stubborn relentlessness of a meal-grinder crushing grain, arms milling relentlessly. He lost count of how many beasts he downed. Behind him, Rama was firing like a line of Mithila bowmen; he could feel his brother's back muscles spasming rhythmically even through his rig.

For the next few minutes, life narrowed to the simple repetition of reach-back-and-pull, string-and-loose. Aiming was secondary. The onslaught was so thick and furious, he would have hit them even if he was stone-blind. That was the disadvantage of their attacking from so close: it didn't give him and Rama much time to string and loose, but then it didn't give the beasts time to dodge either. Soon the ground around him was piled thick with corpses, a natural barrier which new beasts had to leap over to attack, and that gave him yet another advantage. He began slicing off heads and loping off wings even before some of the attackers could launch themselves properly. A bear-faced monkey was crouched to spring when he shot it through one eye. It screeched in a throaty howl as it toppled back.

Even in the thick heat of battle, he could see the grotesque mélange of breeds and species. Leopards with raven beaks. Wolves with snake hoods and rattler tails. Elephant bodies with scrawny human-child heads and forearms. Hairless brutes dripping green ichor and with

437

hair growing *inside* their arrow-exploded chests. Blind civets with the rump of an ass and sabre fangs. The list was endless. The stench and offal of butchery began to coat him as the slaughter went on. Gore splattered over his face and arms; steaming guts strung out over his right shoulder.

The world reduced to the arc of his vision: the half-circle covered by his lethal bow. The twanging of his bowstring became a melody to accompany the dhol-drumming of the blood in his head. The stench of bestial offal and inhuman gore became a familiar perfume in his nostrils; he breathed it in and relished it.

Lakshman had never before felt the red rage of battle-lust but he intuitively knew that this strange new sensation was not unique to him. He let the wave wash over him, carrying away fear, trepidation, anxiety about the outcome, all those before-worries. He became one with the bow and the cord. Each loosing was like jabbing a finger. He tore apart breasts, pierced hearts, tore out throats, ripped open faces, shattered beaks, cracked open skulls. He drank the soma of slaughter, inhaled the drug-dust of violent death, tasted the primordial iron tang of life-blood released by his own actions. He laughed, knowing what kshatriyas down the ages had discovered in the thick of battle: after a point, all men were beasts. Two hands or ten didn't matter. Civilisation was an illusion. Blood demanded blood. Life craved death. The arrow was born to kill, it didn't care whom.

When he lowered his bow at last, it was because the space before him was empty of enemies. There was nobody left to kill.

He stood, feeling the blood rise to his head in a roaring flood. His heart still pounded; his tongue was thick with the scum of his own sour juices. He wiped off a thread of blood that hung from his brow. The jungle was deafeningly silent. The sage was in his mandala behind them, unharmed and complacent as ever. It was only when he turned and looked at Rama that he got the first real shock of the day.

Bejoo was struck on the chest by a fragment of the chariot's wheel. Fortunately for him, the wheel was wooden and his breastplate bronze-iron alloy. Even so, the impact almost unseated him.

What in Shani's name was that? His horse, a Kambhoja stallion that had proved implacable even in the heat of battle, wheeled in startled terror, settling only after he whispered the mantra of Shani, his patron deity, in its ear.

Other horses were neighing and rearing in shock as well, and at least three men lay unseated on their backs, either dead or seriously wounded. One horse had been cut in two by what seemed to be a fragment of the chariot's frontplate, the metal imbedded in its severed neck, its eyes staring up in stunned horror. Of the chariot itself, nothing more than debris remained; it had been shattered and flattened as effectively as a wooden toy beneath an elephant's foot.

What could possess the power to do such a thing? Bejoo rode through his men, who were shaken only by the unexpected nature of the attack, not by the deaths themselves. Death was the inevitable end of a kshatriya's duties; it was the nature of that death that brought honour or dishonour. In this case, it brought only puzzlement. There seemed to be no sign of how the chariot had been destroyed.

One of his horsemen pointed up at the sky above the darkwoods, a bright blue upturned bowl capping the grim grey-green jungle. 'Something came from there,' he said, patting his horse reassuringly. 'Like a siege-machine.'

A siege-machine? Bejoo knew of giant catapult devices that shot large boulders over fortress walls, or at those walls, that could easily destroy a chariot. But if the rakshasas within the jungle possessed and had used such a machine, then where was the damn boulder? All he could see were chariot fragments and the unfortunate remains of the chariot's two horses and two occupants, gore and bodily parts strewn all over, everything covered with a thick layer of dirt.

As he came closer to the site of the attack he wrinkled his nose. That stench! What was that? It smelt like an animal compost heap. And no animal he knew of produced manure of this kind. He frowned. What he had taken for dirt at first was too dark and claylike to be the loose iron-rich soil beneath his horse's hoofs.

Then suddenly he knew. Instinctively, with an unerring certainty born of years of battling strange species and even stranger humans, he knew what had struck the chariot. Wheeling his horse around, he shouted a command to his men, both horse and wheel.

'Scatter! Scatter! Keep apart from one another! Do it now! Scatter!'

His men responded without question or hesitation. But they were hampered by the thick undergrowth that surrounded the path. Even the path itself was grassy and treacherous with holes and stones, and it was impossible to simply turn chariots and ride them through three-yard-high thickets of bramblebush and clumps of thornweed. Still, they did the best they could, as Bejoo rode back to the end of the line, shouting for Bheriya. Where were those elephants? If they had the elephants, they could bulldoze their way into the jungle, and there they might be safer from the menace that he felt certain would strike again. After all, if the enemy knew they were out here, then they would hardly sit idle after that first blow.

He was almost at the end of the line when he heard the sound. It had escaped his attention the first time because it had blended in with the usual forest sounds and he hadn't known what to listen for. Now that he knew, it was distinct, if faint. It rose as the threat approached, and he wheeled about yet again, falling silent. He had already yelled to his men that the attack would come from the sky, but he saw now that the warning was of no use whatsoever. The missile that came arcing over the tops of the trees came into sight only a fraction of an instant before it fell sharply to earth, landing on the back of one horse and the front of another, striking a glancing blow to a third horseman a good five yards away—the thing was enormous, at least ten yards across—and the sound of its impact really was like an elephant thumping its foot on the ground. Except that this was no elephant foot, it was a giant pile of animal manure, packed tightly into a ball and flung at them from over the tops of the hundred-yard-tall trees with deadly accuracy.

But flung by what?

There was no time to think. He spurred his mount on with another mantra, riding to the aid of the fallen horseman, trapped beneath his own mount, its head hacked off and pumping gouts of dark blood, everything coated with a thick layer of brownish-black manure streaked with patches of mucousy slime. He leaped off his horse and began putting his shoulder to the fallen horse, which was still jerking spasmodically in its death throes, the gaping neck notwithstanding. The stench was nauseating and it took all his self-will to avoid turning aside and retching. The man's leg was crushed, he was

441

saying, and Bejoo was bending over to pull him free, helped now by another half-dozen horsemen who had dismounted and come to their aid, when he heard the sound again.

He raised his head, following the sound. It was a faint whistling, like the burring a wasp might make if flying quickly past one's ear. But it was much louder this time.

He stood, staring at the sky above the forest, and his blood ran cold.

The sky was filled with the dark disgusting missiles, all headed directly for the clearing in which his Vajra milled about. He counted three, four, five, then blinked as a sixth one followed its predecessors belatedly.

We're all going to die, smashed to pieces by Asura manure!

442

NINETEEN

'Rama?'

Lakshman stared at his brother uncertainly. Rama was still in his drawing stance, down on one knee, his bow in his hands, an arrow in its cord. His back was still to Lakshman. But even so, his brother knew that something was wrong, something was terribly wrong here.

Did he really do all this?

The thought came to Lakshman not as a flash of jealousy. There had never really been envy between him and his oldest sibling, at least not the competitive urge to outdo which he felt when racing or competing against Bharat, or even Shatrugan. Only a desire to emulate; to do as Rama did. Or as his mother always put it: he wants to be Rama, he only settles for being Rama's brother. So his first thought when he saw what Rama had wrought was not envy but desire. *I wish I could have done that!*

The pile of corpses Lakshman had left strewn across his side was perhaps three deep and ten wide. Thirty, mayhap three dozen corpses in all. He had felt immensely proud when he had risen, heart still pounding with blood-lust, and seen how many of the foe he had brought down single-handed. Thirty bestial attackers! In perhaps as many seconds! With only a shortbow and no place to retreat. Yet he had come off with no wounds—except a scratch or two where a flailing beast had succeeded in pawing or clawing him as it went down in a dead heap— and the enemy had been daunted enough to retreat. It was a victory that bards in winehouses would fight for the right to compose ballads about; a heroic victory.

Or so he'd thought.

The pile before Rama was at least seven or eight deep and perhaps twenty wide. It looked like a small hillock of corpses, piled by some marauding demon in his lair for future consumption. Like the piles of venison, goat and other corpses the royal huntsmen piled up before the kitchens for a royal banquet.

There must have been a hundred and twenty, even a hundred and fifty dead lying there.

The implication was staggering. For every arrow Lakshman had loosed, Rama had loosed five.

But that's physically impossible! I was drawing so fast, my arm and my cord were a blur. How could anyone draw faster, let alone five times as fast?

Lakshman took a step towards Rama, coming into the periphery of his half-circle sightline, and instantly found Rama's bow turned to greet him, the notched arrow aimed directly at his throat. *He moved like a hummingbird's wing! Nobody can move that fast!*

The sight of his brother's face was more shocking than the piles of enemy mounted before him. Rama was covered with the same gore and gristle that he himself was coated with, the inevitable spatters of animal blood and other bodily fluids. But there was so much more of it that for a moment all Lakshman saw was a gore-painted face with two bright eyes shining in the unnatural dimness of the jungle light.

Those eyes didn't look like Rama's. They didn't even look human. Lakshman blinked, wondering if he was still intoxicated with the battle-lust, or whether the sight of so many monstrous aberrations and mutations had driven his imagination over the edge. Rama's eyes seemed almost to glow blue. And in that distinct deep bluish glow, there seemed to float motes of golden light, like tiny shimmering stars suspended in a milky blue substance. As he peered at his brother, the golden motes seemed to be alive, moving with a precision and purpose that was alien, unlike anything he'd ever seen. Suddenly, the pile of corpses, the impossibility of Rama's kills, was forgotten. All he cared about was Rama himself. And he could see that there was something wrong with him. He was about to take a step towards his brother when the seer's voice cut through the deathly silence.

'Stop where you are, Lakshman. He will not hesitate to shoot you down as he shot down all those monsters.'

Rama, shoot me down? Impossible! Yet he could see that it was possible. There was no hint of warmth in his brother's eyes, no sign that he recognised him or cared for him in any way. And that arrow was still pointed at his throat, following his every movement, however tiny, as precisely as if a metal wire connected his jugular vein to the tip of the arrow.

'Rama?' he said uncertainly. 'Put your bow aside. I want to examine you. I fear you may be wounded.'

There was no reply from Rama. The eyes remained fixed, unblinking, their bluish glow unmistakable now. The gold motes swam in their alien patterns, celestial fish in a cosmic emptiness. A statue would have been as responsive.

'He will not answer you, Lakshman,' the seer's voice said. 'He is caught in the battle fever of Bala and Atibala. You felt some vestige of it too when you fought. The maha-mantras take you over at the moment of crisis and turn you into a perfectly efficient fighting engine.

That is what Rama is now, a perfect weapon. Fixed in a state of stasis that will pass once the crisis is truly past. The only reason he does not shoot at you is because he senses your own brahman flow and essential goodness.'

But he's a man, a boy really, not a weapon. This is unnatural. Aloud Lakshman said: 'But then why am I not in the same state? Why can I think and move freely while he sits there like a bowman's dummy, aiming at me as if I am one of Tataka's miscreations?'

The seer sighed. 'The maha-mantras affect each individual differently. In Rama's case, they have taken strong root. Fear not, young prince. He will be as you knew him once the danger is over.'

Lakshman looked around at the silent jungle, the masses of dead corpses. 'But it is over, isn't it? They attacked and we slaughtered them. There were no more left.'

Vishwamitra shook his head. 'Sadly, rajkumar, you are wrong. These were only the weakest and least effective of Tataka's clutch. She sent them first to test your strengths and weaknesses. It is a common battle tactic used when facing a new enemy. The next wave will comprise her best warriors and they will not be as easy to slaughter, nor will they attack in any way you may foresee. Look for yourself. These are mere cubs, not fully mature even by their misshapen standards.'

Lakshman looked and realised that the seer was right. The deformities and bizarre combinations of species had distracted him from seeing this himself; now that he looked closely, he could recognise that the corpses strewn around resembled young beasts. By their colours, their stippling, their only partially formed talons and tusks and horns, he confirmed the truth of the seer's observation.

'You said there were no more than half a thousand of them,' he said, glancing around cautiously now. 'We faced and killed close to two hundred in that first attack. Almost half of their total numbers.'

The seer had seated himself for a while upon his mandala. Now, he rose to his feet, using his staff for support. 'Numbers are not always a true indication of an enemy's strength, rajkumar. These beasts you felled were immature and the weakest of the litter. Also, they were the lesser miscreations of Tataka's unholy experiments. The berserkers that will attack you in this next wave will be more powerful than anything you have faced or heard of before. These will be mixes of the larger, more lethal predators. Elephant and hawk, lion and rhino, shark and falcon, panther and scorpion, piranha and tiger, vulture and hippo. And besides these hybrids, there will be tribrids and quatribrids and even pentabrids too, the engineering so complex and mangled that Tataka herself barely knows the full capability of those new breeds, and keeps them caged. Even as we speak, they are being freed.'

Lakshman swallowed. 'Parantu, mahadev, we do not have that many arrows in our quivers! How will we face such vast numbers?'

Vishwamitra gestured impatiently. 'Arrows? Do not concern yourself with such trivial matters, rajkumar Lakshman. I have seen to it that your quivers shall never go empty. This is the advantage of being in a place where the laws of nature are so disrupted. Even as it makes it possible for Ravana to work his vile sorcery, it also makes it easier to channel the flow of brahman. I have used a mantra that ensures that your arrows are replaced faster than you can loose them.'

The sage fell silent for a moment, his eyes shut, listening intently although Lakshman could hear nothing. He saw Rama's eyes turn sideways for an instant, as if sensing

447

something approaching from that direction. Lakshman looked too, but saw nothing. The jungle stretched yojanas in every direction, seemingly devoid of life. Not even insects or birds stirred. At the very edges of his hearing, he thought he heard something, a very faint sound, like an intensely high-pitched drone. It was more an auditory disturbance than a sound.

Rama's bow turned away from Lakshman, aimed now towards the south-west. *He hears it clearly, while I can barely sense anything.* The motes in Rama's eyes increased their pattern of motion, swirling faster. His eyes glowed bluer, seeming to send out twin searchlights into the gloom of the thick jungle. His lips parted, revealing blood-smeared teeth in a snarl that was so wholly un-Rama-like that Lakshman wondered for a moment what creature this was that had replaced his brother.

The seer opened his eyes and spread his arms wide, crying out. Lakshman saw that Vishwamitra's eyes were bright blinding blue now, like Rama's, and flecked with those same swirling golden motes. The motes rose into the air, in the pillar of sunlight that encased the seer's mandala, spiralling towards the top of the towering trees, reaching for the sky. The sage began reciting a mantra in a piercing tone, shattering the silence of the forest.

//Andh tam pravishanti yeh avidyam upaste//
//Tatho bhuya eeva tey tamo ya u vidyayam ratah//

As the last syllables of the mantra faded away, travelling with shrieking penetration into the depths of the jungle, Lakshman heard the ground-shaking thunder of the next wave approaching.

He fell to his knee, bow in hand, arrow ready, and refocused his attention on the battle at hand.

448

The screams of dying men almost drowned out the screams of their horses. Almost. Bejoo saw horses and riders go down beneath the descending missiles, smashed into ragged fragments of bone, flesh and gore. Chariots shattered. A chariot struck at the back was upended like a child's seesaw, the horses thrown backwards into the air, their rigging snapping like cheap thread. They landed with a ripping sound in a thicket of thornbush, impaled on a thousand needle-sharp thorns, and lay screaming and flailing wretchedly, their skin hanging in flaps, crimson flesh bared and bristling with snapped-off thorns. Everywhere lay the stench of manure, the inhuman fetor of waste matter like nothing Bejoo had ever smelt before.

He had his sword in hand, unaware of when he had drawn it. He almost tossed it away in angry despair: how could you fight missiles from the sky with a sword? Even Kosala steel was useless against this onslaught. *Shaneshwara-deva*, he cried silently, praying to his patron deity, the god of chariot and vehicle, ship and wagon, He whom the Greeks named Saturn after the great planet ringed by the dust of a thousand shattered worlds. *Mighty Shani-deva, grant me a chance to fight the craven perpetrators of this onslaught. Give me death if you will, but a kshatriya's death. Not this defenceless butchery.*

As if in response to his plea, he heard a new sound from behind, accompanied by a trembling sensation in the ground. It was the trumpeting of elephants.

He turned and saw Bheriya riding hard at the head of the elephant squad. The young lieutenant's face was dark with fury as he surveyed the ruins of their proud Vajra. Behind him, the bigfoot squad's lead elephant mahout spurred his beast on with a vigour rarely seen.

Now we have a fighting chance! Thank you, Shani-deva!

449

Bejoo leaped back on to his horse and raised his sword high, pointing it at the dense woods, shouting to be heard over the noise and confusion.

'*Bigfoot! Into the jungle!*'

The lead bigfoot thundered past his horse, its eyes rolling, trunk swirling from side to side. It led its fellows in a headlong charge at the trees. The sound of it striking the first tree-trunk was almost drowned out by the crashing of a new wave of missiles. A razor-sharp fragment of a shield from some unfortunate charioteer whisked past Bejoo's ear, nicking off the lobe. He wasn't even aware of the blood pouring down the side of his head. He only had eyes for the elephants' charge.

Let it work, Shani-deva. Let the bigfoot break through. Much as I hate to die this way, yet I will choose to die here beneath this assault than retreat and leave my duty unfulfilled.

The lead elephant struck the first trunk with a loud crack like a twig breaking, or a spine snapping. The tree keeled over easily, bringing down a ragged line of its fellows with it, raising a cloud of dust and leaves that enveloped the animal. Missiles continued to rain down, claiming more lives and limbs. Without waiting for the dust to clear, Bejoo raised his sword again and repeated his cry, this time for his horsemen and charioteers.

'*Into the woods! With me, into the woods!*'

He rode into the cloud of dust after the bigfoot, into the Bhayanak-van.

They came slowly this time, seething like a living, writhing carpet across the jungle floor. Lakshman saw how easily they clung to the soft rotting soil, their jagged claws and talons digging deeply without effort. They could have burrowed under like their siblings had done in the first wave, tunnelling down and then upwards again until

450

they exploded from the surface. But they chose to show themselves, seeping across the forest like a plague of termites. The seer had spoken truly: compared to these ones, the earlier beasts had been balaks, mere babes. These were much bigger, some towering three and four yards high at the head, their snouted grey heads reflecting their elephantine parentage. Even the smaller ones moved with powerful ease, their actions and features more mature, more sure. They seemed unafraid of his arrows, and even though he sent a flurry into their midst, most only snarled and kept on coming. He pierced both eyes of a beast that was part-stoat part-gharial, but it continued to writhe silently towards him, flicking its leathery tail from side to side, yellow pus-like emissions seeping from around the arrows imbedded deep within its sockets. He downed a couple or three, aided more by blind luck than skill. But the wave of furred and carapaced monstrosities seethed on relentlessly, coming closer by the yard.

He took a moment to glance over his shoulder at Rama. His brother was firing with deceptive calm, each arrow carefully aimed. His bolts unerringly found the vital spot in their targets, making the animals turn belly up and bleating, or fall gasping in their tracks. Every arrow ended a life. Rama shot with a patience that was marvellous to watch; as if the oncoming beasts were merely straw dummies on which to practise his aim. He seemed not to care or fear how little his accuracy was thinning their numbers.

Lakshman glanced at the seer. The brahmarishi was silent now, as if waiting for something, his eyes staring at a point above the heads of the approaching beasts.

They slowed to a halt. The entire line of bizarre hybrids stopped at a distance of about ten yards from where the princes and the seer stood. They formed a perfect unbroken circle around them. Their snouts, tentacles, trunks, faces, mouths, maws issued small grunts and moans and snarls of anticipation. Spittle dripped on to dry leaves.

Lakshman realised with a start that the corpses of the earlier beasts had almost all vanished. When and how had that happened? He saw a creature pick up a fox-cat corpse in its mouth and fling it back overhead. It was tossed and passed back along the seething ocean of hybrids to the very back of the mass, where it disappeared, probably thrown back behind their line. They were clearing the circle in preparation for their attack. In moments, the ground around them was clear, the hundred-and-fifty-odd corpses disposed of. Then they were ready.

Lakshman had already dropped his bow and reached for his sword. The steel glimmered faintly in the dim light, reflecting the blue glow that emanated from both the sage and his brother. He caught a glimpse of a reflection in the mirror-sharp blade and glanced at it quickly, alert to attack from above. Instead, he saw two blue eyes staring back at him. They were his own, glowing now like the eyes of his companions, though not as strongly. He felt the rage of blood-lust come over him again, and raised his sword as the seer began a new mantra.

//Asuryah namah tey loka andhyen tamasavratya//
//Tan asthey preytyabhigshanthi yeh keych atmahanah janah//

Vishwamitra's chant hung in the air for a moment, like a cloud of dust motes suspended in sunlight. Then, as its echoes faded away, the army of beasts charged on the two princes.

The trees were as rotten as they looked. Their trunks shattered like dried gourds when struck by the charging

452

elephants. The large bigfoot leader roared in exultation as he smashed and brought down one towering tree after another, clearing a swathe through the forest wider and more accessible than the overgrown pathway they had followed down the side of the cliff that morning.

Bejoo rode his horse in the wake of the last elephant, careful to keep it close enough to use the bigfoot's bulk as protection against falling trees and yet not so close that the bigfoot itself trampled them under. He slowed his horse as he saw Bheriya riding back to speak to him. The young kshatriya's face was still a mask of rage and shock; he hadn't yet digested the sight of so many of their finest men and horses shattered like clay dolls.

And for what? For nothing. They never had a chance to draw sword or bow. They died without taking down a single shatru. Ah, the shame, the shame.

'How many?' Bejoo's voice sounded nasal and strange to his own ears, the peculiar fetid air of the jungle distorting it, corrupting his senses. He was asking how many of the Vajra's number had survived the sky assault.

Bheriya's face looked ten years older. 'Sixty horse, eight wheel, and fifteen bigfoot. We lost one to a missile before she could enter the woods.'

Bejoo nodded grimly. The stinking assault had stopped the moment they entered the forest; the attackers, those craven wretches sitting in their cosy nooks, undoubtedly knowing that the tall trees would blunt and deflect their missiles. But the relief he felt when the shower ceased and his pleasure at penetrating the jungle were both cut short by the cold shock he felt on hearing the count of his survivors.

'That's more than half our horse and wheel lost,' he said, his voice trembling with rage. 'Someone's going to pay for this. The cowardly bastards, skulking in their crannies!' He roared a cry that rose above the trumpeting of the bigfoot and the shattering of tree-trunks. 'Show your faces, you craven scum! Fight us face to face if you dare!'

There was no reply. Bheriya wiped sweat from his face, smearing a bloodstain. 'What now? Our bigfoot are doing well enough, but they cannot maintain this pace much longer.'

Bejoo restrained his anger and thought his strategy through with icy determination. 'We scout ahead to find the river. We follow its course until we find the rajkumars and the sage.' He grabbed hold of Bheriya's arm. 'And hear me well. I don't care if those bigfoot bash their bloody brains out breaking through these wretched woods. We stop only when we find the rajkumars. Or until we encounter the bastards who were pelting us. Do you follow?'

'Perfectly.'

Bejoo watched him ride away and thought: *Methinks we'll find the rajkumars when we find the rakshasas. And we had better find them quick. Whatever that was, tossing those hardened shit-balls at us back there, it was no siege-machine. Those balls were shaped and pressed by hands, I saw that from the indentations and fingerprints. And if they were ten yards wide at the centre, how large a creature would it take to toss them one after another like confetti? And what manner of Asura would it be?*

He had a grim feeling he would find out before too long.

TWENTY

'*Ayodhya Anashya!*'

The battle-cry resounded through the jungle, rising above the bestial howls of rage and anguish. It came from Rama's throat, booming and reverberating with superhuman force.

Lakshman echoed it as he fought, although his voice sounded shrill and hoarse after Rama's: '*Ayodhya Anashya!*'

Ayodhya the Indestructible.

Behind them, the sage continued his chant, reciting sloka upon sloka, the mantras seeming to change the very texture of the air they breathed, infusing their lungs with raw pure energy, drawn down from the akasa to replace the foul atmosphere of the Bhayanak-van. As Lakshman battled on, his sword driven by a shakti beyond skill or training, he felt the energy gathering around them, growing. He could see the blue glow from his eyes shining on the faces of the hybrids he fought, gleaming back from their inhuman eyes. It didn't seem to frighten them at first, but as the fight raged on, he sensed them growing warier, more cautious. They tried to sneak to the periphery of his vision, to attack from behind, from above, from below, while fewer dared to attack full-frontal.

He swung his sword like a farmer threshing, reaping a bloody harvest. Limbs, organs, guts, fur, talons, and items too alien to identify flew through the air as he confronted and slew one creature after another. He lost count of how many he killed, the bodies tossed back by their fellows, roaring with rage as each new corpse fell. He felt the press around him grow thicker as the hybrids crowded harder and closer, seeking a way through his defences. Even the tiniest lapse would be enough to bring him down with a slash of a razor-sharp claw or beak, or the plunging point of a pointed tail dripping venom, or the fired barbs of a porcupine-lion. But he deflected, cut down, hacked away, sliced off and dealt with every oncomer without mercy or hesitation. He was a fighting machine, as the seer had said, a battle engine driven by the shakti of the maha-mantras Bala and Atibala. And nothing could harm him. Or so he thought in those last moments of blind red rage.

The first hint that he might not be as invulnerable as he assumed came when a cobra-bat swooped from a tree limb at the precise moment when he was battling a wildcat-boar and a bear-stag at once. He ducked in time to avoid the cobra's lunging fangs and the creature swooped past, screeching in frustration as its venom splattered uselessly on the ground. But a searing pain raked his back and he realised belatedly that the batlike claws of the beast's forelegs had scraped him. He felt blood oozing from the scratches and flowing thickly down his side. Still, it was a minor wound and he ignored the pain and fought on with greater vigour.

'*Ayodhya Anashya!*'

But then a gharial-mouthed rhino impatient to have a go at him literally tore its way through the hybrid before him—thrusting its long sword-like snout through the back of the bear-stag to emerge dripping from its belly—surprising Lakshman as it clamped its jaws on his sword hand. Lakshman struggled to free himself and for one suspended instant he wrestled furiously with the gharial-rhino, the dying bear-stag pressed between them, but then the wildcat-boar attacked him with the tip of its jagged horn, missing his abdomen but scratching his hip instead, and the gharial-rhino gained the advantage.

It clenched its jaws together in a bone-crunching vice, shattering his wrist and severing two fingers. Lakshman's sword fell from his broken hand, blood spurting from the severed arteries on to his face, blinding him momentarily.

The next instant, the hybrids were on him, biting, clawing, slashing, tearing. He felt something cold and sharp punch through his back, cracking his ribs and driving their edges into his lungs. Blood gouted from his mouth even as the blunt-edged limb of another creature smashed into the side of his head, cracking his skull open. They devoured him, each beast attacking its own favourite body part, tearing him limb from limb, gobbling his organs as they steamed hot and fresh, crying out their exultation.

He wasn't indestructible after all, it seemed.

Bejoo saw the gleam of water just before his horse broke through the shattered debris of the felled trees, past the bigfoot with its blood-smeared forehead and shattered head-armour. He could barely recognise the river as such, it was so thickly carpeted with moss and rot. But the treeline stopped five yards or so from either bank, forming a pathway through the dense woods, and he could see clear down the course of its flow, into the heart of the jungle. He raised a hand, bringing the Vajra to a halt. There would be no need to keep the bigfoot up front. He would lead the way from here on.

He was about to issue the order when he heard the sounds of battle. He had been in enough blood-fights to know one when he heard it. It was the sound of living creatures locked in a desperate struggle for survival, fighting to destroy each other by any means possible. Only the sound of coupling was as arousing. Sniffing the air like a black mountain bear, he smelled the salty tang of blood from downriver and pointed his sword in that direction, yelling to his dwindled but still determined force: 'Speed! Our swords are needed!'

His horse needed no mantra this time. It galloped forward of her own volition, racing downriver in the direction of the sounds and the scent, her nostrils flaring as the odour of blood reached her. As he approached the scene, he peered through the forest gloom, seeking out the source of the noises. It was a battle, no doubt. But between what manner of creatures he couldn't quite comprehend. The sounds were like a mélange of animal noises as varied as any he'd ever heard. What in the name of the devas were the rajkumars fighting?

He discovered the answer for himself a few moments later as he reached the site of the battle. On the far bank of the rivulet, the most bizarre conflict he had ever seen was being waged.

Rajkumar Rama was standing alone against an enormous mass of beasts. The creatures were so thickly crowded in their eagerness to get at him, Bejoo could hardly tell them apart. Then he realised that his first impression was not a trick of the dim jungle light; these were no ordinary predators. Bejoo's face wrinkled in distaste as he made out the mutated shapes of the creatures his prince was battling.

More amazing than the creatures he fought was Prince Rama himself. The rajkumar was alone, unarmoured, helmless, and armed only with a sword in one hand and a fistful of arrows in the other. Against him were at least a hundred unholy beasts, each lethal enough to strike terror into any regiment of armed and armoured soldiers.

458

Yet Rama fought like he had an army behind him and a shield of invulnerability before him. His sword flashed with such blinding speed that he seemed to wield blue fire rather than forged steel. Everything his blade touched, it slew. The fistful of arrows in his left hand were as effective as any sword, shearing a swathe of bloody death through the pressing beasts. Encircled and outnumbered, he looked like a man wading into an ocean, parting it before him as easily as air.

Behind him, the seer Vishwamitra stood within a column of blinding blue light that rose as high as Bejoo could see, disappearing above the tops of the trees. Golden motes of light swirled around him, like a fly trapped in amber held up to sunlight. He was chanting mantras with the steady ferocity of a general chanting a war cry. To one side of the seer lay a prone form that looked like an animal savaged by a pack of hyenas. Bejoo recognised the golden armlet embossed with the emblem of the House Suryavansha lying amid the steaming remains and realised with a shock that that corpse was none other than Rajkumar Lakshman. Nobody could be torn up that badly and still be alive, could they? His heart sank as he realised that he had already failed in one half of his sworn duty. One rajkumar lay slain, and he was to blame for not being there in time to protect him.

Bheriya was beside him, staring at the fantastic scene across the stream. The young kshatriya's eyes were wide with disbelief, horror and something else. *Adoration*, Bejoo realised, knowing at once that Bheriya's eyes were fixed on Rajkumar Rama. *He has never seen anyone fight like that. And neither have I. Nobody human at least.* He could see the rajkumar's eyes now, blazing with blue fire, filled with the same gold motes that surrounded the sage. *Brahman power at work. What has the seer done to our prince?*

He didn't need to understand or make sense of it all. His warrior's mind needed only to know two things: whom to fight and how. Understanding never made a sword sharper or an arrow speedier. Bejoo turned the head of his horse, riding to the treeline to give himself room, turned again and galloped hard to the edge of the stream, leaping clear across the water, over the raft itself, landing on the far side with yards to spare. He didn't need to wait to see if his men were following, Bheriya had turned his horse immediately after he had. The remaining chariot and bigfoot should be able to wade right through the stream; it was only a yard shallow. He raised his sword and drove his horse forward, calling an invocation to his patron deity Saturn.

'*Jai Shree Shaneshwara!*' he cried, and joined the battle.

//Tasmin tvayi kim viryam ityapidan//
//Sarvah daheyam yadindah prthivyamithih//

Within the cloud of brahman, Vishwamitra vaguely sensed the battle raging around him. Such was the intensity of brahman power: once unleashed, the user lost contact with the material realm. For brahman was beyond space and time; beyond everything that ever was, is or will be. The sage had begun by chanting the sacred mantras of Vedanta; original slokas of his own composition, sacred verses composed in a metre and rhythm that infused them with the power to channel the flow of brahman that sustained the universe. Vishwamitra was chanting the upanisad mantras in order to channel power to the rajkumars, who would use it to fight the enormous numbers of enemy ranged against them. They needed to achieve the fullest flow of brahmanical power, and to have their atmas strengthened so they could contain and endure the rush of shakti, the way a river expanded its banks to accommodate a superior flow.

And yet, some part of Vishwamitra's atma, his divine deathless soul, knew that something had happened in the battle that demanded his attention. Something of great import. Something adverse.

With a great exertion of shakti, he struggled to maintain the channelling while freeing a small portion of his mind. With only as much consciousness as was needed to open his left eye he observed what was happening around him. What he saw was not wholly unexpected.

Rajkumar Rama was glowing with brahman shakti, his arms and weapons driven by the immense vidya of the maha-mantras Bala and Atibala. The results were plain to see. Not one of the horrendous beasts that boiled around Rama like a plague of locusts could harm a hair on his head. He scythed them down like ripe wheat, mowing his way through the field of flesh. And now he was joined by kshatriyas from Ayodhya, the remnants of the same Vajra they had encountered when leaving the raj-marg. The outcome of the battle had never been in question, but now it was certain it would be ended soon. Already, the hybrid monstrosities of Tataka's creation were falling back step by step, unable to match the brutal perfection of Rama's slaying as well as the courageous horsemen, charioteers and elephants of his fellow kshatriyas. Soon it would be over. And Rama would be able to seek out and fight his real foe: Tataka herself. Even at the height of his meditative chant, the brahmarishi's austere face softened in the ghost of a smile.

Then his left eye turned and saw the figure that lay prone on the ground. So near the mandala circle in which he stood, he had ignored it at first, assuming it was just another hybrid corpse. Now he saw with rising disquiet

461

that it was a human who lay there, brutally savaged. The pile of bones and flesh resembled something left on a butcher's slab rather than a human being. Yet there was no mistaking it for one of Tataka's bestial monstrosities. That pile of butchered remains was all that was left of Rajkumar Lakshman.

Bejoo had seen battle-rage before. But nothing like this. As he fought alongside Rama, he felt the raw power emanating from the prince. The rajkumar's sword windmilled through the nightmare menagerie, and Bejoo was left with little to do except stick his sword into a few eyes and guts and lop off anything that came within his reach. He had time to glance at Rama as he fought— drawn by the eternal human fascination for all machines of violence—and what he saw chilled and awed him simultaneously. The look on Rama's face was a grinning mask of exultation. *He enjoys it. Loves the slaughter.*

He saw now that the rajkumar was no longer just hacking down creatures methodically as he had been doing before. He was aiming to inflict the most pain possible. Bejoo watched as Rama cut down two creatures in quick succession, leaving both with terrible mortal injuries, then moving on to other prey. Bejoo dispatched both beasts, wincing as one actually bared its pale white belly to allow him to finish it off. *He's not himself. This is not Prince Rama fighting beside me. This is a creation of the sage, a man possessed by some brahmanical sorcery.*

The battle raged on around them. His horsemen and chariots had ridden into the thick of it and were happy to be able to have an enemy they could fight face to face. Bejoo caught glimpses of spears and maces working, smashing bones and piercing hides. Cries of 'Jai Shaneshwara!' rang out each time a Vajra kshatriya downed a monster. The creatures took some lives too, their bizarre

462

anatomies momentarily catching his men unawares.

In sheer numbers, the animals outnumbered the humans, but Rama's relentless jagganath-like slaughter rate was fast equalling the odds. What had seemed at first sight an impossible scenario now seemed a winnable battle. And the elephants were joining in now as well. They had balked at first, seeing their own species and their cousin-species among the mutated beasts, but their mahouts had used mantras to calm and convince the bigfoot and they were rallying now. As Bejoo glanced back in a respite between opponents, he saw the lead bigfoot smash his way into the thick of the fight, crushing beasts underfoot and wielding a specially designed weapon attached to his trunk: a lightning-shaped length of metal that sliced without snagging or sticking, identical to the vajra on their banner. Everywhere he looked, the Asura monstrosities were being cut down and slaughtered. Rama was no longer the only one wreaking a savage toll.

As if sensing their imminent defeat, the beasts had begun turning tail, cut down as they retreated step by step into the forest. Some were agile enough to dance back and lead their pursuers on individual chases, screeching in frustration when the Vajra horsemen or chariot caught up with them. *They're falling back. It's over.* Bejoo fought harder than ever, the wall of fur and claws breaking before him. Beside him, Rama blazed on remorselessly, chasing down and maiming and mutilating the unfortunate beasts that tried to flee. The creatures raised a volley of heart-rending cries, dying slow, agonising deaths.

Bejoo followed in Rama's wake, slaying as many as he could reach. More creatures were turning now, the line moving back in a unanimous retreat. His men began to raise victory cries as they saw the foe leaving the field. He rested his sword hand a moment, secretly relieved.

He had no stomach for this kind of fight. He was about to call to his men to fall back to the riverbank—they had drifted several dozen yards into the jungle—when he heard the booming.

The next thing he knew, the ground shuddered with an impact so mighty he was thrown off balance. He slipped and fell in the slimy remains of some grotesque monstrosity, cutting the back of his sword hand on a protruding row of spine-knives on the back of the corpse. But he was hardly aware of the pain. His attention was riveted on the shadow that had appeared in the sky.

Hai, Shani-deva. Save and protect us from all evil. What manner of Asura have you sent against us now?

Beside him, the slaying-machine that was Rama Chandra raised his head to glare at the thing that approached.

'*Tataka!*' cried the prince gleefully. '*At last you show yourself!*'

TWENTY-ONE

Bejoo lay where he had fallen, staring up in stunned dismay. The ground shuddered and shook beneath him, tilting him this way, then that. He could feel tiny fissures opening and spreading like spidercracks in the forest floor with each impact. He forgot that he lay in the spilled ichor of the corpse, his sword hand bleeding from the accidental slash. All he could do was lie there and stare up at the apparition in the sky.

He had heard the whispered legends of the Yaksi demoness Tataka, and the tales of the horrors that befell those foolish enough to venture into the Bhayanak-van. But no witness had faced the demoness and lived to describe her. Bejoo himself had always harboured a faint suspicion that Tataka might simply be some insane dasya woman, one of those cannibalistic thugs who had taken to waylaying travellers. Like the highway thugs who claimed to be acting on orders from the goddess Kali herself. He had held an image in his mind of a black-skinned tribal woman in a leaf skirt, body pierced in numerous places by carved bone jewellery, a stout nail-studded club in one hand, a necklace of infant skulls dangling over her naked pendulous breasts, roaring curses in her primitive tribal tongue, her rotted teeth easily mistaken for rakshasi fangs.

465

But the being that bore down on them now was no dasya, highway thug or cannibal tribal. What was she? The human vocabulary had few words for something of such proportions. The term giant seemed laughably inadequate. Words like gargantuan, mammoth, titanic, mountainous came to mind. Surely the apparition before him was the result of some Asura sorcery? Maya. Illusion. A trick of the light. Anything but what his eyes claimed they saw.

But there was no denying it. The creature that approached, making a path of her own through the Bhayanak-van, was all too real. Her head, shoulders and waist rose well above the tops of the highest trees, which were at least a hundred yards high. She towered above the whole forest, her immense bulk blocking out what little light managed to creep through the dense overgrowth. The sun was almost directly overhead, and when her head passed before it, it was eclipsed as effectively as a snuffed-out mashaal. Her shadow was dark and unimaginably huge even in the near-noon light, racing across the forest floor, casting them all into twilight darkness. She was still several miles distant, he realised. She strode through the Southwoods like a Nandi bull moving through a wheat field. The dense woods parted before her like wheatstalks, entire tracts collapsing beneath her strides. The dust of her wake rose like a cloud into the sky, and would probably be visible for a dozen yojanas in every direction.

In fact, Bejoo thought, it was a wonder she had never been spotted from the raj-marg or from any place north of the Sarayu before.

He watched her stride through the forest and suddenly felt foolish: the virgin denseness of this part of the woods was evidence she hadn't been here before. The forest would have been reduced to splinters if she had.

466

The battle around them had ceased. The surviving beasts had fled into the jungle, and his men had stopped to stare up at the new threat that approached.

Bheriya called out excitedly to Bejoo: 'It was no siege-machine! It was her!'

It took Bejoo a moment to understand that he was referring to the manure-boulders that had rained down on them on the outskirts of the forest. Silently, he agreed. This giantess could easily have thrown hillocks at them if she felt like it. Even a small mountain or two. Yes, there was no doubt that it had been she who had flung the balls, shaped by her own enormous hands.

Tataka came to a halt, peering down at them. The cloud of dust created by her passage rose above her head, glittering in the sunlight like a corona of smoke. Her face and body were silhouetted by the bright sun directly above her, and although Bejoo squinted hard, he could only make out her features dimly.

Tataka bent over, reaching down with hands as thick and long as wheelhouses—it was the only comparison Bejoo could summon to mind—and for a heart-stopping moment he thought she was reaching for *him*. But she stopped at the top of a cluster of trees, and parted them like a monkey parting the hair of a relative in search of ticks. She riffled through the trees carefully until she found what she was seeking. Bright sunlight shone down on Bejoo and his men as the giant exposed their part of the jungle. The Vajra's horses reared and screamed in response, terrified by the appearance of the Yaksi. What did the bigfoot make of her? he wondered.

Seeing the commotion caused by her appearance, Tataka emitted a grunt-like sound that Bejoo thought indicated satisfaction. *Or hunger. Maybe she sees us as a tasty snack.* Grasping hold of a clump of trees, she pulled them up with little effort, uprooting and tossing them aside like a handful of straw.

An elephant was caught between the uprooted trunks like an insect tangled in the rakes of a jhadoo broom, and squealed as its feet left the ground. Thick grey legs dangling, it exploded into terrified screams that faded as it was tossed aside with the handful of trees, flying miles away before falling to earth again. When the roots of a tree were yanked out of the ground, two horses were knocked down bodily, their riders violently unseated. Another warrior was killed when his chariot was upturned. An elephant panicked and broke into a headlong run back towards the river.

With startling suddenness, the gloom of the dense jungle was dispelled and Bejoo and his men found themselves in a brand-new clearing, a circular open space about a hundred yards in diameter. The Yaksi peered down, appearing satisfied. The mortals were all exposed to her view, as puny as ants and just as helpless before her prodigious size and strength.

She bent down, her teeth flashing white in her shadowed face. *We're lost*, Bejoo thought, scrambling to get to his feet. There was no conceivable way he could lead his men to kill such a creature. His only prayer was that he be allowed to die on his feet, fighting. He struggled to an upright posture, his sword clutched in his injured hand, feeling impotent as he stared up at the giant Yaksi.

Tataka took a single step into her newly created clearing. Her foot came down yards away from an elephant. The impact shook the earth hard enough to rattle Bejoo's teeth. The bigfoot was thrown several feet into the air, and landed on its side, screaming, but it struggled up at once, both beast and mahout dazed but apparently unhurt.

Horses reared and wheeled, white-eyed. The surviving Vajra kshatriyas stared up open-mouthed.

The Yaksi bent again, and this time Bejoo was certain that his time on Prithvi was ended. He had no means of defending himself and his men against this mountain of an Asura. He clenched his jaw and stood ramrod steady, legs spaced apart to prevent himself from being knocked on his back again, prepared for Tataka's attack and his own death.

The Yaksi turned her head from side to side, seeking out something. *Or someone.*

'Rama,' she said, parting lips large enough to swallow a pair of elephants whole. *And still leave room for celery*, Bejoo thought with dazed bemusement.

Even though spoken from a hundred or more yards high, her breath was strong enough to reach Bejoo. He braced himself, expecting a stench a hundred times as foul as that which emanated from the grotesque hybrids of her creation.

But as the giantess's breath wafted across his face, he blinked in disbelief. *She smells wonderful.* The Yaksi's breath carried the fragrances of a dozen pleasant things. *Definitely clover. And mint. And honeysuckle maybe.* More than the individual perfumes was an odour that he couldn't begin to describe except to say that he knew it all too well. *She smells feminine, like a woman.* Like his wife even, although it felt insane to relate his wife to this towering mountain of an Asura.

Tataka leaned down, her face looming above the clearing. As she came lower, her features grew more clearly visible, illuminated by the reflected sunlight from the ground. She crouched only a few dozen yards above the ground, her face as broad as the diameter of the clearing itself.

'By the red tongue of Kali,' Bejoo muttered to himself, sword clenched in his fist, the hilt slippery with his own blood.

But it wasn't just her smell. It was the Yaksi herself. Despite her size, despite the legends, despite everything he had heard about Asuras in his forty-seven years on Prithvi, Bejoo couldn't deny the evidence of his eyes.

The Yaksi was neither ugly nor malformed. On the contrary, she was . . .

'Atee sundar,' he whispered aloud, as if speaking the words could help him believe the fact. *Beautiful beyond comparison.* So beautiful that it took an effort to wrench his eyes away and glance around the clearing. His men were as baffled as he was. Their weapons were raised and ready for battle, every last one of them willing to fight the Asura to the death, however impossible or futile. But what they were not prepared for was this unexpected reversal. *How could an evil demoness be as stunningly beautiful as one of Indra's apsaras?*

To confound them further, she was making no hostile actions or gestures. If anything, Bejoo realised, she was being as gentle and careful as she could. If she chose, the Yaksi could simply raise a foot and stamp them down like splayed beetles, reducing them to crushed and mangled corpses. Yet even when she had uprooted the trees and foliage to make the clearing, she had done so without directly inflicting any violence on them. All the injuries were accidental. *After all, she can't help her size.*

The thought made him aware of the absurdity of his situation: *I'm justifying an Asura's actions!*

But the fact was as plain as the perfectly proportioned features of the Yaksi's face and body. This was no hideous demoness with crooked fangs dripping infants' blood, clad in human hides. In fact, the giantess wasn't clad in anything. Her enormous body was completely naked of any clothing, apart from a small crown of mogra nightqueen flowers, so redolent they could only be fresh, placed on her bright red hair. This last touch was particularly unsettling. Even Bejoo's wife put mogra in her hair, especially on nights when she knew he was in a particularly amorous mood. It made the Yaksi seem like nothing more than a very, very large and beautiful woman.

'Rama,' she said again, softer this time, her breath as fragrant as a spring field in bloom, her voice as delicate and feminine as a trained gayaka in Maharaja Dasaratha's court. Her bright green eyes were perfectly proportioned, two almond-shaped pools of light and colour. A delicately shaped nose, long ears with pointy tips, a neck as graceful as a swan's, and a body so slender—if that was the right word for a woman three hundred yards tall, and forty or fifty yards wide—that she could have driven any concubine in the maharaja's palace to blazing envy. Bejoo lowered his glance to her more private assets, and was shocked to find himself aroused by the beauty and perfection of her form. Gandharvas created to seduce the devas would have wept for such a body. He glanced around at his men and wasn't surprised to see that several had lowered their swords and spears. *But their level of arousal is rising fast.* He shook his head, trying to clear his mind, and glanced away for an instant, unable to believe the stirring in his groin. *This is impossible. There must be sorcery at work here. How can this . . . this . . . being possibly be Tataka?*

Rama came to his senses in stages, the shakti of the maha-mantras reducing in intensity from a raging glacial torrent to a gushing stream and then a more placid thick-girthed flow, until finally it released its hold on him and he returned to normality.

He blinked in the gaudy sunshine, in full command of his wits again, and remembered what had brought him back to his senses in the first place.

Tataka.

The giantess loomed above him, a sculpted idol of feminine perfection created on a massive scale. He was on his guard, sword still in hand, mind prepared to distrust the evidence of his senses as the result of maya. But Tataka's beauty was overwhelming. It made him hesitate long enough to allow doubt to creep into his mind.

This being can't be an evil demoness, can she?

'Tataka,' he said softly, staring up at the giantess.

She smiled at the sound of her name on his lips. Her smile was a wonderful thing, warm and innocent and full of relief and pleasure at hearing him acknowledge her presence. Except for her size, she might have been any woman, only her ears, the pale whiteness of her skin, the bright redness of her hair, and the faint dotting of freckles on her face marking her as different from other Arya women. That, and the very distracting fact of her utter nakedness.

Beware, Rama. Remember who this is.

'Tataka,' he said again. 'At last I meet you face to face, legendary demon.'

The smile faltered. 'Demon? Is that how you see me, my prince?'

'Rama!' The brahmarishi's stentorian voice boomed angrily through the clearing. 'Do not be deceived by Tataka's shrewd ingenuity. She seeks to distract you with maya. Asuras are masters of illusion. Turn a blind eye to her beauty and femininity and fulfil the duty with which I entrusted you. Slay the monster at once!'

Every pair of eyes in the clearing turned to look at the sage. Vishwamitra still stood on the mandala, but

472

the column of brahman light had vanished. The seer raised his longstaff and pointed up at the giantess, calling out to Rama: 'Do not delay, rajkumar. Remember what I told you: her power is weakest when the sun is highest. This is why she uses this alluring disguise to delay and entice you. Hold fast to your dharmic duty and slay her at once.'

Rama looked at Tataka once again, then at the brahmarishi. 'Parantu, gurudev, she appears to be a woman rather than an Asura. Kshatriya honour forbids me to kill a woman.'

The sage shook his staff in fury. 'Do not be fooled by appearances, Rama. This Yaksi is guilty of a thousand crimes. The devas themselves have sought her destruction time and time again. Remember the tale of Kama's Grove! Of how the devas sought for millennia to rouse Lord Shiva from his million-year tapasya. It was to destroy this very being. Resurrected by Ravana's sorcerous evil, she assumes this bhes-bhav to confuse you. Neither listen to her honeyed lies nor pay attention to her womanly attractions. Take up your weapon now and strike her down!'

A wisp of hair fell across Tataka's face. It hung there for a moment, obscuring her right eye and cheek, lending her an air of allure. 'Would you kill me, my prince? A mere woman?'

Rama looked around, his mind in a turmoil.

'Rama, do not fear her gargantuan size. Even though she has the strength of a thousand elephants, she is no match for you and the shakti of the maha-mantras Bala and Atibala.'

Rama looked at the giantess then at the sage. He scarcely knew whom to listen to or believe now. 'Gurudev,' he said. 'Please, I beg you, do not force me to violate dharma by killing a woman. I have done all you asked and will do all you ask in future. But this command is beyond my ability to fulfil.'

Vishwamitra brought his staff down in fury. Where it struck the ground, the earth itself split wide open with a blast of light and thunder. The elephants and horses, skittish and wide-eyed in the presence of the Yaksi, reared and trumpeted.

'Rajkumar Rama! Dharma is duty performed for the greater good. This duty you must perform for the welfare of all the four castes, for the sake of all mortalkind. A king must do what serves his subjects best, even if it seems unrighteous and distasteful, for such is his dharma. Hear me well, rajkumar. Lord Indra, most honourable of devas, was compelled to kill the daughter of Virocana because she sought the destruction of Prithvi herself, the very planet we inhabit. Lord Vishnu the Preserver killed Bhrigu's wife, mother of Kavya, because she plotted to murder Indra. In ages past, other kshatriya kings and princes such as yourself have committed this painful duty of stree-hatya and they suffered the same doubts and hesitation you are experiencing. You are not the first and you will not be the last warrior to kill a woman. It must be done. Suppress your pity, swallow your misgivings, take up your bow and kill Tataka while the sun approaches its zenith. Kill her now, Rama!'

Tataka rose to her feet, blotting out the sun again. The giantess awaited Rama's decision with a passiveness that was almost heart-rending. *If she was a fanged and clawed monstrosity rushing to tear my heart out, would I have hesitated this long?* And yet, something stayed his hand.

Vishwamitra spoke again, his tone softer and filled with compassion for Rama's plight. 'Rama, listen to me, boy. I know your pain. You are noble indeed to have such lofty ideals. But it must be done, and it must be done now.' The sage paused and then added: 'If not for yourself and your people, then do it for your brother.'

Rama frowned. 'My brother?'

The sage raised his staff and pointed to an object on the ground nearby. 'See for yourself and weep, brave prince of Ayodhya. There lies your courageous brother, Sumitra-putra Lakshman, reduced to a heap of shattered bones and tattered flesh, a victim of this same Tataka. Look at his remains and tell me now, do you still believe this demoness to be nothing more than a beautiful woman?'

Rama was across the clearing and by the side of the corpse with a speed that left the watching kshatriyas blinking in surprise. He bent and tried to collect the heap of gristle and bones that was all that remained of his brother— *my brother in arms*. It was less than nothing, neither a whole corpse nor a bone-white skeleton. Even as the maha-mantras worked their feverish power and the shakti flooded his brain and body, he still retained the ability to recall something of his other identity, the Rama Chandra he was when not under the influence of Bala and Atibala. That Rama brought to this moment a sackful of memories, images, emotions, sensations, half-remembered phrases and words that had seemed insignificant at the time and were more precious than a prayer now. Years growing together, scraping knees and bruising hearts, mastering arts both martial and mortal, learning to kill and learning to love, the importance of family, the necessity of duty, the meaning of dharma, the cycle of karma. It all flashed through with the white-hot intensity of a bolt of lightning leaving the heart of a thundercloud. A clap of thunder followed, deafening. The wheel of time, that great samay chakra which stopped for no man, deva or Asura, revolved another fraction of a fraction of a notch of a turn. He raised the heap of his brother's remains and cried his anguish to the skies.

'*Lakshman!*'

The Bhayanak-van reverberated with his grief.

Rama rose and walked with the bundle of his brother's mangled body in his outstretched arms, an anguished devotee bringing a strange offering to a heartless god. He stopped before the sage, bending his knee. He lowered the remains to the ground carefully, as tenderly as a mother laying down her sleeping infant. Then he bent and touched his forehead to the ground. Grit and dry leaves rubbed against his feverish skin, grinding against the bone of his skull like spices in a silbutta. When he raised his face, his forehead was marked with the grey soil of the haunted jungle, like a Shaivite adorned with ash.

The rage returned with a suddenness that was terrifying as well as thrilling. Pure emotion surged through Rama's veins, rising like a flash flood to overcome his anxieties, guilt and doubts. His fist clenched, seeking weapons, any weapons. His nostrils flared, sucking in air greedily, and he lowered his head to allow the blood and oxygen to reach his brain unimpeded, like a bull preparing to charge.

Even the Vajra kshatriyas took a step back, frightened at the transformation of Rama. Once again he was a being of brahman, a tributary of the great river of celestial power.

'*Mahadev,*' he said, his voice strange and terrible. '*You are supreme in your knowledge of the divine shastras. Brahma himself gave you vidya of all mantras governing life, death, rebirth and resurrection. No task is too great for your shakti. I implore you, return my brother in arms to the world of the living.*'

Vishwamitra shifted his hand higher on the staff, gripping the knob of wound thread at the top. 'There is a price to be paid for every spell that alters the balance of life and death. The Lord of Death, Yama, keeps precise accounts. The scales must ever be balanced perfectly. There are no exceptions. If you would have me apply to him to restore Rajkumar Lakshman to his former state, you must pay the price for his life with another.'

Rama's eyes flashed blue and gold, burning bright even in the light of high noon. '*I will pay the price with my own life if need be.*'

'That will not be enough. The price for resurrection is dear. One mortal soul will not meet Yama-raj's bill.'

'*Then I will offer a dozen souls. A hundred. A thousand! Name the price, Sage, and I will pay it. I will reap a harvest of blood such as was never seen in all the three worlds.*'

'Hear me then. Even all the mortal souls in the world are not enough to satisfy Lord Yama. You could cleanse the world of all mortalkind as Parasurama cleansed Prithvi of every last living kshatriya thrice over, and yet it would not pay the bill for your brother's soul. There is only one life that the god of death will accept in exchange for your brother's.'

'*Name the unfortunate wretch and he will not live to see the sun set today.*'

'Nay. Even sunset would be much too late. Already, Yama is halfway back to Patal on his red-eyed black buffalo, your brother's soul cached in his leopardskin pouch. If he consigns Lakshman to one of the many levels of Hell, it will be impossible to buy him back at any price. The exchange must be done quickly enough to make Yama retrace his steps at once. Within moments.'

'*It will be as you say, seer. Now name the victim who will pay for my brother's resurrection.*'

Vishwamitra raised a hand. 'It is no mystery. There she stands behind you. The one responsible for your brother's death. Kill the Yaksi demoness Tataka, and I will buy back your brother's life from the Lord of Death. Do it now, for the sun is at its zenith, or let the moment pass and go about collecting sandalwood for his funeral pyre.'

Rama stared at the seer. Then slowly he bowed his head once more. *'So be it. Begin the mantra, rishi, I will fulfil my part of the bargain.'*

He rose to his feet, and turned. He strode to the spot where Lakshman had fallen and picked up his brother's rig. He slung it over his shoulders and fitted an arrow to the cord.

Then he raised the bow and took aim at the giantess looming above the clearing.

TWENTY-TWO

Tataka reared up with a cry. 'Sage! You seers have been my bane for too long. Today I shall destroy you and your mortal accomplices. Your kind can never resist the might and fury of the Lord of Lanka! In the name of Ravana!'

Tataka raised her foot, preparing to stamp down on the seer-mage. Vishwamitra stood his ground impassively, reciting his mantras without heed for the Yaksi.

Rama loosed his arrow.

The thin wooden bolt shot up into the sky, and for an instant it was lost to sight, obscured against the blazing noonday sun. Then the giantess cried out with rage and slapped at herself, as if at a mosquito.

Bejoo saw the tiniest of pinpricks appear on the giantess's fair skin, high up on her left breast, a faint red dot. She pinched the arrow with her thumb and forefinger and pulled it free. Against her gargantuan bulk, the bolt was a barely visible sliver, like a needle in a grown man's hand. Tataka tossed it aside.

'Foolish mortal. Do you really believe you can harm me with your weapons? I am Tataka! I have the strength of a thousand elephants. It is not for nothing that I am known as gaja-gamini, the elephant-footed!'

'*An elephant can be killed too, as can a thousand*,' Rama replied, notching another arrow. '*But you can try fleeing with the speed of a thousand gaja if you like. It will not save you, demoness.'*

Something came over her face then, an awareness that the puny human standing before her was no longer the scrupulous dharma-driven prince of Ayodhya who feared committing the mortal sin of stree-hatya, woman-murder. This was a different being altogether, and there would be no arguing with him.

'So be it,' she said, and raised her hands as Rama lifted his bow again. She spread her arms as wide as she could—*wide enough to encompass most of Ayodhya,* Bejoo thought—and brought her palms together with all her force. The effect was like the most powerful thunderclap he had ever heard. The wind from the impact blasted him and his men off their feet, throwing some up into the air to slam against trees and elephants. The horses shuddered and fell over. The bigfoot shuffled sideways, struggling to keep their footing.

At the exact same instant, Rama loosed his second arrow. This one flew straight to the palm of her left hand, piercing the mound of Shukra below the thumb. Tataka hardly seemed to feel it; she was already bending down in preparation for her next move. But suddenly she exclaimed, her voice loud and crashing, no longer modulated gently for their benefit. She raised her left hand and examined it closely. She pinched out the arrow and stared at it for a moment before tossing it aside. Then she rubbed the spot where it had struck, dismissed the prick and turned back to the clearing.

Rama loosed a third arrow. This one struck her right forearm, Bejoo saw, just above the wrist. This time the giantess ignored it, wincing as it pierced her but continuing to reach down into the clearing. She picked up an elephant in one hand, clutched between two fingers like a squirming grub, and raised it to her mouth.

With a single nip, she bit it in half, letting the front half fall to the ground in a mass of bloodied flesh. The back half she aimed and threw at another bigfoot. It screamed as its dead brother fell on its flank with force enough to crush its hip, going down in a heap, bleating helplessly. The lead bigfoot reared up into the air, his eyes white, trumpeting with fury. *This is one battle you can't win, old friend*, Bejoo thought sadly. *Even a thousand elephants couldn't face her and live*. Still he gripped his sword tightly, ready to go down fighting.

The Yaksi raised her foot, causing a riot in the clearing. The horses were reeling and turning, suddenly terrified. *They scent the Yaksi's hostility now*. And he smelt it too, a low, sour odour that was as distinct as the earlier fragrant aroma had been. This was the Yaksi's true body odour, not the sweet scent she had deceived them with earlier.

Tataka brought her right foot down upon three of the Vajra riders with a wordless cry of rage, just as Rama shot his fourth arrow at the same leg. She hardly seemed to notice this one. But Bejoo observed with a start that something strange was starting to happen at the spot where Rama's first arrow had struck.

On the Yaksi's left breast, where there had been the tiniest of pinpricks and a droplet of blood so minute it was barely visible, there was now a dark red patch the size of the Yaksi's thumb. A tiny plume of smoke rose from the patch, and as Bejoo watched, the skin itself seemed to pucker and peel away from the centre of the wound.

What wound? A thistle-poke would cause more harm.

Yet even as Bejoo watched, raising his free hand to shield his eyes from the overhead sun, he saw the dark patch growing, expanding outward. His first impression of smoke was no sun-haze illusion; the wound was starting to catch fire and burn!

The Yaksi frowned, distracted from her stomping and smashing of the Vajra kshatriyas and their beasts. She bent her head and attempted to look at her left breast. She peered at the wound, now the size of her palm and growing with astonishing rapidity, smoke curling up from its puckering edges like a scroll of paper set afire by a piece of glass and sunlight.

She touched the wound tentatively with her fingertips and cried out as the fire singed her fingers as well. Then a curl of smoke emerged from her left hand and she spread the palm, staring at the spot where Rama's second arrow had struck. It was growing too, burning blackly.

Bejoo suddenly began to comprehend what was happening and turned his head to look at the Yaksi's right forearm where the next arrow had struck, then the left foot and finally the right foot where Rama had just shot his fifth arrow. Each wound was behaving in exactly the same way.

It's as if the arrows were pitch-missiles fired into a thatched roof, burning up the skin and flesh like straw. How could such a thing happen?

He turned to look at Rama again, and saw the answer at once.

The prince was preparing to fire a sixth arrow, and this time Bejoo watched him closely enough to see everything he did. Just before stringing the arrow, Rama poked it lightly into his own abdomen. Lightly, but hard enough to break the skin and draw blood.

Bejoo's eyes widened as he saw the tiny pinprick of fresh blood welling up on the rajkumar's flat abdomen. Then he saw that there were identical drops of fresh blood on the prince's arms and legs and chest.

He dipped every arrow into his own blood before loosing it. Bejoo had no idea how that could cause the arrows to act on the Yaksi the way they did, but he suspected it had something to do with the maha-mantras he had heard spoken of earlier. Somehow the rajkumar's own blood was filled with the power of brahman, and by smearing his blood on to each arrow-tip, he was using not just arrows but the very force of the celestial power against the Yaksi.

Tataka's scream diverted his attention back to her.

Bejoo looked up and saw the giantess's five wounds burning freely now, the fires tinged with edges of unmistakable brahman blue, literally eating up the Yaksi's flesh. The one in her chest was a roaring flame now, and Bejoo saw that her chest itself was exposed, the heart and ribcage clearly visible. As she raised her burning left hand in terror and pain, he saw the fire eat right through the palm, exposing sky and a glimpse of sun on the other side. It was an incredible sight.

Rama's blood, rich with the brahman shakti of Bala and Atibala, is eating the Yaksi alive. And the sun god Surya, progenitor of Rama's dynasty, is at the peak of his power, giving the rajkumar the combined strength of mortal and immortal shakti.

Rama loosed his sixth arrow, this time piercing the Yaksi's belly. She screamed, understanding at last what the puny human was doing to her. She pinched out the arrow at once, but already the pinprick was on fire, spreading as rapidly as water seeping across a sloping floor. And then Rama took a seventh and last arrow and pricked his own forehead with it.

'*Now die, Tataka*,' he said. And shot the giantess between the eyes.

Bejoo sent up a prayer to every deva he could think of. With a scream that pierced his eardrums, the Yaksi cried out. Then, with a sound like a waterfall striking a rock, she went up in flames, ringed blue at the edges. She fell to her knees, the impact shaking the earth hard enough to rattle every bone in his body and every tooth in his head.

For one heart-stopping instant, Bejoo was sure she would fall forward, crushing them all. But she groaned, her face a blazing candle oozing molten flesh and running blood, and fell sideways, crashing to the ground in an enormous cloud of dust. After a moment, the forest began to burn around her, a fitting funeral pyre.

TWENTY-THREE

Lakshman opened his eyes, blinking as he found himself looking up at a bright afternoon sky. The ground below him shuddered convulsively. A rattling and roaring filled his ears. From the position of the sun, he guessed it was late afternoon. He sat up slowly, wincing in anticipation of pain, and found himself staring at a curved metal plate not unlike the inside of a battle shield.

He realised he was in a chariot. The sandalled feet of the charioteer were behind his head, stippled with dried blood and cuts and bruises. Blood stained the charioteer's hoary right hand as it held the reins tightly. From the steady rhythmic rocking of the two-horse, Lakshman intuited that they were on a path less smooth than the raj-marg yet not as rough as open countryside.

He tried to sit up and lost his balance, keeling over to the open rear of the chariot, towards the brown earth rushing past at a great speed. A muscled hand gripped his shoulder, steadying him. He turned and looked into the sun-burned battle-scarred face of a grizzled veteran, recognising the man as the same Vajra commander they had encountered on the cliff south of Sarayu just after they left the raj-marg.

'Bejoo-chacha,' he said, surprised. 'What am I doing here in your chariot?'

Bejoo stared at him silently in response. Lakshman frowned, wondering if the man had failed to hear him above the noise of the chariot. Perhaps he was deafened temporarily by some injury; he looked like he had been in a fierce battle.

The grizzled kshatriya blinked at last and looked away, at the road. 'The sage told me to take you ahead. He and your brother follow us on foot.'

Lakshman looked around. He saw they were on a rough but passable dirt path running through lightly wooded scrubland. Another two chariots followed them, both badly battered and one wobbling dangerously. Perhaps two dozen horse followed the chariot, riding in single file, and through the cloud of dust rising in their wake, he thought he could make out the raised trunks of two or three bigfoot.

He turned back to the commander, surprised. 'Your Vajra? Is this all that remains of it?'

Bejoo's jaw tightened. 'Yes.'

'Why did you carry me in your chariot? Why did Rama and Gurudev not rouse me and let me walk? My place is with them, not riding like this.'

Bejoo glanced at him, his eyes flicking up and down as if examining Lakshman carefully. 'You were . . . injured in the battle. Unconscious. Unfit to make the journey on foot. I was ordered to carry you ahead to the sage's ashram.' He added belatedly, 'Rajkumar.'

'I feel fine,' Lakshman began, irritated. 'I could have walked easily. Stop the chariot, let me off here. I will wait by the road for my brother and Guru Vishwamitra and continue on foot with them.'

The commander rode on without slowing. 'Shama, my prince. I have strict orders. You are to be allowed to disembark only when we reach Siddh-ashrama.'

486

Lakshman frowned. 'But we can't be going on to Siddh-ashrama yet. We still have to kill the Yaksi Tataka and her rakshas sons Mareech and Subahu.'

A sudden chill gripped him despite the heat of the afternoon sun. 'What happened to me, Commander? I was wounded, wasn't I?' He patted himself all over. 'But where was I wounded? I feel no injuries on my person. I feel healthy, invigorated, fighting fit . . . and hungry, very, very hungry.'

Bejoo glanced at him curiously, steering the chariot around a bend in the path beside a clump of cherry trees. 'I am sure the rishis at the ashram will provide for your needs, rajkumar. We should reach it soon. The sage said it was about eight or nine yojanas ahead. We have already covered half that distance.'

Lakshman thumped his fist on the dashboard of the chariot. 'I don't understand. Why was I unconscious for so long? What happened after I lost my senses? Speak to me, Commander. Tell me!'

The kshatriya evaded his eyes. 'All I know, rajkumar, is that when my Vajra and I caught up finally with the three of you, you were in the Bhayanak-van and had fought a great battle against Tataka and her minions. We joined forces with you and eventually, by your brother's great valour, Tataka was killed and the Bhayanak-van set ablaze. If you look back, you will see the fire even now.'

Shielding his eyes from the sun, Lakshman peered in the direction the commander had mentioned, and saw the plume of smoke that rose in the distance, several yojanas away. He had missed it earlier because the dust of their wake had obscured it. 'Jai Shiv Shankar! *Hail Lord Shiva!*' he said, unable to believe it. 'Then we won! We fought them all and we won! You said you saw Rama kill the Yaksi?'

Bejoo nodded, looking away. 'I did.'

'Was she as terrible as the tales say? A towering, blood-thirsty, rapacious demoness with the strength of a thousand elephants?'

Bejoo continued to keep his face averted, looking at the road ahead. 'She was the largest living being I have ever seen or heard tell of.'

'And you say my brother downed her? How did he achieve this, commander? Give me the details!' Lakshman slammed a fist into his open palm. 'If only I had been awake to see it. Why did I have to be knocked unconscious at such a time! Rama had to do it all on his own.'

He glanced apologetically at the Vajra commander. 'Although I am sure you and your Vajra must have fought hard alongside him. I can tell that from the extent of your losses.'

'Yes,' Bejoo said shortly. 'Rajkumar, perhaps you would take some rest for a while and allow me to concentrate on steering us safely. I am sure your brother and the sage will answer your questions once we reach the ashram.'

'Yes, yes, of course,' Lakshman said. He felt like singing and clapping his hands. But the commander's obvious depression dampened his enthusiasm. He sympathised with the man's losses. 'You must have lost some fine men in the Southwoods.'

Bejoo was silent for a moment. When he replied, his voice was gruff and hoarse. 'All fine men, some finer than others.'

Lakshman shook his head regretfully. 'When we return to Ayodhya, I will tell my father you fought bravely. He will raise a stone to the memory of your lost men.'

He sighed, folding his arms across his chest, his body rocking with the rhythm of the chariot. 'It could as easily have been me lying back there on the floor of the Bhayanak-van, dead.'

He wondered why Bejoo started suddenly, almost losing control of the horses, and stared at him in wide-eyed shock.

Battle-weariness, Lakshman thought. *The man needs time to recover, that's all.*

They reached the ashram not long after, the sun still high in the western sky. It was not unlike Ananga-ashrama, except that the rishis were devoted to Brahma instead of Shiva, and the ashram seemed more recently built, in relative terms, which meant only that it was a few centuries old to Ananga-ashrama's millennia.

Lakshman refused to take water or food, and would not accept arghya or set foot within the shaded ashram hut until Rama arrived. He sat on a hummock beside the road, waiting. He wished he could take a chariot and ride back to pick up his brother and the guru. The hours passed with agonising slowness, but despite his earlier pangs of hunger, he felt more than able to bear the heat and the lack of food or water. If anything, he felt refreshed and alert. He attributed it to the time he had spent unconscious.

The Vajra kshatriyas tended to their horses and elephants but seemed to avoid him nervously for some reason. Lakshman didn't mind; he was in no mood for talk and he wanted time to try and remember what had happened before he lost consciousness. All he could recall was fighting the hybrid monsters, the blue glow from his own eyes, and Rama's incredible speed, strength and skill during the battle.

The sun was an hour from the horizon when he finally spied the flowing white locks of the brahmarishi and Rama's crow-black hair. Both men were approaching at a pace that was equal to a brisk trot. Lakshman's heart thudded as he saw that Rama was unmarked by scars or wounds. Even the ichor and blood that must have coated his body after the battle with the hybrids seemed to have been washed away.

As Rama came closer, his body glistening with a rich sheen of sweat, Lakshman saw something in his brother's eyes that was visible even from afar, something not like Rama, and a faint uneasiness crept down his spine as he recalled the blood-madness of the battle. But he ran forward excitedly, waving. Rama's face lost its grim expression as his mouth opened in that familiar teeth-flashing laugh, and he ran to meet him midway. They embraced and Lakshman squeezed his brother's sweat-slippery body as tightly as he could.

'Bhai,' he said, fighting back tears. 'It's good to see you again.'

Rama disengaged himself from his grip and looked at him. 'And you too, little brother. So good to see you again.' There was a strange expression to his voice, as if he was trying to choke back sudden tears.

Lakshman turned to the brahmarishi as he approached, joining his hands and bowing his head respectfully. 'Pranaam, gurudev. I apologise for not being in my senses during the battle with the Yaksi and her sons.'

The seer laid a hand on Lakshman's head. 'No need to apologise, rajkumar. You fought bravely, doing more than your share. We all play our own part in each conflict, and oftentimes we serve the purpose of brahman in our own individual ways.'

Lakshman raised his head. 'I look forward to serving you now during your yagna, mahaguru. When will it begin?'

The sage glanced back at the sun hanging low in the evening sky. 'This very evening, Lakshman. I am afraid you and your brother will have no sleep for the next seven nights. You must stand guard and ensure that the rakshasas do not violate the ritual or the altar as they

490

have done at earlier poojas. This is no ordinary havan. It is a maha-yagna that must be completed without interruption.'

'We will not fail you, mahadev,' Lakshman replied.

The seer turned to look at him. 'No, you will not,' he said kindly. 'I am confident in your ability to fulfil your duty to the fullest extent.'

He glanced over Lakshman's shoulder, exchanging another look with Rama. 'I am sure you will be more than a match for Mareech and Subahu when they arrive.

'And now, I will go and purify myself in preparation for the yagna, and you and your brother must do the same. You may perform your sandhyavandana and take your acamana in the sacred confluence of the Ganges and Sarayu. For this is Siddh-ashrama, built on the sacred site where the great Sage Vamana once resided, who as you well know was the famous dwarf avatar of Lord Vishnu descended to earth to regain Prithvi from the demon Bali.'

He smiled. 'But that is a katha for another time. Perhaps when we are done with our yagna and are on the road back to Ayodhya, I may tell it to you. Now, time is short, and much work remains.'

The sage strode towards the ashram, the rishis waiting at its boundaries with arghya jugs and phool malas and all the customary honours.

Lakshman turned to Rama. 'Did he say Mareech and Subahu? But I thought you fought and killed them back in the Bhayanak-van when you killed Tataka?'

Rama's eyes were distant and distracted. 'They fled.'

'Oh,' Lakshman said, wanting to hear more. 'About the fight with Tataka, bhai. After I was knocked unconscious . . . how was I knocked unconscious, by the way? All I remember is—'

Rama put a hand on his shoulder, silencing him. 'Lakshman, my brother. We have work to do. It will be dusk in minutes, and we still haven't completed our evening prayers. Come. We'll talk later.'

'Of course,' Lakshman replied. 'Later.'

They walked towards the ashram together.

TWENTY-FOUR

The first six days and nights passed without disturbance. The yagna went on round the clock uninterrupted, and by the afternoon of the fifth day, Lakshman could tell from the expressions and manner of the rishis and acolytes that everything was going well. Even he could see that the omens were all auspicious, and began to relax.

On the morning of the sixth and final day, Rama woke him with the quiet warning: 'Today, be on your guard.'

The day passed uneventfully.

That night, as dusk began to fall, Lakshman sensed a change in the atmosphere. The hairs on the back of his neck began to prickle, the harsh, plaintive cawing of a crow broke the chirring-chirping sounds of sparrows and insects, and as twilight deepened, he knew that things more dangerous than wolves or cats were abroad.

They came from the sky, appearing out of thin air and flying with no clear means of support. The first was a demon with skin so fair it took him only a moment to recognise it as an albino. Its colourless white eyes were filled with a hatred that was more frightening than the jagged-edged mace it held.

Why does he hate me so much?

Then he remembered and felt foolish. *Because we killed his mother*. That one was Mareech, Rama told

493

him quietly, speaking in the wordless voice that they both had begun to use when under the influence of the maha-mantras.

The second one was completely unlike his brother-rakshas: dark and short and thick-waisted. He carried a weapon that Lakshman had never seen before, a peculiar round astra like a hollow metal ball which covered his fist and most of his forearm. This one was Subahu, Rama said.

As Subahu approached, he raised his hand and swung it in an action similar to swinging a sling. The metal ball unfolded into overlapping layers, each finely honed to razor-sharpness, and from between the layers spikes on thin metal rods emerged, spinning in a synchronous motion that was mesmerising to behold. Lakshman tore his eyes away from the lethal beauty of the astra and concentrated on his own astras.

The brahmarishi had given them their weapons before beginning the yagna. It had been a simple but significant ceremony, attended by the ashramites as well as the Vajra kshatriyas.

'To honour your valour in the Bhayanak-van, for cleansing the dread Southwoods and razing it to the ground with purifying fire, for killing the demoness Yaksi Tataka and ridding the world of her menace, I grant you, Rajkumars Rama and Lakshman, the divine astras of the devas. These mantras I communicate directly to your minds will give you the shakti to call upon any one of a hundred great astras. Despite their name, these are not mere weapons. Each of these astras is in fact a celestial being, a shining demi-god from swarga-lok, the highest of the three worlds. The mantras compel them to serve you at your will. Speak any mantra and the corresponding shining one will be at your command instantly. Accept these divine weapons now as reward for your triumph in Bhayanak-van.'

Lakshman had suffered a pang of guilt. He felt he hardly deserved this recognition after being unconscious through most of the fight in the Southwoods. But when he said as much to the brahmarishi, Rama interrupted and insisted that he should not refuse such gifts. He had agreed only to avoid spoiling the ceremony, but now he was glad the guru had armed them with the astras. As the rakshasas swooped down from the sky, riding through the air by some strange shakti, he stepped forward. He knew what to do. He would use the Manava astra to dispel them both in one blow. It would be ironically appropriate to destroy the rakshasas with the shakti of his ancestor Manu Lawmaker himself.

But as he released the astra at the approaching Asuras, Rama moved in front of him, shielding him. Lakshman cried out in frustration and diverted the astra at the last minute. It went astray, striking Mareech a glancing blow on his shoulder.

Even so, it was powerful enough to fling the rakshas back with the force of a catapult launching a pebble. The demon was thrown a hundred yojanas distant, landing in the Great Ocean, his shoulder shattered. But he was still alive. Lakshman knew this because the astra returned in a flash to him and showed him the result of its action.

Before Lakshman could cry out to Rama to move from his way, Rama had unleashed one, two, three astras in rapid succession. Lakshman stared in disbelief as the astras of Agni, Vayu and Indra struck the rakshas Subahu simultaneously in a magnificent display of coordinated shakti. The rakshas was quartered to the four winds, burnt alive, and his remains reduced to charred ashes by the three astras of fire, wind and lightning.

As suddenly as it had begun, the assault was over. Lakshman blinked, unable to believe the fight had ended so quickly. Around them, the Vajra kshatriyas looked around uneasily, their swords and maces still unsullied, their arrows unshot. They muttered nervously, glancing at the two princes.

When the yagna ended at dawn the next morning, Lakshman turned to Rama and broke the ritual silence. 'Why did you block my way, bhai? I would have destroyed both of them with Manu's astra. They would both be dead now. Instead, you let Mareech escape.'

Rama looked away. 'His injury was grave. He fell far out in the ocean. He won't survive.'

'But why did you do it?'

Rama looked at him. 'I didn't want to lose you again.'

Lakshman felt a surge of anger. 'Just because I was knocked unconscious once doesn't mean I'm helpless, bhai! I can fight as well as you can. I don't need your protection, *big* brother!'

Rama nodded. 'I did what I thought was right at the time. I'm sorry if I hurt your pride, Lakshman. It won't happen again.'

Lakshman's anger faded. There was more to this than Rama was telling him, he knew.

'Rajkumars.'

Vishwamitra's face glowed with a new intensity. The brahmarishi had visibly gained strength during the yagna and now he looked and moved like a man who had shed fifty years—or five hundred, considering his age. He fed them both the prasadam from the yagna with his own hands. Lakshman let go of his questions and doubts as he received the sanctified fruits of the sacrifice and repeated the ritual thanks.

'Your service has come to an end, rajkumars,' the brahmarishi said with a smile. 'You have fulfilled your dharma with great success.' He glanced at Lakshman. 'And great sacrifice. Soon, we will return to Ayodhya where you will resume your lives as royal princes of your illustrious line. Your father will be proud of how well you conducted yourselves on this your first spiritual mission. And the people will rejoice in the knowledge that you accomplished the cleansing of the dreaded Bhayanak-van. No more will Aryas fear to enter those fearsome woods again. In a generation or two, they will be the site of cities as great as Ayodhya and Mithila. And you made all this possible, my young shishyas. You have done me proud.'

The sage beckoned to the Vajra commander, who was standing in line awaiting his turn to receive prasadam.

'Vajra Commander Bejoo insists on accompanying us back on our return journey, and I have consented to allow him to fulfil his orders.'

Bejoo acknowledged the sage's generosity with a namaskar and a bow.

'His associate Bheriya will ride back to the capital to inform Maharaja Dasaratha of the good news, so that when you return home, you will be welcomed back with full pomp and ceremony as befits two victorious princes of Ayodhya.'

He gestured to his rishis, who handed the prasadam to Bejoo. 'Kshatriya, on behalf of all at Siddh-ashrama, I thank you for your service in the duty of your rajkumars. Even though you disobeyed my wishes by following us, your sacrifices in Bhayanak-van more than absolved you of your error.'

Bejoo seemed about to say something, then changed his mind. He bowed his head as he accepted the prasadam.

'You are too kind, mahadev. Will the rajkumars and yourself start your return journey today?'

'Yes, good man. But we shall not be returning directly to Ayodhya. We shall be visiting Mithila first.'

Bejoo blinked. 'But that will take us a full two days out of our way. The Rajkumar Rama Chandra is to be crowned prince-heir on his sixteenth naming day, less than eight days from now.'

'And he shall return in time for the coronation. But this detour is unavoidable. I have important business in Mithila and I would prefer that the rajkumars attend me. After all, do not forget that they are still oathsworn to me until such time as I hand them over personally to their father the maharaja.'

The commander wrestled with his thoughts for a moment, then sighed. 'As you say, mahadev. With your permission, I shall dispatch my associate to Ayodhya at once with this news as well as the earlier information. Aagya, gurudev?'

He bowed to the brahmarishi, then to the princes.

'Thank you for your service, commander,' Rama said formally. To Bheriya, standing to one side deferentially, he added: 'Good journey.'

Bheriya thanked them with a namaskar and both Bejoo and he retreated to the waiting chariots. Bejoo put his arm around the younger man, giving him his last instructions.

'Rama,' Lakshman said. 'Why does Bejoo-chacha look at me so strangely, as if I've grown four ears or something? I just don't understand it. He used to be so nice to me back when we were boys.'

Rama shrugged. 'People change.'

Lakshman wanted to argue that point but Rama had already turned back to the seer.

'Gurudev,' Rama asked. 'If you will pardon my asking, what business requires your presence in Mithila?' The brahmarishi nodded agreeably, relaxed and contented after the yagna. 'I must attend a marriage.'

'A marriage? Whose marriage, gurudev?'

Vishwamitra smiled cryptically. 'Yours.'

The Moon is (Still) a Harsh Mistress

ONE

Bheriya sensed the attack an instant before it came. He and his men were on the dirt path that led up to the cliff. A few yojanas and they would reach the plateau overlooking the Sarayu valley, within sight of Ayodhya. The path was narrow and overgrown, his arms and face criss-crossed with scratches inflicted by some of the more intrusive branches and bushes, yet he rode as fast as the available light and the way would permit, eager to reach Ayodhya and convey his news. *The rajkumars are safe; their mission was a success*. All of Ayodhya would cheer when they heard his tidings; the maharaja would be overjoyed. Then Bheriya could go home to his new bride and they would resume where they had left off celebrating their suhaag raat. He was thinking of just how that particular celebration would go when he saw the movement on the boulder up ahead.

The path wound uphill and turned sharply, following the curve of the cliffside. At the turning, a large lohit-stone boulder protruded, looming over the path. The ambush came from atop the boulder.

At first Bheriya thought it was a deer of some sort. He glimpsed speckled downy fur and large doe-like eyes. Then the creature rose up to its full height, silhouetted against the light of the almost full moon, and he saw its skin ripple, changing in seconds to something quite un-deer-like.

'Rakshas!' he shouted instantly. 'Savdhaan! Enemy above! On the rock!'

His men reacted at once. The moment he yelled, they left the path and began to fan out, separating and encircling the boulder in question, arms at the ready. Bheriya stayed on the path, his spear ready and poised even before the creature moved.

As the rakshasi leaped off the boulder, roaring with rage, Bheriya threw the spear. It sped through the air headed directly for the creature's chest. But at the last instant, the rakshasi twisted and dodged the flying missile in mid air. She fell into the thick undergrowth, vanishing from his sight.

'Surround and destroy!' he ordered. 'Be alert for more enemies!'

He reached for another spear, hefting it expertly as he guided his horse forward. It had been a rakshasi, he was sure of it. He had seen the ugly horned head and the gaping teeth and the unmistakable bulge of its feminine chest. But why had he mistaken it for a deer at first? It didn't matter. What concerned him now was finding the beast and killing it swiftly. And making sure it was alone.

He assumed it was a straggler that had survived the battle in the Bhayanak-van. The Southwoods had been still blazing fiercely when he had left Siddh-ashrama earlier this afternoon, and his party had had to take a wide detour to avoid the enormous swathe of the fire. This creature had undoubtedly escaped both the battle and the fire and was crazed and confused, blindly seeking to avenge its fallen companions. He would soon dispatch it to join those companions.

The sounds of bestial howls and human cries exploded from the thick undergrowth up ahead. He had seen a pair of chariot cutting through the bush on his orders, running to the right. Those were four of his best men. Then the human cries broke off with chilling abruptness, and he knew that the rakshasi had drawn first blood.

'Jai Shani-deva!' he cried, riding into the bush. His horse thrashed through the scrub and trees, and he swatted aside flailing tree limbs.

He came upon the chariots and stopped. They were all dead, slaughtered. Not just the chariot riders and the bowmen; the horses too.

Cursing, he backed his horse to the path, calling to his men to regroup around him. He realised too late that the tactic he had chosen had been the wrong one under the circumstances. It would have worked had there been a whole herd of rakshasas. But because there was only one, the thick brush gave it cover from which to strike and flee, while blocking his men.

'To me! Vajra, come to me!'

He found the path again and turned his horse around, reeling round in circles, trying to find his men or the rakshasi, either of them. All about him, the undergrowth was exploding with screams and cries of pain and terror. Could one rakshasi be doing so much damage? How could she move so fast? She had been relatively small, barely seven feet high, and slender, lithely muscled. But then he remembered her bared fangs as she had leaped from the boulder, gleaming in the moonlight. And those claws, yes, those claws.

He wheeled about, trying to get a fix on her position. He crashed through the undergrowth, finding men unhorsed, their throats slashed, bellies cut, horses disembowelled. All around him, from every direction at once it seemed, the cries of terror continued unabated.

'To me, Vajra!' He was angry now, furious at being duped so easily by a single Asura. How had she known they would separate and fan out? Could a rakshasi know a Vajra's military tactics? Surely that was impossible!

He broke through the bush, finding the path yet again. And stopped.

She was standing in the middle of the path, waiting for him. Her talons and mouth dripped dark viscous fluids in the silvery moonlight. She was crouching like a bear in a river waiting to catch a fish.

The sounds of his men had ceased. They were all dead, he realised.

He hefted the spear in order to judge the throw perfectly. He waited for her to make the first move, determined this time to strike his target. A Vajra kshatriya never missed twice.

Yet he did miss.

And she didn't.

Supanakha licked herself clean. The mortal blood tasted salty and acidic. She spat it out in disgust. She had lost the taste for blood long ago. But there was no way to avoid swallowing some when ripping out throats and slashing bellies. It was that part about killing mortals she disliked, the vile saline taste of them.

The whole ambush had taken only a few minutes. It had been easier than she'd expected. The Vajra kshatriyas had been ill-prepared for the attack, and their leader was disoriented by her part-doe part-rakshasi appearance at first sight. He had acted exactly as she had known he would; she had fought Vajra kshatriyas before. For all their so-called unconventional tactics, Aryas were far too predictable for a truly experienced Asura. She had seen Vajra kshatriyas try the same separate-and-surround tactic as much as three hundred years ago. The outcome of that fight had been the same as this one.

She climbed back up on to the boulder, her claws rasping on the craggy lohit-stone. The moon illuminated her bloody fur, making it glisten wetly. She would sit here a while and bask in the moonlight. Her cousin would probably contact her again tonight, to find out if she had carried out his orders.

Just a few hours away from Rama, and she already missed him. She had followed him down the river yesterday, all the way into the Bhayanak-van. During the battle she had transformed into a langur and climbed a tree, staying high enough to be hidden, low enough to watch.

Seeing him slaughter her fellow Asuras had aroused her powerfully. It had been a thrill to watch a mortal who could stand up to so many of her brothers and sisters and slay them so efficiently. While staying alive and unharmed himself, of course. She had watched and grown more attracted to him than before.

She had a plan. She would speak to her cousin when he contacted her later tonight. Convince Ravana that Rama was now immune to any assassination attempt. That even Kala-Nemi wouldn't be able to get close to him now. With the power of the maha-mantras, the guidance of the sage, and the dev-astras in his possession, Rama was all but invulnerable.

But he could be reached by a woman. Because of her part-mortal parentage, Supanakha could take the form of a mortal woman so convincingly, even the brahmarishi wouldn't know for certain that she wasn't one. That was how she had been able to follow them so closely all the way to the Bhayanak-van. And before that, she had been able to observe them in Ananga-ashrama undetected.

Yes. Where an assassin would surely fail, a woman might succeed. A beautiful young Arya woman who was in some distress, whom they happened to come across while on their journey to Mithila. She already knew they would set out tomorrow at daybreak. She could race ahead of them, just as she had raced ahead of this Vajra company tonight. And ambush them just as effectively. Using deception and disguise rather than surprise and shock.

Supanakha smiled, her teeth flashing brightly in the moonlight. Yes, that was a fine plan. Now all she had to do was convince Ravana. Her smile faded. That was easier said than done. But she would manage it somehow. She simply had to get close to Rama, touch his smooth young body again, feel his heart beating against her breast once more.

Even if she had to tear out that heart a moment later.

After all, she was a rakshasi. And among her kind, there was very little difference between mating and murder.

In fact, she had often found that the latter was far more pleasurable than the former.

She raised her head and howled at the moon, exulting in her recent victory and her forthcoming conquest. The sound carried for yojanas on the still night air. She waited for Ravana to come to her and hear her plan.

All of this was carried with solemn and precious...
...me carrying the maha...
... filling the enclosure... he'd hold... AU...
Sumantra heard?

Rama could scarcely...he had overrun his...
...lead in accusing... too eager to have that...
Manthara-maa? But perhaps...to the maharaja
... which was why she felt a cold chill... but was
...without the restraint...vyn... had raised at first
...the guru's voice...had rung sharp and brittle with alarm
...at this item of information...she'd gone along

TWO

Sumitra-maa was the last to arrive. She had never been to the seal room before and had taken two wrong turns getting here. She scurried in, murmuring apologies for her lateness, and took a seat between Kausalya and Bharat. Shatrugan was the only one standing, his axe slung at his waist even though it was the middle of the night and he was indoors. Sumitra frowned at him, trying to show her displeasure at his wearing a weapon beneath his father's roof. He shrugged. She sighed and looked around at Kausalya.

'Why did the guruji call us here?' she asked, whispering.

Kausalya shook her head. 'I wish I knew. All Sumantra would tell me was that the guru had something important to discuss with us.'

Sumitra looked around. Except for the four of them, there was nobody else in the room. The seal room was an administrative chamber; the kingdom's official seals were stored here. By day, clerks worked at these tables, copying out official writs and proclamations in preparation for the maharaja to apply his official royal seal. Of course, it was usually Pradhan-Mantri Sumantra who did the actual applying, but he consulted with the maharaja. To Sumitra, who had little interest in administrative matters, it was just a large musty room

509

full of big desks covered with scrolls and parchments and writing materials.

'Where are they then?' she asked. 'Guruji and Sumantra, I mean?'

Before Kausalya could answer, the doors swung open again and Guru Vashishta entered, followed by Pradhan-Mantri Sumantra. The guru was clad in his customary white robes, a rudraksh mala around his neck, but was without his trademark staff. Sumitra marvelled at how the guru's clothes could appear so clean and fresh even at this hour of night; surely he couldn't have donned fresh clothes just for this meeting?

Vashishta waited for Sumantra to shut the doors, then he gestured in the air with one hand, reciting a mantra very quickly. Sumitra felt a strange dampening sensation in her ears, as if she had been listening to very loud bells clanging and they had abruptly fallen silent. She saw Shatrugan and Bharat put their fingers in their ears and shake them, as if they felt the exact same sensation.

'A masking mantra,' the guru explained shortly. 'To keep our words from being overheard.'

'You suspect spies within the palace, gurudev?' Kausalya sounded shocked.

Vashishta looked at Kausalya grimly. Even by the light of the mashaals, Sumitra thought she saw new lines of age on the guru's face. He looked as though he had aged several years since she had seen him last. *But that was just this afternoon, when we bade goodbye to Rama and Lakshman.* The thought of Rama and Lakshman brought a lump to her throat and she tried to keep her mind clear of all thoughts, the better to concentrate on what was being discussed.

'Not just spies, First Queen. Traitors too.' He turned to look at each one of them in turn. Sumitra shifted uncomfortably as his hawklike eyes stayed on her a moment. 'This is why I have called you here tonight. To warn you.'

'Who are these traitors?' Shatrugan's voice was soft but his tone was unmistakably angry. 'Show them to us, guruji. We'll cut them down like ripe wheat.'

The guru nodded kindly at Shatrugan. 'Your eagerness for action is understandable, Rajkumar Shatrugan. But these traitors cannot be dealt with as easily as you would like.'

'Why not?' Bharat asked. 'After all, they're mortal, aren't they? We caught and imprisoned thirteen spies in the city dungeon. Why can't we root out and imprison these ones as well?'

Guru Vashishta raised a hand. 'Patience, good Bharat. Hear me out first. I have just had a very disturbing encounter in that same city dungeon. And that is what prompts my speaking to you at this unearthly hour.'

Sumitra noticed Pradhan-Mantri Sumantra shuddering at the guru's words. 'What happened in the dungeon, guruji?' she asked mildly. 'We have heard all sorts of rumours. Is it true that those prisoners melted into milky fluid and vanished down a crack in the floor?'

The guru sighed wearily. 'Rani Sumitra. The truth might be more than you can stand to hear. Especially at the end of a day fraught with so much stress. I understand that the maharaja has regained consciousness.'

'Yes,' Kausalya replied.

'But he is not yet fully in his senses?'

Kausalya paused before replying. 'He is disturbed. It is probably a result of his deteriorating condition. He has been having strange dreams.'

The guru nodded grimly. 'I will go to him when we are done here. But I wish you all to promise me that not a word of what we speak here will reach his ears.'

They all looked at each other uncertainly.

'Guruji,' Bharat asked respectfully. 'How can we conspire behind my father's back?'

'Conspire?' The guru issued a wan smile. 'This is not conspiracy, young Bharat. Conspiracy is what our enemies are brewing right now, even as we speak. But to set your mind at rest, let me remind you that with your father incapacitated, the onus of the kingdom falls on the shoulders of Pradhan-Mantri Sumantra, First Queen Kausalya-maa, and yourself.'

'Me?' Bharat looked incredulous.

'Yes, Dasaratha-putra. For until your brother Rama returns home safe and sound, you must be regarded as the prince-in-waiting.' The guru paused. 'I would not like to explain that part further; I believe you understand it well enough.'

'What did you learn in the dungeon, guruji?' Kausalya's voice was quiet but urgent. 'You learned something from the spies that made you call us together, is it not so? What was it?'

Guru Vashishta turned his ancient eyes on the first queen. 'You are wise beyond your years, Kausalya. The devas have gifted you with an acute analytical mind. Kosala could do worse than to have you reigning as regent after the maharaja passes on.'

Kausalya blinked several times, clearly taken aback at this unexpected compliment. 'I only use common sense, guruji.'

'And you use it wisely.' The guru became suddenly businesslike. 'You are quite right. I learned something in the dungeon that alarmed me greatly. I thought I had the measure of the current crisis. I regret to say I had only part measure of the whole situation. The rot that Brahmarishi Vishwamitra and I sensed is riper than we believed. The Demon Lord of Lanka has his claws far

512

deeper in the body of this great Arya nation than either of us thought.'

Bharat and Shatrugan exchanged glances.

Shatrugan shuffled his feet uneasily. 'Shama, guruji. I don't understand your meaning.'

'I mean only to say that Ravana's influence is far greater than any of us suspected. Not only has he planted spies in the royal court, he has gained influence over the throne of Ayodhya itself!'

Sumitra rose to her feet, gasping. 'Impossible! That would mean—'

'That one of the royal family is secretly loyal to Ravana,' Kausalya said slowly. She reached out and caught Sumitra's hand, firmly drawing her back to her seat. 'Can it be true then, guruji? Can such a thing really have happened?'

Bharat and Shatrugan looked bewildered and angry, respectively. Shatrugan had kept his hand on the shaft of his axe all through the discussion. Now he lifted it helplessly.

'But that would mean . . . that one of us is a traitor!' Shatrugan looked around. 'How can that be possible?'

Guru Vashishta spread his hands. 'And yet it is so. After my encounter in the dungeon, I know this to be true. One of the royal family is a traitor to the Arya nations and a supporter of the king of the Asuras, plotting and conspiring to destroy us all and aid Ravana in his scheme to ravage and conquer the mortal world.'

Sumitra's hands flew to her chest. Her heart was thumping so loud, she was certain everyone else could hear it clearly in the dead silence that followed the guru's words.

She looked around the room. 'But how could any of us be—' She broke off, realisation dawning. 'It's not one of us! None of us would do such a thing. That's why you called us here tonight, to take us into your confidence and warn us. That means that the traitor must be—'

'Kaikeyi-maa,' Bharat said. His face was an inscrutable mask. 'She's the only one left. And the only one with a motive to conspire against the throne. Because she seeks to overturn Rama's ascension and make me maharaja after my father's passing.'

He waved a fist in the air. 'And I would sooner die than see her succeed in her intentions. My mother she is and for that I shall always show her respect. But on this matter I will not support her. Either Rama will become maharaja or Ayodhya will remain kingless. This I swear in the presence of my guru.'

Guru Vashishta spoke quietly. 'Bravely spoken, young Bharat. But you have all jumped too quickly to your conclusions. I fear that the greatest threat to the kingdom and to the mortal world at large shall come not from your mother or any other member of the royal family. The danger shall come from Maharaja Dasaratha himself!'

Jatayu's wings had never ached so much. But then, the vulture had never before flown such a great distance without a break. It would demand a feast from the Lord of the Asuras for flying so long without rest or nourishment.

The bird descended from the thick moisture-laden clouds, its inbuilt sense of direction and distance telling it that the destination was close by. As the vulture emerged from the bank of dark monsoon clouds into the clear sky above the ocean, it screeched happily. Its instincts had been correct as usual.

Lanka lay directly below.

As it circled lower, descending by stages on the wind currents it needed to support its enormous bulk, its keen eyes flickered with disbelief. The sight before it banished even its screaming hunger.

A war fleet was massed offshore of Lanka.

Jatayu had spent half a thousand years scouring the air above Prithvi and had seen countless wars and battles. But never before had it seen a fleet this vast and impressive.

There were ships reaching far out to sea, in endless anchored lines, linked closely to one another with cleverly wrought ladders, like an enormous chain stretching to the horizon and beyond. Jatayu estimated tens of thousands of them, perhaps hundreds of thousands—what did the humans call a hundred thousand? Ah yes, lakhs. More than lakhs, millions. It was impossible to take in the entire size of the fleet; even a bird's yojanas-long gaze couldn't see the end of the chains. And each ship was large enough to carry hundreds of Asuras. Different-shaped ships for different species, hence the variety of sizes and structures of the vessels.

As it flew lower, Jatayu saw something even more mindnumbing than the sheer size of the fleet.

The ships were loaded. It could see the dark, inhuman shapes of rakshasas, Yaksas, Pisacas, Nagas, Uragas, gandharvas and every other Asura species, crowded on those endless decks, all armed and armoured for battle.

Jatayu wheeled barely a few hundred yards above the island now, hovering in the dark thundercloud-shadowed gloom of the Lankan sky, all eagerness to land forgotten. The shores of the island-kingdom were seething with hordes of Asuras waiting their turn to board the remaining ships. The embarking was nearly done. The fleet was almost ready to set sail. As the wind changed, the sound of the hordes came up to the vulture, an overwhelming roaring, like a typhoon at sea. And the stench, the unbelievable, indescribable stench.

There was no doubt about where this vast armada was headed, and Jatayu spoke the name of the place aloud, adding its own voice and foul breath to the malodorous cacophony of the largest Asura army ever assembled.

'*Ayodhya*.'

Its voice was a shrill piercing cry that cut through the gloom of the stormy night.

As if in response, at just that moment the clouds huddled above thundered and began to release their burden of rain. In an instant, the ocean was besieged by a brackish downpour that seemed almost crimson in the gaudy light of the nearly full moon.

516

It was a fitting metaphor for the rain of Asura hordes that would soon besiege Ayodhya. And the ocean of mortal blood that would be spilled by Ravana's invasion.

Jatayu cawed in exultation, and began a slow, victorious descent to the fortress-kingdom of its lord and master.